A Singer at the Wedding

By the same author

*A Concise History of
Irish Art*

A Singer at the Wedding

Bruce Arnold

'Then learn that a man must look to his ending, and cannot call himself happy until he carries his happiness down with him to the grave, having suffered no great misfortune.'

from Sophocles, *Oedipus Tyrannus*

'A child, after all, knows most of the game—it is only an attitude to it that he lacks.'

Graham Greene

HAMISH HAMILTON · London

First published in Great Britain 1978
by Hamish Hamilton Limited
90 Great Russell Street London WC1B 3PT

Copyright © 1978 by Bruce Arnold

British Library Cataloguing in Publication Data

Arnold, Bruce
  A singer at the wedding.
  I. Title
  823'.9'1F   PR6051.R/

ISBN 0-241-89825-0

Printed in Great Britain by Bristol Typesetting Co. Ltd.

Prologue

My father died in the late summer, at the beginning of September. I was not with him at the end. My stepmother was beside his bed in the hospital; I was standing in his garden, among the clematis and roses. It was Alice who answered the telephone, and brought me the news. And she left me alone soon afterwards, standing on the flagged path amid the profuse colours and smells of the flowers he had grown. My feelings were entirely of relief, even of happiness on his behalf. I was glad that he was dead. I was glad that the whole untidy and painful business of his unsatisfactory life was over at last. And for a brief space of time I felt completely, utterly free.

I was free of the past and free of the future. I bent down to smell my favourite flower in his garden, Crimson Glory. And the heavy, sad, old-fashioned fragrance seemed to overwhelm the past, so intense was it, and to suspend the future, so little has the future to do with smells. All that I could think about was the moment of release itself; here, now, he was gone.

I did not need to concern myself any longer with the pain of his suffering, the greater part of which had been mental rather than physical. I did not need to think of what I would do about recording the events, although soon enough I would be embarking upon these words which you read now. I was simply suspended in the shocked relief of the moment itself, a moment outside time, a moment untroubled by shadow of any kind.

The day was perfect, and the most perfect things he had ever made were around me. I thought only of that, and I judged it to be most fitting that the news of his death should have come to me there, among the plants he had grown and loved and cared for during his last years. Gardens had been his only true sanctuary. The happiness that he had derived from them had been the only unspoilt happiness in all the years I had known him.

Everything was still and peaceful. It was already hot, although only a little after nine in the morning. One rose from the bush of Peace in the centre of the small lawn had gone over, and its creamy, tinted petals had tumbled down in profusion on the dry earth. It was a mark of untidiness he would never have permitted. And since he was a remarkably early riser, often up at five in the morning, it made me smile to think that he would have been out on this particular morning three or four times already, and would have cleared away the petals, almost in a mood of anger that one of his beloved rose bushes should have shed its flower in such a way. Of course it would not have happened had he been there. His vigilance would have plucked the flower head from the plant in good time between the moment of its full opening and the final disintegration. And the thought of this made me smile again, and reminded me of an earlier visit that year, in the spring, before the roses had begun to bloom, and when several of the clematis were in full flower. We had come out into the garden together, he leaning on my arm, and as we paused beside one of the half standards, I pointed at the lush green shoot nearest to me, and said to him, 'Look! A greenfly!' And he had responded with much indignation and horror, and had crushed the soft insect between his fingers, and then we had both laughed.

Right to the end, before he was moved to hospital, when he was too weak to stand, he would still ask to be moved in his chair on its small castors out and along the flagged path. And after the difficult manoeuvre he would sit, his secateurs held loosely in his large, slack hands, and would inspect carefully the rose bushes beside the path in the hope that he might find some small task to perform for their greater beauty or health or strength. And generally he found nothing; and sadly, even when he did find some minor detail needing attention, he was usually too weak to perform the action.

His health, before that, had been declining for a year or more, one complication adding itself to another, with no improvements of any kind. But at that time I was living and working abroad, and perhaps I did not take seriously enough the signs that indicated his time was short. Then, in July, things became suddenly worse, and his expectation was reduced to a matter of weeks. I came home to be with him, and we struggled on, amid considerable difficulty, pretending that he would get better, and surrounding him with whatever pleasures were possible during those relentless days.

Eventually he had to be moved to hospital. He became steadily more frightened, and more difficult with everyone. He was not resigned to death. We, my stepmother and I, had promised, he said, that he would never be moved to hospital, but would die in his own bed. 'Take me away, take me away, take me away,' he wailed at us for long terrible moments, on one visit to him together, and we sat in silence, and knew that he had to stay where he was until the end. I felt I had let him down, and I could not remind him that it had been his own wish, when things had become too difficult altogether at home, that he should be moved into hospital. I simply had to sit there and listen to his frightened complaint.

All the years I had known him he had hated physical disability and illness, had feared them in an intense, almost childish way; and now he was being engulfed; and there was nothing we could do.

He was in a hospital on the outskirts of the Somerset town in which he had spent his last years. It was the summer in which General Franco died, and there were some similarities in the causes of death as between my father and the general, though in the general's case life—if it could be called that—was preserved for a longer period of time than was thought desirable for my father. No one regretted this, least of all myself, who wished him free of the burden of unhappiness which he had borne all his life. Though I speak now of that unhappiness with an understanding that might imply I was aware of it over a period of years, the truth of the matter is that I became fully conscious of the nature of his unhappy life only during those last few weeks, and immediately after his death. Even now, going back over all the events I can remember, and sifting again and again through the things he left behind, the snapshots, letters, papers, and his one surviving diary of any importance at all, I still discover gaps in my knowledge and understanding of his life. Yet they are gaps which never really contradict the fundamental thread of unhappiness.

I shall come back to that diary in greater detail later, as indeed I shall come back to many things which I mention now only in an oblique way. During that last illness, for example, I lived at the house with his wife, my stepmother, and with Alice, who owned the house and had known and loved him for more years than any other woman he had ever known, including my mother, as well as his first wife and his third. Since it was now his fourth wife who would sit by his bedside until he died, the possible complexities of the story upon which I hopefully embark may be imagined, but will take time to unravel. That he should have lived out his last days in that particular relationship is a phenomenon in itself. But it is only one of many; and most of them bear witness to the fact that he lived and died an unhappy man.

He feared drowning above all things. He was a naval man, a good naval officer until that part of his life came to grief; he swam well; he had a proper respect for the sea. Often as a child he would caution me, if I went rowing or sailing, or away to summer camp with school friends, of the swift, impersonal hand of water, mercilessly dragging its victims down. And when my son was old enough, in his turn, to take an interest in sailing and swimming, he came in for the same homilies from his grandfather about safety. Well, in the end, my father may be said to have drowned, as his lungs slowly filled with water, his body gradually losing its capacity to deal with the rising tide of fluids. I do not suppose he was completely aware of this. He was drugged anyway. And I mention it more because of my own feelings as I sat watching him during those endlessly hot, cloudless but sombre days in August, conscious of the inevitable tide rising against him.

I used to ride to the hospital each day on a bicycle. It took me fifteen minutes or so. The road went through the outskirts of the town, past houses of various date going back in only one or two cases to the beginning of the century, and mostly ordinary, modest suburban semi-detached homes, with young children playing in the gardens, or in the roadway outside. Day after hot summer day I would cycle along, inspecting the progress of gardens, identifying the flowers and their scents, and preparing myself for the long vigil beside his bed.

My father would see me coming into the ward and watch me as I made my way to his bed. He would stare at me with his grey, angry eyes. He smiled only rarely, and then only in what seemed to be a patronising way. He had no real strength for speech beyond complaint or command, but he liked to be talked to and told things, and he enjoyed his food to the end. For an hour or so at a time I would sit beside him, both of us silent, my hand usually touching his in one of the many grasps that had been part of my life since as far back as I could remember. And occasionally he would squeeze my fingers and nod his head, often without opening his eyes; and when he did that, it served as conversation.

He had a stoic look about him, even in sleep. And he seemed often to be asleep, though in reality it was the vain closing of his eyes against the drowsed confusion of those last days. Once, after a succession of visitors, not all welcome, some tiresome, he lay back, stern, still, cut off. And briefly, passionately, I wished at that moment life would pass from him. Instead, he really did fall asleep, his breath more gentle, his expression more relaxed.

I sat on beside the bed. I had with me a book, one of Hardy's novels, but felt no wish to read. His face was quite peaceful. I tried to think to myself: here is my father dying, and what does it mean? But all that came to me were feelings of futility and impatience. Our time together was ticking away. He was too weak to do anything except smile occasionally and move his hand within mine. If there were secrets about life which he held, then I already possessed them, or would never possess them. If there was anything in my own future about which he was curious, then the time for asking had passed and he knew it.

Once, many years before, he had said to me that in any garden he owned he would plant in some inconspicuous corner a bush of privet. As a child he had memories of the smell of privet in summer in the garden in Folkestone where he was brought up. And he told me often that no smell in the world meant so much to him. 'Nostalgia' he would say. He was fond of the word. Nostalgia. It was enough just to speak it like that. And then he would stare with unseeing eyes into the distance and try to remember for himself the irredeemable thoughts of a child standing on the sour dry earth under the dreary green of a privet hedge and smelling the heavy, cloying scent of the creamy clusters of flowers in mid-summer. In the garden of the hospital there was a bush of privet. And it was fully in flower. And on that occasion as he slept, I eventually left him and walked out in the sunlight of the afternoon and shamelessly picked a cone of creamy flowers from the bush, and after strolling for a while in the sunshine I brought it back to him and laid it on his chest where he was able to hold it. He was awake again. He did not comprehend at first. Then he pushed the flower up to his nostrils and smelt it, and closed his eyes, his face suddenly relaxed. After a while he looked at me, began to say something, thought better of it, and gave a shrug of his shoulders, his eyes suddenly wet with unshed tears. I imagined him to be saying: 'What's the use? You know it all now.'

Well, as to whether I know it all now, the following story will in part reveal. Mutely, I believed, he was urging me to tell it. His inevitable death, staved off by medicine and by his own powerful constitution, had raised in me intimations of mortality. Sitting beside him, quite literally watching the tide rise against him, I was filled with a stronger sense than I had ever had in my life that here before me was a story that I would have to tell. It was a sad story involving a broken and a shattered life. For the first time in my own experience, in spite of the fact that I had grown up with him and had never been alienated from him in affection or in contact, I was becoming aware that he had never really been a happy man. I found it difficult to conceive of this, still harder to explain away my blindness if it really was the truth. I argued repeatedly against it. In all my childhood I had seen my own happiness reflected in his eyes. Yet at that time, the time of his death, talking with his wife and with Alice, and afterwards, thinking over, again and again, all the details, sifting through his life, I accepted finally that this was the truth about him. It shocked me. The very idea that a human being could go through the full compass of seventy-five years, during which reason and passion are exercised on an infinite number of human conflicts, and at the end of it all record, in summary, the simple devastation, 'an unhappy life', was terrifying to me, not least because, by the end of that summer, I had recognised the truth of it all, having been blind to it before then. I suppose I can explain this. I loved him, and for years of my life I drew happiness from him with all the greedy innocence of a child. Even in the most adverse circumstances, that happiness which I obtained was real, and because of this I invested him with a share of it which I believed he got by giving of himself to me. I did not then realise, though I do now, that such a relationship need not necessarily make the giver happy, even though it may provide a temporary joy. I did not know, or if I knew I did not understand, just how much of the rest of his life was torment. Even now I cannot fully understand why. The roots must go back to that child, so striking in appearance, with his brown eyes and blond hair, standing under the privet hedge in summer, before the first world war, in a suburban garden in Folkestone, and recording in his nostrils what was to become the very odour of time itself.

And so, standing there in his garden, among his flowers, the past reasserted itself, and, with it, the future. Would my stepmother and Alice stay on in the house? Would they be able to mind his garden, if only for love of him? No. I doubted that. And I worried about those plants, all of them, and wondered what would become of them. And I think that perhaps I gave thought to them in order not to have to think about myself. For remembering had taken away the freedom which I had felt immediately after Alice had come to me in the garden with news of his death. The intense moment of release, of utter freedom, when the present had dominated everything, was slipping away. Casually, events had linked themselves one to another and had brought the future once more before my eyes, and the future had demanded further details out of the past.

And so I have gone back, and gathered up certain episodes from that time in my childhood when, so I thought, he and I were happy together; when our two lives were bound up as one; and when I first discovered that such a bond was not indissoluble. It is a voyage of discovery, itself prompted by the steadily growing conviction, throughout those relentless summer days, that all the many feelings and beliefs I had held concerning his life, and my life with him, were by no means as I had thought, and that the nature of life itself might just be made a bit more understandable if I could unlock the secret of his own unhappiness.

It begins in winter, in the English countryside, at a wedding, with the snow thick on the ground, crusted with frost. It was a time of innocence. It was a time of learning. It was the time when I first fell in love.

Chapter One

I

We were the choir at the wedding, and the wedding itself was over. On that December evening we jumped down from the Coppinger School bus, and stood about awkwardly, waiting for Parker. We were on the forecourt, in front of the house. The ground was packed with hard snow. It squeaked under our polished black boots. We were gathered in a tight group, close to the side of the bus, and we shuffled our feet in the cold and stamped and jostled against one another. We were insignificant guests now that the service was over, and of no real importance among the crowd that was moving past us towards the house. We stared about self-consciously. Our warm breath hung in sharp white puffs on the frosty air. All of us, even the seniors, were in short trousers, and the pink flesh of hands, knees and faces stood out against the grey colouring of our clothes in the fading light of that winter evening. It added to our raw, impoverished look, binding us more firmly together as a group.

I was standing at the edge of the group, looking out at the guests. An elderly woman, leaning on the arm of a much younger man, was among those who passed us on the way to the reception. She looked directly at me, and paused for a moment. Then she glanced at her companion. 'He's the soloist, isn't he?' She didn't wait for an answer. 'You did sing well, young man.' I smiled and nodded my thanks. For a moment we stood facing each other uncertainly, the old woman's escort allowing himself only the faintest smile of endorsement, unwilling, it seemed to me, to get entangled with the choir boys from Coppinger. I did not know what to say. Only the woman, of an age when the satisfaction of curiosity takes precedence over everything, completed at leisure her inspection of me, then turned away.

I was pleased by her praise, embarrassed at being singled out. I moved in once again with the others, jostling for comfort. It was cold waiting. Yet Coppinger, that gaunt peppering of Victorian school buildings on the rounded top of one of the Cotswolds, 600 feet or so above the sea, with its hardships and its disciplines, had made us all familiar with cold and with waiting. We crunched our way across the snow. Danby, beside me, nudged my arm. 'D'you think we'll get champagne?'

'I don't know. I hope so. I've never had it. Wouldn't be much fun to be drinking just orange, or something like that, would it?'

'But d'you think they'll let us? I've never had it either. It'd be fun, wouldn't it?'

'I've never been to a wedding before.'

'Nor have I. What happens now, like? They make speeches and things, don't they? Read telegrams, and things like that—have a happy married life. Some hope. My Mum's talked about it. She still has photos of hers. We look at them together sometimes.' His voice, North Country, was slow and flat, first mocking, then pensive and regretful.

'It's probably different at a wedding like this,' I said. I tried to hint at superior knowledge. Yet I knew less than Danby. My father had no photographs of that kind, nor had he ever spoken of his wedding. It was an issue locked away in the past, along with my mother's death, and with most tangible reminders of her. I lived over again in my mind the singing of the solo at the wedding service, with all the atmosphere of breath-taking anticipation which always dissolved itself, like acid-sharp crystals of lemonade, into the sweet liquid of sound which flowed out of my mouth and throat and lungs. I remembered again the detail: the faces of guests, the sombre grey and black of the men, the hats, the solid face of the bride, the stony stare of the bridegroom, the high stone columns and arches of the North Cotswold church where the wedding was held; but I could not recapture that feeling of being perilously close to nausea which always resulted from the concentration of so much attention on myself. I said to Danby: 'Maybe it was the last solo I'll sing.' And I allowed a note of regret to creep into my voice.

'What do you mean then?'

'Parker thinks my voice will break soon.'

'Well, it didn't sound like it was breaking today. The bride gave you such a smashing smile when she came out of the vestry.'

Guests in front of us disappeared into the house. We crowded in through the door, in our turn, a gap ahead of us, a few latecomers behind. Sir Joseph Fisher, well inside the low, square hall with its black oak furniture and flagged floor, stepped forward and surveyed us. We were his contribution to his daughter's wedding, the expression of his power and influence. And we had acquitted ourselves well. We could see it in his face, a mixture of pride and indulgence, and a hint of doubt. Would we now become a liability? We were out of our natural element, which was discipline and the hard life, and about to participate at a wedding feast. Could our energies be contained?

'Ah,' he said, feigning jocularity, 'the singers, the Golden Voices of Coppinger, the larks and songbirds from the School on the Hill.'

I was aware of a small group of guests at the door which led into one of the main rooms of the house. A young girl stood among them, with long fair hair. She seemed not to be with any of the adults around her, but to be slightly apart, anticipating some person or event. She glanced occasionally at Sir Joseph. There was on her face that expression of secret, inner equilibrium given, perhaps, to most girls and denied to most boys in those short, stressed years with which childhood is terminated. She was about my age. Her mouth gave to her face the impression that she was on the verge of smiling, but at secret thoughts, and in such a way as to emphasise the aura of isolation which surrounded her. She did not smile, but stood patiently watching.

'Thank you so much, Sir Joseph,' Parker said, his voice slightly breathless. 'Thank you. It was an honour for us all.' There was a pause. He looked across our heads at Philpotts, and appealed: 'Wasn't it, boys?'

There was a murmured response from a few of us. We eased forward. Philpotts was at the back of the group, a more graceful, more mature, less lumpish figure among the ten or so basses and tenors. He was one of three school prefects in the choir, the most senior boy there. In the moment of shuffling uncertainty he spoke. 'Did you enjoy the solo singing, Sir Joseph?'

The question briefly stilled the impatient scraping of feet. Boys at Coppinger did not generally speak to the chairman of the trustees unless spoken to. Sir Joseph looked surprised, not only because of this, but also because of Philpotts's relaxed, well-bred voice. They stared at each other. Sir Joseph looked slightly annoyed. One or two further groups of guests filtered their way through the boys standing in front of him. 'I was just coming to that,' he said. 'Yes. Soloists. Where are the boys?' Danby pushed me forward. 'Ah, yes, there you are.' Kessner stood nearby. 'What are your names?' We told him. 'Mm. Good. Very good. Good show altogether. Now, come on in, the rest of you, make yourselves known, this is Mrs Boyle, bride and groom, you'll find your way . . .' In the surge forward, Sir Joseph put out his hand towards me. 'Hold on, young man,' he said. 'We've a surprise for you.' One or two boys nearby stopped to listen. I felt immediately embarrassed. Announcements of this kind had never, in the past, meant much good to me. I moved a cautious pace forward. I wondered, could it possibly be my father, or something connected with my father? And more forbidding still, would my father—? Impossible. Yet I shivered slightly with apprehension.

I heard Sir Joseph asking, 'Now, where's Babette?' I knew no one of that name. I watched the other choirboys as they moved in towards the reception.

Then I saw that the girl who had been standing watching us, the girl with long, fair hair, was coming forward in response to Sir Joseph's appeal. She picked her way carefully, and with rather obvious composure, against the stream of movement, and I could see that she was conscious of the interest of my friends who stopped and turned, watching her. She looked at Sir Joseph. 'Here he is, Babette,' he said. 'Take him to meet your mother.' Then he turned away to other guests, and left us silently facing each other.

She looked at me for a moment or two, not speaking or smiling. 'Come on, then,' she ordered, and turned away, leading me into the crowded room. I had no alternative but to follow. She went ahead, threading her way between the groups of guests, looking round once or twice to make sure I was with her, but not stopping to explain. We came to a window seat. The curtains had not been drawn, and there was still the strange, pinkish light of the sun shining obliquely across the deep untrodden snow.

'Mummy,' said Babette, 'Here he is.'

I stood still in front of the window seat. Two women were seated there. One of them was the elderly lady who had stopped and spoken to me on the way in. The other, Babette's mother, was a slim and graceful woman in her thirties, dressed in a blue-grey suit, and with a broad-brimmed hat on, the only one of its kind that I had seen that day in the church, and sufficiently striking to bring back to me the precise pew and seat which she, and presumably Babette, had occupied during the wedding service. And in the wearing of this hat, moreover, she was quite distinct in her appearance from what

I understood the fashions in the country as a whole to be at that time, and not just among the wedding guests in that part of the Cotswolds. Yet distinct in a way that made her more attractive, more daring, more beautiful. The visual references by which I might judge her were meagre in the extreme; films, magazine photographs, my own reading—yet they, or some native intuition on my part, invested her now with qualities of romance and beauty. Yet there was in her face a certain sadness, hard to define, which would quite soon become apparent to me in other ways. She looked at me, openly, candidly, without speaking, and I felt radiating from her a relaxed self-assurance which gave depth and definition to her natural beauty.

'So you are George's son,' she said. Her voice was deep, and she spoke slowly, as though savouring the idea, and rolling around in her mind the fact that I was, indeed, George's son. I stood silently in front of her. I still did not know what to say or think or feel.

The greeting—'So you are George's son'—was, of course, a familiar one to me; and not always, in the past, welcome. It echoed many other encounters, and I shivered at the memory of some of them, particularly those that both began and ended thus. Yet with this girl, Babette, and with her mother—if I could only get over the initial awkwardnesses of being introduced, and of understanding why I should be known by them; and assuming that the reasons were not to be the source of shameful revelations—then already I felt a desire to know and to talk and to be in their company. She repeated the words, but this time more softly, as though to herself, yet with greater warmth, with a different, sweeter intonation in her voice: 'So you are George's son.'

'Well,' she said, 'I am Mrs Springer. And Babette is my daughter. And I know your father, and since we are all going to see each other in the coming holiday, it is only right that we should get to know each other a little now. This lady, who thinks so highly of your singing, is Lady Cavendish.'

I shook her hand. Then, uncertain of myself, since Lady Cavendish was the first titled lady to whom I had been introduced in this way I made an awkward little half-bow in her direction.

Babette stepped forward, not putting out her hand to be shaken, but smiling, openly and warmly at me, and saying, 'It's not only Cousin Geraldine that thinks you sang well. We all think it.'

'Come and sit down,' said her mother. She indicated a place beside herself. 'You are still puzzled,' she went on. 'There is more that I must explain.' I could think only of the most obvious answer. I said: 'Well, you must know my father, Mrs Springer. That stands to reason.' I felt, after I had said it, that the expression of logical reasoning was not really necessary. I had never been puzzled about the numbers of women who knew my father and spoke of him in the soft and affectionate terms which Mrs Springer had used. 'Ah, yes. But that's only the beginning of it,' she answered. 'And before telling you about that, please call me Madge.' I frowned at the unorthodoxy. 'Yes, I mean it. I insist.' I felt flattered that one so beautiful should have time to explain herself to me. 'It's very simple, really, your father should have written and told you that we would be meeting; but I don't suppose he did, did he?' I shook my head. 'Well, George is—' she hesitated. 'He's a friend of my sister Ursula. He said to me that you would be in the Coppinger choir. And that you would be singing at the wedding. That's all. And he didn't mention this? He didn't mention Ursula?'

Again, I shook my head. I did not want to confess that I had not heard from my father for several weeks, and that it had been Alice who had written to say that I would be met on my arrival in London, only two days away, when term would finally end. But Alice had not mentioned Ursula. I was bewildered all over again. Who was she?

'Is this your first wedding? Weddings are rather dull affairs. There is nothing to catch hold of. No centre. I suppose the bride and groom must enjoy them; parents must feel relieved; guests must get some pleasure out of it all. But, at heart, I feel there's something artificial about them. My dream for Babette would not be an English wedding at all, but one in France, in springtime, somewhere in Normandy. I see it taking place out-of-doors, in an orchard filled with apple and pear blossom. And it would all be quite formal, with long tables laid out in the sun, and many people laughing and talking, and speeches, and the soft transition from afternoon sunlight and shadows till evening, and time to move in.' She laughed. 'It is quite ridiculous. But there is something slippery in the British character, and it comes out at wedding receptions. You never quite know what is happening, there is just this moving and shifting of people, like an oily sea of deception. Do you understand what I mean?' I looked out wide-eyed, at the oily sea of people, and nodded, more to show willingness, and the fact that I had been listening carefully to what she said, than because I grasped what the national character distinctions were.

Lady Cavendish had been listening to her last words. 'My dear, you are quite wrong. For my sister, Alexandra, and for dear Sir Joseph, it is vitally important, the way things are done. There must be this flow of guests—' she waved her hand vaguely towards the increasingly crowded rooms. 'We must all meet, and be seen to meet.' She looked imperiously at Madge, who did not reply, then at Babette, who did.

'It's not very romantic, cousin Geraldine.'

'Romance! Marriage is not concerned with romance. It is concerned with blood.'

I could not tell whether she was being serious or joking. I was over-disposed, at that time, to take everything seriously. 'No, Geraldine. Please. You exaggerate, I'm sure. But you must not say that to Babette. You make me so sad. Romance will vanish soon enough. Don't tear it away from these children.'

Guests moved about in front of us. Some waved their greetings at Madge, but seemed unwilling to detach themselves from the swirling flow of men and women, seeking out partners, at whom they could shout. My friends from school had been swallowed up in the crowd. Sitting at the edge of the room, listening to the boom of conversation, I felt that I should be making a more positive effort. We had been taught at Coppinger that it was a duty so to do.

'Are you staying here in the house, Mrs Springer?'

'Madge, please, not Mrs Springer. You mustn't call me Mrs Springer. I won't answer if you do it again. Yes, Babette and I are staying here. We shall go back to London tomorrow. Babette's school broke up on Thursday. When does your holiday start?'

'The day after tomorrow.'

'Goodness, that's very late. And will you go home to your father then?'

'Oh, yes.'

'And where will you spend Christmas?'

'In London, I suppose. We live in Clanricarde Gardens. That's in Notting Hill Gate. Do you know it?'

'No. I'm afraid not. What's it like?'

'Well, actually, I can't tell you. My father has moved there since my last holiday. We lived in Kent before that. In the country. In a village. I haven't been to the new . . . the new place.' I felt that I had been tricked into self-revelation, not by her, but by my own desire to make a contribution. Now she sat and waited for me to go on. And I did not know how to describe the new place. I would like to have said that it was a flat with so many rooms. That, I guessed, would be what Madge and Babette and Babette's father lived in, if not in a whole house. Yet in the long catalogue of addresses which I could remember coming home to, holiday after holiday, no London flat had ever featured. We—my father and myself, and at one time my brother—were the insecure, short-term residents of meaner places, at best of double bed-sitting rooms. Once or twice, when my father had been working in the country, there had been what might honestly be described as a flat, in which I had had a room of my own. But that had been a rare and infrequent privilege. I could expect nothing like that now. And even what I did expect, from the address neatly written in Alice's precise hand, seemed remote, coming from behind my father's ominous silence.

'Well,' Madge said, 'Notting Hill's a nice place to live, especially if you're close to Kensington Gardens. Are you?'

'I think so. I'm not sure. My father said it wasn't far.' He had said no such thing. I hoped only that it was true, not for the convenience, but to give support to my rash guess. I wished she would talk of something else, and yet I was nervous of what that might be.

'Have you brothers and sisters?'

How I dreaded that question, too. Why did I have to explain myself so much? Why had she not learnt all this detail already? 'I have,' I said guardedly. 'My sister's been adopted. My brother is doing his national service.'

'And you will see them this holiday?'

I paused. I was beginning to feel the familiar misery of tangled, incomplete, uncertain explanations, when really I should have been pleased at the interest Babette's mother was taking in me. I was pleased. But I was conscious, too, of the inadequacy of my answers, and of Babette, silent for the moment nearby, and almost certainly taking in the gentle cross-examination. The confines of my understanding of myself and of my family were not difficult to reach, and the actual boundaries of that understanding of identity shifted and changed, as I shall show, and were as ill-defined and as open to future alteration as the lines and markings on a pioneer explorer's map; like such a map, however, they had the basic truth in them of first-hand experience. I said slowly, 'No, I don't think so.'

'That's a pity. Who do you pla— go out with during your holidays?'

'There isn't anyone, really. I go out on my own while my

father's at work. Sometimes I go with him. I go to museums and things. I go to the pictures.'

'Well, you shall come and see us. You and Babette can go out together.

'Do you live far from Notting Hill Gate?'

'Not far. We live in Knightsbridge. It's on the other side of the park.'

I looked across the room. In the movement of people a gap opened up, and through it I saw Danby and Eagle. They were looking at me and talking. Babette had crossed from where she had been sitting, and was standing beside me. She said: 'Would you like to explore the house? It's very interesting. There's a big room upstairs. It's where Sir Joseph keeps his collection of eggs. He wouldn't let it be used for the reception.'

'Yes,' I said, 'I would. Will people mind?'

'We don't have to tell anyone except Mummy.'

'All right.'

We stood up. Babette said to her mother, 'We're going to explore the house.'

'Very good, darling. Don't go out in the snow. You won't find me here when you get back, but I'll be somewhere about.' She dismissed us with a gesture of her hand.

II

From the room upstairs we looked out over the snow-covered landscape. The sun had gone down. Remnants of light, absorbed into a violet heaviness, were etched and shadowed with the colours of iron. Yet it was still not quite dark. With almost no intermission, the fading light in the south-west had been superseded by the harder whiteness of a moon that was almost full, and which poured down its colder light upon the great expanse of white snow spread out before us.

Sir Joseph's study was at the back of the house. The parkland stretched away for some distance, dotted with the leafless, spartan bulk of single elms and oaks. Still further distant there were denser woods, then the rounded folds of the hills rising behind. The moon sailed just clear of their soft, curved crests. Its great, clear orb, the reflection of its light off the snow, the precise, dark shadows of the wood, of folds in the landscape, and of occasional buildings, gave to the picture before us the sharp contrasts of a wood engraving. Had anything moved across the snow, had a badger or fox or rabbit stirred out into the frozen wilderness, had rooks or magpies flown down to hunt for food among the occasional tufts of vegetation that had pushed through the heavy, smooth blanket of white, we would have seen each movement quite clearly. Yet we watched and waited in vain. Nothing moved in the stillness of nightfall.

We stood side by side in the darkness of the long, low room. Babette had turned out the lights. We had inspected Sir Joseph's collection of birds' eggs, and found them very dull. We could hear the steady drone of noise from the reception below us.

I had been nervous at the lights going out: the action represented conspiracy to me, and possibly the prelude to confidences, even romance. Yet all Babette had said was that its reflection, on the snow under the windows, would be seen, and that we would be brought back into festivities in which neither of us was particularly interested.

I admired her practical approach. We did not speak. We were unwilling to move away. Something held us in front of the window: the stillness of the landscape, perhaps, the panels of yellow light stretching out across the snow from the windows of the rooms below us, the gentle rise and fall of sounds echoing through the old building. There was, for me, contentment in the slow passing of time. I was absorbing a relationship that seemed quite different from any experienced before. For the moment I did not want to test it or explore it any further; I just wanted to let it hang there in the air between us. Questions, however, crowded in and spun about in my mind. Who were these people, so suddenly thrust into my life? I was unnerved that Babette should be connected, however remotely, with a former landowner of these very fields and woods and hillsides. For West Aston was the village in which the wedding had taken place, and Nether Barton was only two miles beyond. Who was this girl, younger than myself, who could call Lady Cavendish 'Cousin Geraldine' with such ease and naturalness, while I could only bow awkwardly? Perhaps more important: how long would these people stay part of my life? It had always been an important consideration in meetings with those who knew my father. What kind of people were they? For being of a certain 'kind'; being 'our kind', or 'not our kind', had been a touchstone used by him on many occasions. It had not escaped me that this particular method of judgement was deployed for rejecting or dismissing people for reasons that had little or nothing to do with the 'kind' of people they were, but was connected with their willingness or otherwise to fall in with my father's plans. Even so, I was conscious of being with people whose background was new and exciting and a bit unnerving. Indeed, my very nerves seemed to tingle at the closeness of this girl, Babette, standing so still beside me that I could hear her breathe; and in this state of excitement and anticipation of something—I did not know what—I let out a sigh of frustration which caused her, in the strange, cold light of the moon which flooded through the tall window, to turn her calm, serious gaze upon me.

'What's the matter?'

'Nothing.'

'There must be something.'

'No, really.'

'But you don't just sigh for nothing. No one does.'

'I wasn't sighing for nothing.'

'What were you sighing for?' She paused. The tone of her voice changed. 'You don't have to tell me if you don't want to.' She looked away into the distance. 'I wish something would come out in the snow,' she went on. 'Some animal. It's all so frozen and still.'

'Babette.' It was the first time I had spoken her name. 'Don't you think it's strange my father not telling me about you and your mother coming down here?'

She nodded, slowly, a reflective expression on her face. She seemed to have infected me with a sense of pleasure and excitement; how, exactly, I did not know. Should I reach out and touch her hand and tell her the moment was important? I did not dare. Should I praise the landscape before us? I could not gather together the words. Instead, I asked her: 'What's your aunt like?'

'Ursula? I never think of her as my aunt. She is "my dear friend". She teaches in a school. She's artistic. Mummy says so. I do too. She has sad eyes, and a soft voice like my mother's. But she's not elegant in the same way, not like Mummy. People think her bohemian in her dress and appearance. I only know what it means from looking at her. If somebody said to me what's bohemian, I'd take them to meet her, and say, that's bohemian. I think Mummy would be more bohemian in her dress if she were not elegant, but she is elegant because that is what Daddy likes.'

I knew what bohemian meant. And I understood elegant. 'I think your mother's beautiful,' I said.

'Do you?'

'Yes. Easily the nicest looking person at the wedding.'

'Including the bride?'

'Oh, I don't think much of her. She comes to the school sometimes with her father. She taught the juniors for a while. She's known as "The Horse". Is she a *special* friend of your mother's?'

'That's a cruel name for her. I hope I'm never called anything like that.'

'Why isn't Ursula here today?'

'Her school hasn't broken up yet, and it was impossible for her to get away.'

'And your father?'

'He's in America. He had to go over for some negotiations. He works in the Foreign Office.'

From the window we saw where the curtains were now being drawn in the downstairs rooms, leaving only the moonlight spreading its cold colouring across the untrodden snow. I asked: 'Should we go back now?'

'Do you want to?'

'No, of course not.'

'We'll not be missed.'

'I only wondered . . .'

'What time do you have to leave?'

'I think at half-past six.'

'It's a bit like Cinderellas at the ball. If you don't go by then you'll all be changed back into . . . rags.' She faltered before finishing. The last word was no more than a whisper. And she looked down and was silent.

I felt my cheeks redden, and was glad of the darkness. She began to look up again, and out of the window. I said: 'Is that what you think of us?'

'Don't be silly. It was only a joke. I didn't mean anything. It was just that Sir Joseph said it,' she went on hurriedly. 'Last night. He said, "Let the Cinderellas come to the ball." There was quite a discussion. Mummy asked him what he meant, and he told us all about the school.'

'And we were the Cinderellas?'

'I suppose so. It was at dinner.'

'Did you have dinner with all of them?'

'Yes.'

'What was it like? You know, he's the senior trustee. I think he's the chairman. At school they all say he's very rich. He's a Member of Parliament.'

'I know. He said the school had changed a lot since he became the chairman. What did he mean? He said it was awful during the war. He made it sound really horrible. Was it? Were you there then?'

'Yes,' I said. 'I came during the war. I've done five years.' I wanted to tell. I wanted her to know about myself.

'What do you mean, done five years?'

'It's the way the boys at Coppinger talk about the time they've been at school. Some come when they're very young, you see. Our prefect, Philpotts, talks about vintages; says 1944 was a good vintage.'

'And that was your year? Was it terrible then?'

'No. Not *terrible*.' I searched in my mind for a way to explain how it was. 'You see, the boys at Coppinger have all lost one or other parent. Or else something has gone wrong at home. They're not orphans exactly. It's not an orphanage, but it's not a proper school, either.'

'And you? What about you?'

'What about me?'

'Well, you don't have a mother. But how did you come to Coppinger?'

It was something of an effort to tell her. I remembered every detail. I remembered coming in mid-term. I remembered the clergyman who had brought me, a young, gaunt-faced man, with a limp that must have excused him from the war; he had a bony Adam's apple; and was full of questions. But how it had all been arranged was not clear in my mind.

'I remember coming,' I said. 'Every detail.' And I told her about it.

A few things I held back. I said nothing of what had gone before. What I told her then was not the full answer to her question. Apart from the fact that I did not know the full answer, there were aspects of that period of my life of which I felt ashamed then, and for which, in any case, the words seemed too brutal. Even as the decision to hold back registered in my mind, so too did the sudden fear that she knew already, had learnt from source, as it were, knowing my father through this woman, Ursula.

That name haunted me already. It made me think of water, and of drowning. She was becoming, in my mind, a creature of myth, a strange, willowy water-sprite, with long hair and penetrating eyes, a half-smile on her lips, enigmas in her heart.

I waited to see whether Babette would betray any detailed knowledge of myself. But she did not refer any further to what I had described. She simply said: 'I suppose in a way you were lucky?'

'Yes, I think so.' I felt relieved.

'I wish you could come to us for Christmas. Where do you normally go?'

'We usually stay in London,' I said. I hesitated, leaving an echo of indecision, of uncertainty in the air. Her wish surprised me. It offered prospects far more exciting than had previously been there for the forthcoming holiday.

'Just you and your father?'

'Yes. Or sometimes there's Alice. She's a friend. She's very nice. She always gets me extra presents, and takes us to a show.'

'But what do you *do*?'

'We have a good time. We have Christmas dinner. We have presents before that. And in the afternoon we go for a walk. And we listen to some of the shows on the wireless. They're always good at Christmas. And if I get books given me—I always do—I read them.' It sounded lame, even as I said it. I did have a good time, it was true. But I could not explain to her what it was that made it all right. I did not fully know myself.

'We go to Granny's,' Babette said. 'It's nice, but everyone's nearly a hundred, and they're always having drinks and going to see relations and talking about the family. There isn't anyone of my age. Mummy's often said that she wished she could find someone of my age to join us.'

'I wish I *could* come.' I felt, even as I said it, that I was betraying my father's and Alice's good intentions. Yet I meant it. I sensed in Babette a new world, quite different from my own, and I yearned for it, without understanding what it was.

I knew only that the life that revolved around my father and Alice was a claustrophobic one. It was enclosed. It was sterile. It suffocated me. I knew this because my father had said as much, and because I knew of other worlds into which, together, we had briefly penetrated, with greater joy and greater freedom, only to be as swiftly expelled again. But they had been clandestine. This new world, inhabited by Babette and Madge and Ursula—normal, acceptable, 'real' people, I thought—was different. It exercised a formidable magnetism upon my senses.

'Where does your grandmother live?'

'On the South Coast. We go in summer as well. But it's very crowded then. I like it in winter, when it's deserted.'

I went up close to the window. I pressed my head against the cold glass, but it did not still the pulse of excitement in my brain. I yearned for romance and magic, and it seemed to me that it was near. Near but intangible. I looked out at the moon; it offered me no encouragement, and no answers.

'What does your mother think of my father?' I asked.

'Mummy says your father's in love with Ursula.'

I turned from the window pane, misted by my breath, and stared at her. She was looking out at the snow.

'She said that to you?'

'Well, not actually to me. She said it to Daddy once and I heard. She doesn't mind me hearing things like that,' she added, defensively. 'She doesn't want Ursula to marry your father.' Her voice was quite natural. She was merely stating a fact.

It had occurred to me on occasions, that my father might marry again. But with the passing of the years since my mother's death the possibility, as far as I could judge, had grown more remote. There had been many women in his life, but only Alice had been constant. And her constancy, I knew, was in part sustained by its half-hearted reception. There had been passing associations, mostly discreet, although I could remember the shock of one day surprising my father with one of our many landladies on his knee, his arms around her, her tear-stained face pressed against his cheek, tears whose meaning I never discovered. Her eyes had opened first in a shock equal to my own, then in shame, the shame of impropriety, where in fact there was so little. What stimulated it must have been my childish expression of surprise and curiosity.

Then there had been Laurie, a friend who had emerged occasionally during the year or so before that winter from the unsympathetic background of his drinking. Laurie epitomised for me a streak of vulgarity in my father, developed out of the need to be well-liked in hotel-bar and public-house. With a capacity for making easy and superficial contact with people, he combined gallantry with women, and an intelligent and sincere response towards men. But these predispositions, serviced by charm, did not blind him to the cold, hard reality. He knew that they could rarely lead anywhere. Laurie, in my mind, matched up with a whole host of similar, and unfortunate impressions: the rank stench of stale drink in the early morning, secretive searching for money through the pockets of clothes discarded by my father the night before, and his own bitter self-criticism. To him, however, she represented something different. I remembered an occasion, after I had said something about Laurie, something marginally disparaging, my father had taken my shoulder and stared into my eyes, with an odd, sad expression on his face. 'Old scout,' he had said, 'she understands me. When all the others reject me, she'll still be there.'

'When all the others reject me . . .' Was I included? And what about Alice? How could he possibly imagine that there would ever be a time? Or did he mean others, leaving us two out? Deep down I believed that our life together, father and son, had some invisible constant factor to support it. I had to believe it. What else was there?

'When did your mother die?' Babette's voice came from far away, breaking in on my tide of anxious self-reassurance.

'Six years ago.'

'Wouldn't you like it if your father married again?'
'I don't really know.'
'Mummy says your father's a very passionate man. She says she's frightened of him. She keeps saying it to Ursula. Daddy just shrugs his shoulders.'

I felt embarrassed by her frankness and turned again towards the window. The sky was clear. Nothing moved. The spectral vision of trees, and distant woods, and hills rising behind them, together with the occasional far-off light of a lonely farmhouse or cottage, made all such complications in life seem unreal.

'I'd like to leave tracks in the snow down there,' I said.
'Well, let's. We'll tramp our initials there.'
'But your mother said not to go out.'
'She won't mind, when I tell her.'
'Are you sure?'
Babette smiled. 'Come on,' she said.

III

Our feet were wet when we came in, twenty minutes later; our faces flushed. The lawn at the back of the house was marked with our initials, tracked out in great lines and loops through the snow. We both felt a bit overwhelmed by what we had done to the lawn, and wondered if we would get into trouble.

We tried to wipe our shoes dry, but my socks were heavily flecked with the melting snow, and we both left marks on the polished floor. My feet were cold. The sense of power, as I had stamped round with my black boots through the white wilderness outside, was transformed into a feeling, now that I was inside the house, of clumsiness. We stood unnoticed at the side of the library, within a shallow bay of bookshelves, and we were ignored by the guests, who represented to us, coming in from the silent cold, a wall of deafening noise, and impregnably solid flesh. The volume of sound had risen appreciably, anyway; but to us, after the dead stillness of the deserted rooms upstairs, and the cold, vibrant loneliness of the moonlit lawns under their blanket of snow, it became now an oppressive assault on our ears. Babette went to find her mother. Flushed and hot in the warm and crowded room, I waited for her return. I stood, edged in against the bookshelves, watching the faces of the guests. Although I knew that the mouths, moving in animated conversation, were responsible for the noise that roared in my ear, the two were separate. Individually the mouths were dumb, except when occasionally a shriek or bellow of laughter could, by chance, be connected with some gaping red orifice. This was not often possible. And the more I stared, the more detached what I saw became from what I could hear, until I felt dizzy from it all. I bent once to brush my socks. I could feel the dampness of melting snow soaking through. I noticed the broken puddles of water from my black boots on the polished floor. Surreptitiously I shifted the sole of one foot backwards and forwards across the wetness in a guilty and futile attempt to rub it away.

'Hello! What have we here? Where have you been? Who are you, boy?' I froze at the icy jocularity of the voice which questioned me in what was almost a drawl. I knew that voice. Lady Fisher was standing beside me with Colonel Savage, one of the school trustees. It was the latter who had spoken, a familiar, threatening look on his face: that of a man of authority on the hunt for misdemeanours.

Savage was tall, with a big-boned, taut-skinned face. His grey eyes had an unfriendly lidded look about them.

'I've been exploring the garden,' I said. A few guests nearby turned and looked at me, then backed away when they saw the state of my boots. Colonel Savage himself stared forbiddingly down at the puddle of water. From being protected in the bookshelf recess, shielded by it and looking out upon all the noise and action, I was now exposed within it and trapped.

'And who are you?' Colonel Savage went on. 'What's your name?' The final word was dragged out, filling the bubble of silence in which I felt I was standing. With the nasal 'a' exaggerated, the word became grotesquely distorted. In the midst of growing panic, I had a fleeting urge to laugh.

I told him. 'I'm from Coppinger.'

Lady Fisher looked at Colonel Savage. 'These Coppinger boys!' she said. There was a hint of despair in her tense, tired voice. Colonel Savage's chin set in a firm, hard line. I watched the muscles move under the tight surface of his cheek. 'I told Sir Joseph,' Lady Fisher went on, gripping Colonel Savage's arm. 'I told him. Glasses have been broken. And one boy was sick. And now this. Somebody had better get my husband.' The appeal was vague, but a young, fair-haired man went off. The Colonel was beginning to bristle with indignation. He had the appearance of a man over-conscious of his own authority.

'We'll get to the root of this, Lady Fisher. I'll find out what's been going on. I have experience of these boys. There will be no lies told to me. Coppinger boys all over the house. I told Sir Joseph myself it was wrong. Completely wrong. Now then, young man, just where have you been?'

I looked round. Where was Babette? Did she exist, or had I dreamt the whole thing?

'I didn't do anything,' I said. 'We just thought it would be fun to go out. We were looking at the garden from one of the windows, and I wanted to walk in the snow.' I looked up into the cold grey half-lidded eyes. In the hope that it might ameliorate things, I added a belated 'Sir.'

'Looking at the snow, eh? And what rooms were you in?'

'I went to see Sir Joseph's collection of eggs.' In my mounting panic I felt that a more expansive and totally truthful confession was called for. Only complete directness and honesty would appease this angry man.

But I was wrong. From the expression that kindled in the large, cold eyes, I knew I had made a mistake. The muscles under the flushed skin of his cheek began to thud steadily. I felt he was being unnecessarily stern. I wondered why. Had he drunk too much champagne, and was it taking him this way?

'You did what?'

'I went to see—' I began.

But the Colonel had no patience to hear again what he had already heard quite clearly. 'You went to see Sir Joseph's collection of eggs? And who gave you permission to do that? Eh? Who? Who?' His voice began to achieve the hoarse proportions of a shout.

I could not answer. I felt a constriction in my throat, which by this time was quite dry.

Suddenly an extraordinary thing happened, taking everyone, myself included, entirely by surprise. The Colonel, with a kind of twitching in his flushed face becoming more noticeable, stepped forward and struck me across the cheek. I was still frightened of him, but now, in addition, utterly surprised at his action. In stepping away from him on the smooth wooden floor, made wet around my feet by the melted snow from my boots, I lost my balance, slipped and fell. The slap sang in my ears. I felt the sting of it and the shame of it. I wanted to cry out.

The circle of guests, who had become silent and intent as Colonel Savage worked himself towards this final climax of rage, now seemed frozen into immobility. They became a single mass of humankind swimming before my frightened eyes. No one remonstrated or came to my defence. They did not move or speak. To me they resembled a cardboard cut-out of a crowd for a model theatre. In my mind they were permanently linked together, and later, in my memory, small, so that if one could have been able to take hold of the elbow of the woman who had been standing at one end, and then lifted, it should have been possible to hang the whole group up sideways in the air, reduced suddenly to Tom Thumb proportions. They were that part of humanity whose rôle is to be an audience for life's dramas: curious, fearful of involvement, passive, and, in time of crisis, having no function beyond the dubious one of looking on.

In my confusion I saw Philpotts easing his way through to the front, a puzzled frown on his face. In his movements he was never precipitate. 'Get up,' the Colonel was shouting. 'Get up, boy. I'll get to the bottom of this. Turn your pockets out.'

'I think that's enough, Colonel Savage,' Philpotts said. 'I think you can leave the boy alone now.'

For all the youthfulness of his eighteen years, emphasised by the grey school clothing, and by the dark, curly, crisp hair, he looked equal to the occasion.

His intervention was ill-received. Colonel Savage pointed a trembling finger at him. 'Who?' he asked, in his shrill voice, 'Who do you think you are? What do you mean by interfering? I shall have you punished. I shall have you expelled.'

My face stung from the blow I had received. My head swam. I felt dizzy. I was conscious of the Colonel's long, bony fingers gripping my arm. I felt no great pain, but there was a singing in my head, and a strange numbness which deadened the voices around me. It seemed also that a zone of nervous silence was spreading among the guests who had witnessed the incident. Beyond it, a long way off, there was still the hum of the reception. I saw Madge, and then Babette, small and distant, just as she had appeared first to me when we had arrived. She moved through the taller men and women and stood staring at me, a puzzled look on her face.

Philpotts, calm and unruffled, crossed over and stood beside me. He continued to look into the Colonel's face, his eyes maddeningly direct. 'I don't think so,' he said. 'I don't think it would be wise to carry this any further.' To me, just then, he was the manifestation of wisdom in an unwise world. I felt my arm being released.

Colonel Savage's jaw chewed minute particles of nothing. Lady Fisher put her hand on his arm. 'The boy's right,' she said, 'they are our guests. We asked them here—for the singing,' she added lamely.

It was Madge who brought the episode to a conclusion. 'I think we are all being rather silly,' she said; then turning and facing everyone, she went on, her voice slightly raised, though her tone was one of conciliation, 'He was with Babette. She took him to see the house. Then they went into the garden. They have done nothing wrong. I'm sure of that. You've done nothing wrong, have you?'

I shook my head. I felt the tears pushing into my eyes, and wanted to blink them back. I felt overwhelmed by this sudden rescue.

Madge went on: 'I think you should apologise for hitting him, Colonel Savage. He didn't deserve it. Don't you agree, Lady Fisher? What did he do that could give the Colonel such offence?'

Nobody answered. Nobody knew. Our choirmaster had at last appeared from one of the further rooms. The Colonel decided in favour of a little face-saving. 'Get these boys out of here, Parker. It is time to go. Get them back to Coppinger. Quickly.'

Philpotts looked at Mrs Springer. Then at Babette. He put his hand on my shoulder. He did not lower his voice. He just said, 'Are you all right?'

'Yes.'

'Good.' He looked at his watch, then at Parker. 'Perhaps it *is* time for us to leave.'

Parker's mouth framed words, but he thought better of it, and turned to where Danby and Eagle and several of the other boys had gathered to listen, their eyes wide with nervous curiosity and fear; yet also with relief that, while Coppinger was obviously in the thick of something, they themselves were only on the fringes. He told them to go out to the bus. They turned, unwillingly, and walked a short way before stopping once more to see what would happen. Parker looked across to where Philpotts was standing with his hand still resting on my shoulder, and gestured to us to come.

Philpotts said, 'Do you want to say goodbye to your friend?'

Madge bent down towards me. 'I think you'd better go with the other boys now. Does your head hurt?'

'No, it's all right.' I said it slowly, shyly.

'I hope you'll come and see us in London,' she said. 'Babette, you'd like that, wouldn't you?'

'Oh, yes, Mummy.' To me she seemed close, and yet infinitely far away.

'I'm sorry you got into trouble,' she said. 'It was all my fault.'

My lip quivered. I shook my head. 'It doesn't matter,' I said. It was all I could think of to say.

IV

The moon floated higher now above the snow. The bus moved away from the house, gathering speed. The trees threw down their sharp shadows. These moved towards us across the glistening ground, became a blur, and then moved rapidly away in our wake. Across the flat meadows, deep in untrodden snow, silent and still in the frozen cold, could be seen the warm yellow light from the house and the movement of people at the door as other guests took their leave. But the trees broke the image more frequently, and soon there was a dip in the ground and the house was lost to sight.

We travelled at first in silence. Philpotts sat beside Parker in the front of the bus, but neither spoke. Everyone knew, by the time we had all climbed into the bus, that there had been a row. The whispering had sped like lightning among the other boys on their way from the house, and already distortion and exaggeration were taking over from the inconclusive and unfinished events at whose centre I had stood. The drama of Kershaw being sick, and of Jennings breaking a champagne glass and spilling champagne down the trousers of one of the guests, was swallowed up in the larger drama of Philpotts quietly putting one of the trustees in his place.

How did he dare? What would happen to him? Would there be a school meeting? Would the headmaster punish us all? Boys began to whisper among themselves, and these were the questions they asked.

They were being asked in a vacuum. What had I done? How had it all started? The whispered explanations continued.

Danby, beside me in the bus, said, 'What happened? What did you do?'

I told him, but only about exploring the house and looking at the collection of eggs. I said little about Babette. I made her incidental to the adventure of roaming first among the rooms of the mansion, then of trampling and kicking in the snow. I described carefully what had passed between Philpotts and Colonel Savage.

'He said he'd have Philpotts expelled?' Danby asked.

'That's what he said.'

'And do you think he will? Do you think Philpotts will be sent away?'

'No,' I said. 'They wouldn't dare. They wouldn't want the school mentioned in the papers. It happened once before.'

'But not like this. I hope you're right. He's pretty good, old Phillers. But Parker's in a paddy. He'll have us all in a ditch before we get back, the way he's driving.'

Eagle leaned over from the seat behind where I was sitting. 'What's she like?' His unerring accuracy went to the heart of the matter in that single question. I remembered the moment at the reception when the crowd had parted, and I had seen Danby and Eagle together, watching me. It had been Eagle who had summed things up. He was from Shoreditch. There was a teasing sharpness in his voice. He meant his question to be heard by others in the bus. He leaned close to me, waiting for an answer that did not come. Then he went on: ' 'Er muvver's a smasher. A bit of all right. I'd go for 'er, if it was me. The girl's a bit young, but not for our Casanover 'ere,' giving my shoulder a push before he sat back again in his seat.

Danby said, 'What *is* she like?' His Yorkshire accent added a sympathetic plaintiveness to his question. 'I don't know, Danners,' I answered. I could think of no satisfactory way of describing what I thought of Babette, even to Danby. What I thought was still too much in the heart's imagination. 'Her father and mother know my father. They live near us in London.' And then, the wish outdistancing the fact, I added: 'It's possible we'll go and spend Christmas with her family.'

'Did she ask you?'

'It was discussed. Of course, it can't be decided without my father.'

'I've never been away for Christmas.'

'We usually have it in different places.'

Danby looked at me. 'What do you mean?'

'Well, we go away for Christmas sometimes. You know, go to the country from London. Or, if we're living in the country, go up to London.'

'Who's we?'

'My father and me.'

'I thought you had a brother?'

'Well, he's usually away at Christmas.' The geographical and emotional dispersals of my family in different directions sounded to me somewhat superficial and glib.

Eagle's face re-appeared over the back of the seat. This time he spoke more quietly. 'What's she like, mate?'

'She's all right,' I said. I wanted to say no more. I had no more to say. I distrusted Eagle. He was bigger than I was, a pasty-faced chubby boy who sang alto, who had fat cheeks and small eyes, and who was a pander to one of the school bullies, and the epitome of treachery.

Foolishly, with the desire to lay a false scent, I said: 'Her mother wouldn't let me call her Mrs Springer. She told me to call her Madge.'

'Fancy!' said Eagle. 'Madge! I wish she'd said that to me. I wouldn't mind calling 'er Madge.' His throaty laugh was forced and lewd. He subsided once more into his seat.

The bus drove on through the snow. It skidded once, and

Parker slowed down. Philpotts sat beside him, looking straight ahead. Neither of them spoke.

Gradually, the rest of the choir relaxed into silence. There were occasional bursts of laughter from the back, where the tenors and basses, none of them of Philpotts's seniority in the school, had monopolised the seats, and were talking in low tones.

Danby nudged me once, and pointed out of the window. We were passing an ancient circle of stones, standing out in the snow beyond a dry stone wall. They looked eerie in the bright light of the moon.

'I wouldn't fancy being on my own out there,' Danby said. 'Would you?'

'No. It looks pretty spooky. Do you think it's haunted?'

'I don't know. They say you never count the same number of stones.'

We relapsed again into silence. I felt tense and excited, fearful of both past and future events. My thoughts turned over and over. Names ran through my head. Babette, Madge, Philpotts, my father, Alice, Christmas, the looming sharp, pale face of Colonel Savage, the imagined face of the unknown Ursula.

The small battered bus slowed down for the entrance to the school. We looked out. The lights in the houses reminded us that it was still quite early in the evening. Through the brightly lit, uncurtained windows we could see the bustle of end-of-term activity, the cleaning out of lockers, the trade and barter of goods, the ragging; that mood when discipline is lost in excitement.

Parker drove up through the houses, scattered among the leafless trees of the school grounds, to the main office building of Coppinger. It was usual, on such occasions, for boys to be dropped off at their houses, or near them. But Parker, grim-faced and silent throughout the journey, was in no mood for such courtesies. And nobody suggested that he might stop.

'Straight back to your houses,' he said, after the bus had

stopped. 'No loitering. And be sure to report to your housemasters when you get in.' He turned to Philpotts. 'I'd like you to come with me while I put the bus away, Philpotts,' he said.

Philpotts stayed in his seat. 'Right you are, sir.' His voice was relaxed, almost sleepy. The rest of us climbed out, and stood round in the snow. It was very cold, the air sharp and crystalline, the shadows around the big Victorian office block precise and angular across the white courtyard. The snow, pressed down by other vehicles, crunched under the wheels of the bus as it moved away. We watched it until the tail-lights disappeared behind the corner that led to the garage. In the silence our feet squeaked, and we stamped.

'What do you think will happen?'

'What does he want Philpotts for?'

'Will he get the boot?'

'Don't be wet. He's all right. Parker'll just square him up.'

'What do you mean, "Square 'im up"?'

'Just tell him to leave everything in Parker's hands. Parker's scared, can't you see?'

'I didn't think—'

'You're dumb. What's the use talking to you.'

'What actually happened? Did you see, Smithy?'

'No. I wasn't there. I was at the champagne.' Smithy's comments were concluded with a well-timed, well-executed belch.

We moved away in groups from the main building. The figures of the boys were clearly visible against the moonlit snow, and the sound of voices carried clearly in the still night air. High above us all the great school clock chimed eight. We could see its face quite plainly. The sound was crystal sharp in the frosty air.

Eagle, Smith and Jennings, with Danby and myself, walked slowly down towards our own house. We were half-hoping Philpotts would catch up with us. He was head of the house. We wanted to know what would happen.

'There isn't much time, is there?' Danby asked. 'If we go home the day after tomorrow, what could the boss do on the last day of term?'

' 'E could do somefink, if 'e wanted to,' Eagle said. 'Don't be daft. 'E's good at last minute dramas. Remember the time when the money was stole. 'E got that back, didn't 'e?'

'I hope nothing happens,' I said. I was afraid now for Philpotts more than for myself.

We came to the house, and stopped and turned. We could see Philpotts striding across the snow towards us. He had taken a short cut under the trees. We waited for him. From the house came the sound of laughter and shouting, the slamming of doors, the movement of boxes, the hollow echo of voices in the tiled washrooms and lavatories. We had no wish to go in without some word from Philpotts about what Parker might have said.

He came up to us. 'It's no night for gathering out of doors. What are you all waiting for?'

'We were waiting for you. Is it all right? What . . . what did Parker say?' It was I who spoke, looking up at him and feeling much more directly involved than any of the others. I noticed he was smiling. Danby and the rest watched us, as we stood face to face.

Philpotts said, 'Of course it's all right.' He spoke for them all to hear. 'A couple of expulsions, yours and mine, a few resignations by trustees. A row in the papers. We'll have the *Oxford Mail* down, and there may be questions in Parliament. But there's nothing to worry about. Nothing in the least serious. Nothing that won't blow over in a week.'

Eagle laughed nervously. 'You're 'avin' us on, ain't you?'

'We'll have to see,' he said. 'Now you can all cut along inside.'

They turned and went. I stood still in the snow, looking up into Philpotts's face. 'Is it really all right? I mean . . . there won't be any trouble?'

'I don't know,' he said. 'Nor does Parker. He doesn't want

it to go any further, but it depends on Colonel Savage, and Sir Joseph. If they ring up the head in the morning, then there could be trouble.' He paused. 'If there is,' he said, 'will it have been worth while? Is she a nice girl?'

'Yes,' I said. 'Yes. She is.' I looked with gratitude at Philpotts. 'She's super.'

We turned towards the house. He put his hand on my shoulder, and I was stirred by a sense of privilege. What had the guests at the wedding got that I had not got also? That Philpotts had not got? They could do nothing now. Term was ending.

'I did nothing I wouldn't do again,' I said. 'And . . . and thanks for what you did.'

'I did nothing I wouldn't do again,' Philpotts said. 'So that's all right, then, isn't it? And we can jump the next hurdle when we come to it.'

Chapter Two

'Go on.' The voice in the darkness sounded impatient.

I was tired. My head throbbed. I regretted my role as dormitory entertainer.

'Ssh.'

'They fought on, the steel flashing in the moonlight. He had to win. He had to find Dubois' weakness. There had to be one. Most of his own strokes were simply to defend himself against the flashing speed of the other man.' I paused once again for a moment, and tried to moisten my lips. I was thirsty. I could feel the tension in the room as the others listened. 'Alan looked up into the arrogant, sneering face. As he did so he saw the expression change. It all happened in a single moment of time. The confidence was replaced by fear. But it was too late. He plunged his own blade deep and true into the bunched lace at the other man's throat. Dubois' heavy breathing became a bubbling gurgle. Blood splashed from his mouth. He fell sideways, choking, dying. Through the haze of pain and relief he saw Anna running towards him across the clearing, her face in the moonlight ready to cry out to him, her arms reaching out towards him. He felt for his shoulder, damp with blood, and quickly pulled out of it Dubois' rapier, which he threw down across the other man's body. It was all finished. He had won in the end.'

I stopped and lay still in bed, a throbbing sensation going through me. I thought of Anna, tending Alan's wounds, of the sympathy between them, the expressions of love, and of relief. But I could not, or would not phrase them, thereby extending the story still further. It was better, I felt, to finish abruptly.

'Tell us anuvver.'

'Go on, tell us another.'

The appeals were echoed through the dormitory. Normally I liked telling stories. I liked being the one they mostly asked. There was the time before the story, when the appeals went round in the darkness. And the time of indecision and uncertainty, when nothing seemed to be there of which to make a story. Then came the inner decision: yes, perhaps *that* would do, followed by a certain element of coyness and procrastination, until, at the right moment, the events were launched. The best time of all was when it was over, and one lay in the silence, savouring the warm feelings of accomplishment. Yet, somehow, in spite of this, that night's story had been ground out against the grain.

Now, looking up, I could see the vague outline of the high-beamed ceiling of the room. Coppinger houses had been built in the mid-nineteenth century. They were plain, solid, Victorian structures in granite, with mullioned windows, hammer beams, pitch-pine panelling. Through the window at the end of the dormitory shone the moonlight, falling across my bed and giving enough light for me to see the shadowy figures of the other boys in the iron beds that lined the walls. Danby was beside me. He said, 'Is there no more?'

The headache I had had in the morning had returned again. 'No,' I said. 'There's no more.'

From somewhere below in the house we heard the distant sound of voices and laughter. It came in waves and faded again into silence.

'Gaffer's telling his stories,' one of the boys said. 'That means the seniors'll be coming up soon. He never goes on long once he gets onto them.'

'I wonder what they've been drinking?'

'What'll Phillers say when he finds he's got an apple-pie bed?'

It was the night after the wedding. The next morning we would all be leaving for the Christmas holiday. The excitement of it had rippled through the dormitory in waves.

I had heard nothing further during the day. My head had been aching when I woke up that morning. I had reported it to matron, who had given me aspirin and told me I should not have drunk so much champagne. Her words made me wonder whether the blow struck by Colonel Savage had been real at all.

'Did you 'ear any more about the wedding?' Eagle asked. His uncanny sensing of the thoughts passing through my own mind bewildered me.

'Nothing's going to happen,' I assured him in the darkness of the dormitory.

'Bet somefink'll 'appen between you and that girl. Will you see 'er in the 'olidays?' It was Eagle who spoke from the other side of the dormitory.

I felt a flush of embarrassment.

'What girl's this?' said one of the boys.

'Yes, what's all this about a girl?'

'It was someone 'e met. 'E won't tell us about 'er. Keepin' 'er very secret, 'e is. Very secret. What's 'er name, eh? 'E won't even tell us that.'

'I did tell you, Eagle,' I said. And then, more loudly, 'Her name is Babette.'

Some of the boys repeated the name, dwelling on it, teasing me with it. But it was half-hearted. I almost wished I had gone on with the story, inventing something to command their interest.

'Tell us about her.'

'Go on. Tell us.'

'There's nothing to tell. Her mother knows my father. That's all.'

'That's a bit la-di-da. "Her mother knows my father".'

'Tell us anuvver one, do! There's more to it than that. What were you doin' to get Colonel Savage all worked up? What went on?'

'Oh, shut up. I don't want to talk about it.'

'Oh, *really*. "I don't want to talk about it."' Someone in the darkness gave an exaggerated imitation of my voice. 'Must be serious. Are you meeting her during the holidays, old man?'

'Course 'e is.'

'Leave him alone,' Danby said. 'It's his business. She's his friend.'

Gradually they quietened down, and began talking among themselves. I lay on my back, looking out at the sky. I tried to gather up again the threads of my story, Dubois choking on his own blood, Alan lying wounded but triumphant, Anna coming towards him. On such a night, I thought, just like this, the moon as it is now, the stars pale. I was Alan, and I could feel quite suddenly the pain in my shoulder. I put my hand to it, twisting in conjured anguish. Anna's face was the face of Babette. I felt my heart thud with emotion.

Eagle was right. Something must come of it, in the weeks ahead, on holiday in London.

I could so easily people the city with my fancies, and now she was a part of them. I could picture the two of us, Babette and myself, in Church Street going down towards Barkers, on Campden Hill, walking in summer sunshine up towards the tennis club there, in Kensington Gardens, going towards the Albert Memorial, among the trees, beside the lake, out in a boat.

It never occurred to me that she might know all these spots equally well. In my mind it was my city. She would be brought to a deeper knowledge of it by me, and only by me.

Then it welled up within me, the desire to speak of her, extol her merits. I spoke quietly. 'I hope to go and spend Christmas with the girl I met, Danners. I really hope so. She said she hoped so, too.'

'You told me so. On the way back from the wedding. Have you fallen for her?'

'Well, I like her. I like her a lot. But you won't say anything, Danners? About staying with her for Christmas?'

'Of course I won't. Is she really nice?'

'Yes. She is.'

'And her mother?'

'Yes. I like her, too. It's her sister who is a friend of my father's. But it's all happened recently. I don't know any of them. I haven't met any of them. This was the first time.'

'Are they rich?'

'I don't know.'

'I expect so if they go as guests to a wedding like that.'

'Yes, I expect you're right. It doesn't matter to me, of course. I don't mind whether they're rich or poor.'

'Where do they live?' Danby asked.

'Well, they go to have Christmas on the south coast. But they have a flat in London.'

'Do you live in a flat?'

'Yes,' I said. 'We live in a small flat in London. Just my father and me. It's near Hyde Park. It's in quite a good area called Notting Hill Gate.'

From his adjoining bed I heard Danby suddenly say: 'You're right lucky, to live in London! Whereabouts in London are you?'

He knew nothing of London. He travelled home by a different route, never touching the metropolis. And the nuances of district or of habitation meant nothing to him.

'We've actually moved to a new flat since the summer holidays,' I said. 'My father had a job in the country, in Kent. But he gave it up. He said he couldn't face the winter there.'

'Why? Isn't he well?'

I felt my face redden in the darkness, and was glad of the concealment. I recalled, all too easily, the early weeks of the term now ending, the coming of autumn colours to the

Cotswolds, and no word from my father. How well I knew the stages, the silence as the bouts of drinking became more frequent, more excessive. Then the first evasive letter with its change of address, the apologies, the small amounts of money —conscience payments—the little parcels of chocolate, carefully, methodically wrapped, the feigned illness to account for it all. I could detail the slow progress of recovery, the lapses, the false starts, the growing confidence. Part of my nervousness, preparing to go home for Christmas this time, was due to the feeling that a full cycle had not been quite completed. Else would I not have had some warning of Babette's descent on the wedding with her mother? I had told my father all about it, writing a slow and arduous Sunday letter each week, telling of the choir practices, the different anthems, my own solo. Surely that had registered? And my father, at his normal best, dilligent and thorough, would surely have related it all. Surely?

In the darkness I said to him: 'My father suffers from asthma a bit.' Asthma! A good word for it!

Below us, in the house, the party for the senior boys was coming to an end. We heard the laughter, the mixture of familiarity and respect with which the house prefects and monitors said goodnight to the Gaffer. Then the sound of them coming up the stairs.

The dormitory was quiet. We waited for Philpotts. Voices passed on the landing. There were snatches of conversation and laughter. Then these died out in goodnights, and silence prevailed. It was minutes before Philpotts came in. He walked slowly down the length of the dormitory towards the window, and stood looking out. I watched him. Then he turned and stood for a moment, his eyes adjusting to the gloom after the landing lights. Then he lifted himself onto the window-sill. I felt him rest one foot on the end of my own bed.

'Are you awake?'

'We're all awake.'

'And you've been talking.' He looked at me. 'Have you been

telling one of your stories? Full of blood and death and beautiful girls?'

'Yes. As a matter of fact, I have.'

'It was good, Philpotts,' Painter said. 'Full of blood. But only one girl. He didn't tell us what happened in the end.'

'I did,' I said. 'That's not true.'

A brief argument ensued on the merits of the story. The final judgement was favourable, though some were still not completely satisfied at its abrupt conclusion. Philpotts sat in silence. He was clearly visible in outline against the light from the window, a stocky, unathletic figure, relaxed, amiable, self-confident. 'Left it to your imaginations, did he? A festering thought.'

'What was the party like, Philpotts?'

'As always,' he said. 'A performance by your house-master. He regaled us with many stories, as he invariably does. And who are we to compete? Have we fought battles in the jungles of Burma? Have we engaged in sharp conflict with the fiendish Japanese? No. We are at a disadvantage on such occasions. We drank the Gaffer's famous end-of-term wine cup. We ate his sausage rolls. We listened dutifully. We laughed.'

'Did 'is daughter come?' Eagle asked.

'Yes, Eagle, you lecherous monkey. The nubile Janet made a brief, dramatic appearance for us, danced and sang, did her one and only striptease act, and then went away, Barnwell and Hodges whooping after her.'

Weatherby asked, 'Did she really dance and sing, and . . . and . . . do an act, Philpotts?' The others laughed at him.

'What else could she do?' asked Philpotts. 'She has heard the stories even more often than we have. She didn't stay long.'

I asked him: 'Was Parker there?' Parker, as well as being choirmaster, was house tutor.

'Yes, he was.' He spoke quietly. Some of the other boys began talking among themselves. But most lay listening. I looked over at Danby, who was in the bed beside me, and saw that he was lying on his side, watching Philpotts. Philpotts went on: 'Nothing will come of the row at the wedding.' He paused. 'How's your head?'

'I have a headache. I had one this morning. I got some aspirin from Matron. She said it was the champagne. And it went away. But it's come back again tonight.'

'Hitting someone like that on the side of the head is dangerous.'

'Is it? What can it do?'

'Oh, it's just dangerous. It might damage your brain.'

'I don't feel it's damaged. It seems to be working as usual.'

Philpotts laughed. 'That's not saying a great deal.'

'I'm worried,' I said. My voice was quiet. 'What about Mrs Springer? What about Babette? It would be awful if they were involved.'

'The whole thing enrages me. What are we, at Coppinger, that we have to be treated like a charity school, out for a binge? If we are untrustworthy, just because of being here, then it would have been better if they'd left us in the homes we came from.' Philpotts looked directly down the length of the dormitory towards the darkness at the end. It was as if he saw in the darkness ahead of him the enemy: privilege.

'From the very start they made us feel we were different,' said Danby, who had been listening.

'We're different all right,' Philpotts said. 'We'll be carrying this school on our backs for the rest of our lives. We're different because we're at Coppinger. It means that we've been plucked out from some family background that went wrong, and given the privilege of this place. That's how the trustees see it. That's how other people who know the school see it.'

I could only understand part of what Philpotts was getting at. Yet I suppose I looked in admiration at the bigger boy. I remembered my conversation with Babette, standing in Sir Joseph's study, above the laughter of the wedding guests, high above the untrampled snow. I remembered being disconcerted that she knew already all about us, knew what kind of school Coppinger was, knew why we were there. I accepted what Philpotts was saying, yet could not see it as the burden it was becoming for the older boy. For me it was a natural enough state, better by far than the last I had known. I could only judge it in that way. I remembered something of the life from which I had been plucked, and I would rather that I did not remember it. *That* was the real burden, not Coppinger, but what Coppinger had replaced.

'When will you leave Coppinger, Philpotts?'

'At the end of the summer term.'

'Will the school be any help in getting you a job?'

'Of course not. How could it? I shall be doing national service first anyway. Then Oxford.'

'Oxford?'

'If I get in. I'm reasonably confident that during two years in the army I can make good the intellectual deficiencies of Coppinger.'

Oxford was a Mecca for all of us at Coppinger. At half-terms we made trips there. Boys hitched the twenty-odd miles. Runaways were usually caught there. The choir's annual outing was to the New Theatre. I had seen *The Marriage of Figaro* on one such occasion. Yet few boys went to the University.

'Will you be working for that until the summer?'

'Yes.'

What did they think of Philpotts, the other boys lying there in the darkness? I felt their gradual exclusion from the conversation as I received his brief answers to my questions. I was closer to him than the others. I knew I was held in special affection, had been teased before now because of it. There were occasions, rare fortunately, when Philpotts's fairness towards me was in question because of it. But I did not mind. I was grateful that this friendship did not impose upon me too much of the physical proximity that with other relationships like it in the school gave rise to snide jokes and dark suspicions. It was better to have sentiment and poetry rather than a familiar hand around my shoulders.

What I wanted to know was what Philpotts was feeling. What did he think? What were his ambitions? In the quiet of the dormitory, with the conversations around us dying into the warm silence of sleep, with Danby beside me drifting into the stillness of measured breathing, his eyes closed now, one hand hanging out of the side of the bed, with the moonlight, cold and pale, gleaming down through the small panes of glass, I felt drawn closer to the older boy. Boy! What a foolish term for this tousled eighteen-year-old, with his heavy shoulders, his love of sarcasm, his dreams of Oxford.

'Will you be in London at all, Philpotts?'

'I may be. Or I could come up. We could go out for the day. See a film, perhaps.'

'I'd like that.'

'So would I. We'll do it. We'll fix it up on the journey tomorrow.' He stood up. 'I'd better unravel my bed. I suspect it's been tampered with. There aren't many awake now to enjoy my discomfort. A strange ritual.' He sighed, and stretched, and eased himself down from the window-sill. 'Goodnight,' he said, ambling slowly away between the beds to the other end of the dormitory.

'Goodnight, Phillers.'

Chapter Three

I

Those of us who were travelling by the London train were strung out the next morning in the sunlight along the road to the station. Our luggage had gone ahead of us in school transport; so had the prefects who travelled on that route, among them Philpotts. It was a privilege the handful of senior boys welcomed, for the station was well over a mile from the school. The rest of us welcomed it, too. It lifted the last restraints from our shoulders.

We laughed and sang in the clear morning air, shouting with raucous enthusiasm. There was a mood of infectious gaiety, a determination to throw off the last, thin shackles of authority. The sun was up in a pale blue sky, still quite low above the sleepy limestone cottages of the village, yet shining with dazzling brightness on the fields deep in snow, on the ribbon of white roadway ahead of us, and on the black branches of the hawthorn hedges where the direct warmth of its rays had begun to melt the thin ridges of snowflakes that decorated the leafless wood in a delicate tracery of white. The drips of falling water could be heard occasionally as we passed along. But few heeded them. Instead, we jingled what remained of our term-time pocket money and listened with unchecked tolerance to the boastings and the stories, the plans and the regrets, the unimaginable mystery of what lay ahead of us all, the relief at what we were leaving behind.

Many years later—indeed, not long before my father's death—I faced, suddenly and fortuitously, an occasion which highlighted the strange atmosphere which seems to surround us during schooldays. It was a couple of years before my father died. I had gone to visit him, and we had enjoyed two or three days of unbroken October sunshine. We had talked gardening, looked at his stamps, discussed my career, and gone driving in a hired car in the Quantocks. He was already then physically restricted, his legs giving him trouble as a result of poor circulation, so that he was virtually a prisoner of the house. Inevitably, the time for departure came too soon, and some expression of his, I cannot remember what, mildly hinted at the possibility that we would not have many more occasions like that. As I walked away from the house to catch the London train—he always waited at the gate until the turning in the road shut him from view—I was struck, vividly, forcefully, and quite without the usual preamble which leads to such thoughts, by the feeling that he had taken on —been forced to take on—precisely those limitations and restraints which, in childhood, are imposed by parents and schools on children. He had become me, and I had become him. That was exactly how I felt. I was the man of affairs, striding away under pressure of business and responsibility; he was the child all over again, yearning for the unattainable, yearning to be other than what he was. So that when I use the phrase 'unimaginable mystery', I am referring to the amazing vortex into which all our reactions, to the very slightest things, can be concentrated. Take that moment, on the road from the school to the station; it was the mystery of freedom that filled us, stimulating us as the scent of prey stimulates the hunting animal: to answer no bell at seven in the morning; to choose what food to eat, and when; to attend no lessons; to indulge in no sport; to fret away no endless hours at the homework tables; and not to be sent to bed. Gone the smells of cleaned and polished floors, the disinfectants, the carbolic soap, the heady smells of polish and leather in the bootrooms, the sourness of stale sweat in the changing rooms of the gymnasium. Gone, above all, the circumscriptions of discipline. We were on our own.

Kessner and I walked side by side. We did not talk much. Kessner was younger than I, and from another house. We had our singing in common, sharing Wesley's 'Love One Another with a Pure Heart Fervently', at the wedding, but not much else besides. I had said goodbye to Danby earlier, and had seen him leave for a train that passed through the same station on its way north well before daylight. I liked Kessner well enough, I supposed. (He was about a year and a half younger than I.) He had a fine voice, lighter than mine, but of a high quality, and Parker had made it clear to us both that he would be the next lead treble. I knew that Kessner could not equal the bell-like tone of my own voice, and was glad of that. But I knew also that my position was transient; my pre-eminence could not last. And though I would have liked it to be different, I knew my treble days were numbered. Kessner had time on his side. Did I feel resentment? Being out of the choir was being pushed into a wilderness. And yet could I blame Kessner for that? I would be lucky to last through the summer, to take part in the concerts then, before those hoarse squeaks and sore throats which I had heard so often in others, descended on me, and carried me over from childhood into youth. It was a Stygian passage, one of no return. And, oh, how much it mattered to me, being the best singer in the choir, and how much it would mean to lose the distinction for no other reason than the onset of years. My father was proud of my voice; displayed it as though it was a visible thing. It was to me my one secure justification. I could not offer my father any sporting skills; I could not emulate his past triumphs as a rugby footballer, or as an athlete. But I could bring him this—for a short time more, anyway.

'Do you sing at home, Kess?' I asked.

'Oh, yes. I sing in the choir. My mother arranged it.'

'Do you sing solos?'

'Sometimes. What about you?'

'No . . . There's nowhere I could. You see we live in a flat in London. I don't even know where the church is.'

We walked on through the snow together. Going down the road ahead of us was Eagle. He was with Grainger. Grainger was between fifteen and sixteen, big for his age, a clumsy, noisy, aggressive boy, red-haired and with many freckles. He attracted around him a group of younger boys who fed on his words and sought the protection of his crude strength. There were five or six now, clustered around, and listening as Eagle spoke to him, the clear cockney inflection drifting back to us as we followed along the snow-packed road towards the station.

'They're talking about the wedding,' Kessner said.

'Everyone's been talking about it,' I said. 'It's amazing the head hasn't heard. He usually picks up things like that jolly fast. I thought he had yesterday. But nothing happened.'

'It's too late now.'

'It's all blown over. That's what Philpotts said. He told me Parker'd spoken to him, and nothing's going to happen.'

'I'm glad.'

'So am I.'

Kessner nudged my arm. 'They're talking about you. Eagle's telling Grainger about the girl you met.'

I shrugged my shoulders. So what? School was over. What could they do? Even so, I felt a slight tremble of fear. Out on the open road to the station, term ended, the school discipline and security left behind, and Philpotts far ahead of us getting the luggage organised, there was time and scope for trouble. I slackened my pace, and Kessner with me. Boys were stretched out in small groups ahead of us and behind.

'I hope they don't throw us in the snow,' Kessner said. I did not answer. It was my own fear expressed. Under the hedges the snow had drifted, and was deep. I did not relish torture of the kind outlined by my smaller companion.

I noticed Eagle glancing back towards us once or twice, his face bearing an expression of sly vindictiveness. Other boys looked round, though Grainger paid them no attention, slouching on with large, ungainly strides. He was a boy perpetually outgrowing his clothes, and careless of them anyway. His socks were down in sloppy untidiness around his grubby black shoes. His hands in his pockets pulled out the sides of his baggy, creased trousers.

They were walking noticeably slower now, and, slowing up too, we heard the sound of another group of boys coming up behind us. We were in good time for the train; excitement about getting away had made sure of that.

Grainger, still without looking back, began asking Eagle questions. 'So, what was she like, Eagle?'

'Ooh, a bit scrawny.' He filled the word 'scrawny' with the cockney sound of his disdain.

'Flat-chested you said, didn't you?'

'Well, somefink beginnin' to 'appen, I'd say.' Eagle laughed. So did the others.

'And this is the girl-friend, is it?' He stopped then, and turned. Though I had slackened my pace, along with Kessner, there was no possibility of avoiding Grainger. We came up towards him, and I met his gaze. Grainger stood directly in my path. I went to one side of him to get past. Grainger moved over to block my way. I crossed to the other side. Grainger crossed, too. The group of boys who had been with him stood back from their leader, but sniggered their encouragement. Eagle watched me, the sly look still on his face. I glanced only briefly at him.

I stood facing Grainger. I did not say anything. I did not look directly at him.

'I asked you a question.'

I then looked up. 'I didn't hear any question.'

'You should wash your ears out, then. You're too busy dreaming about her. The question was: who's this girl-friend of yourn?'

'I don't know who you mean,' I said.

'You're going to make me angry, little man. You wouldn't

want to make Grainger angry, would you? Uncle Grainger's your friend.' The boys grouped behind him sniggered more loudly. He pointed back towards them with a thumb over his shoulder. 'Hear that? My nephews, see? *They* don't make Uncle Grainger angry. They seek to please him. Now, why don't you? Uncle Grainger likes to be pleased.'

I still did not answer him.

'I want to know, see? I have a genuine interest, like my friend Eagle here. We are concerned with your welfare. And with your friends. So let's hear a bit about this little girl of yourn. What's her name, Eagle, did you say? Pipette, eh? Long and thin, with a bulge in the wrong place.' He laughed raucously, and the others joined in.

Kessner looked nervously at me. I felt my face reddening. 'That isn't her name.'

'What is it, then?'

'It's none of your business.'

'Ooh, lip, eh? Dear old Uncle Grainger's getting cross now. He doesn't like lip.'

'Come on, Grainger. We'll be late for the train.'

He ignored the suggestion. 'A little girl, I understand. No breasts. That right? I, personally, like a girl to have a bit of shape, something to get hold of in a dark corner. Seems it's different with you. Are you sure she's a girl? Just your kind. That's your trouble. Well?'

I confess I was afraid. I looked then at Eagle, and he turned away. They will not humiliate me, I thought. They can do what they like, but they can't make me answer. I said: 'I don't know what you're talking about, Grainger. I haven't been listening.'

'Why are you blushing, then?'

I felt my cheeks redden still more.

Grainger turned briefly towards Kessner. 'And I suppose you heard nothing either, Kessner?'

'We—we . . . just heard the . . . the last bit,' Kessner said. He stammered from fright.

'Just heard the last bit, eh? And what was that about, Kessner?'

'It . . . it was about her not having . . . about her not having . . . being well-developed.'

'Not having any tits. That's what it was about. And you heard, both of you. And what was the name of this titless wonder, then? Come on, I'm losing patience. Let's have it.'

He stood there, ominously gross in appearance, a heavy, loutish boy, equally assured of his physical strength as he was of his intellectual limitations.

I knew I should be launching myself at the other boy, striking out and closing his filthy mouth, with brave, useless blows. In films it was done. I had seen such a fight in *How Green was my Valley*. I had read of it in books. But I was afraid. The big, ugly bulk of Grainger frightened me. I would not be humiliated, but I could not fight him.

'He's looking flustered, isn't he, boys? Looking a bit hot under the collar? Red in the face? Lost your voice, then? I think a nice dose of cooling snow might bring it back.' He advanced on me. 'Come on, Selby; and you, Cox. Get him.'

They got hold of me. I struggled, but it was no use. The three boys bundled me across to the snow at the edge of the road and pushed me towards the deeper drifts under the hedge. They were not very enthusiastic about it. There was a train to catch, they were in their best clothes, and, while they feared no retribution, their demonstration of physical power provoked none of the refinements that might have been used under other circumstances. Floundering in the snow, I felt I was drowning. I looked up at Grainger's leering mouth, his cruel eyes, and then these, too, vanished as a heaped handful of snow was rubbed into my face and I was left.

Kessner helped me out. 'They're gone,' he said. Together we watched them hurrying away. 'They're just awful, rotten bullies. Sods.' Kessner was normally timid and nervous. In his anger he made small punching motions in the air with his boyish fists.

I didn't speak. I shook out my coat, then shrugged my shoulders at Kessner. The last stragglers for the train came up, and looked at us curiously. They had seen what had happened, but they were indifferent. One of them said, 'Come on, you two. You'll be late.' We all moved off again, beginning to trot.

II

We were still in good time. We claimed our luggage and stood in groups on the platform. Two porters were there. The station-master, a fat, red-faced man, with his podgy fingers tucked in between the buttons of his waistcoat, watched us sternly from outside his office. The train was a 'schools special'. It had made its noisy way from Hereford, picking up an excited cargo of both boys and girls, and the Coppinger boys were the last to be gathered in. A bell rang, and far up the line the black engine appeared round the bend, clearly etched against the white landscape, and coming on towards us, its clean, precise puffs of smoke heralding its still almost silent approach.

Philpotts came towards us. 'Hello, Kessner,' he said. He looked thoughtfully at us both for a moment or two. 'You two can come in our compartment if you want to. There's enough space.'

I thanked him. Kessner nodded.

The train came in. Two carriages were reserved for the school. There was a scramble for the doors, then for the compartments. I struggled with my case which was heavy. It seemed always I had so much, every corner of my case filled with 'things'—made, found, swapped, acquired in some way. It was as though I carried with me a modest environment, as does the experienced traveller, setting up photographs, books, trinkets, etceteras, at each resting point. I was similarly equipped. I pushed in behind Kessner. Philpotts was already there. He lifted our cases for us, and told us where to sit.

It was comfortable and warm. It smelt of going home. It smelt of privilege and of normal human life coming back to us again after the monastic, antiseptic wood and stone of school. It was a smell that had a distant, welcoming, half-forgotten familiarity. We sat down and looked around. Beatty, one of the school prefects and head of a house, was sitting in a window seat. He was already smoking a cigarette and reading a copy of *Lilliput*. He had his feet up on the seat. He nodded at us, but said nothing. There was Molik, an Indian boy, a monitor. He stared at us. There was a slightly forbidding coldness in his expression. I wondered if he resented our presence; if, perhaps, he would have chosen some other junior boy to share the compartment instead.

Philpotts stood in the doorway watching the platform, making sure everyone was on the train. Then, at last, we heard the heavy banging of doors, the shouts of porters, and a long, shrill blast on a whistle. The train began to move out. Term was finally over.

'Why are you looking so untidy?' Molik asked.

'He was thrown—' Kessner began. Then stopped.

'I didn't know I was untidy,' I said. I pulled at my jacket and felt for my tie. It was loose, and had slipped under the collar of my shirt. I stood up and straightened my clothes, then looked into the mirror that was fixed in between brown photographs of the River Severn and of Hereford Cathedral. My hair was untidy, and I attempted to straighten it with my hands.

Philpotts held out a comb. 'Where were you thrown?' he asked.

'It was nothing. I just had a row on the road to the station.'

'Who was it?'

'It doesn't matter.'

'Kessner, who was it?'

'It was Grainger, Philpotts.'

'Need you have asked,' Beatty said. 'That lout should be in

a reform school. He gives me more trouble than the rest of my house put together. That so, Molik?'

'It is. He's a most disturbing influence. No doubt about that. I'd like to see him out of the place, altogether. But he'll go this coming year, anyway. What he'll do, God alone knows. And I've no doubt God worries about it.' There was a pitying expression on Molik's delicate, thin brown face; he seemed genuinely concerned at the unpropitious options open to Grainger starting out on his life in a few months' time.

'Did he hurt you?'

'No. Just threw me in the snow.'

The train gathered speed. Its shadow, and the shadow of the smoke from the engine, fled across the snow-covered verge and the fields. I was fascinated by the silent, shuddering movements of dark and light. Occasionally, as the train passed a building or wall close to the track, its shadow came suddenly up towards us and was close and blurred to indistinction. At other moments, passing over a bridge or viaduct, running along the top of the embankments, the shadow fell far away below us, and the impression was of less urgency and less speed. But the pattern of sound was soon an established, regular, monotonous one. And the feeling was of an assured, firm vigorous tugging towards London.

I had nothing to read. The book I was just starting, *Dark Hero*, was packed in my case. I sat forward on the seat, staring out of the window. Molik had begun to read a copy of *Picture Post*. Philpotts had a novel of Anthony Trollope in his hand, but kept putting it down and looking round at the others in the compartment. He was not ready to read.

Outside there was still excitement and movement. Boys jostled each other in the corridor, headed off noisily, first in one direction, then back. Shouts and screams echoed down towards our compartment from further up the carriage. Once a group of boys began fighting and banged into the door. Philpotts looked up at them. One looked in and pulled a face. But they went away.

Philpotts got up and pulled down the blinds on the corridor windows. 'I have done my bit,' he said to Beatty. 'I've got them all onto the train, and their luggage. They can't get off again until we reach Paddington, assuming they don't throw themselves off. I think I can wash my hands of them all now.' He leaned against the door and looked out over the snowy landscape. 'It will melt. It probably has melted in London. Where is it you go, Beatty? Essex somewhere, isn't it?'

Beatty grunted. He did not look up from his magazine. Molik turned a page of the *Post*, glanced briefly at Philpotts, then across at Kessner and me. Then he went on reading. The two of us sat together, uncertain of what we should do or say. We had nothing to read.

'How many times have you made this journey?' Philpotts asked, looking at me.

'Not often. I didn't always come to London.'

'Why not?'

'We didn't always live in London.'

'Oh, I see. And you, Kessner?'

'I've . . . I've only been at the school two years and a bit. C . . . Counting there and back this must be the seventh time.'

'How long have you been at Coppinger?' I looked up at Philpotts, straight into his eyes. He should know the answer. He had heard it before, but then probably had forgotten it again. Why, anyway, should he take the trouble of remembering such things?

I sat there for a moment or two adding up the years in my mind. It took no time; and yet I took time about it. I was savouring my wealth of Coppinger experience. I was remembering things that did not really need to be recalled. They were always present, just below the surface, ready to be invoked as part of the immediate and continuous past. How vivid the day of my arrival still was to me. Would I ever forget in all my life, the smell of the junior school, the waves of it as they hit me, that strange moment of being handed over, the knots in my stomach, the emptiness in my heart, the dryness in my throat? 'You know about this boy?' the clergyman had said. And the matron—in my mind now I could see her, though she had since gone from Coppinger, her stern eyes staring through the dark brown spectacles she wore across her straight nose as she nodded and said, 'Yes. Yes indeed. We know all about him.' She had said no more to the young curate who had brought me from London, but had turned to go back into the house. 'Come along now,' was all she had said. And I had wondered to myself: how does she 'know all about him'? Yet I did not doubt that she knew. And the conviction haunted me for days and weeks of painful adjustment after that. Thus my life at Coppinger had begun. How stern she had been, the formidable Miss Coghill. And yet, it seemed to me, remembering, that during the time I had been there she had softened. Or so I thought. And so had her two assistants. I could not define it or explain it, but I could remember the different episodes—in a sense with a hint of shame—and they added detail to the transition at that time, for the junior school, perhaps for the whole school, out of war and into normal life again. That strange house at Coppinger, tucked away in a fold of the hill, some distance from the other houses and the older boys, how violent and vivid a reef of memory it would always remain.

'Seven and a half years,' I said.

Beatty looked up from his magazine. So did Molik. I was already a vintage child, though still junior to them.

'You were there before the war ended, then?'

'Yes, Philpotts. I was. I came first in 1944. It was February. It was the middle of term. It was cold, but there was no snow.'

'Why did you come in the middle of the term?' Molik said. 'That seems unlike Coppinger. A bit irregular.' He was that type of boy, much put out by irregularities. Reputedly an efficient prefect, Molik was good at preparing house lists and organising house duties. His sense of efficiency was bruised, it seemed, by my inconsiderate behaviour, even though that behaviour lay in the distant past.

For me the question bit more deeply. I did not wish to remember the circumstances, much less explain them. 'It just happened that way,' I said. 'There must have been a vacancy, or something.'

Molik did not look convinced. But he did not bother to press the point. 'What happened to the staff there?' he asked.

I looked at them. Beatty had stopped reading. Philpotts was watching me. So was Molik. 'They all went, eventually,' I said. 'They all left. I think they were sent away. We never heard why. Were you in the school then, Molik?'

Molik shook his head.

'You were, Beatty, weren't you?'

Beatty said he was. 'I remember there was some kind of gossip. Not giving you proper food or something, wasn't it?'

'That's right. It wasn't that they were mean. They didn't take it for themselves. It was just their way of discipline. They had these rules, you see. There were other things she punished that way. It was a favourite way with her. When Merchant first came he heard of it. She was told not to deprive any child of food. Well, she had no other way of keeping order. And the boys knew, anyway.'

'How did they know?' Molik asked.

Slowly I looked up at him, then at the other boys, including Kessner. They were all listening. Philpotts was watching me.

'Yes, how did they know?' Philpotts asked.

'Well, it was a relation of Merchant's he brought in to teach us, that was after he became headmaster of the senior school. She was his sister-in-law. She used to ask us all about the school. And then I suppose she told him. He didn't come till after the war ended, did he? That's when it changed.'

I chose not to tell them everything. I chose not to tell them of what seemed to me now a shameful thing, the breaking of the old order in the junior school. I remembered them all in so many different ways. Miss Coghill, sharp and birdlike; Miss

Chance, with her long eyelashes and red, red lips, a far from glamorous woman, even so, trying to compete with Jean, the maid from the village, whose full breasts and sultry face were objects of total admiration among all the boys; and Miss Evans, from Cardiff, sweet and faded. In those days, before the war had ended, they had reigned supreme in the isolation of the junior school down the hill, an isolation broken only on Sundays when we all trooped in crocodile up to the main chapel, our hair plastered down with melted margarine, our highly polished Sunday boots pinching our feet, our clean rough grey collarless shirts itching against our skins under the blue jerseys we wore, the caps on our heads stiff with old, congealed grease. Merchant had changed all that; had brought in new people first, then new disciplines, until finally they had all left.

Was I ashamed of the way it had been done? Was I afraid of the relish with which the alleged 'horrors' of our life were recounted to Miss Wilkes, whose sister was married to Merchant? Did I remember with pity the occasion, one evening, when Miss Coghill, her voice strangely subdued, even pained by what was going on, told us that we had been guilty of betrayal? She had chosen the moment well, too well. She had herself become the victim of it. I remembered it all so clearly, the summer evening, gathering in the playroom of the house before going to bed, and being read to by her. But 'with pity'? She cannot have been all that bad to have read to us before our going to bed, to have read *The Coral Island* and *Martin Rattler* and *Ralph Rashleigh* and *With Shield and Assegai*. That night she had been reading *Scott of the Antarctic*. And purely by chance she had reached the moment of Oates's disappearance into the darkness and the blizzard. We had watched in total, absolute fascination as the eyes of this stern intractable woman had reddened behind the glasses, and the tears had appeared. Miss Coghill's voice trembled, and she stopped. We sat still while she paused in her reading. Then she looked up at us, and her voice was clear again, and direct. It pinned those that were guilty in their seats, myself among them. 'There are boys here,' she had said, 'who have betrayed us.' She looked slowly round the room. 'We have always done our best for you. Perhaps it has not been perfect. But these are difficult times. And some of you have seen fit to complain about us outside the house. I don't want to know who or why. I know how. We are all very sad about it.'

We had stood up after that for prayers, a very subdued gathering.

We sang Thomas Ken's evening hymn, our clear, treble voices filling the large playroom, drowning the sounds of the summer evening which we had heard through the open windows during the reading. 'Teach me to live, that I may dread The grave as little as my bed . . .'

'It must have been strange at Coppinger during the war. Was it, Beatty?' Molik asked.

'The staff were all drunks and deadbeats. They've gone now. I suppose it was the same in many schools. You hear some odd stories from some of the other schools, too. It wasn't just Coppinger.' He went back to reading his magazine.

I did not look at Philpotts. I knew the older boy was watching me. I had told Philpotts much more about the junior school on other occasions, and I was nervous now to look at him in case his eyes might hold in them some hint of criticism or blame. I looked instead out of the window at the passing countryside.

The train sped on through Oxford, and beyond. The bright sun shone down on the snow. It was melting from the rooftops and the roads that the track crossed. The carriage had settled down. Only occasionally did boys move back and forth. I sat back beside Kessner and looked out of the window. The three older boys read. Beatty smoked another cigarette. He offered the pack to Philpotts and Molik, but both refused.

I said to Philpotts, 'Do you go to another station when you get to Paddington?'

He nodded. 'Victoria.'

'What train do you catch then?'

'It doesn't matter. I can suit myself. They go every hour.'

'And there's nobody waiting to meet you?'

He shook his head. 'No. Nobody meets me. I shall just go home. My mother will be there.'

'Is it just you and your mother?'

'Yes.'

I wondered what that would be like. I felt a twinge of envy. I tried to imagine Philpotts's mother. I would have liked to have asked about her. Yet I could not think how, not in that place, with the others there. She would be, I thought, a fine woman, gentle, tender, understanding; and Philpotts would make decisions for both of them, guiding his mother and helping her. And their life together would be peaceful and settled. I looked at Philpotts. He was reading his book and did not look up. What was it like, I thought, coming home from school always to the same house, to the cottage in Sussex that Philpotts had once described to me? What was it like, I thought, to know that it would always be there? That she would always be there? Was it this that gave him his cool assurance, his air of knowing precisely where he was going? For he did know, just as he knew that he would travel to Victoria, catch a train south to Steyning, and find things there just as he had left them in September. Did knowing this make Philpotts what he was? Had it been the security of this at his back that had sustained him when confronting Colonel Savage?

I wished I had the same assurance, the same relaxed confidence.

The train pushed on through the Chilterns, through Reading, and down through the Thames valley. Its vigorous, urgent drive towards London was pleasing. It was a warm and comfortable sensation, going home. There was no slackening of pace, and therefore no grounds for impatience. I counted the regular, hypnotic sounds from the wheels; I swayed from side to side with the motion of the train; I closed my eyes and fitted short phrases to the sounds I heard, singing them to myself in my mind as the carriage wheels beneath us repeated each double click across the gap between each double length of line: 'I'm go-ing home, I'm go-ing home; I'll see Babette, I'll see Babette; and Ur-sula, And Ur-sula; it's Christ-mas time, It's Christ-mas time; And then New Year, And then New Year; I'm com-ing home, I'm com-ing home'.

I sank back against the cushions of the seat. The wheels across the rails, steady and even in their message, read back to me the words I had given them. But the iron track had not quite remembered the lesson, so that I had to go over everything again. And the second time it was much clearer. It was like learning lines in a play. Knowing them created the character, gave reality to the words: if I said it enough times—'I'll see Babette'—then I would surely see her. If I said 'I'm coming home' enough then surely home would be there for me when I arrived? Of course it would. And so would my father, there at the head of the platform, as fixed as he had always been.

The train drew nearer to London. The beeches on the smooth Chilterns, the hard-surfaced, rolling mounds of chalk, gave way to the engrossment of fields and buildings, cemeteries of innumerable dead, factories, warehouses, the dark markings of packed humanity. The numbers of railway lines on either side of the train multiplied; routes converged, the proximity of the land they passed through was pushed away by walls and shunting yards, tattered boards carrying advertisements, open areas filled with waste and scrap. The rhythm changed, the even language of movement was broken up.

The train slackened speed. We had come through the suburbs and were close now to Paddington. There were only traces now of snow on the buildings. The sun still shone, but through a haze of mist and smoke. Beatty stood up and stretched. He opened the window and flicked the end of his cigarette out across the rails. Then he turned and reached for his coat. Molik did the same, and the rest of us.

In the bustle Philpotts put a hand on my shoulder. 'Will you write, if I write to you?'

I nodded. 'Of course.'

'I'll come up after Christmas. I have your new address. I'll let you know when I'm coming.'

III

Children spilled out in hundreds onto the platform, dragging their cases or rushing to the luggage van for trunks. Parents moved up and down the platform. Beatty produced a pork-pie hat, a bit crumpled, and put it on before giving us a wave and disappearing into the crowd. Molik stalked off. Kessner was pounced on by his mother. I looked round for my father and decided he must be waiting at the end of the platform. He usually was. I looked up at Philpotts.

'See him?' Philpotts asked.

'I think he must be at the end of the platform.' I felt nervous. What would I do if my father had not come? But my father *always* came.

We set off together, part of the stream of parents and children, the different schools now mingled. I knew my father would be there. I knew it. I knew exactly how he would be standing, his feet apart, his hands in his coat pockets, his head jutting forward. A colossus, whose legs spanned my world, whose hands had held me so often, whose head had dictated my attitudes, whose heart had taught me love. I hurried to keep up with Philpotts. The case in my hand was awkward and heavy. I refused help with it. Then I saw him. He stood just where he should have stood, where he always did, in the wide gap at the end of Platform One. His eyes fixed on the middle distance, just where we were walking, the familiar angle of his head, the loose, dark grey coat, and his hands pushed down hard into his pockets.

I raised my own hand. The groups ahead of us were splitting off to left and right, the crowd between thinning out. Surely he could see me? But no. I dropped my hand again and changed the case over from right to left. Then I touched Philpotts's arm. 'There he is,' I said. I pointed, my hand sore from the handle of the case. We hurried on. Then I hesitated. I felt a prickle of unease. That fixed gaze, that solid, impregnable stance, those shoulders, the feet firmly planted in their polished brown shoes, all were as they should have been; yet the colossus had *swayed*. All was not right, although all was as it should have been. My father's eyes were glazed and half-shut. His face was set in a faintly bewildered but untroubled mask of resignation. I clutched again at Philpotts's arm. 'Oh, Philpotts. Help me,' I said. 'He's drunk.'

The note of desperation in my voice was understood immediately by the older boy. Philpotts said nothing. He did not check his pace, nor look down at me. He just reached out and squeezed my arm briefly and moved on directly towards the island figure in the stream of boys and girls and parents.

'Hello, sir,' he said. 'My name is Philpotts. Here's your son.'

My father had already by this time seen me, and dimly and slowly had raised a hand in greeting. The presence of Philpotts put him out. He turned puzzled eyes towards the older boy. He felt some explanation was needed, but could not be sure whether it should come from Philpotts or from myself. 'My son,' he said, putting a hand out towards me, drawing me in and embracing me. It was a claim rather than a statement of fact. There was a certain belligerence in his voice. 'My son.' He looked down, as if to make sure. Then his voice softened. He was convinced, and he saw no immediate challenge to his statement from Philpotts. 'Well, your father's had a bit too much to drink. He's a bit under the weather. Who's this? Philcox, did you say?' He turned his puzzled eyes once more towards the older boy. His voice was slow and slurred, the accent flat, the words exaggerated.

We stood, an island in the stream of moving people. They

must all realise, I thought, all of them. How shameful. I blushed with the shame. What must Philpotts think? How did he look upon me now, my older friend? I could smell the drink on my father. I wanted to hide my face in the rough, dark grey wool of my father's coat. Instead I pulled away and turned my reproachful face up towards him, my eyes now filling with tears. Angrily, I tried to shake them off, to will them away.

'Philpotts is the name. Philpotts.' He spoke slowly, and with emphasis, as if to a child. I wondered how it was that Philpotts understood things so well, knew just how to speak to my father when I myself could say or do nothing. 'We're in the same house. I have to go on to Victoria Station soon, but I wanted to meet you. I thought perhaps we could all have a drink together in the buffet.'

My father looked slowly down at me. He frowned. Then he looked away again. To his muddled brain the mention of a drink established Philpotts in his mind as a potential ally. 'That sounds a good idea,' he said. 'A good idea. Yes. What do you say to that?'

I nodded. It was a means of escape from our present onlookers. I could not trust myself to speak. But I had stopped the flow of tears. Anything was better than this vast and public auditorium, where all eyes must be on us as we stood there, all ears acutely tuned to my father's deliberate, slow, carefully accentuated phrases. People like Eagle would remember it all next term. They would relive it for me, torment me with it. What had I done to deserve this?

My father lifted my case. It was no weight to him. Philpotts walked slightly ahead of him on one side. I was on the other. I did not want to, but I took my father's arm, more to steady his deliberate yet uncertain steps than for any affection I felt at that moment.

We went into the high, echoing station buffet. In spite of the flood of people outside, it was only half full. I sat down with my father, Philpotts went off to the bar. One or two groups looked over at us with idle curiosity, but I stared back with an expression of cold defensiveness on my face, and they lost the determination to indulge their vague questions about the three of us. I looked over at my father, watched him as he fumbled through his pockets, found cigarettes, then a box of matches, and, after three unsuccessful attempts, lit a cigarette and drew deeply upon it.

A conflict of emotions burned within me. This was *my* holiday, I thought greedily, *my* Christmas. It was such a brief affair. Each day had to be weighed and measured. There was no room for catastrophe and the attendant waste. I wanted to love this man. I did love him. Yet I was tormented by passionate anger. How did he dare to so shame me? What would the boys think? What would they say next term? What did Philpotts think, buying liquor for a drunk man in a station buffet on his first day home from school? I could not bear to look at my father, except covertly, swift, sidelong glances at the blue-grey pall of smoke that hung about him, the wisps that curled around those broad, relaxed fingers, the twin plumes of inhaled smoke that came from his nostrils and went up in a thin veil before those unseeing eyes.

It was Philpotts who broke the reverie. 'There you are, sir,' he said. 'A brandy. And there's a glass of cider for you.' He put the drinks down on the marble-topped table. Then he drew up a chair and took a sip of his own beer. He looked at me, his face quite calm. Then he raised his glass. 'Chin up. It'll be all right. Happy Days.'

'I am all right,' I said. I lifted the cider and sipped from it. In a way I was all right. I was absorbing the shock of the encounter, suppressing the feelings of shame and betrayal. I was getting ready to go on.

My father roused himself suddenly. He raised the hand with the cigarette in it, inspected the end of it, flicked ash deliberately away from him and looked at us. It was as if he was coming back from a great distance, up from the depths of thought. His eyes were no longer glazed and unseeing. Scales of confusion seemed to have fallen away. He was still deliberate and slow. He looked first at me, and made a half-gesture towards me with his hand, wanting, it seemed, to reach out and ask for a measure of forgiveness. But the movement ended with his hand resting on the table close to the untouched glass of brandy. Then he looked at Philpotts. 'Philpotts,' he said. Then again: 'Philpotts. Yes. He has written about you. You are a singer, no? And head of his house?' The strain of remembering seemed, for a moment, too much. He looked on round the buffet, at the bar, at the other people, at the clock. It was high up on the opposite wall, and he stared at it. His lips moved. He muttered quietly to himself. 'Must I hold a candle to my shame?' He looked again at the older boy. 'This must end, Philpotts,' he said. 'This must end now.' He put his hand into his pocket, took out a ten shilling note, reached over and pressed it into the top pocket of Philpotts's coat. 'You have no cause to be buying drinks for men like me. Where do you live?' Philpotts told him. 'You a good sort? Eh?'

Philpotts nodded. 'I hope so,' he said. A slight smile played round his lips.

'Good. Glad to hear it. Come and take my son out. He gets lonely sometimes. Ring first. Number's 7645. Bayswater.' He drank off the brandy at one swift gulp. It went down his throat like water. He dropped the cigarette on the floor between his legs, stood up, took the case, and turned to me. 'Come,' he said, and strode out. He did not look back.

'Goodbye, Phillers,' I said. 'Thanks ever so much.' I held out my hand to the older boy, a suddenly formal gesture that surprised Philpotts into taking it.

He laughed at me. 'God love you,' he said. 'I'll come up after Christmas.'

Then I left, hurrying, still hurt and awkward with shame, after the already vanished figure of my father.

IV

The taxi moved out through the slush of melting snow in Praed Street. We drove through Sussex Gardens and on to the Bayswater Road. We sat in silence. I looked out at the bleak, leafless trees in the park. It had clouded over a bit, and the sun had gone in. There was still snow on the grass, but it had melted from pavement and walls and pathways, and the wheels of the cab hissed their way down towards Notting Hill Gate.

My father called out, 'Right here.' But the driver had already slowed, and we turned across the traffic into Clanricarde Gardens. It was a deserted, graceful cul-de-sac, lined with tall, stately houses, each doorway a pillared, ornate structure, bearing above it a balcony for the first-floor front room. And it was into one of these that we went, up the dry, airless, carpeted stairway, and in through the numbered door.

Home. Two beds with quilted counterpanes. Two pairs of windows, opening to the floor, and leading out onto the stone balustraded balcony. The windows were curtained in white at all times, and with heavier, gold drapes to pull across at night. In the corner of the room stood a cubicle. Concealed within a wooden hide-all, was the wash-basin. There was a double gas-ring, a cupboard for eating things, a wardrobe, chests of drawers, tables, chairs. The floor was carpeted. The colours of things, chosen to fit an insipid, undemanding cycle of tastes, had faded and blended in the grime of post-war London. There was nothing actually squalid in my father's choice of habitations. The components were already familiar to me. I had experienced them so many times, and this room, already becoming part of me as I slowly inspected it, was also part of an unchanging pattern of faded gentility that fitted my father's tangled pretentions.

Home. It had meaning only in his person, as he stood now

on the hearthrug in front of the unlit gasfire, staring down at me. My hopes and anticipations for Christmas blurred by fears of something going wrong, I looked back at him. I tried to choke back the tears, but could not. I tried to stoke the fire of my anger, my sense of outrage, my justified reproaches, but could not. 'Dad,' I said, wanting to say more, and not knowing what to say. 'Dad.' And I flung myself into his outstretched arms, and burst into tears, my sobs shaking my whole body.

'It's no good, old son. It's no good. It's no use pretending. Toynbee used to point his finger at me and say: an old dog like you can't change. He was right. You must learn from my mistakes. That's all.' He paused. Then he spoke more quietly. 'Don't cry.' To me it sounded as if my father meant the opposite. I cried anyway. And he went on: 'One day, old son, you'll get past this. You won't cry any more. You'll just look at me. And I know what the look in your eyes will be like. And I won't be able to say anything or do anything, because I'll know you're right. I'm afraid of that time. I'm afraid of that time, when it comes.' I tried to shake my head, but my father held it pressed against himself, and tightened his hand against the gesture of denial, knowing it to be false. 'We'll be all right. We'll be all right, you and I. We'll make the grade. We'll come out on top. Don't cry, old son. Don't cry. Don't cry.' The voice was still slurred. Yet I felt reassured. I was reassured, in a strange way, by my own tears. Not being able to cry still lay in the future. And it was true, we would come out on top, so long as we stayed together. And I would learn. Yes, I would. But I let the tears come, and I listened to my father's promises. I had heard them so many times. They had never heralded any change in the basic pattern of our life together. Yet still I believed what I heard. What else would there be if I did not?

What else would there be? This was home, this familiar smell, this tobacco smoke, alcohol, sweat, body warmth, the easy, relaxed, strong embrace, the rich and persuasive voice. It was what I knew best. It was the best part of all that I knew. In due course I was comforted. I stopped crying.

'I must rest for a bit now, old son,' my father said. 'I'm tired. You unpack. Put your things in there. That table is for you. But keep everything shipshape.'

I was hungry. It was lunchtime, and school breakfast had been early and hurried. But I did what I was told. I unpacked carefully, putting my meagre school clothes away, arranging my books and note-paper and pencils the way my father did. I took from my case the carefully-packed model I had made for Alice, for Christmas, and checked that nothing had broken. I was absorbed in what I did. When eventually I looked over to the bed in the alcove I saw that he had fallen into a deep sleep. So, I thought. Home.

I explored the 'kitchen', a curtained alcove with gas-rings, a rack for crockery, saucepans, a frying pan. There was a loaf and butter and cheese, tea, milk, sugar lumps, Bovril in a pot, and some apples. Cautiously, I began to prepare myself some food. I lit the gas. Put water on to heat. Spread butter on the bread. Sliced cheese. Each action had a certain pleasure for me, it demonstrated my liberty, my right to choose and decide for myself. It was so different from school. It was home.

Afterwards, I wandered round the room, touching, inspecting, checking that 'home' was all that it had been last time. The bric-a-brac was the same. The photographs, in their Boots frames, the same: myself, as a child, with Melanie, being bathed by my mother as a baby, playing on the sand at Bognor, standing beside a large pig on the school farm, relic of a half-term visit my father had made. And above the fireplace, a photograph of my mother, in profile, Eton crop, handsome features, a stylish study, flattering in the firm lines of nose and chin. Oh, you were a handsome woman, I thought, before time wore you down and death took you!

I was checked as I looked up at the photograph, not by thoughts of her, but by the realisation that I could not recall her as a person at all. Though I had been six years old when she had died, and therefore, one might imagine, capable of storing up some memory of her flesh and spirit, I could not, then or at any time later in my life, recall her as a person real to me. Always, I knew her through my father and through my brother. Always, she was remembered for me, but not by me. My heart was blank about her. The knowledge of her which I had, was knowledge without feeling.

Perhaps it was the same, even when she was alive. Perhaps even then, since I adored my father and was his favourite child, even in early childhood I responded to my mother only indirectly, through him most of all, but through Francis and Melanie as well.

This possibility—for it is only that; I cannot recapture or recall that time—is frightening to me, even now. It represents a cutting of my mother out of my life, not just from the time of her death, early enough though that was, but from before that event itself.

Looking at her photograph, then, and always since then, has had precisely the same effect upon me: I never really knew her at all.

My father's things were laid out on a desk between the windows. I ran my hands across the smooth, worn, faded green morocco writing case. I did not really dare to touch it. I had never opened it. I could remember it as far back as I could remember anything. I knew some of the things that were inside: identity card, ration book (my own emergency coupons would go in there, too), post office savings books, my father's and my own. More vaguely I was aware that certain letters of 'significance'—I did not know their significance—were kept there, sometimes the odd bit of money, some old naval documents, 'things'. Looking down upon the smooth grain of the leather, at the half-pint milk bottle in which two pencils and a pair of scissors stood, at the sheet of blotting paper, at the bottle of Stephens blue-black ink, I began to relax. This was my father's life, spread before me on a table, summarised, checked out in 'things'. This was our world. Nothing much mattered outside it, so long as the inside remained unchanged. I felt no real curiosity to inspect further, to know all the details contained before me in papers and letters. I did not need to feel curiosity about my father. I knew him, and I believed that my knowledge, built on emotion, was absolute. If I did not question the foundation, why should I doubt the detail?

I moved away from the table. My father stirred and snuffled in his sleep. I sat down on the hearthrug in the warmth of the gasfire and looked into it, listening to the faint hiss of the jets. Safe, intact, separate from my other world, with my things gathered now with those of my father, I was home at last.

Chapter Four

I

'Alice? Marry Alice? Never!' My father stopped under a gas-lamp at the beginning of the deserted street down which we had turned. He spoke with exaggerated deliberation, a hint of mockery in his voice. There was something enormously wrong even in hinting at such a thing. Yet there was no easy way of explaining to me in words what it was. Perhaps there was no way of explaining it at all. Alice was there. She was part of our lives. My father needed her. Presumably she needed him as well. So why all the fuss?

He stood apart from me, one hand raised to emphasise the point he was making. He paused, in silence, searching in his mind for some further phrase that might ameliorate the excessive force with which he had rejected the idea of Alice as wife. It did not come. He let his hand fall.

'Never?' I asked. It was not doubt that prompted the question, but loyalty to Alice. In my heart I thought that I knew, even then, all the answers about her. I did not, of course. I expected no further answer to my question. I spoke in order to offset the shadow of guilt hanging over me, that on this our first night together again, the ritual tribute visit to Alice, the giving of news, the discussion of holiday plans, was being replaced by a visit to another woman. As it turned out, the order in which we were doing things was fortunate. But far more immediate were the simple feelings of relief and excitement that instead of seeing Alice we were on our way to visit Babette's aunt, Ursula. And those feelings were heightened by the thin, faint undercurrent of betrayal.

'I cannot change the way things are,' my father said. 'We are really the captives of life, men like me. We think it is different. But it is not. In a thousand years I cannot love that woman.'

'Alice loves you,' I said. 'She's told me.' I looked directly at him. The light from the streetlamp, a soft, pale glow, fell more on my own face than on his, since his back was to the lamp-post, and his gaunt features were heavily shadowed. Was there a note of accusation in what I said? Even as I spoke the simple words, which time would teach me to accept as almost the full summary of Alice's character, I felt the distance and the difference between my father and myself. One did not really converse with him. There was a godlike intractability in the things he said and the attitudes he adopted. Even then, saying what little I had to say about Alice's feelings, I was conscious of the thread of defiance he might detect in my continuation of a discussion which should have been closed by the statement that he could never marry Alice. Yet I was determined to challenge, even if ever so slightly, the sage-like finality of his words. I wanted to assert, I suppose, firmly if also very delicately, that I stood there before him, and I was to be considered. Fresh home from school, and from the company of Philpotts, Danby, Kessner; still smarting with the shame of his drunkenness at Paddington; I could not yet look upon him with the warmth and trust which had been in my expectation as the Christmas term at Coppinger had drawn to a close. And I wanted him to know.

At that time in my life I had gone through a certain amount of ill-health. I had arrived at Coppinger under weight and small for my age. Quite usual illnesses—measles, chicken pox, mumps and such like—had left me still weak and frail, prone to dizziness and fainting. During the summer of that year I had spent something like six weeks in the school sanatorium with a protracted series of things, beginning with a bad throat infection. There remained vividly in my mind from that period of time the experience of lying in bed, suffering perhaps from a temperature, and raising my hand before my face in order to experience that strange and terrifying illusion in which one's fingers become disproportionately huge and frightening, great swollen masses of flesh, heavy and unmanageable, which, looming only inches before the eyes, seem in their threatening proportions, like towers that will fall and crush one into oblivion. I had something of the same set of feelings, looking at my father after I had spoken of Alice's love for him. Had I gone too far? Was he likely to react fiercely or quietly? Would he loom large and ferocious before me, or melt into the normal and comfortable proportions that I loved?

He did the latter. But the relationship between those who are closest together for long periods of their lives is such that the choice between a highly distorted view of one by the other and a more natural, relaxed 'normal' view is often precariously balanced. I always felt, coming home on holiday from school, that this was the initial problem that needed to be sorted out—exactly where did we stand, in relation to one another? And to some extent, as he turned from me, there in the street under the lamplight, and shrugged his shoulders, and set off again, that was the principal activity in which we were both involved.

In the line of his shoulders, the hang of his head, the downward thrust of his hands into the pockets of his overcoat as he moved away from me, I detected a familiar, stubborn bullishness. Perhaps also a hint of shame. I knew I needed to be cautious. I followed him.

'So there's nothing to be done?' I was hurrying to keep up. He shook his head.

'Will we see her?'

'Yes, of course we will. She's looking forward to seeing you. She has an outing arranged for after Christmas.'

'But before then? Will we see her before then?' Was the urgency just to see Alice? Was it an instinctive desire to make good my advantage in the progress towards a working holiday relationship between my father and myself? Or was it, perhaps, just my nature, seeking to establish certain future details which would make me slightly less vulnerable to the haphazard ways he pursued? After all, Alice was one of the few permanent things in my life's pattern just then. Familiarity had taught me already, in the few years we had known her, that it was the symbol of something other than my father on which to depend that mattered far more than the person of Alice herself. She was permanence and stability to me, to us both. She was, I mistakenly believed, a possible route to other and more normal branches of life.

These are much more than the thoughts I had at that time, if thoughts I had at all. Yet they are not far removed from the roots of anxiety by which I was governed in those years. Time has provided the substance for dissecting and building up again the possible motivations of the child. And time is said to bring wisdom. Yet what I believe to be the truth about that time now is no less muddled and diffuse and perhaps morally shabby than the differing instincts which governed me then in my view of Alice, a view inevitably coloured by one dominant fact: that my father rejected her love while at the same time depending upon her for money and help and comfort. And as if this were not enough material, on its own, to make up a truly frightening emotional conundrum, there was now added the fact of Ursula, towards whom we were making our way.

'We'll go to see her tomorrow or the next day. We'll see.' He looked back at me, still following on behind him, and a sharper edge came into his voice: 'Come on, now. We're late for Ursula.'

So I caught up with him and took his arm. The night was warmer than the morning had been. The snow melting on the hawthorn hedges was a long way away. There was slight fog, now, and all traces of snow in London had vanished. Hopes for a white Christmas had melted too. The pavements were damp, and reflected the pale, soft light from the street lamps in their uneven surface.

The street we were walking down was a turning off the King's Road, somewhere not far from the Town Hall. The few shops at the corner were closed. Past them was a school, and opposite, much further down the street, towering up in the uncertain, reflected city light, was the great black outline of a church. We passed few people. The scene was ours. Coming from countryside, still unfamiliar with this, I thought of it as a 'scene', a film set, something that was not necessarily quite real. Did people go to the church or attend the school or buy from the shops? Or was it just an avenue of make-believe leading us to Ursula's home?

My father walked with an easy, relaxed swing in his stride. There was a nautical heritage in the slight flexing of his knees, the left one more than the right, at each pace. I measured out my own stride against his, my hand still on his arm, and I was determined to keep quiet. Yet I could not help noticing also, glancing sideways, a pensive expression on his face. His head was turned down and some of the jaunty optimism and certainty that had stopped him under the lamplight, moments before, had faded. I allowed time to elapse, ground to be covered. It seemed that I had dared much already. Then, gently but firmly, I held him back with my hand, and made him turn and look down at me, in the dim, pale glow of another street lamp.

'What's the matter, Dad?'

His face was stern, his eyes cold, and still a bit bloodshot from the drinking, but sharply penetrating. I felt within myself a righteous strength. I could force him to answer me. I still possessed in that moment of delay a moral superiority: not one that could be over-indulged any further, but a pressure that could exert some tribute to the small position I had in his world.

'Dear old son,' he said, 'when you look at your father and ask him "What's the matter?" like that, he knows that you know. Your eyes tell him. You see into him, don't you?' He paused. His own eyebrows went up and his forehead was suddenly furrowed across all its width with wrinkles of resignation. He sighed, puffing out his cheeks, blowing the air slowly from between his lips. Then he shook his head. 'I shouldn't have been drunk at the station. I don't know what that fellow thought. Philcox, wasn't it? He's a special friend, isn't he? You admire him, look up to him. Well, if he's a good friend, it won't matter. And if he isn't, it won't matter either. And all the others? Don't worry about them. They'll have forgotten, all of them. It will all be the same in a thousand years, my son, all dust, all forgotten.'

His voice had risen as he spoke, and he had begun to enjoy being himself again, throwing before me his perpetual, 'thousand year' measure of life's absurdity. But then he paused again. And when he spoke it was with a quietness that was infinitely more memorable. 'Yet the real thing is the fact that you'll remember it all, won't you?'

'It doesn't matter, Dad. It doesn't matter any more.'

'You're wrong. It does. It matters to you. You'll remember. And you'll go on remembering, all your life. I can see it in your eyes. You'll frighten people with your eyes, one day, my son. Even those you love, and those who love you. Well, it's ended, now. There'll be no more drinking. It's in the past. From tonight, no more. I swear it. On my honour. Your father is done with all that.'

I looked at him and tried to believe him, or, rather, tried to hold back the disbelief, as I had done so many times before. And I was partially successful, as on other occasions. This time it *would* be different. It *was* different. There was Ursula, Babette, Madge, that whole family. It was not just Alice. Something that had not been there before was now at stake. And although there was the urge to laugh—I had it so often in the face of my father's solemnity—it was this time a desire to laugh *with* my father, the two of us, together, laughing at all that lay outside us, laughing at the mountain we were hoping to shift, laughing at our own impossible dreams.

In my heart I knew it was all a long way from laughter. It was the ending of one tempestuous bout. That was all. There was no need to look into the future. There was no point in doing so. There was nothing to be learnt from looking back. I did not know how it had been this time, nor how it would be from now on. I knew only that the hard, damp, cold flagstones were beneath my feet, that my father's arm was there to hold, that a new adventure lay before me, that I would see Babette soon, and that for as long as it all lasted I would be happy.

'What time are we to be with . . . with Ursula?'

'Now. Come.'

We came to a terrace of houses. Most of them were in darkness. The houses stood opposite the church we had seen from the end of the street. He turned in suddenly, and knocked loudly three times on one of the doors. The great hollow boom of the hooped brass knocker echoed up through the dark, empty house. We did not stay by the door, but stepped back onto the deserted pavement. My father looked upwards towards a lighted window at the top of the house. Presently it opened, and I saw a woman's head and shoulders. There was a pause, then something white fluttered in the darkness, and I heard the sound of the keys as they hit the ground. Neither Ursula nor my father spoke. The head vanished and the window closed.

'Come,' he said.

He unlocked the door. In the dark hallway he struck a match. A gas bracket, similar to those at school, stood out from the wall above an old mahogany hall table, but he ignored it, and moved forward towards the stairs—I stumbling after him.

I was puzzled. Perhaps I was a little frightened. There seemed to be no other people living in the house. It was totally dead and silent. I kept close to him up the stairs. There was a smell of musty neglect. In the light of the matches he struck on the way up, all the doors looked unused, permanently closed on dead secrets. The wallpaper was of an ancient brown colour, ornately patterned, badly stained, and peeling in places. The stair carpet was worn, in places threadbare, and in places gone altogether. At last we rounded the final stair, and our way was softly but more evenly lit by a gas mantle that burned beneath a red shade. A door at the top of the last flight of stairs stood open. My father went on and up and in, sure of himself, sure that I would simply follow. This I did. We walked into the main room of Ursula's flat, and stopped, and stood there, side by side.

I caught my breath at the warm welcoming comfort of the room, its walls a deep, daring crimson, its furniture a profusion of rosewood and dark mahogany, its decorations a treasury, to my eyes, of silver and glinting glassware and old china. In one corner the great curved trumpet of an old gramophone loomed out at us; on the wall between the two curtained windows, from one of which the keys had been thrown down to us, was a small display of what I was later to learn from Ursula were early daguerrotypes, framed in ornate gilt and brown velvet. Of many more things I was to learn their particular and sometimes complex stories. At just that moment, however, I was filled with a sense of awe at the richness, and, I had to be honest with myself, the sense of sin. Such luxury, in my uninformed and puritan imagination, could not be unconnected with a certain measure of wickedness.

The shaded gas-lamps threw a soft, warm light over the room. At the end burned a gasfire. And in front of it, seated on the ground, a magazine opened on the rug beside her, sat Ursula.

She looked up at us. 'It's a long time since you've been to see me, George. Several days.'

He didn't answer her. I watched both of them.

'It must be all of a week. I've been lonely. Are you sorry?'

'Ursula, my love.' He held his hands out towards her. It was a gesture of apology and of command. 'This is my son. This is Ursula. Give her a kiss.'

I came forward into the room. I felt my cheeks redden. I held out my hand. Ursula got up and took it, and held it briefly in hers. She said: 'Babette's told me about you. She says you have a lovely voice, and sang so well at the wedding. Did you like her?' She tilted her head sideways a little when she asked the question, and looked into my eyes.

I nodded. 'Yes.'

'And she likes you. She's looking forward to seeing you again.'

'Where is she?' I half expected Ursula to produce her, and fulfil the promise in what she said.

'Oh, she's gone to her grandmother's already, with my sister, Madge.'

'Oh.'

Ursula crossed over to my father. I watched them as they kissed. I watched her lips as she turned them towards him, and his own met hers.

She was wearing black, a full black skirt, a shiny belt and a jersey. Her waist was narrow, and it accentuated the mature fulness of her body, its supple strength, its physical capability. When they had finished kissing she rested her forehead on his shoulder, and seemed about to speak. Instead, she disentangled herself from his arms and crossed to the door. 'I bought some supper after you phoned this morning. But I didn't know quite when you'd come. I'll get it ready.' She went out.

My father took off his coat. I did the same. We stood looking at each other.

'Shall I hang them up?' I said.

'Yes, do. Out there. You'll find hooks.'

I took my father's heavy grey coat over my arm and went out to the small hallway of Ursula's flat. I saw through one doorway a bathroom, its fittings ancient and angular and dilapidated. Through another was the small kitchen. I hung the coats carefully. Then I turned towards the second door. Ursula's back was towards me. She was busy at the stove.

'Can I help you?'

She turned for a moment towards me. 'Come and sit here. There's no room anywhere. I'm so chaotic. No, there's nothing for you to do. But you can talk to me. Tell me about your work at school. I'm a teacher. Did you know that?'

'Babette told me.'

'Of course. I felt sure your father wouldn't have told you. He's no good at giving practical information, is he? Do you find that?'

I did not know what to answer. I had never thought of my father in that way, as giver or withholder of information. 'I didn't ask him about you.'

'He thinks it's irrelevant. It's not facts with him. Facts with him are stepping stones to something else. Once used they can be forgotten. They are always there to go back to. I hope you're not altogether like that. With him, it's feelings. "Emotion is all"!' She threw up her hands, looked across at me, then laughed. Her voice, I noticed, was unusually deep, and I was moved by the sound of her laughter. 'I teach music in two schools here in Chelsea. And I have private pupils. I have to think of dull things like facts.' She paused. 'I give Babette piano lessons. Did she tell you that?'

'Yes.'

'Now tell *me* about *you*.' There was a note of challenge in her voice.

I stared at her. She was preoccupied with pots and stirring and turning down the gas flames. The smells made me hungry. I could think of nothing to say. All there was to know about me could be examined and dealt with in a few moments and was worthy of no one's attention. Here was real life; what I had been engaged in at Coppinger was something quite different and far less significant. She was only being polite asking about it. All I could do was look at the waves of hair that fell upon her shoulders. She had a habit of throwing her head sideways, with a little twitch in the gesture which set the dark brown hair swinging away from her for a moment, and then settling again, full and soft and alive. Her mouth was like Babette's, the same suggestion of a smile, an indulgent, almost mocking smile, when in fact there was no smile at all.

She looked across at me. I thought she was going to press me for an answer to her question, but instead she said: 'Are you hungry?'

I nodded. 'Yes, I'm afraid I'm very hungry. You see, I didn't have any proper . . .' my voice tailed off.

'Go on,' she said. 'You didn't have any proper lunch? Why was that?'

I felt confused. 'Well, we went straight home. And my father—Dad—was very tired and wanted to rest. And I couldn't really go out. And there was only some cheese and stuff. It didn't matter, you see. I wasn't hungry then. I had quite enough. But it's just that I'm hungry now.'

She frowned. 'I hope I have enough.'

'Oh, I'm sure you have. I mean I'm *hungry*, but not actually *starving*.' I laughed nervously.

'No. You don't look as though you're starving. But we'll get something ready very soon.'

'Are these houses very old?' I asked.

'They're eighteenth-century. I believe they date from about 1740. Do you like them?'

'I don't know. They do seem a bit spooky. They don't seem to have many people living in them. Don't you feel a bit nervous?'

'Nervous? No, not really. Lonely sometimes. When George doesn't come to see me. But why would I be nervous? I have the house to myself. I like it here. I like the room. I like the view across the road, the church tower and the trees. No, it's more than liking, really. I love it. I wouldn't change it.'

'How old is the church?'

'Oh, it's not old. It must be about a hundred years. Nothing like as old as the houses.'

'Have you always lived here?'

Ursula looked at me. There was a thoughtful expression on her face. She pondered the question for a moment or two. 'What a lot of questions,' she said. 'Yes, I've always lived here, since I came to London. But I won't be able to stay much longer. The houses are condemned. They will soon be pulled down and some awful office block built in their place. Then I shall have to move.'

'Where will you go?'

'I don't know. Probably a modern flat.'

'But it would be so different. Wouldn't you miss the gaslight?'

She laughed. 'Yes. I'd miss the gaslight most of all. It's so soft and generous, isn't it? I've always loved the pale soft glow. I feel it flatters me.'

'Are there many houses in London that still have gaslighting?'

'I don't know. There may be thousands. They didn't put in electricity here because these have been due for pulling down for a long time. It wasn't worth it, I suppose.'

'I've never been in a house in London where the lights were gas. We have them at school. But they're changing over to electricity. They're doing it house by house.'

'What do you like doing?' Ursula asked.

I looked at her and frowned. 'Do you mean when I'm on holiday?'

'Yes. What will you do with yourself?'

'Well.' I paused. 'I go around. See things. Visit places. You know.'

'What places do you visit?'

'I usually go to museums or galleries. I like looking at pictures.'

'Do you? I do, too. Would you like it if we went together?'

I nodded. 'I'd like that very much.' I did not know if I really would. But it seemed the polite thing to say.

Ursula took a last look at the stove, then turned back to me. 'Come,' she said, and led the way through into the main room of her small flat.

He was standing in front of the fireplace. He was smoking, and holding in his hand the *Radio Times*.

Ursula said: 'Am I allowed to offer your son a small glass of sherry before his dinner?'

He looked up at her, then at me. 'Would you like that?' he asked.

'He cannot decide unless it is offered.'

'Then, by all means, offer it.'

She turned, her face laughing, and held up a bottle and a small green glass. 'Well?' she said. 'Would you like some sherry?'

I nodded. 'Yes, please.'

She poured out the small glass of sherry and gave it to me. She poured some for my father. 'I'm not sure it's as safe to offer it to you,' she said.

'You may well be right. He has more discretion than his father. A very civilised drink, old son. A little sherry, a little wine, in moderation.' He held his glass and bent his red nose towards the rim. He waited until Ursula had filled her own, then raised his. 'To moderation.'

'What a fraud you are, George,' she said. 'You're quite terrible. And hopeless, too. Isn't he?' she asked me. 'Say he is.'

I looked across at him. At that moment he had eyes only for Ursula. I raised my own glass. Tentatively, a little nervously, I toasted him: 'To my fraudulent father!'

We all drank.

'No more, though. In all things, my son, be moderate. Look upon your father and say to yourself, that is how *not* to do it; that is how not to live, how not to behave. Your father's life should be an example to you. Mine is: an example of the road to excess, which is the road to ruin. And I'm only saved from that by the love of a good woman.'

The quizzical semblance of a smile was on Ursula's lips as she watched him. She looked steadily into his eyes for a moment before speaking. 'Rubbish,' she said. 'You do talk the most awful nonsense, George. I sometimes wonder how you can possibly take yourself seriously, whatever other people may think. Now, you can both stay here and I'll bring in some supper.' She went out.

II

We had wine with our meal. I felt very grown up. I did not like the red wine as much as I liked the sherry, but I enjoyed it well enough. Ursula told me it was from Italy. 'It comes from Piedmont,' she said. 'It's a bit rough. I sometimes dilute it with a little water.' She showed me how much, and I did the same. I thought it tasted better that way. We ate spaghetti. I twirled it around my fork, copying her, and splashed sauce on my chin. I suppose I ate a great deal. She joked about my appetite. I told her how awful the spaghetti was at school, a sprawling mass of worms in brown gravy. It was she and I who laughed and talked together, while my father looked on, indulgent, but tired. She mocked him occasionally, teased him for neglecting her, then looked at him with concern when he did not finish his food. It was at that moment, their eyes softened by tenderness, meeting across the table, and myself watching suddenly from the outside, that the thought passed through my mind that the difference in age between myself and Ursula was almost certainly less than the difference in age between my father and her. I knew it was an inconsequential fact. It reminded me of a particular kind of mathematical problem. And I tried to construct a formula which would express the impact that time would have on such a relationship as ours might become. But it was too difficult, or too transient an idea, and I abandoned my endeavour. Yet it pinned in my mind my father's mortality, and struck a chord of anxiety in my heart: the reddened, handsome, bullish, fighter's face; the wise, expressive eyes; the ragged evidence, in the broken blood vessels of his nose and cheek, of a lifetime's fluctuations of temper and indulgence.

Ursula divided, with scrupulous fairness, the last of the bottle of wine. She gave us cheese, but I could by then eat no more. Then she put grapes on the table, and I helped myself to them, one by one.

'Try taking off a small bunch,' she said. 'That way they look nicer. I hate the little wet pobbles sticking up on a bunch of grapes.'

I did so. I approved of the suggestion. It seemed a natural enough respect for visible order. I felt comfortable and relaxed.

'Now tell me,' she said, when we had finished, and moved to the fire, and I was sitting on the floor, my head resting on the edge of the sofa which was also her spare bed, 'Now tell me, what happened at the wedding?'

I told them. They listened in silence, my father frowning, Ursula occasionally nodding, or saying that it was just as Madge had reported it. Eventually I finished.

'You were brave to stand up to them.'

'It wasn't me, really. It was Philpotts. He stood up to all of them.'

'That's the boy who was at the station?'

'Yes, Dad. That was Philpotts. You called him Philcox.'

'Well, why didn't you tell me all this? I should have known.'

'What chance have I had so far to tell you anything?'

'Chance? What do you mean, chance?'

'Well, you were asleep this afternoon. Then we came out. And I was telling you about other things.'

'But this wedding business. I like to know. Have to be kept informed. Might need to do something about it.'

My father was adopting an attitude. It was a self-conscious process. 'I don't think there's anything to be done, Dad. It's all over.'

'Can't have a son of mine being struck on the head by some bullying army type. Jumped up fellow, I've no doubt. Got too high a regard for himself.' He paused, frowning at the reported indignity visited on his own flesh and blood. 'And Madge was there for all this? Did she know it was happening?'

'Not to begin with. She only came over at the end. If she had been there, or Babette, it wouldn't have happened. It was just that I was a Coppinger boy, on my own. They thought I must have done something wrong.'

'I'd like to get my hands on this Colonel.'

Ursula laughed. 'I don't think you would,' she said. 'And it would do no good. What use is muscle against prejudice? It only deepens it.'

'I'd get satisfaction out of chinning the bastard.'

'I wonder,' Ursula said. 'I wonder, would you?'

We talked of other things. Mostly, I listened. I felt drowsy in the heat from the gasfire and began to relax for the first time since coming home. I was content. I didn't want to talk any more. I closed my eyes. Through my drowsiness I was conscious of my father and Ursula, but couldn't take in what they were saying. I thought of Babette. It was easier to re-create memories of her, and then embroider them with my own imagination. I entered the fantasy world of make-believe, and trod deeper into its dappled shade. After a while I fell asleep.

III

I woke to hear Ursula saying to my father, 'You won't drink any more, George, will you? Please?'

'Moderation,' he replied. 'Moderation. The grail of my

life. I see it always before me, Ursula, tantalising, glowing in the darkness that surrounds it, just beyond reach. There it is. I know it. I seize it for a while. I enjoy the peace it brings, the safety, even the prosperity. Modest prosperity, of course. But still it is there. And then something breaks.'

He spoke quietly, with that sincerity which is unique to the conversation between two people, and which any third disrupts by creating an audience. And, though my eyes were closed, I could picture in my mind the lost expression in his face.

Ursula waited a while. Then, very tentatively, she asked him: 'But what is it? What is it that gives? Why? Tell me. I want to understand.'

'I don't know,' he said. 'I just do not know.' He paused. I imagined the bewildered expression on his face, and my heart went out to him. 'When I'm drunk,' he said, 'I feel free. I don't have to be tidy. All my things . . .? Do you understand?'

She was silent. I would have smiled, even laughed, if I had not felt the pity of it all. I thought of the half-pint milk bottle with his relief pen standing in it. I thought of the green morocco case and the lists all clipped together. How could she understand that? She had never lived with his lists.

'I can't take it. You do know? You understand, George?' There was a pause. Then she spoke again. 'What's to be done?' Her voice was resigned. My eyes still closed, I read into it a note of despair.

'Moderation,' my father said, in a tone of oblique hope that was all too familiar to me. 'Balance in all things. It is all that is left to me. Otherwise, I am lost.'

'But do you mean it?' she asked.

'Mean it? Of course, Ursula, my darling. Of course I mean it. Moderation. Oh, damn. Oh, dear God. You are so right, Ursula, so right in the way you are. And I am so wrong. Come and kiss me.'

There was a pause. I opened my eyes and looked up at

them. They were in each other's arms. Just briefly I watched them, then closed my eyes again.

I heard her say: 'You know I love you, George?'

'Yes.'

'And will always. You know that?'

'Yes.'

'Whatever happens . . .' She paused. Though I did not look, I could imagine her head turning away from his face and resting on his shoulder, looking out at her room, perhaps even at myself. Then she added, in a tentative, uncertain voice, 'I suppose . . .' And she stopped. It could have been a question, or the beginning of a phrase of doubt, or of sad speculation. I sensed the love in her voice, but behind it, all too clearly, the hopelessness of that love, and the despair. And it came to me, as I lay on the floor, feigning sleep, that she was more bewildered than I was. She had not lived with the carefully folded clothes and the relief nibs. She had not had her life ticked off on a list. Lying there on the floor, I was overwhelmed by the sadness of what I heard. It did not really matter what she supposed. It was her despair that mattered.

My father seemed to have caught the same hint of desperation. 'What do you mean?' he said. 'What do you suppose?'

'I suppose,' she said, and she spoke slowly, as though the burden of truth was about to overwhelm her, 'I suppose time will just pass, and we shall go on, you and I, George, getting a bit older, a bit more frightened, able to solve nothing, to—'

'Nonsense!' he said. 'Nonsense!'

'It's true. It's true. You don't realise. You hold on to your son, but you don't realise. It is only a matter of two or three years before he will leave you. He's not a child any longer. He'll have university to go to, or his national service. It's still a conscious effort on your part to credit him with the maturity he has. You must realise, George, you are growing old.' She laughed suddenly. 'Oh, dear. What am I saying? Not old. Older.' There was a nervous hesitation now in her voice.

Though in its quality it was much like Madge's, I could distinguish between the calm, practical confidence of the one and Ursula's tentative, uncertain exploration of her relationship with my father.

He said: 'I hate old age. I shall never be old.'

Ursula sighed. She spoke slowly. 'You will,' she said. 'We all will. And what will it all have come to, in the end?'

'It's what we make of it,' he said, and paused. She was silent. 'There's my son,' he went on. 'There's his life to consider. I may not have come out too well myself. But there's him.'

'But it's us, George, it's us. Do be sensible.'

'Sensible? What do you mean by that?'

There was a long pause. Then Ursula said: 'That's the trouble. I don't know.'

'It's the kind of advice Robert would give you, isn't it? Be sensible!'

'I suppose so. Yes.'

'The trouble with Robert is, he's so *safe*.'

'No, George dear. He's not safe. Poor Robert is vulnerable, and in a way that you never will be. You don't understand Robert. You don't want to understand him. You think he disapproves of you. It may well be the case. And you know he has some substance, being Madge's husband.'

'I don't give a shit for Robert.'

'You do, really.'

They could not agree, and were both silent. I opened my eyes. I looked at them, where they were, still thinking I was asleep, their conversation ended in a suspended argument which left them both smiling, him in defeat, she in subdued knowledge that her words were accurate: he did not dismiss Robert as totally as that.

I moved my hand, and they both turned.

'Who is Robert?' I said.

'Robert's Madge's husband,' Ursula said. 'Why do you ask?'

'I heard you talking about him. I've been asleep.' I had not intended asking the question. It had just been blurted out. 'His name woke me. It reminded me of someone at school.'

Ursula said: 'You're tired. You should both go home.'

I got up and sat on the edge of the sofa. Ursula came and sat beside me. 'Tell me,' she said, 'would you like to come and spend Christmas with us? It's a very simple family affair. It's the same each year. Babette will be there, of course. Would you like to?'

I looked up at my father, standing in front of the fire, his face set, hard and without expression. I questioned him with my eyes, but only briefly. I wanted a reaction from him, some instinctive sign of approval, but I did not want to give time for doubt to creep in, or for some remembered obligation to Alice to emerge. It was foolish of me to imagine that such a thing would occur. I turned quickly back to Ursula. My cheeks were flushed. My eyes shone. 'Oh, Ursula, I'd love to come. I really would.' Then I turned back, 'Can we?' I asked.

My father nodded. 'Yes, of course we can. What is there to stop us? That's very kind of Ursula. You must thank her.'

It took something away from the enthusiasm with which I turned back to Ursula, this command to thank her when I was going to do it anyway. 'Thank you ever so much, Ursula. It'll be absolutely super. Babette told me it was on the south coast, your mother's house, where you all go for Christmas.'

'Did she?'

'Yes. We talked all about Christmas. I told her I thought we would be staying in London.'

'I know. She told me.'

I blushed. I was asserting my own claims to be considered more. Without consciously remembering what Ursula had said about me while I had apparently been sleeping, I was giving them some indication that no longer was I a purely passive element in their lives. I, too, was involved; even my affections were tied up. Mercifully, neither pushed the point, though I fully anticipated my father's clumsy, bluff comments.

'When will you come?' she said. 'I go down tomorrow evening. Madge and Babette went down today. Robert can't come until the day after. You could come with him.'

'What's wrong with tomorrow night?' my father said. 'We'd come down with you.'

I looked up at him. 'What about Alice?'

There was silence between us all. The only sounds in the room were those of the softly hissing gas jet and the fire.

'You want to see Alice, don't you?' Ursula asked.

'Yes, I do,' I said. 'I must. I made her a Christmas present at school. I shall have to give it to her.'

'Well, then you must see her. Of course you must.' Ursula looked up at my father. 'It would be better to come down with Robert. You can phone him and find out which train he is taking. And now you should both go home.'

IV

Driving home in the bus through the wintry streets we said little to each other. I sat looking out through the window. We passed occasional knots of people, still lingering outside the pubs, which had closed. The streets had dried out, and there was a cold wind which caught at the raincoats and flapped them against the legs of the people still standing in determined groups. I wondered what they were talking about. They reminded me, all too vividly, of the occasions when I also had waited patiently on the fringes of such crowds, or had tugged with less patience at my father's arm, anxious to get him away from them all, with their tedious, boring, foolish talk, and go home. And I suddenly remembered that it had been on such an occasion, perhaps a year before, perhaps more, certainly in London before we went down into Kent, that my father had first introduced me to Laurie. The knots of people standing in the streets reminded me of her. There was a bitterness in the memory, and a relief that it was distant now from me, not just in time, but in circumstance as well. There had been something which she had said, something shocking to me at the time. I did not wish to think of it. She represented a 'commonness', a vulgarity from which I expected to be shielded. These were things I feared. She loomed in the background of my life, a dark spirit.

I looked at the passing streets, mostly deserted from one pub to the next, but with little forlorn gatherings still persisting outside closed doors as we sped by. Occasional fragments of newspaper or other street rubbish blew against the fencing that surrounded bombed-out sites on our way, or caught itself around lamp posts. We sat on the top of the bus. My father was preoccupied, and sat forward in the front seat, his elbows resting on his knees, a cigarette in his hand. Without turning towards him, I could see his profile reflected in the side window of the bus against which I leaned my own head. The thin veils of blue-grey smoke trailed up around his stern, expressionless face, the hooded, inward-looking eyes, the veined, red complexion, the prominent, slightly hooked nose.

'This fellow Robert,' my father suddenly said. 'He's all right.' Then he was silent again.

It was obvious to me, from the way my father spoke, that Robert was by no means all right. I turned away from the window and waited. My father went on: 'It's just, well, he's a bit of a stuffed shirt. It's these people that get into the Foreign Office. They're all the same. They're all on the old school tie network. I've known them all. They forget I've been to a public school. And to Cambridge. They think to themselves: Good old George, he's one of us, but gone a bit off the rails. I've known them all. Know the type. Can't stand 'em, really. Too bloody polite. Well, Robert's a bit like that. Always very correct. "Have a sherry, George, old boy," he says. It just bores me. Madge is too good for him.'

'He wasn't at the wedding.'

'What?'

'He wasn't at the wedding. Only Babette and her mother. I haven't met him.'

'Oh, yes. The wedding. I'm not sure I shouldn't do something about that. A son of mine being beaten about the head by a fellow of that kind. Should be more responsible. Same type, I suppose. Abusing his position. Think they can do what they like, trustees, I know all about them. So Robert wasn't there, you say. Where was he? You'd think a bloke like Robert'd be there, hobnobbing with the M.P.s.'

'Babette said he had to go to America.'

'I see. Funny bloke he is, Robert. Don't altogether trust him. I don't know what it is. Something about his eyes. I never know what's going on behind them. Of course, he doesn't approve of me. Never has done. Thinks I'm just a bad influence.' He paused, and looked ahead at the swaying street down which the bus was furrowing its way. 'Can't blame him, I suppose. Your father's a bad lot, really. Incorrigible.' He threw down the end of his cigarette and looked out through the side window of the bus. It had turned up from Kensington High Street into Church Street. 'Let's walk the last bit,' he said. 'Fresh air. Good for us.'

I swung my way along the top of the bus behind him, and down the steep stairway to the platform. The wind was cold on face and hands. I wished for a pair of warm leather gloves. We got down at the stop and walked along together. I pushed my hands deep into the pockets of my raincoat.

'You don't mind about going to see Alice, Dad, do you?'

He stopped and looked down at me. The hard, inscrutable expression on his face softened. He smiled first, then laughed. 'You're a good old skin,' he said. 'A good old skin. At the end of the day there'll always be you. You'll be loyal to your father. You'll stand by him when the others don't.' He looked up into the night sky, his chin jutting out, as if he was challenging its loyalty and its determination to stand by him when things went wrong. I remembered the many times he had said the same words before. I hoped what he said was true. 'Of course you must see Alice,' he went on, looking down at me again. 'You want to see her, give her the Christmas present you've made. You must do what you think is right. You must stand by your principles. Not like your father.'

There was a mellow look of fatigue in his face. It was an expression I usually associated with the aftermath of drinking, just as I associated these expansive and deeply confidential sentiments with the same period of retrenchment. It made me suddenly think of the morning, and feel again the sharp twinges of shame with which our first encounter had been surrounded. It would be different the next morning. Tomorrow we would make a fresh start. A new father, somewhat more ruthless perhaps, swifter in decision, sharp, strict even, in his discipline over me, would emerge to build up again the shredded fragments of his life at the end of a bout of drinking. I tried to remember: what had it been like before Alice? How had my father paid for a room to live in then? How had we survived the weeks of carousing, the accelerating spiral downwards that still, years on, made me wince at the memory? How had we done it? And, I remembered, unhappily, through veils of time, that in reality we had not. I remembered the separations, the charity, the loneliness, the puzzlement, the anguish of being left with strange people in strange places, nothing explained, no warnings, no understanding of how I felt. I remembered just enough to prefer to forget.

'Will I ring her tomorrow?'

'Yes. We'll ring in the morning. Go and see her tomorrow evening and go down with Robert the next day. We'll have a good Christmas. We'll have to get presents. What will you give to Babette?'

'I don't know, Dad. I'll have to think about that. I don't have much money.'

'Nor does your father, old skin. He's a bit broke. It's a bit of a problem.' He paused. 'Wait a moment, though. I put some money into your Post Office book. That was before I left Kent. Only you can take it out. I'd forgotten.'

'How much do I have?'

'There's a few pounds, anyway. We'll get by with presents. You see if we don't.'

Chapter Five

I

His singing woke me the next morning, his voice gently invading my dreams. He was shaving as he sang, and the words were mingled with fragments of humming as the razor rasped across the skin around his mouth. The thread of words was broken by this, but it did not matter. The song was infinitely memorable to me.

> 'Mm . . . mm . . . are grey dear,
> I don't mind the grey skies;
> Mm . . . mm . . . mm . . . sonny boy . . .'

I lay in bed. Through sleepy, contented eyes I watched him as he stood, stripped to the waist, in front of the washbasin. Drinking had given him a belly, but otherwise his body was lean and spare. He was then about fifty.

He raised his chin up towards the glass, and drew the razor down through the white lather towards his Adam's apple. Two triangles of white shaving soap remained, only one of which was visible to me. I was comforted by the familiarity of what I saw. The gasfire was on. The room was warmed by it. It was warmed as well by the golden glow from the lamp above the washbasin which reflected on his skin, still bearing the residue of sunburn from that summer, spent in the hop fields.

Behind him, however, there was a different light. There, one set of curtains had been drawn, and through the full-length windows, and the discoloured net curtains stretched over them, there came the cold grey light of that winter morning.

I was home again, a state of mind more than anything else, and never so vivid to me as on each of those first mornings, holiday after holiday, waking always to a new variation of sounds and prospects, coming up from sleep by degrees to a comprehension of the best happiness I then knew, met as I did so by songs, stories, reminiscences of Toynbee, observations about Alice or other women, and questions about school, work, health. I savoured the thought of these as I lay there, my father still not aware that I was awake, still preoccupied with the smoothness of his own chin.

He sang the fragment of song through again, this time without interrupting himself. His voice was soft and warm in my ears. Then he was silent, inspecting his face, pulling the skin tight over different parts of his jaw. He began to lather it again.

He started on another fragment of song: 'We'll gather lilacs in the spring again . . .' He brushed the thick white lather over his chin and neck. I looked at the table on which my father kept his things. Some newspapers were piled there. They had been opened and folded carefully. Beside them lay a pencil, neatly placed on top of sheets of papers. There were several small piles of pennies. There was a letter, already opened.

I moved, and stretched out my arms. I saw him watching me through the mirror. He had stopped humming. The reverse image of his face in the glass, itself not quite as familiar to me, was made even less so by the quizzical expression in his eyes.

'Awake, old son? That's the spirit. You've had a good sleep. It was a late night last night. Ready for some breakfast?'

'Mm.'

'Busy day, today. Got to get on now. Turn over a new leaf. Sort things out.' He went on shaving.

I got out of bed and crossed over to the window. People were leaving from some of the houses and setting off towards the Bayswater Road. Many carried umbrellas. The streets were wet and a fine rain was falling. There was a universal colouring of grey over everything.

'Have you been out already?' I asked.

'Yes. I was out to get the morning papers. And to get some coppers. Must make some calls.'

'What time is it?'

'About half-past eight.'

I crossed to the table and looked down at it. The newspaper was open at 'jobs vacant'. Several of them had been squared neatly in red pencil. The only letter, lying on one side, was in a long, white envelope. The address was typewritten. Printed at the top were three names, 'Wharton, Reynolds and Smedley', and underneath, in smaller letters, 'Solicitors'. I stared down at it. What did it mean? For a moment I thought of asking, then decided against it.

'Shall I put the kettle on?'

'Yes. There's some bread in the cupboard. You could make some toast. Would you like toast? There are eggs, too. And a pan for them.'

I began to get breakfast ready. I started the kettle, and a pan to boil eggs. Then I sat down on a rug in front of the gas-fire to make toast.

'I found your Post Office book,' my father said. 'It's there, on the table. Under the newspapers, I think.' He was washing the shaving soap from his face. He used a large flannel cut from a towel. Glancing up from the fire, I watched the steam rising from it as my father buried his face in it.

'Watch that toast. Don't let it burn,' he said, then buried his face in the flannel once more.

'Don't worry. I won't.' I looked at it, on the end of the wire fork. It was tinged golden. I felt the heat of the fire on my face and listened to the slow even hiss of the burning gas. I turned the toast.

'How much is in it?' I asked.

My father's face came out of the flannel, red, smooth, shining, crisp-looking. 'Seven pounds and three shillings,' he said.

The comfortable, vibrant odour, which seemed to suggest the invigorating release of energy, filled the room. There was an easy relaxed capability about him. Recovery was on the way. Grandly, confidently, on the morning of yet another new life, he was offering me seven pounds three shillings of my own money with which to buy presents which we would give jointly to members of the Brooke family.

'What presents will I get?' I asked.

My father paused, inspecting his face carefully. 'We'll have to think about that,' he said.

'Do you smell differently as you grow older?' I asked.

'Do you mean the smell of a person, or the way he uses his nose?'

'The smell of a person.'

He shook out the flannel and draped it carefully over a rail beside the basin. 'I suppose so.' He gritted his teeth. 'I do not want to be old,' he said, into the mirror. He bared his teeth and inspected them. 'I cannot stand the smell of old men.'

I knew the smell he meant from Tessier, the French master at school. He was an old man, in his eighties, and there was something rank about the smell that came from his body. If I pressed my own hand or arm or shoulder against my nostrils, the scent was sweet and good. Emanating from my father now was an equally good, though different, mixture of shaving soap and water and invigorated flesh.

I finished one piece of toast, and speared another slice of bread on the fork. 'Shall I put the eggs on?'

'No. I'll do it. I'll make the tea, too.'

'How much will I spend?' I asked. 'And what will I buy?'

He put the eggs into the saucepan of boiling water, and took the lid off the blue teapot, ready to warm it. Then he crossed over to the wardrobe, and from a shelf in it he took a clean shirt and shook it out. He looked at me. 'We'll have to make a list,' he said. And he smiled. I looked back at him, trying to express in my face resignation, but succeeded only in returning his smile. He unbuttoned the shirt.

Lists. They featured so much in my father's life. It was almost as if they determined its shape and pattern. Was that an exaggerated claim about their importance? Perhaps. Yet at times I saw them in my mind as the only guardians of sanity, the creators of order in a sea of passionate chaos and emotional rebellion. For as long as I could remember there had always been, on the tables of the innumerable rooms we had shared, a sheaf of papers held together with a bulldog clip, and listing certain directives for the day.

They were an evasion. I had already decided that much. I had seen, years before, sandbags piled up as protection from blast; lists were the same: a barricade against the blast of reality. Reality dictated that one remembered important things; the rest were dealt with when, and if, possible.

Yet I could not dispute the existence of those lists, and their importance. They were in my head, a part of my life, always written in that particular, flamboyant hand: things to buy—that was reasonable enough—people to telephone, clothes to wash, bits and pieces to mend, newspaper articles or books to read or return to the library, letters to write, an infinity of equal obligations. They were all mingled, sharing parallel importance, struck out when completed.

When my father was drinking there were never any lists. Years later, when I gathered together all his diaries after his death, I found in their pages a more permanent echo of this fact. For there, interspersed across the years, coming as interludes between the pages of ephemeral notes of a most mundane kind, were blank spaces—weeks, occasionally months—which coincided with bouts of heavy drinking.

Our breakfast was on the table, the eggs cooked, the tea made, the toast propped up against the marmalade jar. And my father stood over me, in front of the fire, and smiled down, his face all shining and sharp and ruddy in the yellow glow, his great barrel-chest and muscular arms relaxed and easy, his belly, heavy from the weeks of drinking, pressing against the belt of his trousers. He slapped his stomach and looked down. An expression of surprise appeared on his face. 'Oh dear,' he said, and looked at me, as if he had not noticed before the changed shape of his own body. 'What would Toynbee have said?' I looked blankly at him. Though I knew Toynbee by reputation I could not answer. 'Toynbee would have said: "Is anybody underneath?"' He laughed, and I burst out laughing as well, remembering one of his stories about Toynbee. Looking down at himself his eyebrows came up in an expression of pained surprise. 'You shouldn't be there,' he said. 'It won't do. I was once so fit. And now look at me. Weakness of the flesh. Well, it must be put right. Work! Work and moderation!'

We finished breakfast. I made out the list: Ursula, Madge, Babette, Robert, Ursula's mother, and another sister whom we had not met. Her name was Jennifer. She was the eldest.

I was overawed at the prospect of strangers. How would I behave? Would I know what to do, what to say? I had never been away for Christmas in my life. I had never stayed with a family. I was solitary, self-conscious, completely without roots. I was, in truth, a kind of well-bred vagabond. 'Going away' had no meanings except sad ones: I had left only one home, forever; and that had been on my mother's death. I went away from my father, to school, regularly: and it was most painful. That was the sum of my experience of 'going away'.

The echoes of Christmas itself were sad ones. I could draw little encouragement from them in the past. And in the present they represented occasions for polite suffrance. Far away, in the distant past, there were memories of the three of us as children, with mother as well as father, swirling together in a rapturous tumult of excitement, of gifts and games and hardship and love. But it was more than half my lifetime away. I needed to be reminded of how it had been. And even when that happened, and when my father talked of how we behaved, I knew enough to see that it was the fun, the happiness, the humour, that was stressed. And they all belonged in the past.

My father was making telephone calls. The phone was in the hallway, outside the room, and he came in and out, making notes, gathering up piles of pennies, crossing off the various jobs that did not suit, or had already gone. I put down suggestions, and asked him for approval.

'That sounds grand, old son,' my father would say. He was preoccupied. He crossed through another of the entries. 'They're no good. That's one at half-past ten. Another at twelve-fifteen. Both in Knightsbridge. That's good. Now, I'll phone *them*.' He went out again.

I wondered what I would give Babette. It was the most difficult present of all. It had to speak for me, say exactly so much, and yet be balanced evenly against the unknown present she would give me. Such balance was most important. I had also decided that I would choose presents from myself for Madge and Ursula, since I knew them both, but share in my father's gifts for everybody else. It did not occur to me that I might be eking out the seven pounds three shillings for some time to come, nor that the sum itself was anything but riches for what had to be bought. Like my father, I was prodigal. The rightness of the gift was what mattered.

'That's Swan & Edgar's at two-thirty,' my father said, with some satisfaction, coming back in. 'They want a salesman in the furniture department. They'd be good to work for. I must just go through these again.' He lifted the papers and began checking them through. 'There's another. Used to know the manager there.' He was really talking to himself; and there was a sustained urgency in the flow of his words, almost as if they were partly responsible for vitalising his actions. He was strung tight with anticipation.

'Does Robert smoke?' I asked.

'Hm? No. I don't think so. Perhaps cigars at Christmas. But you can't be sure. I should have asked Ursula.'

'What will you give Alice?'

He paused. 'Alice?' He looked at me. Then it was no longer a question. 'Alice,' he said, his voice flat and tired. 'She deserves better than she will ever get from me. And she must know it.' He paused, and his hand, irresolute, suddenly flaccid, came down on the table and rested there among the pennies and pencils and papers. 'You tell me, my son, what shall I give to Alice?' He looked at me, then he began to gather the papers in front of him together into a single pile. In sharp contrast now to his actions moments before, there was a listless, indecisive appearance to what he did. There was doubt, uncertainty, an indeterminate pledge towards Alice, both unfulfilled and impossible.

I looked back at him. I shared his guilt. My concern was for him, not her. 'If you like,' I said, 'I'll choose.'

'Yes. You choose.'

'And what shall I get for Ursula?'

'You decide them all.' He turned once more to the notes in front of him. He finished tidying the papers. He reached for his green leather case and opened it. I watched him as he tucked the solicitor's letter carefully into one of the pockets. Then he closed it and held it for a moment, staring down. I was standing by the bed, watching him, waiting for him to turn. After a moment or two he did, and looked across at me. His eyes were still preoccupied with thought of some kind, complex, to judge from the expression, and, I guessed, concerning myself. But he said nothing. Instead, my father shook his head, replaced the leather document case, squared it off against the other things on the table, and then tapped it twice, as if, by magic, to seal in its secrets. Though many times tempted, I was well-schooled in my father's heightened sensibilities towards the physical order that surrounded him, and the slender, inner privacy which that wallet represented, and had never ventured to pry. And though curious, I did not so intend now.

'Presents,' he said to me. 'What's the point? I can never think what people want.' He looked at me. There was an accusing expression in his eyes. 'What do you want?' he asked.

I shrugged. I did not know what to answer. There were many things of course. But in a situation as unstable as ours, one in which my own Post Office savings book was the only source of immediate money for presents for other people, what possible scale of values could there be against which I could name a gift for myself? I just looked blankly back into his eyes. I wanted to shield him from the supposed fault of never knowing what people might want, and of not being able to do anything about it, anyway. At the same time I had the sudden urge to laugh, and knew that, if I did, we would both dissolve into a joyful bout of cynicism against outworn human symbols, conventional values, habitual, tribal absurdities. But I did not want that. I was bewildered enough, myself; but at the same time I could also see that my father's regret at not being 'good at' presents indicated a dilemma for him as well. And on top of all this I was so desperately anxious to give to Ursula and Madge and Babette presents that would be 'right', even memorable, that I conditioned myself to resist the temptation to make little of the problem. It went even deeper. Briefly, but sternly, I was struck by what my father's confessed inability meant: it was an admission that he could not see into those for whom he acknowledged love, or at least affection, deeply enough to understand what *their* desires and *their* wishes might be. These things, the penetration, the sensitivity, the richness of feeling, the flexibility, understanding, sympathy, were denied him. He might seem to stand aloof, untrammelled by concern for the public futility of trifling gifts —so false, he had often said—but at times like this, before the solitary, astute audience of me alone, the inner frailty showed through, and with it a kind of shame.

I agreed that I would see to the presents. I had my own

list, like him. I had my own ideas now, about what I would get for each of these strange new people who had come tumbling into my life. The prospect of a day's Christmas shopping, on my own, in London, thrilled me. I wondered how much I would spend.

'Right,' my father said. His hand came down thump on the table. He looked down at his papers and notes. Then he took up my Post Office book and passed it to me. 'There. That's your day. At the end of the street you turn right. The Post Office is about a hundred yards down on the right. Draw five pounds. You cannot draw more. The rest I leave to your discretion, my son—your youthful wisdom.'

He stood up and crossed to the basin. He looked himself over carefully and critically. Then he took up the pair of stiff-bristled hairbrushes and attacked once again with brisk hard strokes the already carefully brushed hair and moustache.

'You'll hurt yourself,' I said.

'Must look the part, old son. Must look the part. Crisp, cool and efficient. That's your father. Super salesman. Must give the impression they can't do without me. I'm doing them a favour, applying for their job. I should, in reality, be the managing director, but a certain difficulty having occurred earlier in my life . . .' He looked down at me. 'How's the general appearance, then?'

'Very impressive, sir,' I said. 'We must ask you to step up to the boardroom, right away. We have promotion in mind for you. It's upstairs for you. No need to be sticking round here, on the shopfloor, along with the ordinary men. We have better things in view. Come this way, sir.' I opened the door of our room with a flourish and inclined my head. We looked at each other.

'Let the day commence,' said my father.

'Aye, aye, sir,' I said, and followed him down the stairs and out into the street.

II

There was a festive warmth in Oxford Street, in spite of the wintry weather. The morning rain had cleared, and a watery sun shone through fitful clouds. The decorations, the window displays, were more elaborate, richer, than I remembered them a year before. The street was crowded with people.

I threaded my way through the crowds, determined to conceal my inner excitement, that bubbling, tumultuous sense of exultation that I felt. In my pocket I had money, vast sums it then seemed. I had keys for our new home. I had my list. Wide-eyed, I stared from side to side, missing none of the colour and excitement. Yet my own face was made solemn by the intensity of emotions within me. In my heart, just then, I was listening to the steadily beating wings of freedom. The day was mine. London was mine. Every detail was there to be absorbed. My macintosh was buttoned and belted. I wore a carefully tied scarf. My shoes were well polished. The creases in my long trousers were pronounced, giving a stiff, unused look to them. Thus it is, in those painful learning years, that circumstance seems to force upon us an inflexibility of character, a remoteness, a self-contained intensity of reflex that is there even in what is usually described as normal circumstances for the adolescent: a sense of him housing a coiled spring of action, held by a shallow ratchet, worn down already by time. How much more, as I plotted that day for myself, did it emerge in me, in the careful tidiness of my appearance; in the direct, solemn, searching, polite gaze with which I greeted my surroundings. Experience had conditioned me to solitude, and solitude had made joy a secret thing. It was not to be read easily in my eyes. It was not often to be shared.

I say it now without self-pity—quite the reverse, since things have turned out well for me—though perhaps I felt self-pity then: but I had never known, away from school, friendship prolonged and enriched by time. There had been friends, yes. There had been boys and girls of roughly my own age in the different places in which my father had worked. Yet nothing had been allowed to last, and therefore little had been permitted to fade naturally away in the flux of time; it was always snatched, chopped off, broken. It always left uncertainty and a sense of deprivation.

I remembered, yes, but always with a heightened feeling of unfair loss. There had been girlfriends—long village conversations on hot summer nights, snatched, clumsy kisses, the sticky holding of hands, August expeditions to swim in the slow, green pools of the Evenlode—and how vivid were the memories (how much could 'being in love' mean at eleven and twelve years old) when being parted from those round whom they were created was so ruthlessly inevitable.

I had never once in all my life gone back. Never once. Perhaps some day, in the distant future, I would. But I could not, then, foresee it as a reality. And the effect of this was that each experience got bottled up in my memory as just that: 'an experience'. The alternative, something richer, deeper, more prolonged, a more complex part of the texture of life that was added up, month by month, year by year, eluded me. I knew it only within the catchment of school: and that, also, had its terminal date.

Did it slacken such feelings? Did it reduce or undermine them? Memory told me that it did not. My longing to see Babette, my fear about that longing, my special concern over her present, my excitement about the coming Christmas visit, told me it did not. But it told me to be guarded, and it was responsible for the hungry, solitary, searching look I cast about as I threaded my way up towards Selfridge's through the thick crowds of people.

And so I bought presents. Carefully, methodically, as my father, by example and injunction, had taught, I went through the list, striking off each person. I chose carefully.

With Babette, with Madge—I still found it difficult in my

mind to think of her as 'Madge'—and with Ursula, choosing what to give was easier than with the others, whom I did not know. I had bought for Ursula a French pottery dish, patterned in blue and white. The assistant, wrapping it, had said what a good choice it was, and how much taste I had 'for a young boy'. And I had disliked her instantly for the qualification she put on her compliment, though I accepted it as deserved. I bought for Madge a blue glass bowl. In a large and crowded Oxford Street bookshop, I searched among the volumes of poetry. I had not the courage to buy for Babette an anthology of love poetry. I pondered over Shakespeare's 'Sonnets'. Then I chose two slim volumes of somewhat contradictory character, *The Hunting of the Snark* and *Songs of Innocence and Experience*.

I finished shopping, and it was not yet time for lunch. I decided to go home, and get rid of my parcels. The afternoon would then be free. I had spent just over three pounds. I had kept all the receipts. I could offer to my father, if it was demanded of me, an exact account of the morning's purchases.

III

'Well, what sort of a fellow was he? You say he had a beard? A *beard*? What sort of beard was it? Was he clean? What were his clothes like?'

I felt very uncomfortable. I wished that I had not told him. 'I've told you all I can remember. It was nothing, really. We just met. It was in the open, by the Round Pond. He was sitting on this seat. He looked sad and lonely, and I thought—'

'You thought? Sad and lonely? You obviously didn't think at all. How many times have I told you? How many times?'

I sat in an armchair. The fire was hot, and my cheeks were red. Why did he go on so? I had met the old man in

Kensington Gardens, and talked with him for a while. That was all. I wasn't ten any more. I was thirteen, I would soon be fourteen. I could look after myself. I looked across at Alice. She had stopped preparing the table. She saw the appeal in my eyes, but said nothing. We had come separately to her bedsitter. I had arrived first, punctual as I always was, as my father had conditioned me to be, shy with Alice to begin with, comparing her and the place she lived in with the fresh memories of Ursula and Ursula's flat, and finding Alice's wanting in magic and mystery and excitement, if not in comfort. And then my father had come, full of fierce energy, the self-righteousness of sudden reform stridently clashing with the equally fresh memories in my mind of the swaying colossus greeting me at the station. I had had time to tell Alice about that, and to mention visiting Ursula. I saw now, in Alice's eyes, something of the same scepticism which I felt.

'I think we can sit down now,' she said. She stood behind one of the chairs, her beautifully kept, rather plump hands folded in front of her. She had none of the lithe grace of Ursula. To my eyes she was motherly in shape and appearance. She had resigned from any romantic combat. She accepted Ursula and the others, just as she accepted his drinking, as part of him. There were no ultimatums.

It pained her; I knew this from things she had said to me, from reactions to my often clumsy mention of other women whose relationships with my father I understood only dimly. But it did not curtail nor limit her devotion. And she had the indestructible asset of her permanence. The others changed; she did not. Always, in our lives, mine and my father's, there was Alice.

My father was loath to give up the attitude he had struck, standing in front of the fire, looking down at me, teaching me what not to do by admonition. 'Your father knows,' he said. 'Trust him. He's been in the world a long, long time, hundreds of years, knows its ways, sonny boy. You may laugh at him, but while you are young take good advice. Old men, sad faces, beards, *beards* in this day and age, half-glasses, mittens, I *know*. I know it all.'

We did sit down. Obediently I drank my Campbell's tomato soup. My father said that everything was excellent. There was a glass of orange squash for me, water for Alice and for him. And we finished the meal with plums from a tin.

'You must be very excited about going away for Christmas,' she said. Was there a frosty hint of resentment in the way she said it?

'Yes, I am.'

'I was hoping, of course, that you would both be here. I shall see less of you than I usually do. But that can't be helped. I've so little to offer you. It will be much more exciting on the South Coast. And then you have a girlfriend now, don't you? Is she pretty?'

I nodded.

'Well, that's nice,' Alice said. 'But you won't forget we have a date, will you?'

'Oh, no. Of course not.'

'New Year's Day.' She paused, and looked across at my father. 'When do you have to come back, George?'

'Depends which job I choose.'

'Which will you choose?'

'I think it will be the Kensington store. The wage isn't as good, but the commission's better. It's a question of relying on old George's ability to sell. We've got to get back on our feet, old son, haven't we? Get the old man in trim again, back on an even keel.' He brought his big hand down gently on top of Alice's, where it rested on the table's edge. And I noticed the quick fervour with which she responded to his touch, turning her palm towards his, clutching at him for a few brief moments, her eyes suddenly proud.

Just before half-past eight Alice turned on her radio.

'What's on?' I asked.

'What's on?' my father repeated. 'Why, it's "Take It From Here". Didn't you know? Best laugh on radio. Mustn't miss it.' He sat down in the armchair beside the set, stretching his feet out before the fire. His hand went out to make a minor and unnecessary adjustment to the tuning.

Alice began to clear the table. I helped her. Our care to make no disturbing noise was exaggerated. In the tiny kitchenette off Alice's bedsitter she whispered instructions to me, and I put things away. 'Alice?' I whispered, half closing the door, 'Dad's not in any trouble with the law, is he?'

'No, my dear. Not that I know of.'

'He'd tell you, though, wouldn't he?'

'I'm sure he would. Why do you ask?'

'I expect it's nothing really. It's just, well, he had a letter this morning from a firm of solicitors. Their name was on the envelope. I saw it.'

She looked at me, no expression on her face. 'Did you say anything to him?'

'No. I just saw it. I didn't mention it. He put it away.'

'Well, I'd forget about it, if I were you. It can't be anything big, or he'd tell us about it.'

The programme started.

In spite of our lowered voice, or perhaps because of the whispering and movement, our concern not to disturb his engrossed attention, we did manage to annoy him, and he turned in irritation and told us to shut up and sit down and listen. The order was peremptory. We did so. I wanted to listen anyway.

I had felt deflated during supper. The comedy cheered me briefly. There was a brisk, wholesome vulgarity to the absurd events. The story wound itself rapidly into knots of comic tension which then exploded into laughter. There were even moments when the principal actor himself was overwhelmed by the urge to laugh. I had lived with my father's passion for radio comedy since wartime days, when we had listened to ITMA, when my mother had been alive.

It ended. My father turned it off. He looked at us both, his face still smiling. 'Nothing does you better than a good laugh.

Eh? I must say I like Jimmy Edwards, and Ron and Eff.'

I nodded.

'And now,' Alice said, settling herself in anticipation, 'tell me about your term. How has it been?'

'Tell her about the wedding. Positive triumph. Son of mine. Amazing. Do you know, Alice, he sang the solo at this wedding. In front of three hundred guests. It was reported in *The Times*. And the *Daily Telegraph*. It was really a big affair. Titled people. But you tell her. Go on.'

I told Alice about the wedding. I modified the story to fit it more closely to those aspects that appealed to my father—the number of guests, the house, the titled people who had been there, the amount of champagne—and I said little about Madge and Babette. I described the row. Alice listened very carefully. Occasionally she said 'Goodness me!' or 'How exciting!' or 'What an adventure it must have been!' I enjoyed telling her about it. My father's interest had grown and expanded, and when I finished he cut in.

'That's the way. Good lad. Always stick up for your rights. Let no one push you around. I'm proud of you, old skin. Chip off the old block. Think of him, Alice, singing there on his own in front of three hundred guests. He's his father's son. I can see that. Only he'll go right where his father went wrong. That's the difference. You'll come out on top, my son. No question about that. No question at all.'

Alice smiled and nodded her approval. 'And did anything happen after that?' she asked. 'Did you get into trouble? Was the matter taken no further?'

'I thought I might. I was worried all the next day. It was the last day of actual school. But nothing happened.'

'You must have been relieved.' It was not an invitation to reply; there was no encouragement in Alice's voice to continue that particular conversation. I had noticed on occasions before her ability to terminate sections of an evening with a solid and irreversible finality. Enough, I felt from her manner, had been said about Coppinger.

My father asked Alice about the situation at her office. She worked in the City. She was private secretary to a merchant banker, a Jew, infinitely wealthy in my judgement. My father periodically asked questions about him, but Alice's discretion —which was profound—revealed nothing beyond a few personal idiosyncracies of behaviour and taste, none of which seemed particularly romantic or dramatic to me.

I felt that we were 'getting through' the evening tolerably well. I was conscious of 'it'—the evening—in a way that I knew was unnatural; and yet it had always been so with Alice. I could predict, even now, what was yet to come; and, sure enough, she began to put her sewing—intricate, detailed, beautiful, precise work—away in its bag.

Then she looked at me, and smiled. 'Would you like to play crib?' she asked.

I nodded.

We moved back to the table. My father had once again picked up the *Radio Times*, and was scanning it through. Then he turned his attention to the *Daily Telegraph*.

Alice used her beautifully kept hands with a determination and precision which was at odds with her generally slow and docile movements. There was a clipped secretarial efficiency in the way in which she now placed the cribbage board on the table where we had eaten, shuffled the cards, and, on winning the cut, dealt. She wore a colourless nail varnish and no rings on her fingers. Her nails were carefully shaped and short.

She played cribbage in a cool and practical way, and I loved watching her hands picking out the little ivory sticks and counting them carefully along the holes in the cribbage board. She won the first and then the second game. I felt that I was warming up, and I managed to win the third.

We paused, and Alice said: 'Have you heard the joke about the elephant in the department store?'

She looked gravely at me; equally seriously I stared back, and said that I had not. She told me. It took some time. At the end I laughed, perhaps immoderately. The story was not altogether a success. I could think of no anecdote to offer in exchange which was untinged by some questionable element.

Alice said: 'Then there's the one about the Irishman who went to Moscow.'

When she had finished, my father, who had clearly been pondering in his mind, no doubt helped along by some story or other in the *Daily Telegraph*, further ramifications of the Coppinger wedding saga, said: 'This fellow, Willcox, Philcox, whatever his name is. Is he in your house?'

'His name is Philpotts, Dad. He's head of our house.'

'Does he sleep in your dormitory?'

'Well, it's *his* dormitory.'

'What kind of a bloke is he?'

'I don't know, really.' But I did know. I knew what my father's suspicions were. I understood the anxiety that had prompted his anger about the old man in the park. I sensed the vague feelings of unease which my father occasionally had about Coppinger. It was, after all, a 'special school'. Was everything quite 'straight' there? At the same time I knew that almost nothing I could say about Philpotts would reassure him, suspicious of culture, a hard man bred in a hard world, in his own schooldays and at college a good boxer and rugby player, how could he accept Philpotts, who despised sport, loved music and theatre, and wrote poetry?

'But what do you mean, son?' my father asked, frowning, a stern edginess coming into his voice. 'You don't know what kind of bloke he is? You must know. Is he a sportsman? Does he play rugger?'

'No, Dad. He doesn't play rugger at all. He doesn't like sport. He used to have to play, but now he's senior enough to be excused.'

'What *does* he like? Has to like something. Must have interests. Sounds a queer fish to me.'

'He likes music. He plays the piano. He's good at acting. He wrote a revue for the house two terms ago. It was awfully good. He did a Noël Coward act. It was very funny. Everyone said it was the best thing in the show.'

'Hmm. Noël Coward.' My father's frown deepened. 'And I suppose he writes poetry?'

I felt myself blush. 'Yes,' I said. I looked at Alice, vague appeal in my eyes.

'Not every boy can be good at sport, George,' she said. 'He's a good friend. That's what matters.'

IV

It was not late when we left, and we set off to walk up Holland Park Avenue. It was cold. There was fog in the air. The wind of the daytime had died out. I had arranged to call on Alice at her office the next day, leave in the present from my father which I had chosen that morning, as well as my own, and collect her presents for us. In the moments of departure from her, my father had delayed in the doorway, and I had heard the crackle of notes. He now walked beside me, a spring in his step, confidence in his gestures. He put his hand on my shoulder. 'I'm sure this fellow, Philpotts—that the right name?—is fine. You mustn't worry about what I say. I'm anxious for you, old skin, that's all. You're all I've got. I don't want to see anything happen to you.' He paused. The pavements gleamed ahead of us, reflecting the dim, blurred street lights. Occasionally, the headlamps of cars and buses, furred and indistinct, shone out as they passed by, their tyres hissing slightly on the surface of the road. 'But this old man. Now, he's different. You watch your step there. Promise me that, won't you? Promise.'

'I'll be careful, Dad. Just don't you worry.'

Chapter Six

I

The road climbed steeply from the station. On one side there were railings, and the ground fell away in a tangle of leafless shrubs and dead hummocks of grass, with occasional glimpses of the hard rockface through the rank, dead winter covering. It was indistinctly lit by the pale white street lighting. As we trudged upward the train moved out with slow, noisy, laborious puffs of white smoke which caught the reflections of light on the platform before being dissipated in the breeze.

I could smell the clean sea-smell on the wind. It was fresh and invigorating after the train, and it intensified my excitement. We climbed in silence. I could hear my father's breathing. It came in short, and increasingly strenuous puffs. He was, as he had said once already since leaving the station, out of condition. It was towards seven in the evening. The streets were deserted.

'Excited?'

I nodded. My father had rested one hand on some railings and was breathing deeply. We each carried a canvas bag with zip fastener. In addition, my father had a carrier bag hooked onto one finger. In it were our presents, which I had carefully wrapped.

We walked on.

'Not far now,' he said. 'The next turning, and then the seventeenth house.'

'But it's not number seventeen they live in?'

'No. But it's the seventeenth house on the right. I counted them last time. You can check if you wish.'

'Why ever did you do that?' I asked.

'I don't know, old son. I like to know these things. Everything must be in its place with me, everything shipshape. Count them off, you know exactly where it is.'

'But it's not going to move, is it?'

'Never can tell,' he said. 'You never can tell. Stranger things have happened.' He said it seriously, even sadly, as if nothing in his life was safe, nothing could be relied on.

'What's it like, Dad? The house?'

'You'll see.'

'I can't wait.'

Then, as he offered no information, I added: 'You're all puffed. It's as if you'd been on a cross-country run.'

He grunted. 'Steep climb,' he said. 'I must be growing old. A lifetime of punishment.' He put his hand on his chest, and then raised it, the finger pointing up the hill in front of us. His voice deepened, and he changed its inflection. It became sonorous, full of portent. ' "The disability of self-indulgence" as old Toynbee used to say, pointing his finger at me accusingly. "George, you'll be for the high jump. Make no mistake." ' Then he sighed. 'But it was Toynbee, wasn't it, old skin? He made the jump. Toynbee, poor bugger, went the way of all flesh. You remember the last time we saw him? Well, perhaps it's best not to remember too much.' He paused. 'And so the years pass . . . carrying us . . . and our small mercies . . . towards the grave . . .'

He stood for a moment, surrounded by suburban evening quietude, and turned towards me. I could see his chest rising and falling, hear the heavy short breaths, sense the physical strain. My father occasionally ballooned out his cheeks in a great puff of air from his lungs, and then breathed in deeply. He had paused to regain his breath. Yet he could not fully accept the sensation of incapacity, and was persuaded to give it some dramatic purpose, even if only for my benefit. He looked solemnly at me, and put down his canvas bag and the carrier bag, and raised both his hands in an expansive gesture: 'Don't do what your father does,' he said. 'Don't take his example. Ever.' There was a deep and sombre penetration in the tone with which he uttered the final word. 'Be guided by his experience. That's all right. Quite a different matter. But don't follow it. Mark well what I do, and learn from it what not to do. That is my lesson for you, my son. Your father is too old now to be other than what he is. Too old and tired. Life has no more surprises for him.'

'But you're not old. You're only just over fifty. You shouldn't talk like that. It's like when you talk about dying.'

'Your father is what he is. He has seen it all, passing through his fingers like grains of sand. Families, people, houses, events, jobs, life itself, like tiny grains of sand. And you are all I have left.'

I looked at him, moved by the glow of what he chose to believe was wisdom, secure in the feeling that I, of all the strange people in the mighty living world, was supremely important to him. I did not doubt it. I looked at this stalwart figure, labouring under the misconception that he was old when he was not, that he was wise when he was not, that he had experienced all of life's tragedies which he had not. And I was secretly a little dismayed to think that he also laboured under the belief that his son could conceivably learn from his errors, and not imitate at least some of them, since it was, contrary to his hopes and expectations, my desire to carry through into my own life at least part of the melodrama, part of the make-believe, part of the self-delusion, part even of the foolishness, and, hopefully, all the passion and all the feeling.

To my father, wisdom was passion, and passion was the only wise course. 'Follow the heart,' he had so often said; and to 'be passionate' was an injunction that had rung in my ears as far back as my innocent memory could take me. I had heard much of this without understanding it. But it did not matter. I could store up the tablets of the law. Thus wisdom was passion. Thus, passion inspired instinct, and was inspired by it. Instinct guided my father, and he had often said as much. And though originally, perhaps, I had let the truth trickle in only slowly, realising that, like an animal, this violent, gentle man vacillated between terrible and wonderful reactions, between base and noble instincts which produced in me an increasingly wide range of judgements, some of them dismissive; yet, increasingly, as the years passed the combination of the two won my admiration. It was his nature to be thus. Prejudiced, I compared my father with others, and found not him but them incomplete.

We walked on together. I counted off the houses, checking to ensure that the seventeenth house would be there, that Babette, her mother, Ursula, the others, would be there; that Christmas itself would be there, real and not just a dream, so uncertain was I of those things that existed outside the two of us.

II

It was Babette who came to the door. She was dressed in blue, and wore an Alice-band in her hair. Her face was serious. She looked first at my father, a quizzical expression in her eyes which gave way to one of relief. She looked at me. 'Happy Christmas,' she said. 'Mummy wouldn't let me come down to the station on my own to meet you. Please do come in. My father is coming down on the next train and Aunt Ursula's already here.'

'And how are you, Babette?' My father bent down as he said it, put his arm round her shoulder and kissed her.

'Oh, your moustache is bristly, George,' she said.

I waited for him to encourage, from me, some similar demonstration of affectionate greeting. I tensed in expectation, remembering in a tumbling sequence of instantaneous recollections those occasions in the past when I had been made to blush in confusion at my father's impetuous forcing of premature demonstrations of feelings which I did not have, or did not wish to express according to his dictate. The very quality in him, of forceful and spontaneous emotional response which I was to admire more and more as time went by, in those days was more often the cause for bewilderment and embarrassment. Not so at that moment. All he said, moving on into the hall, was 'Say hello to Babette, and give her a kiss.'

I said hello. We smiled at each other. We did not kiss.

The expression on her face was different, and understandably different, from how I remembered it at our first encounter at the wedding. Then, she had been solemn and detached, and a little imperious; now, she was warm and direct and welcoming, though still preserving, perhaps, an indecision about where we stood with each other. Does this sound pretentious, to invest an encounter between children, remembered from long ago, with the same time-suspending drama that accompanies the second and subsequent meetings between lovers? I do not know. But I remember how desperately important it was. I remember how my heart surged forward in response to present reality taking the place of my memory of her, and of her indicating that, at the very least, we were friends.

I could not know what was transpiring, at that moment, in Babette's heart. Was there trepidation there, too? Was there relief? Or was I simply, in my own real need, investing her with doubts and indecisions which simply did not arise? Would there be, I wondered, an opportunity for the privacy and the conversation, once again, that had already invested with magic my memory of the exploration of the house on the now distant night of the wedding?

Madge appeared. 'Lovely to see you,' she said. 'How are you?' She looked at me, and walked towards me, her hand out. 'No more fights?' She let my father kiss her. He held her close for a moment, then she pushed him away. 'You can save that for Ursula,' she said, laughing. 'She'll be down soon. Come on, Babette, we'll show them their rooms.'

I felt an immediate sense of pleasurable anticipation. Rooms! It quickened my interest, the thought that I would have a room of my own. We climbed the stairs, the four of us together. Then Madge took my father into one room, and I followed Babette up another flight to where she opened a door for me and stood back to let me go in.

I felt self-conscious, standing in the room, in one hand the canvas bag, in the other the carrier full of presents, my macintosh still on, and buttoned up, and belted, my scarf tied at the neck. I did not look at Babette though I knew she was watching me. Instead, I stood in the middle of the small, top-floor bedroom, and gazed slowly round. A patchwork quilt covered the bed. Against one wall and between two dormer windows stood a small bow-fronted mahogany chest of drawers. On top of the chest was a little shield-shaped mirror on a stand. On the wall beyond the bed were photographs; they seemed to be family groups, and were old, and a bit faded. The room, which was under the roof, a true attic, had sloping angular ceilings, low and cosy. They had been papered in a pattern of flowers and ribbons, and the curtains at the windows were striped in yellow and brown. There was a low bookcase filled with books. Rush matting was on the floor, and the boards under it were stained and polished. My eyes absorbed it all hungrily, moving from one part of the room to the next. I said nothing, and Babette was silent too, leaning against the jamb of the door. Finally I turned round towards her.

'I did the holly,' Babette said. 'There aren't any flowers, you see.'

I noticed the berried holly in a small vase on the bedside table beneath a lighted bedside lamp. I looked at her, still holding my canvas bag and the presents. 'It's super,' I said. 'It's a lovely room.'

'You look awfully silly,' she said, 'still holding your things like that. And you've still got your coat on. Shall I help you unpack?'

I thought for a moment. I dearly wanted Babette to stay with me. At the same time I was shy about my possessions, and there were the presents. I shook my head. 'I shall be all right,' I said. 'Will I just come down then?'

She nodded, then reached for the door handle. 'Don't be long.'

My heart thumped with the excitement, and the effort of controlling it. So this was how it began, I thought, a family Christmas. Babette seemed so grown up, so natural, so relaxed. I was puzzled by the ordinariness of it all; how could so many normal, ordinary things be so exciting? The door was a door, the house just a house, all the things that people had so far said or done were completely as one would expect. Yet in spite of this a tinge of special magic, like the glow of light catching on the deep green of the holly leaf, at the curved, shiny surface of the red berries, seemed to colour every person, every word, every thing revolving now around me. Would I be able to tell her of the sensations I felt, just then, standing foolishly in that room? How could I express the flood of comfortable warmth which I derived from something that was theirs, and of course hers, always? What was it but ordinary human living, with passion and tension and crisis all present, though somehow given a balance which I did not easily understand. Possibly I would have blamed my father for this lack of understanding which derived from the extraordinariness of his way of living, had I been able to stand back and make the necessary judgements. Instead, I could only revel in the fact that these ordinary things were at least as wonderful as I had hoped; the strange, rambling Victorian house, my own room, tucked up under the eaves, and Babette; assured, gentle, constrained, and so pretty; she turned all the rest into a whirlpool out of the centre of which she smiled at me and quietly said, 'You look awfully silly.' I said it to myself as she had said it: 'You look *awfully* silly.'

I unpacked my things. I took off my coat, brushed my hair and washed. I left the presents in a pile on the bed. I inspected the books and the photographs. I began to know more about their family, and to feel more at home, though the phrase 'at home', when I thought of it, caused me to falter. I heard my father calling outside, his own voice subdued, and I opened the door and answered him.

'My room's super,' I said, when my father appeared in the doorway. 'What's yours like?'

'Oh, all right. Comfortable. It's just below yours if you want me.'

'What will I do with the presents?' I pointed to the pile of gaily wrapped parcels on the bed. 'Shall I bring them down?'

'No. Not yet. Wait until after dinner. It will be time enough then to come up and collect them.' I stood across the room from him, looking at him, and I suppose I felt small and unimportant, thankfully letting my indecision be resolved by him. He sat down on the chair just inside the door. He spread his feet out, and leaned forward, his elbows on his knees. There was a rock-like firmness about him. He filled the room with his own physical presence. He was one of the elect, those who determine the flow of their own lives, and the lives of those around them. He knew what he wanted; or, at least at that moment, I thought that he did. I was comforted by the feeling of assurance which this gave to me.

My father took out a packet of cigarettes and put one between his lips. The crack of the match on the box was decisive, so was the way he drew the smoke deep into his lungs.

He held the cigarette loosely between his knees, so that the plume of pale smoke rose up, veiling the down-turned face, the well-brushed hair; and the blue of it, the smell of it, romantic, evocative. Yet was it a symbol of solitary strength and introspection, or was it a sign of doubt, uncertainty, even nervousness?

It did then occur to me that my father might be nervous. And the possibility made me more fearful than I had been of the Christmas now before us both. There was a difference between us. I could still claim some indulgence for my age and inexperience in most of the things that I might do. But my father was 'a man of the world'; or so it would always be argued. He had 'seen life'; he knew what it was all about; he told me as much, often enough. He had known the romances and the tragedies. And this vast reserve of direct experience on which my father's human judgements were based was distributed liberally. He was not shy of recounting evidence of his worldliness.

The reality, I felt, had positively to be faced; it was a reality of being among ordinary people who behaved towards each other, loved, liked, tolerated each other, in ordinary ways. And however exceptional all this might be to me, to my father, I felt, it was an even more considerable challenge to his capacity to adapt downwards from his vast experience of having 'seen it all, often and often,' to the more normal exchanges of a family Christmas in the house of an English doctor's widow in a seaside Sussex town in the mid-twentieth century.

In those moments, as I stood watching him, an image presented itself and made me shiver. It had already, at that time, long been part of me. It would, in time, become as permanent a memory itself. But just at that moment, as if designed to underscore the thin ice of happiness, it forced its way into my consciousness. I saw it as a barrier between my life, between our life, and that of the people with whom we had come to spend Christmas. It was a warning of impermanence. It was a warning I wanted to ignore, yet could not. The image always seemed to present itself to me as a sequence from a film: first, I see my father, striking an attitude. He fills the frame, his whole body vibrant and intense, one hand raised in a gesture designed both to silence interruption and to focus attention on what he is saying. The other hand holds a glass.

The camera of my eyes tracks backwards and embraces more of the scene. It is a bar, filled with people. The group around him is attentive, and I hear in my mind the collective approbation for 'George', 'good old George', 'always good for a story', 'never stands on ceremony', 'gallant with the ladies', 'has seen life', 'is generous—oh, so generous—when drinks are being bought and he has the money'.

And the camera tracks on backwards, as the story is told. A door intervenes. The figures are smaller. I am outside. My father still holds the centre of the group, Laurie is part of it, and they are all bathed in the warm and languorous light of the bar. But it is now a smaller pool of colour, surrounded by shadow. And there, in the foreground, is myself, at the edge of the doorway, waiting, staring in. I suppose I am waiting to be noticed. I am staring at a scene of which I am inextricably a part. I tug ineffectually at my father with my eyes. But I am ignored. I smell the familiar mixture of odours that floats out from the throng of drinkers. I yearn; I hope; I am impatient.

The image was dispelled suddenly by my father's voice: 'What's on your mind, old skin?' He looked at me with concern. The question itself had, by the raising of his eyebrows, caused his forehead to wrinkle, and the light from the bedside table sharpened the shadows. I recalled, suddenly and vividly, those occasions in childhood when I had stood close to his seated figure and run my fingers across the surface of his forehead, alternately commanding him to make the ridges and then to dispel them. The game, then, was one of delight and laughter, the child having absolute power to command, by virtue of love, certain trivial actions.

What was on my mind then was an uneasy feeling that I needed to caution my father in some way about the evening which lay ahead of us. And I suspect now, though I did not at the time, that he realised this. For he sat on after asking me the question, an expression of kind enquiry in his eyes, of patience, of reassurance. It was not that I did not know what worried me; I wavered because I feared that my voice might falter, and my uncertain confidence dissolve. It was a ridiculous fear. I could tell my father anything. Yet, though my mind clearly told me this, physical instinct indicated the possibility that the expression in my face might well crumple into that uncoordinated ugliness of early adolescence, before the appropriate lessons in dissembling have been learnt, before a fuller use of one's face and eyes and hands and lips has been mastered. How I envied him his ability to strike an attitude, to hold an expression, and compared it with the innocence and directness which seemed to make my own situation so difficult.

Yet things had to be said, even if the saying of them was imperfect in some respect. 'Dad? If we are having music or singing after dinner, or anything like that, you know, charades, or different people doing things, you won't push me into it, will you?'

'Your father wouldn't do that, old son. Always stand by you, support you.'

'But that's just it, Dad.' I faltered. I could not quite bring out what I wished to say, that his support was often too enthusiastic, and embarrassed me.

'But you like singing. You sing so well. You have talent. They all know about your solo.'

'I know all that, Dad. I don't mind about the singing. In fact I'll like it, I know I will. It's just that I don't want you to push me. That makes me nervous.'

'Nonsense.' He drew on the cigarette, looking away from me. 'You should be proud of your father when he stands up for you. Not many will in this life. It's a serious matter, making your way in the world. You must seize on any help you can get.'

'I know, Dad. Only here it's just for fun, isn't it? It's not like a competition.'

He stood up. 'Come. Let's go down. Leave it to your father. He knows best.' And down we went, through the tall, old house, towards the rich smells of dinner and the voices of the family.

III

'It is good to be together again, at last.'

'How do we manage it? It seems more difficult each year.'

'There were times in the war when we didn't. Remember?'

'There will be again.'

'God forbid.'

'It shouldn't be thought about.'

'But mostly—'

'Yes?'

'Bread, Madge?'

'No, thank you.'

'A perfectly delicious soup.'

'She's awfully good, Mrs Drake.'

'Isn't she?'

'Mm.'

The words and phrases seemed to fall without effort, like the prodigal descent of autumn leaves, creating a soft cushion of warmth and comfort. I was seated next to Mrs Brooke, on her left side. She had Robert, her son-in-law, on her right. And she had placed my father directly opposite on the far side of the large round table. It could have seated twelve; there were only eight of us around it that night. It seemed to me that Robert should have been in my father's place. And I would have been happier with my father closer to me than he was. Yet this view, mainly prompted by my slight sense of isolation, was already being dispelled by Mrs Brooke's gentle kindness towards me.

'It did all seem easier then.' I heard Madge saying.

'Ah, but Father was alive, and we were much younger. How we chattered our afternoons away, along the seafront, flinging pebbles into the waves! We thought time stood still.' Ursula paused, her eyes remembering, her face momentarily sad. 'How wrong we were! How foolish! There we were, marooned in the midst of, well simply acres of time; hours, days—even weeks—not really knowing what to do, except to engage in endless talk and laughter.'

'You don't regret it, the squandering of time, then. I don't think you regret it afterwards, either. It's part of being young.'

'Do you remember those long bicycle rides we used to take?' Jennifer asked. 'Up into the Downs. Even at Christmas time. How huge and ghostly the beech trees could look, in the late afternoons, in winter.'

'Don't you think,' Mrs Brooke said, turning to me, her soup finished, her lips tapped once or twice with the edge of her starched napkin, 'that this is the best time of all, Christmas Eve, when there is more or less nothing more that can be done, the presents all bought, the arrangements made, all things—we sincerely hope—properly attended to, and ready for tomorrow? This feeling of anticipation, of having gathered ourselves together and closed everyone else out for a little while? And not knowing what tomorrow will bring?'

'Is it that anticipation is better than fulfilment?' I asked. I did not quite know what she was trying to say, but my own trite words, remembered from more than one occasion in the past, seemed to relate to her feelings, though at the same time to take away all the warmth and immediacy.

She smiled. 'Yes,' she said. 'Something like that. Perhaps, though, we don't quite have to be so uncompromising. The way you put it makes it seem as though an unavoidable disappointment is lurking for all of us tomorrow. I trust not.'

'I didn't mean that,' I added, hurriedly. Yet if I did not, what exactly I meant was beyond me to explain. 'I have not had Christmas like this before,' I said. 'Not since my mother died.' I spoke quietly, intending what I said to be heard only by Mrs Brooke. It was an intimacy designed to compensate for the previous remark, and express my trust in her only. Madge, on my left, was speaking anyway, with Ursula, beyond her. But I did notice Robert, who was finishing off the last spoonfuls of soup, glance over towards me. 'I mean,' I said, 'not a family Christmas.'

'Well, I hope it will all go smoothly and happily, for everyone's sake.' She spoke with finality. The course was concluded.

I looked round me, inspecting people and things with a deep sense of comfort. I felt blanketed in the warm colours of the people seated round the table, of the table itself with its glowing, polished surface, and the silver and glass and ironstone dinner-ware with which it was so richly burdened. There was the single source of light, a low-slung, heavy, complicated contraption, of weights and cords, and a delicate gathered curtain of red silk, from which the diffused rays of light spread over the surface of the table, and up into the faces of those seated at it.

I was persuaded of the existence of an order, a dignity, a 'rightness' in everything. It was not just the 'things'; not just the satisfaction and the human warmth; but something deeper —that came at me from the distant past, when my mother had been alive—a cloak of certainty which had eluded me ever since.

The soup was cleared away, and there followed, for me, the unprecedented phenomenon of fish. I listened to the flow of conversation, the remarks and allusions to local and family friends, as the daughters, regathered after many months, took possession again of their own past, an event from which my father and I, and even Robert and Babette perhaps, were partly excluded.

I considered Robert. He had shown only a perfunctory if polite interest in me when we had been introduced earlier in the drawing-room, and he had frowned slightly and glanced sternly at Babette, when I had accepted a glass of sherry from Ursula. He had shown, so far during the meal, a somewhat odd detachment, making a few comments here and there, but not apparently wishing to let himself become involved in family matters.

There was a sleek look about him. He belonged to a class of men not at all familiar to me, a class of men who wore the outward marks of success in this world with an easy nonchalance. In my mind I used those words—a phrase worthy of Jeffrey Farnol, a writer whose books I had been devouring—and looking across at Robert I applied them now. They were almost, but not quite correct. The word 'easy' did not rest naturally upon him. He had that slight self-consciousness of achievement. I classed him with 'the City', with the lawyers and accountants, politicians, men of social substance, men from whom the Coppinger trustees were drawn, men for whom my father sometimes worked, men with whom I had, as yet, enjoyed no familiarity nor friendship. He sat now, just the tiniest bit isolated, with his plump, cleanly-shaved cheeks, his black hair, slightly curly at the ends and carefully brushed, and wearing a dark blue suit with waistcoat, a pale cream silk shirt, and a deep red, patterned tie. I thought of the tie which I had eventually bought as his Christmas present, and wondered now, would it please him, or would it be quietly rejected? I stared for a moment at his small plump hands. How different they were from my father's. My father's fingers were big and spade-like and rough and strong; Robert's were smooth and small and pointed.

'It is quite obvious, Babette, isn't it? I should have cancelled my trip to America, and attended the wedding of Sir Joseph's daughter. Clearly all the excitement was there. I could have forgotten the cold war in favour of the reality of our young friend's'—and he nodded towards me—'David-and-Goliath struggle with which we have already been much regaled.' He proceeded to masticate the last forkful of fish from his plate while he looked round the table. Then he put his fork down again noisily. I noticed that my father had stopped eating and was staring across the table at Robert. It was clear on other faces that the air had quickened with expectation. Robert himself had noticed this, and there seemed to me almost a smacking of lips in the way he continued.

'Diplomacy,' he said, 'despite the tension suggested by journalists, is becoming very dull. I would even say, *entre nous*, that we diplomats spend most of our time seeking to give weight to the ephemeral shades of meaning that emanate from politicians' speeches.'

There was a slight rustle of impatience, and in the moment of pause which followed Robert's observation, Jennifer began to speak. But she was not allowed. The peremptory, abrupt way in which he raised one hand for silence restored his audience to him. 'How much better,' he went on, 'to have been in the romantic, dreamlike, snow-covered Cotswold Hills: to have gone to Great Aston for the wedding. Now that would have been dramatic!' There was an echo of mockery in his voice. He smiled around the table, and crumbled a piece of bread in his fingers. Then he looked at my father. 'And I must say, George, it was a pity you weren't up at the wedding yourself. But then, of course, you weren't invited, were you? You missed a performance of note by your talented young son, according to Babette. That's so, isn't it, my dear?'

I did not fully understand the tone in Robert's voice, though it reminded me of Colonel Savage. There was enough relaxation in it to allow the mockery to be taken in more than one way. It was not necessarily sardonic, though I guessed it could be quite bitter.

Babette treated his question quite normally. 'Yes,' she said. 'He sang very well. Didn't he, Mummy?'

'I think he sang like an angel.'

I felt their eyes on me. I looked down, a blush of embarrassment flooding my cheeks.

'Don't look down at your plate, my son!' It was my father, calling out from his position across the table from me. He seemed enormously distant and remote. 'It shows ingratitude. Complimented by the prettiest girl in the room, and he looks down into his food. He's not his father's son.'

It was the tone in his voice which, above all, I most dreaded, and it compounded my feelings of embarrassment.

Jennifer said: 'Leave him alone, George. You would almost certainly have looked down at your plate at his age.'

'Am I right, George,' Robert asked, 'in thinking that you referred to my daughter, when you mentioned the prettiest girl in the room? Or did you mean my wife?'

Again, the echo of mockery. Again, the ambivalence of feeling behind it.

'Why, Robert, Babette of course.' He looked directly at her. 'She has the bloom of youth in her cheeks and the light of love in her eyes. She has the world at her feet; she has the greatest ally of all at her right hand, that old mischief-maker, Time. Moreover, child—and mark the words of one who has lived richly, and knows most, if not all of the answers—the life you have before you is wonderful, so wonderful; you must live it to the full.'

Her laughter became entangled in the final, resonant echoes of his pronouncement upon life, for she had seen the humour in his pretentions to knowledge and wisdom, and, unlike me, she was not inhibited from the most natural response, which was to laugh first, and then imitate; and this she did: repeating exactly his words, following his emphases, every shift and nuance of sound, her voice sinking to a deep and vibrant imitation of his own on those last few words . . . 'and you must live it to the full.'

Everyone laughed. How I loved her at that moment, her mouth softened in real, if mocking, affection for my father, her head turning, first away from me, so that I could see the perfect profile of her face, and then back towards me, so that I, too, could be bathed in the warm affection of her eyes.

But was it really 'wonderful, so wonderful', for everyone? Must life truly be lived 'to the full'? Or was this ordinance about the conduct and direction of one's life, which I had heard so often from his lips in the past, though never before directed at someone I loved in the way that I thought I loved Babette, in reality a direction to her to follow an example which it would in actual fact be madness to follow? Even as I joined in the laughter I had before me the image of possible catastrophe. I had the knowledge that life was not always, for everyone, a wonderful experience. There was Alice. Could not Babette, in her turn, years further forward, be hurt in a similar way? Were there not, even then, at that very table, people who concealed behind their laughter the anguish of some deep and unrequited yearning for events in their lives which had not materialised in the way wished for, and would now never materialise? I could guess that Jennifer had suffered in some way, that Madge was not entirely happy. And I knew that Ursula wavered on the brink of a decision that probably offered her pain either way; just as I knew that Mrs Brooke would never again enjoy the lightness of heart, the companionship, which marriage had given her, and widowhood had taken away. I looked with a certain envy at my father's face, as he gazed at Babette, an expression of such unmitigated softness in his eyes, his emotions running together as visible emblems of the gratitude he felt for her direct response. Why did I, for that moment, so unquestioningly exclude him from the unhappiness with which I so easily invested others around that table? I cannot answer. Only now, looking back, does it seem strange to me that I did not suspect that, behind all the self-dramatisations, even deeper shadows lurked.

It was because of a nervous expectation that my father would notice my own rather solemn face, that I turned away from him to look at Robert, and was surprised to see that he, also, was not joining in the general laughter round the table. His eyes, quite cold in their expression, were fixed upon Madge. And I felt strangely hypnotised by the frigid blankness in his gaze, surrounded, as it was, by the well-fed, assured framework of his face, the clean, discreet, comfortable smugness of his hands. But the expression, with all that it revealed, was short-lived. Even as I watched him he adjusted, and came back once again, with a slight smile, to worry at the edges of what he had missed. He clasped his hands together, and they rested upon the edge of the table, from which he had gently pushed forward his plate.

'You children,' my father resumed, looking from Babette to myself, 'will have wonderful lives. It is all so different, now. When I was your age I would never have sat at dinner like this. My parents were not as remote as some, but being a child was, I think, more of a penance then.'

'Oh, George, I cannot imagine you as a child,' Jennifer said. 'You must have been dressed in knee-length, buttoned trousers, and a kind of Norfolk jacket, with one of those strange floppy peaked caps, all in matching tweed. Am I right? And your mother? What was she like? We want to know, don't we?' She looked round the table. No one contradicted her. All were seated in a kind of anticipatory stillness, the fish course finished.

Mrs Brooke said: 'Yes. Tell us, George.' And I detected in her voice a note of serious inquiry, as though my father's childhood might reveal to her certain valuable information about this man who loved her daughter. 'But let's first clear away this course, and serve the beef. We're going to get you to carve, George, while Robert deals with his own best love, the claret that he advised my husband to buy long ago.'

The beef was brought in by Mrs Drake. My father got up and went to the sideboard. He picked up the knife and felt the blade with his thumb. Then he honed it briefly on the steel. Mrs Drake told him she had already sharpened it, and he smiled at her, and replied that he was just getting into practice once again. The sound of steel on steel took me back to early childhood, when we had all been together, and when he had played a game at Sunday lunch, reciting some forgotten poem, lines of doggerel no doubt, and pointing the quivering blade at each of us children in turn as we sat round the table with my mother. He did not do anything of the sort now, but the mere memory of it pleased me, just as it pleased me to see him so obviously at home in this house, confident, the more significant of the two men there, at least in my prejudiced view.

'Shall I help?' I said.

'That would be kind,' said Mrs Brooke.

'I can never understand why Robert hates carving,' Madge said. The tone in her voice made others look at her. She was smiling at her husband. Surely she knew the answer, I thought.

He was pouring a half-glass of wine for Babette, an action I found vaguely surprising. 'Really, dear, you know it's just something I don't like doing. I can't explain it. An aversion. A psychologist could explain it.'

Ursula said, 'It's meant to be a very revealing sign of character. Men who carve well are usually men of decisive, aggressive natures. Are you decisive and aggressive, George?'

'It's you who should be answering that,' Madge said. 'Come on. Tell us. Is he?'

'Let him answer. He's even better qualified,' Ursula said.

My father finished serving a plate, and watched me while I carefully took it up in my hands. Then he laid down the knife and fork and turned to face the table. 'But of course,' he said. 'You should all know it. Am I not obviously a man of decision?' He paused. 'And look where it's got me.'

There was silence during our first attack on the roast beef. Just the clink of knives and forks, and of other almost imperceptible movements. I noticed my father drinking his claret, and pausing to absorb the flavour, an unexpected act of pleasure in him, and I felt disarmed and happy. He was so mellow, so much at home. Dinner seemed already to have gone on for a long time. Yet his more expansive gestures, the air of relaxation and confidence which surrounded him, set me entirely at my ease.

He paused, and lifted his glass, and looked round at the table. 'This is all marvellous,' he said. 'I wish you all a happy and memorable Christmas. It's so good to be part of your family. Isn't it, my son?' I nodded and raised my glass as well. 'To you all!' he said, and we both drank.

'We have decided that we shall have a Christmas Eve concert after dinner,' Mrs Brooke announced. 'All are to take part. No exceptions. So you must all think of what you are to do.'

'What will Robert do?' Madge asked. 'What will you do, darling? How will you entertain us?' There was a laughing, teasing note in her voice.

He looked across at her. If he was uncomfortable he concealed it behind his cold and baleful eyes. 'I really don't know,' he said. 'I'm not at all good at this sort of thing. It just isn't my strong line. I feel at a bit of a loss.'

Babette looked first at her mother, then at him. 'Daddy will tell a story. Or recite a poem. I shall help him.' She put her hand on his arm, and he touched it for a moment with his fingers.

I was watching, and she suddenly looked directly at me, her eyes wide and serious. I thought, in that moment, that perhaps something was not right between Madge and Robert, and that Babette herself was conscious of it. She smiled, just briefly, and took her hand away, and then looked down. I felt a surge of envy at the touch of her hand on her father's arm. I felt proud of her for standing up for him.

I was glad when Ursula began to speak about a certain Uncle Jeremy, whom they would be seeing during the Christmas holiday. I was able to feel absorbed once again by the Brookes and the Springers, and overlook the disintegrated fortunes of our own family. The family conversation swirled about me. It was new and strange; so settled, so firm, so ordered.

I watched Robert carefully as he drank his wine. Robert had called it 'claret', 'a good, robust '37'. I did not have the courage to ask what he meant, and I felt I was being rude, staring at Robert as he drank. But Robert was supremely unaware of me. He buried his pale sharp nose in the mouth of his glass, and it seemed to twitch. Then he closed his eyes. He took a sip. He held the liquid in his mouth, shifting it from cheek to cheek. Finally he swallowed. This was not the way Ursula and my father drank wine.

Mrs Brooke said to her son-in-law: 'How is it, Robert?'

He nodded several times before he spoke. Then he said: 'Mm. Good. Very sound. Just right for drinking now. Reginald had very good taste. Cheval Blanc was, and is, excellent. I shall be glad myself when things get back to normal again, and such wines as these are in reasonable supply once more.'

'You must advise me on what to buy. Our stocks are not what they were.'

'What do you think, George?' Robert asked.

My father took up his glass. His sniff was peremptory. He took a gulp. 'Excellent. Couldn't be better.'

I remembered the wine we had drunk at Ursula's. There had been no comment then. We all paused and took sips. I could see no real difference. It seemed less sharp than the wine Ursula had given us, but that was all.

We finished the beef, and moved on to pudding.

'Have you always lived in London?' Mrs Brooke asked me.

I glanced up at my father. He had drunk several glasses of wine, and Robert was refilling his glass. I was left to fend for myself. I noticed Jennifer looking at me, and Babette beside her. I turned back to Mrs Brooke. 'Mostly,' I said. 'You see, we move about quite a lot.'

'What do you mean by that?'

'Well, Dad—my father—changes his job quite often. We were in the country last holiday. Down in Kent. Now we're back in London. We mostly live in London, though. For as long as I can remember.'

'And are you lonely?'

I looked across at Babette. She smiled, a questioning, pensive smile which I found difficult to understand. 'Yes, I am, sometimes. I don't mind though. I'm used to it.'

'Loneliness should never become usual,' said Mrs Brooke. She rose from the table. 'Come along then. Let us go and look together at what music we have. It's getting late and we still have the presents to arrange.'

IV

I think that I continued to feel nervous with Mrs Brooke, perhaps on account of her kindness towards me. I did not know how much she knew about us. I did not know how she regarded the relationship between my father and Ursula. I did not know myself how to regard it. There had been other women, some of whom I had liked. But there had never been this involvement with a family. And it was immeasurably exciting to me. I had to grip my hands to assure myself that it was real. I half feared that if I failed in my behaviour towards this grand old lady with her gentle eyes, her firm control, her cool judgements, that I would be rudely awakened, and find myself suddenly back in the faded, airless gentility of our room in London.

We had moved into the drawing-room. I was anxious to sing my best, my very best. Mrs Brooke sat herself at the piano, and turned over a book of songs. 'Now you must tell me the ones you know,' she said.

I chose 'Allan Water'. Robert came in with my father. Then Babette. They applauded. I felt no real nervousness. Babette came and stood beside me and we sang 'The Bonnie Earl o' Murray' together. In the middle of it the sisters came in. They were laughing and talking, and then suddenly quiet. They grouped around the piano and we sang, all together. I watched Mrs Brooke as she played, her graceful hands strong and sure on the keys. The piano was black, a boudoir grand. I read the name in gold letters, 'Bechstein'. It was the same make as the best school piano, the one kept for concerts. I knew from Parker that it was good. Jennifer, who had a rich, deep voice, sang 'Blow the Wind Southerly'. My father and Robert, amid much laughter, sang 'On Ilkla Moor Baht 'at'.

The pauses between songs grew longer. Eventually Mrs

Brooke stopped. She looked round at them all. 'We've all done our share. It's your turn now, Ursula.'

Ursula played Brahms. And then Madge, who did not play as well as Ursula, but looked as if she might have played better, and might well have done had life been different for the sisters, played the Brahms G Minor Rhapsody. I lost myself in the sweep of the bass, the firm thump of the tune, the sudden soothing persuasion, the questing, teasing progress: doubt, uncertainty, resolution.

'And now it's time for the presents.'

We brought our presents down. The top of the house was cold and quiet. I hurried back again. We laid out the parcels under the small Christmas tree.

'We must have some carols,' said Jennifer. 'It wouldn't do not to have carols. Will you play, Ursula?'

We sang carols. I wished with all my heart that the evening would never end. I wanted only to hold Babette's hand and my happiness would be complete.

She sat beside me while they were singing. When they had finished, while the others were talking and Robert was pouring out drinks, she said: 'Shall we go down to the sea tomorrow, early in the morning?'

'Can we?'

'Of course.'

'What time?'

'I'll call you. I have an alarm clock. Granny says breakfast will be at nine. If we get up at eight, that will be enough time.'

'Is it a sandy beach?'

'No, it's pebbles.'

'Pity.'

'It's still nice.'

'I wasn't thinking of that. I was thinking of making tracks in the sand, like we did in the snow.'

'There's a pier.' She offered it as a consolation.

'Isn't it closed? I thought they closed piers in winter?'

'The end is closed, the concert hall. But you can still walk out along it.'

'I like your grandmother.'

'I love coming down here. Mummy always seems to be different down here.'

'How do you mean?'

'I don't know, really. She's more relaxed. She never plays the piano at home.'

'What about your father?'

'Oh, he doesn't change.'

Madge came over to us. She knelt down on the carpet in front of where we were sitting. 'Happy?' she asked. I nodded. 'And you, Babette? Has it been a nice evening?'

'Lovely, Mummy.'

'Are you looking forward to your presents?'

'Oh, yes, of course.'

She paused, reaching out and taking Babette's hand. 'I think you should go off to bed now.' Madge kissed her daughter. 'Goodnight, darling.'

We said our goodnights. On the landing I wanted to take Babette's hand as her mother had taken it; kiss her, even. We lingered for moments there, then parted. Toiling up the stairs to my own room, I reassured myself that in due course I would do so, that I would hold her in my arms, and kiss her lips. It was as much as I could, or would, imagine.

V

I was running through the snow. It was deep, the drifts hid the ditches, and I fell again and again. In the distance was the church. I could see it through the trees. I knew I would be all right there. But I couldn't run fast enough. I could hear Colonel Savage behind me, shouting, 'How dare you, boy! We'll get to the root of this! How dare you!' When I reached the church door I could not open it. I cringed, waiting for the

Colonel to strike me. But instead he took me by the scruff of the neck and pulled me away from the door. Then he opened it and together we went in. Colonel Savage marched me through the church. It was filled with people. The choir were all there, except for myself. We came to the communion rail. The Colonel turned me round to face the congregation and shouted hoarsely at me 'Sing, boy!' The music began, but when it came to the time when I should sing I opened my mouth and no sounds came out. I felt again the rising tide of panic. The noise made me dreadfully dizzy and hot. Colonel Savage raised his arm. There was only one escape, to run into the sanctuary and throw myself down before the altar. I fumbled with the catches on the communion rail, and rushed forward, shouting 'Help me! Help me!' But there was no floor in front of the altar, and with a sickening lurch I fell forward into the void, still crying out, 'Help me! Help me!'

'All right, old son. All right, old skin. All right. All right. Take it easy. Relax now. Dad's here. It's all over.' Coming up out of black treacle, scratched by the terror of drowning, I clutched at the big, warm, friendly frame of my father. I buried my head in the rough texture of his jacket. I smelt on him the faint mixture of brandy, cigar, cigarette smoke. I felt sweat inside my own pyjama jacket, tears on my cheeks, a dryness in my mouth. I felt a great, overwhelming sense of relief, and I sobbed it out against my father's chest.

'It's the excitement, George. He stayed up very late.'

I listened to Ursula's voice. I was comforted by the note of concern. My father was stroking my shoulders and back, murmuring gently to me. I felt a churning in my stomach. 'I think I want to be sick.'

A basin was produced. I heaved tidily, obediently into it.

'There's a good lad,' my father said. I wiped my mouth. Ursula brought me a glass of water and I drank thirstily from it. 'You couldn't have timed it better if you'd tried.'

I lay back and smiled up at them. I felt suddenly very tired.

'How pale you are,' said Ursula. 'Are you warm enough?'
I nodded.
'All right now?'
I nodded again. They sat for a few moments on the edge of my bed. Ursula was leaning against my father, her head on his shoulder, watching me. I felt a deep sense of security having them both there. Colonel Savage was vanquished. It was still Christmas Eve. The holiday was just beginning. At eight Babette would wake me up, and then Christmas itself would begin.

Chapter Seven

I

'Wake up!' I felt myself being shaken, and struggled up from the final layers of untroubled sleep. 'Wake up!' A hand rested on my shoulder. I opened my eyes. Babette was frowning slightly, her face turned sideways, and brought quite close to where my head lay, still pressed deeply, comfortably, into the soft whiteness of the pillow. I could not, at first, understand the closeness. Then I remembered that we had to be up and out and down to the sea and back again for breakfast. She smiled as I watched her. 'You're an old sleepyhead,' she said. 'Don't you remember? We said we'd get up early and go down to the sea.'

'Why are you so close?' I asked, not so much out of curiosity as from a desire to stretch out the moments of stillness and communion. I had not, as yet, moved. The bedclothes, the eiderdown, were hunched over my shoulder. I was warm, and felt safe.

'I'm kneeling down, you ass,' she said, 'trying to wake you up. Are we going to go? Do you still want to?'

I nodded and smiled at her, beginning to raise my head from the pillow and to move my arms from under the heavy warmth of the covers into the cold air of the attic room.

Babette got up and crossed to the window. 'It's after eight,' she said. 'It's still not light.' She drew the curtain. 'Nobody else is awake. How long will you be?'

I sat up. 'I'll only be a few minutes.'

She stood for a moment by the window, looking across at me. 'Happy Christmas.'

'What?'

'It's Christmas Day. Happy Christmas.'

'Oh. Happy Christmas to you.'

'I'll wait downstairs.'

By the time I came downstairs, I felt light-headed, my stomach empty and slightly uneasy. I hoped it would not make me dizzy or cause me to faint. I was susceptible that way; and the previous night's excitement, to which my father had attributed my nightmare and its sequel, had left me feeling weak. I told Babette, and she was suddenly overcome with concern, and doubtful about the advisability of going out at all. But I insisted.

'I'll get you something before we go, then. What would you like? Are you sure we should go out?' She moved round the kitchen table, trying to decide. Then she brought out and gave me bread and honey, and a glass of milk. 'Mummy says simple food is best,' she said. She watched me as I ate. She took an apple to keep me company. 'What made you sick?'

'I don't know. My father says it must have been the excitement. I had a nightmare.'

'Did you? What happened in it?'

I told her.

'How did you really feel when all that happened at the wedding?'

'I didn't really feel frightened. I knew I hadn't done anything wrong. It's just that—well—no one believes you when something like that happens. Sometimes you don't even believe yourself. You get so confused. It must, at some time, have happened to you, being accused of doing something which you haven't done, and then, in the middle of it all, beginning to think that things have all gone wrong, and perhaps you did do something, by accident. Do you know what I mean? You're left all alone. That's the feeling I had, with everyone crowding round and staring. You don't trust yourself any more when that happens. You feel dizzy, confused, choked. That's how I felt in my nightmare last night. I felt that same choking sensation. Have you ever had that?'

She had listened silently, nodding occasionally at what I said. She nodded more vigorously now, and said that she had once or twice felt the same. I finished the bread and honey and drank up the milk. 'Should we go now?' I felt much better. It had helped, to talk with her.

We listened for a moment in the hall. We could hear faint sounds from somewhere upstairs. Nearby, the grandfather clock ticked out majestically. Through the fanlight above the door came in the first grey light of day.

We left the house quietly, and hurried down the road which my father and I had climbed the evening before. The air of mystery and adventure that had been bestowed upon it by the slight hints of evening mist and the infrequent and uneven glow of lamplight was now replaced by the settled certainty of ordered gardens and still, silent houses in the growing light of dawn. We turned off the road along a path which led to a footbridge over the railway. From it the deserted streets sloped gently away in front of us. Eventually, round a bend, among shops and other seafront establishments, closed or boarded up against winter and the holiday, we came out on the broad open roadway that ran along the front.

'We'll have to hurry. I don't suppose breakfast will really be at nine. More like half-past, or even later. But we'd better not be too long. They'll only worry. Particularly your father. He's the worrying kind, isn't he?'

'Yes, I suppose he is.'

'I guessed as much.'

'When do we unwrap the presents?'

'We have them after breakfast.'

'There's almost nobody about,' Babette said. 'How strange it is. So deserted.'

I did not answer her. I felt intensely excited. I had been

beside the sea on so few occasions in the whole of my life. There had been a holiday from school once. There had been a visit to Devon. And as an infant, with no memory of it, but with faded photographs of my father sitting on the pebbles at Bognor nursing me to prove the fact, there had been the holiday well before the war began, a holiday which Francis occasionally remembered in order to tease me; in all probability the only holiday which we, as a family, had together during my mother's lifetime. I remembered my words to Mrs Brooke, the night before, about anticipation, and I strode out with a spring in my step, beside Babette.

We crossed the road to the broad, deserted promenade, with its lamp posts and ironwork, its seats and urns. And we stood together, arms leaning on the railings, the pebble beach below us, the hissing, flopping, gently thumping waters of the full-tide close by. Together we stood, not too close, gazing out towards the horizon. The light, sharp and intense in those moments immediately before the appearance of the sun itself over the edge of the horizon to our left, intensified lines and shadows around us, giving an edge of blue to objects; it touched the wisps of cloud with shadowings of mauve; these, in turn, changed to dull, then to brighter pink.

Almost at our feet the grey waves continued to break in a half-hearted way, the shadowy curve of water running along the surface of wet pebbles, the foam hissing softly among them. The front stretched away to our right, out seaward, and the uneven line of buildings was broken by the solid, majestic bulk of the principal hotels. The nearest was painted white, and part of it stuck up, tower-like, with the name, 'The Royal Hotel', in black Gothic letters high on its wall. It was of a 1930-ish design, distinctly reminiscent of the huge white superstructure on a cruise liner. Beyond it were the other hotels, then houses, then modest cliffs at the furthest tip of land, concealing the coastline beyond.

'Look now, the sun's coming up,' Babette said. 'It will catch on the highest buildings first. Let's watch.'

The white bulk of the hotel was tinged with shadowy, opalescent pink. Because of the mist the sunlight was diffused, and there was no clear line as its rays extended downward. We turned towards the sea, and waited. Presently, the disc of reddish gold, its edges blurred, appeared above the horizon. It was day.

'It's like magic, isn't it?'

'It is magic.'

'Look how the buildings catch fire.'

'And look at the sea, all golden. And the sky. How quickly the clouds seem to change from mauve to pink, and pink to white.'

Babette turned towards me. 'Your face is all glowing in the sun. I can see it reflecting in your eyes. Can you stare straight at it?'

'Yes, I can. The morning mist is like a filter. No, I can't any more. You try. Let me look into your eyes.'

She turned her face towards the sun and the sea. At first she closed her eyes and held on to the railings. I leaned beside her looking into her face. Then she opened them and stared fully into the ever-increasing light. I watched the reflections in the black glistening pupils of her eyes, half closed again, and then blinking slightly. Her face shone with the sharp golden light, and the morning breeze, strangely mild for mid-winter, lifted her fair hair and blew it back from her face.

She closed her eyes and laughed. 'I can't look any more.'

The sun had risen clear of the horizon's distant line, forging its way upward through the low, thin traces of sea mist. Its light gathered strength. The surface of the sea bore the hammered-out pattern of its increasing brilliance.

'Can we walk along a bit?' I asked. 'Have we time?'

'We can't stay too long. We can go down as far as the kiosk. Then we can come back along the beach.'

'Is that all?'

'Yes.'

'Not just a bit further?'

'No.'

She was definitely in charge. I wanted to stretch out as much as possible the time we would be alone together, but conceded that she must know just what time permitted. As well, I wanted her hand in mine, and did not know how to achieve so momentous a change in our relationship.

A man passed below us on the beach, his feet crunching among the pebbles. Then a boy, younger than myself, went by. He had a young puppy on a lead. The lead was new, and the puppy and the boy were in dispute about its function. We stopped to watch.

'Would you like to have a puppy?' she asked.

'It wouldn't be possible,' I said. 'Not in London.'

'But people in our flats have them.'

'We only have a bed-sitting room. Double. I'm sure pets wouldn't be allowed.' I knew they would not. 'Besides, my father doesn't like animals.'

'Have you always lived in different places? Always moving, like you said, last night, to Granny?'

I nodded. 'Yes,' I said. 'I suppose so.'

'Always?' she persisted. 'Even when you were little?'

'Oh, no. It was different when my mother was alive. Then we had a house. It was in South London. Sometimes we go back there. I wish, sometimes, it was like that again.'

We had come to the kiosk, and stood now at the top of some steps that led down to the beach. We looked at each other. Babette had her back to the sea, and the sun caught in her hair, edging it with white and gold. I had to screw up my eyes against the sharp winter sunlight still flashing and gleaming low across the sea. It reminded me suddenly, vividly, of a painting I had once seen in an art gallery of two girls running along a pier in slanting sunlight. The picture, as I remembered it, was neither of winter, nor of the dawn. There were yachts in it, and other people. It was surely of late afternoon in summer. But something about the long shadows, the pink light we had watched slowly fading into the sharper whiteness of day, echoed in my mind, back to that image of freedom evoked by the partially remembered figures of the young girls, running hand in hand.

'Couldn't it be? Couldn't your father marry again?'

'Do you mean Ursula?'

Babette nodded. 'They are lovers,' she said. The phrase sounded strange coming from her mouth. It was said calmly, lightly, factually. I was faintly shocked. At that stage, for me, it was a description of people inhabiting the world of the imagination, not the world of life. It was all right to think of the chaste lovers of Jeffrey Farnol, the less chaste ones of Peter Cheyney. But my father? Ursula? That was a different matter. And I was not entirely free of confusion about the exact meaning. Did it mean *that*?

'Are they?' I asked, foolishly.

'Don't be silly. Of course they are.' She turned suddenly, and ran down the steps. 'Come on,' she called up at me, 'we must hurry. I'll race you back to the other steps.' She disappeared among the pillars which lined the lower walk, and which supported the edge of the main promenade. I paused for a moment only, then followed her, emerging onto the beach to see that she was already well ahead of me. Then I gave chase. We arrived almost together at the next set of steps, and climbed up again, breathless and laughing. 'We must hurry back,' she said. 'They'll be wondering where we've gone.'

'Do you think,' I asked, 'that my father will marry Ursula? What does your mother think?'

'I don't know. They talk about it, but mostly in fun. Mummy says she's never met anyone like your father before. She doesn't know what to make of him. Perhaps they'll just stay the way they are. What difference does it make? When I look at them I only wish that Mummy and Daddy were like that together.'

'Aren't they sometimes?'

She shook her head.

I took a deep breath. I touched her arm, and she stopped and looked at me. 'Are *you* happy?' I asked.

She smiled at me. 'I am just now,' she said.

'But at other times? At home? With them?'

She looked at me queerly then, her head on one side. I felt suddenly near to her, and was afraid. My throat tightened. I could hear my heart beating. She turned to go on, without answering me. I fell into step beside her, and took her hand in mine. I waited for her to pull her hand away again, but she did not. My heart flooded with pleasure.

We climbed the hill in the cold Christmas morning air, in silence, puffing out the visible expression of our excitement and energy, our bodies adjusting to the new conjunction, our steps harmonising on the pavements. It was only at the gate of the garden in front of the house, with a squeeze that was returned to me just as firmly, that I released her fingers, buckling the memory of them, and of that occasion, carefully away in my heart.

II

As a child one wonders about others, not about oneself, since the reality and importance of others is greater. The problem is how to understand them, and how to relate to them. Perhaps, even, how to be like them. On that Christmas morning, after we had finished breakfast, and had gathered together in the drawing-room for the presents, I felt this desperate need to understand in order that I should know how to feel, and how to behave towards them. Is it this need which makes us doubt increasingly, during adolescence, our ability to feel naturally and to be natural? There are too many questions.

In the midst of the confusion and excitement, which was for me a kind of camouflage or protection, I felt a shiver at my own nature, that seemed to be residing outside, unable to join fully in the joy and enthusiasm. I was conscious, guiltily so, that I was putting on a kind of performance: that the clear, sharp eyes of different members of the family at different times were on me, questioning and measuring my responses, and that I was responding to *that* rather than to any overwhelming surge or thrill of pleasure. I listened to the calls from Madge, sitting at the foot of the tree. She read out:

'"To George from Ursula, Christmas, 1949". There you are, George. See what Ursula has given you.' And Madge handed up to my father the slim package wrapped in blue tissue, and tied with a red ribbon. She and Babette knelt among the profusion of parcels at the foot of the tree and took turns in reading off the labels and handing out the presents.

Robert had just opened his gift from us: 'This is perfectly splendid, perfectly splendid. Very good of you both.' He held the tie unenthusiastically in one hand.

Babette called out my own name. She knelt with the present in her hand, but did not attempt to read the label. I crossed over from the chair where I had put my other things, and took the package from her. It was her gift. I guessed that. I thought at first it was a book, but it felt soft and flexible. I went back to unwrap it on my own.

'But it's beautiful,' I heard Jennifer saying. 'I've never seen anything like it. Wherever did you get it?'

'Oh, Robert found it. He always knows the best people to go to. I feel quite envious of his contacts.'

'I thought you'd like it,' Robert said. 'It's rather good, you know. First period.'

'Oh, Babette, how clever you are!' said Mrs Brooke, 'your painting has come on amazingly well since the summer. And I'm so glad you remembered the one I liked best.' She held up a picture by Babette which had been framed.

I looked up in sudden surprise. Across the room the 'painting' appeared to me a mass of greens, cool and limpid. How little I really knew about her. I looked across at her. She was smiling at her grandmother, and I noticed the small dimpling of her cheeks at the corners of her mouth, little half-moons of pleasure. She turned suddenly away and took up another parcel.

'Aunt Jenny,' she said. It was one that I had parcelled up.

I took her present from its wrapping. It was a leather writing-case, with pad and envelopes in it. I could not bring myself to call out my thanks across the room. I felt shy and exposed and embarrassed, even more so in face of her gift, than I had felt already since the giving of parcels had begun. I could feel my own heart beat. Could I get up and cross over to her? Would the others look at me? Surely not. They were moving about, laughing, talking, turning over the wrapping paper, generating confusion and excitement and a welter of coloured paper and string and ribbons. I slipped behind Mrs Brooke's chair, where she sat in patient, benign expectation, and knelt on the floor beside Babette. 'Thanks ever so much,' I said. 'It's really a super present.' I meant it, and yet I could feel the embarrassment of my thanks tugging my mouth into an awkward, churlish expression over which I had no control.

'You'll have to write to me now.'

'Yes, I will. Of course.'

She looked calmly, directly into my eyes. 'That's why I gave it to you. Here you are. This is from your father.'

Blushing, feeling foolish without understanding why, and resenting the way I felt, I looked down at the package in my hand. It was small, but firmly, substantially wrapped in stout paper and in string that had been knotted and knotted again. I took it away.

'George, dear, come and sort out some of these presents,' Madge said. 'I want the chance to open mine.' She got up.

'Robert shouldn't have bought that, Madge.' Mrs Brooke said. She was holding a silver rosebowl in her hands. It was plain, with rope edging round the top. It gleamed among the turbulence of wrapping paper. 'It is really too exciting.' She seemed, to me, genuinely moved by the gift. More colour had come into her cheeks than I had yet seen there.

Around each of us the profusion of coloured debris increased. Down the long room towards the window that faced south, and through which came the sun's rays, each chair stood within a growing mound of wrapping-paper, out of which small, tidy piles of presents had been rescued and stacked, carefully by some, with no concern by others, but each pile kept apart from the growing turmoil of tissue and boxes and ribbons and string, and in some cases stout cardboard, corrugated paper, stamps and sealing wax.

I struggled with the tight wrappings on my father's gift. Babette left the tree and came to a chair close to me to undo her presents. For a moment she paused and watched. I expected a fountain pen from the small, oblong package. But instead, I pulled out a wrist-watch. It lay in my palm staring up at me, the second hand clicking relentlessly round its black face. My first watch. I couldn't speak for a moment. Then: 'Babette! Look! A watch! It's what I wanted more than anything! I never expected it. Never.' I held it out to her, and she took it and admired it. I looked down at the stiff, plain white card that had come out of the box. On it my father had written: 'To My Dear Son from his Loving Father, Xmas 1949.' The handwriting was big and bold, the capital letters standing up firm as sentinels, the X of Xmas and the date scored heavily into the surface of the white card.

No, I had never expected it. How could I have done, in the circumstances? Where had the money come from, but from Alice? I looked across at my father and saw behind him her benign shadow. I felt strange in that company, bewildered and momentarily sad. My father had taken over the distribution of presents as though engaged in nautical strategy, passing out family gifts with abrupt efficiency, and a trifle heartlessly.

Babette handed me back the watch. 'It's a lovely present,' she said. Then she turned her attention to her own parcels.

I did not look at her. I put my hand down and took the

watch and held it and went on staring across the room between the figures of Jennifer and Ursula, who were talking, past all the profusion, at the kneeling, busy figure of my father. I watched him in silence. Everyone in the room seemed occupied. Then our eyes met. For a moment my father's expression was one of surprise, perhaps at the sadness in my own face, perhaps at the sudden questioning my glance must have implied at how the watch had come to be bought. My innate sense of discretion pushed me out of my chair and across to where he had half-risen. I put an arm round his shoulders and hugged him briefly. 'It's a super present, Dad. What I wanted more than anything else.' Then, more quietly, 'And I didn't think it would be possible this year . . .' My voice tailed off into silence.

'Not possible? You underestimate your father.' He stood now, a present in one hand, the other on my shoulder. Still speaking quietly, and only for me, he went on: 'Leave it to him. He'll always find a way. He always has, eh?' And he smiled down at me, and hugged me, almost roughly, then held me off and looked down at my face. 'Put it on, then.' I did so.

Madge turned to me. 'Is that your father's present?' she asked. 'May I see?'

I showed her.

'Do you like it?' Ursula asked.

'It's terrific. Just what I wanted.'

I felt slightly embarrassed at my mixed feelings, sadness and joy inextricably intermingled. I found it difficult, if not impossible, to escape the feeling of insecurity which emanated from the knowledge that I belonged in this place at this time, only because my father belonged, and that his belonging there was a phenomenon of curiously uncertain substance.

I carried my presents upstairs and brushed my hair ready for church. I put on my coat and went down again. Robert was alone in the drawing-room, standing with his back to the fire. I hesitated at the door.

'All set for church then?'

'Yes, Robert.' The name came uncertainly to my lips. I could not find it easy, as Babette found it easy to call my own father George, to address her father as 'Robert'. And I felt that Robert, in his turn, found it just a shade too familiar.

'You'll enjoy the Christmas service.'

'If it has carols I will.'

'There'll be carols, of course. You'll have all your favourites. And your father's sonorous notes of last night can be applied with a religious connotation. Is that a possibility, do you think?'

I frowned slightly at the tone in Robert's voice. He reminded me of one of the masters at school. And what did he mean by saying 'you' all the time? Was he not coming to church? 'I suppose it is,' I answered. 'But my father's not very good at carols.'

'Hm. A strange lapse. They provide us with fine music. Look at those.' He pointed to the mass of Christmas cards above the fire. 'Jolly, red-faced, eighteenth-century coachmen, for the most part, achieving the impossible, singing lustily and laughing heartily at the same time. And what is it that gives them so much pleasure? Carols.'

I looked towards the door. It was time we started. 'I don't mean he can't sing them,' I said. 'It's just not his favourite sort of singing.'

'Don't worry. We're in good time. Too early, in fact. The women of the house will keep us waiting until the last possible moment.' He paused. 'You and Babette went down to the seafront this morning, I'm told.'

'Yes.'

'And how was the seafront?'

'It was—' I hesitated, 'it was all there.' He raised his eyebrows with an expression of inquiry, and I realised that my phrase, awkward and not very explicit, might also seem impertinent. 'What I mean is, it was just as I expected it to be, just how Babette described it to me.'

We stood in silence. I felt increasingly awkward with him, and wished that someone would join us. We seemed to have been standing there together for a very long time. Eventually I said: 'It was a lovely morning. We saw the sun coming up.'

'It's still bright.' He nodded towards the window. 'We shall all meet up after church and go down to the front.'

I looked at him, puzzled. 'Meet up with who?'

He smiled indulgently. 'You don't realise. We go to different churches. You'll go with my mother-in-law, and my wife, to St Andrew's. Babette and I go to Mass.'

This was a blow. The information complicated my view of things, since at that time I was passing through an erratic but forceful phase of religious enthusiasm, of a broadly evangelical kind. I suppose I was lurching my way into a faith of some kind, but not of wide enough compass, then, to appreciate the possibility of Mass on Christmas Day.

I said: 'Does . . . does your . . . Mass begin at the same time?'

'Yes,' said Robert. 'And finishes at much the same time, too. You could come with us if you wanted. But our carols are not sung to the same high standard.'

'Then couldn't you and Babette come with us?'

'Well, no. That wouldn't do.'

At that moment she entered and I heard the others in the hall. Mrs Brooke was giving instructions to Mrs Drake at the kitchen door.

'After church,' Babette said, 'we're all going down to the seafront for a walk. You're to wait for us. I'll see you then. Do you like my hat and scarf? They're a present from Granny.' She threw an end of the scarf over her shoulder.

We all set off from the house. I walked beside Madge. 'I didn't know Babette was a Catholic,' I said. 'It seems odd going to a different church.'

'It's a bit of a nuisance,' Madge said.

'He said I could go with them. But I didn't think I could.'

'You mean you wouldn't know what to do?'

'No. I've never been to Mass. Is it true, you can go if you are different, I mean, if you are Protestant or something else?'

'Oh, yes. Of course. I take Babette when Robert's away.'

'But why don't you go with them now?'

She appeared to find my question difficult. After a pause she said: 'I like Mr Taylor at St Andrew's better than Father O'Connor. I don't trust men with red hair. And it seems worse when they're priests.'

We walked down the hill in the sunshine. The light came in across the sea, reflecting in its surface. The sun was bright, the sky clear and sharply blue. It was cold and still. Groups of people moved down towards the Christmas service. The bells of the church rang out.

I kept pace with Madge. Ursula and my father were ahead of us, Ursula's arm through my father's; behind came Jennifer and Mrs Brooke.

'Does Babette talk about it?' I asked.

'Talk about what?'

'About being a Catholic. And you not being one.'

'We try not to talk about it. It's very boring.'

The church was crowded. The heat from the pipes that ran under the floor rose up through the cast-iron grating and kept in circulation the mixed smells of sanctity—the dust, the embroidered, horse-hair hassocks, the wood and stone, the faint intrusions of damp over many years. The sun's rays slanted in through the stained glass windows along the south side of the church, and the dust rose up and hung in the light, its myriad slow-moving particles glinting in the sharp glare of the cold winter morning. I felt a firm sense of my own importance, standing between Mrs Brooke and Madge in the family pew to which we had been shown by the verger. I sang out confidently. I tried hard to feel the full weight of meaning in the prayers. And I listened for all the echoes of familiarity with which the service was studded, for in most of its features it was the service of morning prayer. Into it had been inserted an anthem, 'Glory to God', extracted, with recitatives, from *The Messiah*, and sung indifferently by a choir predominantly of women. Under my breath, I sang with them, but their singing made me critical. They lacked the necessary attack on that first 'Glory . . .' I saw, clearly, in my imagination, the figure of Parker swinging his legs over the organ bench and crossing the school chapel to tell us all just that. 'More attack. Drop down on the note, boys. You are birds of prey. Pitch it here. Do you understand me? Pitch it here.' And he would tuck his chin in, stare at us all over the tops of his glasses, and tap with his finger on his high forehead, close to the receding line of thin hair.

We did not stay for communion. We stood outside in the cold sunlight, our breath hanging momentarily on the clear air. My father and I moved away and left the family to exchange greetings with friends at the door.

'Well, now,' he said, 'and what time is it?'

I told him.

'All in order, is it?'

'Yes, look.' I held out my thin wrist in front of his face. The large, cheap watch, with its black dial and luminous, heavy figures, looked altogether too big for me. My father looked at the watch, then at me, then seized my hand and held it firmly in his own.

'That's the stuff, son. Life grows more difficult, but we shall not be put down. The world was made for you, not you for it. Remember that.' His hand came down on my shoulder, heavy, sure, possessive. He looked down into my eyes. Then he laughed. 'What a sentimental old fool I am. But it's yours. Never forget.'

'How could I ever do that? You say it so often.'

'It's the most important lesson.'

I could not answer. I did not believe it to be the only lesson, or even the most important, but I could not argue alternatives. I looked up and smiled, laughed almost, a laugh as much *at* my father as *with* him. The world was, quite clearly, made for people like my father. His survival was a predictable miracle. But I had no intention, even then, of depending on miracles. Nevertheless, I made a note of the advice, misleading though it might be.

'What a lot of people they know,' I said. 'I wonder where Babette is. I want to go down again to the sea.'

My father did not notice the 'again', though he was meant to. 'People,' he said, 'people, people. They give me claustrophobia. I feel as if I'm going to drown when I see so many people, all knowing each other. Tribal. That's what it is. The herd instinct. That's what religion is all about.'

'There's more to it than that, Dad.'

'You'll learn, my son. You'll learn. I've seen it all. You think there's more to it. There's not more to it. Loneliness. A desire to be involved, to be seen doing your bit. Sanctimoniousness. This is what's brought these people here to worship.'

Already 'these people', breaking away from the crowd at the church door, were passing us. One or two attempted greetings, or smiled. Most stared at my father, overhearing an occasional fragment of our conversation.

'Keep your voice down, Dad, please,' I said. 'They'll hear you.'

'Let 'em hear. Why shouldn't they? It's all about them.'

'Those aren't the only reasons, Dad.'

'What others are there?'

I looked up at him and hesitated. There was a look of determination in my father's face, of truculence, of challenge. He was adopting the stance of argument, one leg slightly forward, the knee bent. It was clear to me that a policy of appeasement would be best. Yet I could not let the matter pass just like that.

'Love of God,' I said.

My father laughed derisively. 'Love of God! Do you really think anyone comes to church for that? Love of God! That's the last reason in the world.'

'I do,' I said. 'I come for that.' I knew my voice lacked conviction. I was too conscious of the people nearby. Conviction, anyway, would aggravate things. And conviction, just then, was more than I felt. My mind was on other things. Down the road Babette was coming towards us, with her father. I would happily have gone with them to Mass. So what God exactly did I love?

'You go for the singing, my son. That's what you love above all else. And so you should. It's what you do best.'

I could not deny it. The feelings of guilt rising within me were cut short by Mrs Brooke and her daughters joining us.

'How wise you were, George, to avoid that,' Mrs Brooke said. 'Let me take your arm. Let us go down to the front for a while.' Her step was firm and graceful. Like her daughters, her movements were supple and relaxed. Beside my father, who wore the punishment of fifty years as proudly as she carried the cares of seventy, she looked strangely youthful, her age an indeterminate, irrelevant thing, just as his was.

We were all spread out now, in twos and threes, making our way towards the sea. Jennifer walked beside me. She had deliberately singled me out as her companion, saying that she wanted to talk to me. Without looking at her, I was thinking all the time about her sad face, and the things that had happened in her life, hinted at by my father, briefly referred to by Babette.

'And what do you think of our choir?' she asked.

'I think they're quite good,' I said; but I spoke without conviction.

'Do you mean that?' she went on.

I sensed in her voice a faint desire to pin me down. I answered more guardedly: 'Well, yes, they were all right.'

'They were all wrong,' she said, looking at me. 'Not a voice among them worth noticing. Hymn singers. They shouldn't attempt Handel. It was beyond them.'

'We did that at school—'

'And did you sing any of the recitatives?'

'Yes.'

'Well you can't possibly mean what you say about them being good.'

'No. I suppose not.' I shrugged it off with a slight smile. I felt I had been admonished, but not to the point of embarrassment; almost the reverse. I was being led by her towards a more honest expression of my feelings. I would learn in time to like this quality in Jennifer. She had the habit of telling others that they could not mean what they were saying, having arrived at this conclusion by questions and answers that were clear and logical. She would then break off, and lead more gently into another subject, ameliorating the sharpness. She did this now, as we all crossed over, in the bright morning sun, and started to walk down the promenade, in sight of the dazzling surface of the sea.

'You're not an only child, are you?' she asked. She seemed, from the way she expressed herself to be implying that being 'an only child' could well become, under her scrutiny, a serious handicap.

I shook my head, disowning the possibility. 'No,' I said. 'I have a brother and a sister.'

'And where are they?'

'My brother's spending Christmas in Shropshire. He's in the Army. He doesn't get much leave. He couldn't get off this time.'

'What's his name?'

'Francis.'

'What about your sister?'

I looked out at the sea, then ahead of me to where my father and Mrs Brooke walked on, arm in arm. 'She's adopted,' I said. I cast my mind back, searching for memories of her. There were very few to recall: a little child of two, fat and placid, seated in front of the fireplace, in our first and only family house, under the tired, resigned eyes of my mother, not many months before her death. Why was it always that I remembered Melanie in this way? The dark rug, the wire fender, the gloomy atmosphere of the room, the glow of the fire, my mother, her careworn face framed in straight black hair, pausing in the work she was doing—she was always active—to stare down at her youngest child.

'Do you ever see her?'

I shook my head.

'Of course not, if she's adopted. How silly of me. But sometimes these things are strangely ordered and—' She broke off. 'Do you miss her?' she asked, looking sideways at me.

I looked back at her. 'I don't know,' I said. 'I suppose I do.'

'That's a strange answer. Don't you know? What about your brother?'

'Francis doesn't get on with my father,' I said.

'Do they see each other?'

I shook my head.

'Do *you* see Francis?'

'Oh, yes. We went to the same school. He only left this year. National Service. At half-term he came down to the school and took me out. He said he'd do the same next term if he could. And we write to each other.'

'That was nice of him. Surely, it must have been his first leave? And he chose to visit you. I am envious. Would you believe that? Would you?' she laughed. 'Yes. It's true. I always wished for a brother. And I always imagined him older than me. I never wanted to be the eldest. But of course you can't order these things. You must accept what is. And so I had to be an eldest sister to Madge and Ursula.'

'My brother wants to go into politics.'

'Oh? And how does he propose to do that?'

'I don't know really. He seems set on it. I suppose he'll find a way.'

'It isn't easy. It's not like teaching. You have to make your mark. I expect you have to know the right people, as well?'

'Francis doesn't think he'll have any trouble.'
'How old is he?'
'He's nineteen.'
'At nineteen there are no troubles. At thirty-three he may find things rather different. Which party does he support?'
'Oh, he's a Conservative.'
'And do you think that's the right thing to be?'
'I don't really know.'

The others in front of us stopped. It was time to turn back. We stood in an uncertain group in the pale, sharp light of late morning, looking back at the buildings along the Front, looking out over the peaceful sea, inspecting the other groups of people out walking. I crossed to the edge of the pavement and looked down over the railings at the beach. Babette joined me.

'Are you hungry?' she said. 'I'm ravenous.'
'So am I. Will it be Christmas dinner when we get back?'
'Yes.'
'Will there be crackers?'
'Yes.'
'And what happens after?'
'I expect we'll play charades. We usually do.'

III

'His Majesty has made a truly wonderful recovery,' Robert said. He was standing in front of the fireplace. It was shortly after three o'clock. We had been listening to the King's Christmas Message on the wireless, and the set had just been turned off.

It puzzled me, the way he said the words 'His Majesty', softly, unctuously, implying in some strange way, a degree of personal intimacy that was obviously in doubt, as far as I was concerned, since I could not believe he had even met the King, a matter, admittedly, which I had no way of checking or questioning. Why did he not simply say 'He', or 'King George', or simply 'the King'? It was as if some kind of private knowledge of the true nature and extent of the King's illness—which, indeed, had been of national concern—had somehow been conferred on Robert by virtue of his position as a diplomat. He underlined this implication by the way he spoke, and seemed determined to challenge everyone to speculate otherwise if they dared. Well, it was my father who did so.

He was stretched out in a low armchair, his feet extended and crossed, his hands behind his head, his eyes half-closed. He looked at Robert. 'He is not much longer for this world.'

In the quietness of the room, disturbed only by the faint hiss of a damp log which had recently been added to the fire, the words had about them the sombre ring of eternity knocking at the doors of all our lives.

The King mattered then. His very remoteness made him precious to us all, as had his illness, which had been most serious. I had seen him, yes, on two or three occasions, when taken by my father to Parliament Square and hoisted upon his shoulder at the State opening of Parliament or some municipal function at Westminster Abbey—there had always been room and time enough in our lives for such outings—and I knew, in my own mind, what constituted the man: his thin, ever-boyish head and face, his discreet, charming smile, the gentle, restrained way in which he lifted his hand in answer to the cheering with which his passage through London was invariably greeted. Yes, these things were part of me at that time, and would remain so through manhood, and probably until my own death, whether I wished it or not. But it was more, now. Those words, coming from the wireless cabinet, itself a dignified, old and well-tried object, standing on its own; those words, dropping with gentle, measured conviction into the otherwise silent room—those references to children and the happiness of the young, to national tribulations and to 'my peoples'—had gathered us all together in feeling and sympathy.

Afterwards, my father expressed cynicism about the annual speech. He could combine, to a strange degree, sentimentality about human feelings and human motives, with scorn for the genuineness of those attributes. And he said later that it was all a kind of contrivance, and was, each year, so that in countless homes the length and breadth of England, families gathered in the closing light of the Christmas afternoon, replete with food and drink, to hear comfortable words from their sovereign in an atmosphere designed to make them respond according to certain well-tried rules. Well, if it was so, it was so. The fact was, in its own fashion, in that post-war period, it worked. In as far as I can remember, we subscribed willingly. What the King had said to us carried the bell-like resonance of truth. And we believed in these things as the words faded into the national anthem, and then silence.

Robert clearly doubted my father's gloomy forecast, and seemed to feel that an official attitude in support of the idea that the King's recovery had been total, was required. This was quite unnecessary, I thought, in the midst of his own family. Surely, there, he could speak openly, and not give the impression that he was part of an inner circle, privy to the King's real state of health? Or was it just for my father's benefit? Robert's next remarks suggested this to be the more likely motivation. The faintly absurd hints of an intimacy which, if I had believed it to be the true picture (which I did not) would have been most impressive, carried no weight. 'My dear George,' Robert said, his elbow settling among the Christmas cards on the mantelpiece, 'I would venture the opinion that you are not in full possession of the real facts. His Majesty's illness has been grave. Most grave. Of that there is no doubt. But his recovery has surpassed even the most optimistic expectations in official circles. I have it on the best authority.' He paused and looked round the room.

The slanting light of the sun, low in the south west—there was less than an hour's sunlight left in the day—stretched far into the room, yet with only a feeble strength. We were all there together, satisfied at the advancing stages of the day, thinking and acting, listening, and occasionally talking, with a lassitude that was one of satisfaction.

My father said: 'I am glad, Robert. We are all glad. You are probably right. I know nothing about it. Absolutely nothing. I am in total ignorance of these things, while you possess all the facts. But I felt just now that I was hearing the voice of an ageing man. And I fear that it may be the voice of a dying man.' He paused, and there was silence for a moment or two, with Robert looking down at him. Then he went on: 'Whatever it is, the voice is one out of which the inspiration to go on has begun to drain. Some of the horsemen are riding by.'

He spoke slowly, his deep voice rising out from the depths of the armchair. Usually I associated this mood with the gross, and ultimately absurd exaggerations to which he was prone, and which he enunciated more or less privately, ending, more often than not, in laughter and self-mockery. But this was different. And the moments of silence gave validity to the prophetic tones.

I puzzled about the 'horsemen', but it was Babette who asked him: 'What do you mean, "horsemen riding by"?'

'The four horsemen of the Apocalypse. Death, famine, plague, war.'

My own blood thrilled at the words he used. They sounded so romantic, so terrifying, so final.

Robert shifted, and laughed in a forced manner. 'You are too melodramatic, George. You take a theatrical view of things—divorced from reality.'

Mrs Brooke stood up. 'Children,' she said. 'I want to go walking. I think the beech avenue, up at Corleys, and then down to the cliff's edge at Lovers' Seat. It will just be dusk when we reach there. Jennifer? Will you get the car out?

Perhaps,' she said to me, 'you will help with the garage doors?'

Alone with Jennifer I felt I could ask what the Apocalypse was. I had already in my mind a vision of riders upon warhorses, going forth with the swords of death, famine, pestilence and strife raised up in their gnarled and cruel hands. But I felt that I needed a more detached and academic definition.

'Oh, dear,' Jennifer said, laughing, her hands on the steering wheel of the car as she prepared to back it out of the garage, 'what a huge question to ask! The Apocalypse isn't really a *thing*. You *could* say it's the end of the world. I think that's the way your father thinks about it, especially when he talks about the horsemen of the Apocalypse, those strange creatures who accompany chaos in the world. But it is really an idea about the world. I don't even know if I can explain it.' She stopped talking for a moment as she steered the car round in front of the hall door, and stopped it, and turned off the engine.

'Please try,' I said. 'The only idea I have of it is these four horsemen, giant figures, galloping up and down.'

Jennifer looked quite seriously through the window of the car. 'That,' she said, 'is really how it was considered for centuries. Now, no one considers it at all. Very foolish of us. Sad, as well. We have moved, too quickly, from too much belief to none at all. You see, it is really more a way of thinking than anything else. An apocalyptic vision is one that sees a revelation of things which are to come, or have been in the past, as part of a huge and pre-ordained scheme for humankind. All things are, and have been, and will be, according to a divine pattern. It is spread before us always. We cannot change it, or alter it, or bend it.'

I tried to grapple with the vast territories of thought which Jennifer's words opened up to me. Time stood still. Her life, and my life, and all the lives of the people in the house who were just about to join us and set out for a Christmas walk in the encroaching dusk, were suddenly pulverised by the idea that everything we did was governed by some kind of pre-ordination. We were nothing more than grains of the finest dust in some huge quarry over which God—or perhaps a less benevolent deity—laboured with great pounding pieces of machinery, shaping some kind of final destiny in which the dust—since He must be conscious of every tiny particle of humanity—would be finally gathered together as part of an ultimate design.

Yet how could I fit my father's life into that? And all the others, too? I wanted to ask: 'Do you accept the idea?' But I could not. My reasoning was confused. To begin with, there was no time; the family had already gathered on the steps, and I had to climb out of the front seat, beside Jennifer, and wait to be told where to sit. Besides my hesitation went deeper than that. Her words had struck sympathetic chords in me which I did not wish to explore lest her understanding of this particular view of the world should not support my growing belief in it. She could, as a schoolteacher, explain it so well. Suppose, then, she believed something quite different? Suppose she left my apocalyptic intuitions high and dry? I felt that I could not risk it, and that if I wanted to explore it all further, I would have to do so with care, choosing my time in the future.

And yet of the three sisters, it was she who somehow seemed to offer me a more fertile field in which to allow my ideas and understanding to grow. As the car moved slowly up through the town, with all of us squeezed into it, and out along the high cliff route; as we walked and talked after getting out of it at the chosen place; as we came to the cliff's edge and to 'Lovers' Seat', and looked down upon the sea, and the sweep of the bay, and the pier, and the setting sun; as we registered to ourselves and to each other our approval of the occasion, I dwelt in my own mind on what she had said, preparing myself for further examination. And it so happened, when we were walking back towards the car, with the last low beams of sunlight catching on the silvery whiteness of the trunks of beech trees—many of them inscribed with transient summer messages, memorials to faded and forgotten love—that Babette and I found ourselves either side of Jennifer. I asked her: 'You know what we were talking about, don't you? the end of the world, and all that?' Jennifer said yes, that she did remember. 'Well, what I want to ask is this: do you believe it? Do you think that some all-powerful being has arranged everything? And that we are all moving towards an end which has been mapped out for us from the very beginning?'

'We begin life,' Jennifer said, 'by believing that questions like the one you have asked have answers. And we can end it believing the same. My grandfather, Babette's great grandfather, who was a clergyman, died believing that he had fulfilled, if badly, a life-work given him by God. But when you ask me, "Do you believe it", I cannot say. It seems to me just one of the ways the world has taught itself to see itself. In any case what I believe or don't believe isn't really of any very great significance.' She smiled, tenderly and softly, and took Babette's hand in hers, swinging it, almost with a violent intensity, and looked ahead, as with quickened pace, we walked on.

I could not, after that, pursue any further with her my unsatisfied curiosity. I would with Babette, but that would be a different thing. She, like myself, would have answers because she would not have had to test them. But Jennifer, who had tested a number of things in life, declined to explain herself, perhaps because she could not; perhaps because it came too close to her inner feelings. The thought filled me with a sense of sadness. The more I wanted answers—and the demands for them seemed then to be beating down upon my head like hailstones—the more difficult and elusive and contradictory those answers seemed to be. At almost fourteen years old, I was grappling, often frantically, with the problems of other people, while those around me, with the single exception of

Babette, seemed to prefer to remain unaware of them. It was not a satisfactory state of affairs.

IV

'Do you like it?' I said.

'I love it,' she replied. She had been looking at one of my two Christmas presents to her.

'We could read it to *them*,' I said.

'Should we? How would we do it?'

'Well, Lewis Carroll says it's in "fits". We could do a fit each' I suggested.

'Who would start?'

'You.'

'No, you.'

'Girls first,' I said.

'Not in things like this. You must take the lead. Otherwise I won't do it.'

'All right. Shall we try it?'

We sat side by side on Babette's bed. We had returned from walking, all crushed into the big Vauxhall, warm and sleepy. And when we arrived back at the house a mood of still greater lassitude had descended upon everyone and there had been a mute and swift dispersal of people to rooms in order to rest, leaving Babette and myself on our own.

The bright afternoon light had faded into dusk, softening the features of the room, intensifying the physical presence of Babette, sitting so close to me. I felt a nervous relief at being away from everyone else. The events of the day were crowded together in my mind, a host of images: morning sun reflected in the sea, the ghostly gleam of slanting light on the naked grey branches of tall beech trees high up on the downs, the puffs of white breath on the frosty air, the wavery voice of my father singing, Brahms, prayers, Handel, presents, laughter, people. It had all brought Babette closer to me than I had thought possible. And yet, at the same time, she was still distant enough to have built up within me waves of passion and tenderness that were now ready to break.

I loved her: innocently, without experience, not merely for her companionship, but in confused recognition of the fact that she was the most approachable symbol of this Christmas. I yearned to establish some kind of bond between myself and her, a bond that would survive on its own into the unpredictable future.

The most important moment in my day had been when my hand had closed over hers, early that morning, and I had felt the magic of her response. That had warmed my heart ever since. Mountains of hope and expectation had been built around that symbol of affection, our clasped hands. Every word and gesture passing between us had been related to it in my mind. Yet I knew only my own feelings. What of hers?

'Come on, then. What are you waiting for?'

I sensed again the feeling I so often had about her, both then and later, that she was laughing at me, that she knew what was going on in my mind, a mind made slow by trepidation. I did not resent the feeling. I came, in due course, to make light of it, even to revel in the idea that I was the object of her mockery, since it was inspired by love; or so I believed. But on that afternoon it pushed me towards some kind of resolution. I looked into her eyes. 'You've no idea how much I like you,' I said. There was silence. I felt a thudding in my chest. Could she hear my heart beating? Would she laugh at me? Would she turn her face away? Should I ask her? *What* should I ask her? Were my arms long enough to reach across the small gap between us? 'I want to kiss you, Babette.'

She half reached towards me with her hand, her eyes still seriously looking into mine, her lips parted as if to speak, but not speaking.

Awkward, blushing, afraid, I put out my hand towards her shoulder, held her, and clumsily kissed her, half on her lips, half on her dimpled cheek. It was difficult, side by side, on the edge of the bed. I could not risk any readjustment in our positions. I was acutely conscious of my body, of the hard, unmanageable expression of desire. I did not accept this ungovernable side of love.

'Hold me tight,' she said, 'hold me tight.'

'I love you, Babette,' I said. And the enormity of that statement silenced me. I could think of absolutely nothing more to say.

After a while she pushed herself gently away from me and put her two hands into mine. I held them tightly. 'Who do you like best in the *The Hunting of the Snark*?' she asked.

I thought for a moment. 'The Baker,' I said. I felt foolish at the sudden anti-climax.

'Why the Baker?'

'Well, they're all onto him. They make him cry. And all those coats he has. And trying to wink with one eye. And then in the end he's the bravest, isn't he? It's the Baker who finds the Snark, isn't it?'

'The Boojum, you mean.'

'I wonder if it really was a Boojum.'

'Perhaps you're one,' she said. She laughed into my eyes. She made me feel so happy. I was secure. My joy flooded through me. I wanted her to laugh at me again. It made me feel safe, somehow. It relieved the tension, the anguish of my uncertain hope that all this would last for ever. I could not help but remember my father in the drawing-room, after the end of the King's speech that afternoon, warning us all, it seemed, of the transience with which everything we did was surrounded.

'When did you first . . .?' She frowned, not knowing quite how to finish that most ancient of questions. 'Was it . . .?'

'Since the wedding. Since we explored the house that day. Since we walked in the snow. I never thought we'd be having Christmas together.'

'I did.'

'Babette?'

'Yes?'

'Do you believe that things are arranged to happen for us? Do you believe our lives are mapped out ahead, all the people we meet, the places we go to? Do you believe what Jennifer said?'

'I don't know.' She was silent for a moment, looking down at her hands still held in mine. 'Do you?'

'Yes. I think I do. I think this was all arranged to happen a long time ago, I mean, us meeting.'

'But what happens next?'

'I don't know. I'm worried about that. It's one thing to believe that it was all planned long ago. You meet, and you part, and you meet again. And it's as if somebody had settled it, and kept the plans in some kind of huge box or chest. But it's still all in the past. It doesn't make it any easier to know what has been decided for the future. That's if it's true. I mean, about it being planned. Who has the plans? Who knows what lies ahead?'

We sat in silence. I think, looking back, that I was never again to want something with quite the same passionate singleness of purpose that I felt then. I did not know precisely what it was. It included Babette; indeed, she was at the centre of it. But she was a focus for something much broader which I could not hope then to analyse or understand. I suppose the greater part of her concern was over my bewilderment. She could not possibly have the same yearnings. And so we sat and were puzzled, and could not predict the future.

Even if we could have done, would I then have understood what I understand now? Events, as they turned out in those months which ran from Christmas to Easter of the following year, were to condition the way in which I should live the whole of my life afterwards. I did not know this for a long time to come. I did not know that already it was too late, and that what I wanted was impossible to have, and had been impossible for many years. I simply hoped, and prayed, that life would now take a new turning.

'You mustn't worry,' Babette said. She could see from my face that I was doing so. 'It'll turn out all right.'

'It's just I never know what happens next. Never. It was all right before. But now it's different. I want it to stay like this, and I can't be sure that it will.'

'And before this? What about before? Had something that you wanted to hold onto gone when you came home?'

I nodded.

'Tell me,' she said. 'What sort of things? Were there girls like me?'

I blushed, but smiled at the same time. She did not really understand. 'That would be telling, wouldn't it?'

'Yes, it would. But you must. I want you to.'

I sat for a moment, deep in thought. Then I recounted some episode from the past, trivial in detail, momentous in what it had meant to me. She listened in silence.

'How old were you?'

'I was ten.'

'What happened?'

'He started to drink. I don't remember what it was. Something about being made to work too hard. "They're taking advantage of my strength" he used to say. He's very strong. He used to work awfully hard there. It was towards the end of the holiday. The girl had been told not to see me, to keep out of my way. But we used to meet and talk. And I knew from the things she said that my father would be told to leave. That *we* would be leaving. It didn't happen until after I had gone back to school. Then one day a letter came, and there was something in it about everything "falling through" at that job. And the address was somewhere else, and I knew that I would never see her again.'

'Did things often "fall through"?'

'Always. Always, always. Nothing ever lasted. Never. There would be some row, usually over nothing in particular, and, after it, drinking. Then it would all break up.'

'Did it happen while you were there?'

'Sometimes. Not often.'

'And you don't mind talking about it?'

'I don't usually talk about it. But I feel you know anyway.'

'I wish I was like you sometimes. I wish things changed for us a bit more. It must be very exciting.'

I looked at her in astonishment. 'Do you really think that?' I said. 'Don't you like knowing, when you come home from school, that everything will be the same? What about your room, and all your things?'

'I don't think they matter very much.'

'Mine matter to me.'

'You shouldn't let them too much.'

'That's what he says.'

'It's true.'

I was silent and filled with doubt. What did I have if I didn't have 'things' to spread out around me in every new home?

'Do you think you'll be remembering me in a few months' time like you remember that other girl?' Babette asked. 'Or do you think our paths will cross again, and go on crossing?'

I turned to her. I wanted to kiss her and reassure her that this was different, but her solemn, questioning eyes checked me. Physical reassurances were not what she was seeking. I said: 'It *can* be different now. *We* can decide. I'm almost fourteen. I shall write to you. I shall write letters all the time. And next holiday, and the holidays after, I shall come and see you. That's all.'

From below in the house we heard Madge calling. It was time to go down. We stood up. I was still holding Babette's hand. I picked up the book. 'We'd better bring this,' I said.

She said, 'Yes.' But she spoke absently, as though it did not matter any more. There was a strange expression on her face, puzzled, pleased, regretful.

I felt awkward doing it, but I reached out and put my hands on her shoulders. 'And will you write to me?' I asked. 'Will you?'

She nodded, and smiled, and, stepping close to me, put her arms round my neck, and kissed me; and we clung briefly and awkwardly to each other in the silence of the room, until we heard Madge's voice once again, calling us down.

Chapter Eight

I

'And do you really have to go, George?' Babette asked. 'Can't you stay one more day?'

He looked up at her from his travelling bag, which was now almost full, and into which he was carefully placing some of the presents he had been given. Then he sighed. 'I wish I could, my chickadee, I wish I could.'

Although I had watched them together many times during those few days, and had come to accept their natural and easy friendship, and the way in which they both bridged the gap of years between them, it was only then that I thought, directly and consciously, of the fact of Babette seeing him as a 'person' rather than a 'parent', and the difference which this made.

He continued getting ready to depart. He looked across the room to where I sat, hunched and silent on an ottoman, my knees tucked up underneath my chin, thinking to myself. I could smell in the room his smell of shaving soap and tobacco and much-worn cotton shirts and much-polished leather shoes.

It was already dark, and none too warm in the bedroom. Babette was standing at the foot of the bed. She had helped to pack the clothes, and now handed him his pair of hair-brushes and his comb. He bent down to tuck them into the side of the bag, then stopped and stood up and looked at

Babette. 'You'll have *him*,' he said. 'Isn't that what you want?'

'It'll be different here after you've gone.' There was a gentle hint of accusation in her voice.

'Yes. More peaceful.'

'Just different.'

'Babette, my sweetheart, you are the soul of tact. You see everything, you watch, you understand; then you reserve judgement.' And then, smiling, 'Now he never reserves judgement, does he?'

'Which is best?' Babette asked.

'My son will have a stormy life. He knows it. I have said it often enough. People don't like to be judged. He has a way of looking—I can't describe it—I can only feel it—but there are times, Babette, when he looks at me and I, even I, am frightened by his eyes.'

'That's not true, Dad. You're not afraid of anything.'

'It is true. It is. You see my frailty. And you condemn it.'

'And is he right, George?'

'It's not true, Babette,' I said.

'He is right. Of course he is, child. That's what frightens me.' He sat down on the edge of the bed, and began to zip up the bag. Then he looked carefully round the room. 'Mustn't forget anything,' he said, almost to himself. 'Must leave everything shipshape.' He looked up at Babette's face, then across at myself. There was a mock solemnity in his voice when he spoke again. 'Learn from my failure,' he said. 'Pity me, child.'

Babette looked over at me. Her face was troubled. She crossed over and sat down on the bed. 'You don't need to be pitied, George,' she said. 'Pity's a bad thing. Mummy says no one should be pitied. They should be loved for what they are.'

'And judged for what they are?' We both looked up at him, curious at the growing melodrama in his voice. He stared across at us.

'I don't think your son does judge people, the way you say.' Her voice sounded uncertain, defensive.

There was silence for a while.

He looked once more round the room, then carefully finished closing up the bag. 'What time is it, my son?'

I consulted my watch. 'Seven minutes and twenty seconds past nine.'

'Time to go. Will you both come down to the train with me?'

'Aunt Jennifer said she would take you down in the car.'

'Let's walk instead.'

Secretly, it was what we both wanted. But it also occurred to me that my father really wanted us to see him off; that perhaps, when all was said and done, the company of myself and Babette was preferable to him than that of either Ursula or Jennifer or some other combination of adults in the family. The thought pleased me, because it satisfied my wish to be alone with Babette.

We followed him downstairs and into the drawing-room. The rest of the family was there.

'I'll take you down, George,' Jennifer said, getting up from the piano.

'No need. I shall walk. We've lots of time. The children are going to see me off.'

Ursula crossed over to him. She put her hands out and adjusted his scarf. 'Do you really have to go, George dear? Can't you stay until tomorrow?'

He looked down into her eyes and shook his head. 'Must. My new job. Have to be ready for it all tomorrow. When will you come back?'

'After the weekend. We'll all be up then. Your son will return on Friday, in time for his outing.'

'I hope he behaves himself.'

'We don't want him to be too good, George. Do we, Babette?' Madge spoke from where she was standing, beside the fire. She had been looking down into its flames. 'He must have some fun in your absence.'

'I want him to behave as a son of mine would.' He said it

192

as though such behaviour was definable; as though his own code was clearly consistent, and there to be followed with ready understanding by myself who stood at his side. I was prepared to read in their faces some hint of amusement at the absurdity of the remark. But there was none.

Only Madge responded directly. She said, in a quiet voice, 'He behaves very well as himself.'

'Drink before you go?' Robert was standing beside the table, a glass in his hand. He raised his eyebrows politely, but there was no enthusiasm in his voice.

'No thanks, Robert. Must be getting along.' He crossed over to Mrs Brooke. She was sitting in a chair beside the fire and had watched them all without speaking. 'It was good of you to have us. It was a wonderful Christmas.' He held out his hand awkwardly.

'Haven't you a kiss for an old lady?'

'Of course I have.' He bent down and kissed her. Watching, from beside the door, I thought how unlike my father not to have kissed her directly and with the full and generous warmth which was so much a part of his natural approach to women. And then the consideration came to me that Mrs Brooke, unlike so many women in his life, was of an age almost comparable to what my grandmother would now be, had she lived, and that my father must look upon her with a measure of filial respect, heightened in part by his love for Ursula.

He kissed Madge and Jennifer, and shook Robert's hand. There was a flatness in the atmosphere, a curious artificiality. My father was sad at leaving. I could see it in his eyes. But he also hated the formalities of departure, always had done, as long as I could remember. It was a very temporary parting, except from Jennifer and her mother, and this made the occasion awkward. He was, I felt, saying goodbye to an atmosphere, a house, its aura, with the possibility—always to be faced—that it would not be visited or enjoyed again.

'Come, children.' He turned briefly at the door and looked once round the room.

Ursula came out with us. They kissed. Babette and I moved on into the garden. I looked back at their figures silhouetted in the light from the hall. My father's bag was heavy in my hand.

It was cold, and there was a hint of fog in the air. It blurred the street lamps down the hill from where we stood. In the moment of waiting I reached out for Babette's hand, and she squeezed my fingers, then let them go. Then he joined us, and we set off down the road.

'Mind how you cross the roads. That's the first thing. Right?'

'Right.'

'Look after Babette. Don't fall into the sea. Don't talk to strangers. Don't catch cold. Help in the house. Be a good boy. Behave yourself. You'll make sure he does all those things, won't you, Babette?'

'Of course, George. Every single one of them.'

He laughed as we walked along. 'You won't, of course. I know that. You'll both do what you like. And good luck to you. But if I say these things often enough it's just possible some of them will sink in. We all have to learn the hard way. That's what life is about. I never took my father's advice. Always thought he talked a lot of nonsense. I don't see why you should take mine, good as it is. You're growing up now. You've got your life before you. So have you, Babette. Make the most of it. But do everything in moderation. Everything.'

We tramped on together through the wintry night. The lights of the town were blurred and indistinct. From the last part of the hill we could look down on the station. There were a few cars, and people; the train was already standing at the platform.

'Will there be many on it?' I asked.

'I don't know. But I don't suppose it will be full.'

We waited while he bought his ticket. Then he turned to us with sudden resolution. 'Go on back now,' he said. 'It's too cold to stay out. I'll see you after the weekend. Don't dawdle on your way up the hill. Goodbye.' He bent and kissed Babette. 'Look after him, my dear.' Then he gave me a hug and kissed my cheek. I felt the scrape of his bristles. 'Be a good boy.' Then he turned from us and went through the barrier.

We did not go immediately, as he had told us, but followed as far as the ticket barrier, where we stood side by side, watching his gradually retreating figure. He walked on down the platform in the direction which the train would take. He seemed unperturbed about finding a seat, hardly looking into the carriages. His step was heavy and yet easy, his legs flexing as his feet met the ground, his left knee giving in a slightly more pronounced way. Then abruptly he stopped, and opened a carriage door. He paused and looked back. He seemed to me a long, long way away. He saw us, and raised a hand, just once, in the air, his face solemn. We waved back, but almost before we had raised our own excited hands his dropped, and he climbed aboard.

We turned away, and lingered in the ticket hall, under the baleful, yellowy-white light of the station. We were unwilling to go before the train left. A few late stragglers were hurrying in, their money ready for the ticket office, their eyes on the clock.

'Is he sad at leaving?' Babette asked.

Her question was difficult to answer. Yes, he was sad. Had he not looked it? Had not every phrase he had uttered been imbued with tell-tale echoes of regret and self-pity? Had he not displayed all the appropriate signs of a heavy heart? Yet that, precisely, was what worried me, and turned Babette's innocent and straightforward question into a challenge, to me, to understand and explain my father's character. Like so many simple and straightforward questions this one could be disposed of very rapidly, and more or less honestly by saying that he was sad. He had enjoyed himself, and now he was leaving. Yet it was one of those occasions when the very simplicity of the question begged deeper consideration, and when that deeper consideration, once embarked upon, opened up fathomless caverns of speculation.

For I did not come anywhere near to understanding the workings of my father's heart. And the older I grew, the more difficult it became. Whereas with others—Philpotts, Alice, my housemaster at school—time brought out a constancy of behaviour, a consistency of emotions, so that their characters seemed to be made up of layers of experience which all folded into one known centre; with my father the opposite was the case, with all the different facets of his make-up struggling to separate themselves from each other, so that his sadness, or his anger, or his selfishness, or his generosity, pulled him away from the predicted course of his life in great lurches which repeatedly threatened the balance of the whole. Exactly the same character pattern, after all, dominated my father's drinking habits, which were either so excessive as to suggest that death was not far distant, or so prim and cautious as to place him on the fringes of membership of the Ivy League (of which, indeed, he had once, urged by his mother, become a member). And in either case, there was an element of action for its own sake, including the blindly-besotted gulping of drink that was clearly useless for any purpose whatever, since the point of absolute inebriation having been passed, further drinking was simply a suicidal expression of a basic character flaw which demanded 'total' self-realisation. I could not express all this, and did not try. I simplified and temporised by reframing the question for Babette.

'I honestly don't know what he feels. I don't know if he's sad or not. I think he's thinking more about the job which starts tomorrow than he is about us. Anyway, would *you* know what your mother felt, if she was leaving you, only for a short while?'

'She'd be relieved, silly.'

'Really?'

'You mean like tonight, at the end of Christmas?' I nodded. 'Oh, then she'd be sad. And I would know.'

'Well, that's the difference. I don't know. It's not just now, not just this time, here. It's always. I have the feeling that he's playing some kind of game. That what's happening isn't actually real to him.'

I looked into her eyes as we stood there. The busy, last minute passengers stared curiously at us, so intense were we, so concerned with our talk. We heard shouts from the platform, then the whistle, then the loud hiss and puff of the engine. A brief glance assured me that the train was moving out. I turned towards the station entrance and walked slowly towards it, Babette behind me.

'Do you get homesick when you leave him? When you go back to school?'

I nodded. 'Yes, I do. I hate it. The going.' I paused. 'But it doesn't last long, I like school really. It's just the change, from being able to do what you want to do, to being told to do things. It's a shivery feeling, for a while. It used to be worse still . . .' I tailed off in sudden indecision.

'How was it worse?' Babette asked.

'Oh, it just was. It's a long time, you know. I started going to Coppinger when I was seven.' I remembered how tears then used to ease the anguish, but how much longer it took. I remembered the nibbled finger nails, the acrid smell, waking up to be afraid each morning.

'You must have been very small,' she said. And then, 'Come on. We'd better go straight back, or they'll be worried.'

We climbed the hill in the cold. Our breath was visible in the foggy, damp air. It was difficult to see more than just a few of the lights of the town from the turn in the road. There were not many people about. We passed one house where there was a party, and paused to look in through the window at the silent, excited faces.

'They do look silly, don't they?'

I nodded. 'Do you get unhappy when you go back to school?'

'Not really. Things just go on as normal.'

'That must be nice.'

'Sometimes it is. Not always.'

I wondered what she meant. Her life seemed to me then very different from my own. It did not appear to have, as a natural ingredient, the climaxes which were so much a part of my own experience. Yet could it be that different? I wanted her to volunteer more detailed information about herself, but so far this wish had proved too difficult to express, and she had made no natural offering of the inner trepidations which I guessed she must feel about some things, above all, perhaps, about her parents.

'Do you want school to be over?' I asked. 'For ever, I mean.'

'I think it will be more fun when it is.'

'I don't really want it to end. I don't know what I shall do then. Most of the boys who leave go into the Army. But they say it's not much fun.'

We came to the gate, and turned in. I held her back for a moment from the door. She looked into my eyes in the gloomy half-light of the distant street lamp. She was the same height as myself, slighter in build, and yet already betraying, in her face and neck and figure, the intrusions of womanhood. I just wanted to look at her, and reassure myself about myself.

'Will we ask Mummy if we can go to *Brief Encounter*? It's on down the road. She'll have to bring us. It's an "A".'

'What's it about?'

'It's about two people who fall in love. They keep on meeting together. But it's no good. It has a sad ending.'

II

Robert left the next morning and took with him that aura of slight fussiness and formality which had, to some extent, overshadowed us all. For him and his cases the car was necessary. He acquired an air of importance when he put on his bowler hat, and he took up his briefcase as though it contained public responsibility. Suddenly the gap between my world and that of Babette widened. It was no comfort to remember the unexpected warmth and egalitarian rivalry he had displayed towards my father when talking of their schooldays, at lunch, the day before. That brief episode had been the nearest they had come to each other; both on common ground, remembering common standards of behaviour and judgement. But it had not lasted, and was soon dispelled. Once again, he had become a minor plenipotentiary of power, a figure in the landscape of hierarchy and ambition, a cog of some moment in an extensive piece of machinery.

We all walked out into the pale, cold morning fog. We were spaced out between the front door, beyond which Mrs Brooke resolutely refused to advance, and the front gate, where Madge fussed and teased him into the car. Her wave of farewell was an off-hand gesture, and she had turned to go in, with no intention of looking round, before the car had moved away. Only Babette stood and watched her father disappear.

We did not go to the station; Jennifer had business to do and could not bring us with her. Instead we sat in the drawing-room, before the fire, with the radio on, and read books.

The atmosphere had already changed in the house. The sisters laughed more. They talked about local people. They relived their childhood in brief, vivid portions.

We all went to see *Brief Encounter*. Jennifer said that I would not like it. She was right. Love, for me, then, was not associated with a station buffet or a circle seat in the Regal.

Yet Ursula liked it. So did Madge. It was real to them. They both said, afterwards, laughing, that it had made them cry. It had not made Babette cry, but she had liked it. We sat in the warm darkness of the cinema, side by side, our fingers intertwined, perpetually readjusting our hands to make sure that contact and response were maintained.

It was a matinée performance. It was dark when we came

out and the streets were wet. It had stopped raining. The cinema was down towards the older part of the town, beyond the pier. It was in a street that turned off from the seafront. The cold, hard weather that had lasted over Christmas had broken. The wind had swung into the south-west and was gusting up the Channel, bringing heavier seas. We could hear the waves breaking on the pebbles, dull solid thumps followed by the sharp, sibilant hiss of water draining down through the filter of stone. It was blustery but not cold, and our coats flapped and the hair of the women was blown back from their faces.

We stopped outside the Cadena Café. Madge put her hand on Ursula's arm. 'Let's go in and have some tea and cakes,' she said, 'like we used to. It's such a long time since we came down here.'

We found a table in the upstairs balcony, close to the balustrade. The comfortable, rich smells of coffee and cakes rose up to our nostrils, mingled with the sound and sight and bustle of the late afternoon shoppers crowding in. And for a while we just sat and watched.

'We know no one in this town any more, Madge,' Ursula said. And she sighed. 'Isn't it strange? Feeling like visitors in the place we grew up in.'

'I don't regret it for one moment. All the awful people always asking about father's health. It was very dreary. I don't know how Jennifer stands it.'

'She says she likes it.'

'I'm sure she does, Babette, if she says so.'

The waitress came with tea and a plate of cakes. She bustled round us. Ursula asked for more éclairs.

'You can pour, sister dear,' Madge said. 'I'm going to be greedy, and take that cake. What about you?'

'I don't think I'm very hungry, thank you, Madge,' I said.

'Are you all right? Do you feel ill?'

'I'm all right. I just don't want anything to eat.'

They all looked at me.

Ursula said, 'Are you wondering how your father's getting on in his new job?'

'I wasn't, actually. I expect he's all right. He usually is, at the beginning.' I felt strangely cold about him just then. I could not work out whether this was because of my youth and lack of experience, or whether it was the reverse; whether the very variety of my experiences, always on the coat-tails of my father's ambition or passion, had deprived me for ever of the ability to enjoy naturally, and for its own sake, the simple experience of taking tea and cakes in an English café in a provincial seaside town on a December afternoon. I felt ponderous and awkward and out of place. And I anticipated a conversation about myself, and my father, with questions which I would not wish to answer, and comments which I would not wish to endorse. Part of my misery was the feeling that what was denied me—the ability to be wholly part of the occasion—was what, at that moment, I wanted most in all the world.

'It'll last this time, I'm sure it will,' said Ursula, squeezing my hand impulsively.

I looked into her eyes, grey and sad, and read there the doubt which her words had failed to dispel, either for me or for herself. 'It won't, Ursula,' I said. 'You know it won't. It never has. Why should it now?'

We were all silent. My words were like a glass falling and breaking at a party, silencing everyone for a brief moment. I continued to look into Ursula's eyes until she could not watch me any more, and looked down at her plate. Madge, also looking down, spoke quietly, softly, tentatively, as though she, with her elegant feet, was stepping cautiously out among the broken fragments, seeking to start things again. 'Tell me,' she asked. 'What happens? What goes wrong?'

I looked at her, then looked away at the crowded shop below the tea-room balcony where we sat. How could I answer? One of the few constants in my life was that dark centre of self-destruction in my father. There was a geometric precision about the laws which governed its operation upon us both. But at that time I did not know it, and would not have accepted it, in spite of the evidence already available. Indeed, my own passionate commitment at that time, even as Madge asked the question, was towards events and decisions which would, as I hoped, change for ever the course of our lives. How could I tell her what '*happens*'? Yet I did, after my fashion. 'I do not know,' I said, and I spoke with resignation. 'It could be anything, anything at all. I don't usually know what it is. He'll tell me a bit about it, long afterwards perhaps. And sometimes, even later, I'll hear more, and it'll be different again. He doesn't tell *all* that happens. He doesn't like people giving him orders, just for the sake of it. And people do that, you know.' I looked round at them, as though they might not fully believe this particular enormity of human character. But all three of them were watching me with serious concern. 'He talks about them, the people that employ him, "cracking his nerves". It's a favourite phrase. When I hear it, I feel that it is a sign of time running out.'

Ursula smiled, and briefly pressed my hand in her own. But it was a sad smile. 'You have to believe it will be different now,' she said. 'I believe it will.'

Could I detect in her voice, in her eyes, in the pressure of her hand upon mine, a faint indication of despair? How well did she know my father? His energy and passion, yes; the driving forcefulness of his mind, yes; a certain appealing simplicity—that of the social buccaneer or gipsy—yes, even that. But what of the flaws? Who knew of these well enough to have replaced despair, little by little, with stoicism? Only, perhaps, myself and Alice. Who could love him well enough to accept him, knowing that there would be no change?

'I hope it will,' I said.

III

It was my last day. I was to return to London that afternoon on the train, and I was filled with a restless inner dissatisfaction that time was running out, and that I had not used it properly enough or fully enough. I had not done all the things which I ought to have done. I could not immediately think what they were. It was a conscious effort to try remembering them in my mind, and for a while I did, but put like that—to have walked the seafront again its full length, to have climbed up from the fish harbour to the cliff path—as things worth doing they seemed flat and detached now, hardly even worth regretting not having done. And so I gave up. They were, in any case, too many. They were the diversions of weeks or months, years even, compressed into a few days.

It was mid-morning, and I was listlessly wandering in and out between the study and the conservatory. Babette was painting at the study table, her watercolours laid out before her, a drawing board, with paper pinned to it, propped on her knee, and some still life objects arranged on the table in front of her.

I felt an almost peevish resentment at her preoccupation. I had said I would go, but she told me to stay. I had stood behind her, watching her work, but she did not like that, and I moved away through the open door into the conservatory, and stood there, in the sunlight, mollifying my hurt feelings among the sweet smells which filled the still air. The sun, which was low and brilliant, warmed the conservatory as well as filling it with strong light. The shelves were mostly filled with geraniums, and I plucked from one plant a soft indented pale green leaf, downed with faint silvery colouring. I crushed it in my finger and sniffed, with surprise, at the peppermint flavour. It filled my nostrils with its sharp and sudden and unexpected odour. I folded the leaf still smaller, crushing out of it the essence it contained, redolent for me in later years, of winter and of Christmas, and let fall upon the red tiled floor the little bruised fragments.

I did not want to leave. I did not know how I would fill the remaining days before returning to school. My father would be at work. I would not always be able to see Babette.

I remembered I had promised to go out with Philpotts on one day after Christmas. It seemed, at the time, a welcome, even a flattering prospect. But time itself had deadened the anticipation, and the days of Christmas had changed the relevance of Philpotts. He was more distant, and more reduced in my eyes, and I felt a sudden stab of remorse at this: it was unjust to change, yet I could not help myself. The reality of the young, self-possessed girl, sitting quietly, thoughtfully, diligently painting in the next room was uppermost in my emotions, and as I paced aimlessly to one end of the conservatory and looked out at the garden lit by the hard, low, wintry light, catching on the bare branches of trees, seeking out and eliminating the white dusting of frost on the sullen green of the winter grass, I felt all over again the longing and the yearning which her warm affection for me had not lessened.

'Will you become a painter?' I asked. I had come back to the door which led between study and conservatory, and was looking into the comparative gloom.

Life stretched ahead of us, filled with innumerable and unknowable years. I wanted to know, so that I could feel that I was a part of her future.

She nodded, still absorbed in what she was doing, still surrounded by an atmosphere of assurance which had, up to then, made me hesitate about interrupting her. For much of the time her head was on one side, her teeth gently biting into her lower lip, punishing it. On the table in front of her she had arranged some things, conventional still-life objects, I thought, a blue earthenware coffee pot, a white bowl of tangerines, a wine glass and an empty bottle into which she had poured water. Yet for all the predictability of subject, and the pitfalls of facile representation, she had already managed a freshness of colour which clearly pleased her.

'How will you do it?' It was a challenge issued; a requirement that she should state her capacity. Ever since first meeting her, at the wedding, I seemed to have been answering such questions, but never asking them.

She finished a sweep of grey wash across the top of the paper, then stirred her brush in the water, and gently kneaded it dry on the edge of the glass jar. She looked across at me. 'I shall go to art school.'

'Do you want to be a real painter, living by it? Like . . . like . . .' My words tailed into silence. I did not know what was involved or how it worked. I had only the very vaguest notions.

'Yes,' she said. 'In my life, that is what I want to do and to be. I know that it's going to be difficult. You have to be good. But I shall be good.'

I hesitated in the face of her determination and compared it with my own uncertainty. 'What do painters do if they aren't good enough?'

'They teach. They teach even when they are good. That's what Ursula says. She takes me to exhibitions quite a lot in London.'

'It seems to be in your family, teaching.'

'Yes.'

She looked at the painting again. Then she started to mix orange with brown and to work on the shadows under the tangerines.

'Why do you bite your lip like that?'

She shrugged her shoulders. 'Concentration,' she said.

'What do you think about when you're working like this?'

'Nothing in particular.'

'I wish I knew what I wanted to be.' I paused. She didn't answer. 'You're lucky to be so sure. I wish I was sure like you are.'

She touched in an edge of deep orange, then inspected it, her head again on one side.

'What do the boys from your school do, mostly? Do they go to university?'

'Coppinger boys? University? I wish they did. My brother's going, after National Service. He was the first in four years, and he only made it because he did another year in a different school. Philpotts is going. He's awfully clever. He won a scholarship. Most of the boys go into things like engineering. I don't really know what they do. They seem to get into National Service, and then vanish for a few years. The ones that come back on Old Boys' Day have jobs and money. Some even have cars. That's more than the staff have. But I don't really know what many of them *do*.'

'And you? Will you follow your brother to university?'

'I hope so.'

Babette went on with her painting for a while, then stopped. She put it down on the table and rinsed out the brushes.

'Finished?'

'Yes. Do you like it?'

'I think it's super. You'll easily be a painter when you grow up. Do you paint in oils?'

'Yes.'

'Do you like it as well as this?'

'Sometimes. It depends. Today was a watercolour day.'

She got up, and came towards where I was leaning against the side of the door. She was carrying the drawing-board with the watercolour pinned to it. I backed into the conservatory, and she followed me out into the sunlight, sighing with relaxation at having stopped. She put it down on a table, and we both looked at it.

'Shall I sign it?'

'I think it's awfully good. I really like it very much. I envy you, being able to make something that will last, like that will, and all the others you have done. And the ones you will do.'

'Would you like it?'

'Do you mean, give it to me?'

'Yes. A keepsake for this holiday.'

I was deeply moved. 'I'd like that more than anything.' She could have given me drawings or paintings out of what she had done in the past, and it would have meant much less. This was different.

'I shall always remember you,' I said, looking down at the painting, 'as you were this morning, sitting in there. When I look at the tangerines I shall smell geranium leaves, and the blue coffee pot will remind me of the warmth of the winter sun. Did you know,' I went on, 'that you bit your lip while you were painting, and put your head on one side? Like this?' And I imitated her. But instead of looking down at the painting, as she had done, I looked across at her, and into my eyes I attempted to concentrate all the love I believed I felt, the deep longing to belong, the sensation of impending loss that was even then beginning to steal up on me as I realised that these were my last hours there with her.

'It's for concentration,' she said. 'I told you.'

I nodded.

'It helps me to paint.'

'It must.' Could she not read my eyes? In my shyness I felt that the gap between us, that brilliantly lit space of air in the conservatory, was widening. I wanted to reach out to her, and stop the moment right there.

'The painting is quite dry now, isn't it?'

I nodded. 'Yes, it is. It's quite dry.' How I envied her. How surely, how certainly she seemed to know where she was going, what her life would be.

'Should we roll it up? How will you carry it to London?'

'We could roll it, and put paper round.'

'Let's do that.'

'I wish I wasn't going,' I said.

'But we're coming back after the weekend. We can do things together then.' She smiled, sadly, fleetingly, into my eyes.

'Will it be the same as here?' I asked. 'Will it?'

'I hope so,' she said. 'Yes, I hope it will.'

IV

I left on the train in the afternoon. I felt a deep sense of loss, leaving them. I felt it about all of them. I could not believe it would be quite the same, ever again. They would try, and I would hope. But these few days, like fruit in autumn, had gathered and swelled and ripened, and were now harvested. And the future was something different. Other clouds, other seasons, other dispensations hung over it. I could read the affection for me in their eyes, as well as, or so I imagined, the doubts they must feel about me and my future as my father's son. George and Ursula had brought me there for that Christmas; would they ever bring me again, together? Or would the usual painful pattern of my father's capricious life destroy all this as it had destroyed so much before? No, not destroy it. That was not quite what I meant. I had learnt how to avoid that, how to store up for myself, against future disruption, the magic of the good times, by committing them deeply to my memory, harbouring them safely in my own imagination. But it could be no substitute, at the time, for the warmth and the reality of my feelings. Only in retrospect, in a year's time or in two years, looking back, comparing, assembling Christmases future and past, like Scrooge, would I be able to feed on the safety of the heart's storehouse. Now, faced with the reality of departure, all I could think of was the immediate, huge loss. I had been so completely engulfed by them all, I had become part of their lives, I felt sure of it, and I had learnt enough of the rich continuum of what they did and were, to know that it was not just an experience, a Christmas holiday, from which I was departing just as they would depart, but a family and a collective life that would go on after my departure, and irrespective of whether or not I would ever come back into it again.

I looked round at them in the drawing-room after lunch. I

wore my coat buttoned up against the cold. Babette had hers on, too, and was coming down to see me off.

'Goodbye, Mrs Brooke,' I said. 'Thank you ever so much for having me. It was a lovely Christmas, the best I've ever had.' I said goodbye to the others.

'You'll come and see us next week, won't you?' Madge asked. 'Babette will arrange it with you.'

'Tell George I'll ring him on Monday night,' Ursula said.

'I'll tell him.'

'Goodbye,' said Jennifer. 'Give your father our love. Wish him good luck with his job. We all want it to work out successfully.'

They came to the front door. I stumbled on the pathway, and Babette held open the gate, as I turned and looked once more at the group of women, easy, relaxed, pensive in their expressions, resignedly part of something I would give so much to be possessed of. I waved, my vision blurred by unshed tears.

She came with me to the station. To begin with we didn't speak. Then, at the turning of the road, she looked at me. 'Don't be sad. You'll come for holidays like this again, won't you?' She took my arm, and I felt for her hand and held it in my own.

'I hope I will.'

'Well, we'll do the same again, at Easter or in the summer. I'll make sure.'

'But suppose . . .' I tailed off. I could not contemplate the awful possibility of my father and Ursula either drifting gradually apart, or, which was much more likely, breaking with the sudden, abrupt finality of so many of my father's decisions.

'Suppose what?'

'Suppose my father and Ursula . . . well, suppose it doesn't work. What happens then?'

'That needn't stop us.'

I did not answer. What she said reassured me, but the reassurance was overshadowed by my knowledge of the past. There had been so many other occasions like this. Not as real, but with an embarrassing resemblance. Nothing had survived from them. Why should it now?

There were only a few people catching the train.

Her lips were cold on my cheek as she kissed me goodbye. It was an awkward moment. Our farewell was brief. Feeling suddenly protective towards her I said: 'Hurry back home, Babette.'

She laughed. 'You're so like your father. Don't be too like him.'

I walked to the train, conscious of the shadow of blood, and imitating, for her benefit, my father's seamanlike step, the slight give in the left knee, the head jutting forward, so that when I turned at the carriage door and looked back down the platform, she was laughing, and waving at me, and I laughed as well, and waved back. And for a while after that, as the train pulled out of the station and out of the town in the slanting afternoon sunshine, I felt all right. I watched the still, sharp landscape flying past, the leafless trees, the lank, discoloured grasses, the solid brown furrows of ploughed earth, the remnants of frost that were still to be seen in the lee of hedges and banks. Then sadness overcame me, and in the deserted compartment, looking out through the grubby window of the railway carriage, all I could see began to blur into a watery mist, as I let the tears come.

Chapter Nine

It was their conversation that decided me, so I thought. Hearing them together, and simply not believing that there was anything in it: no feeling and no relationship; above all, no love. I am as saddened by the memory as I was by the time itself, and I look back with greater regret in the light of what happened afterwards. And because of this, in my mind I sat away from them, erecting a barrier of imagination to protect myself from that in which I no longer had any faith.

I am even conscious, as I write now, of the awkward and uneven nature of that evening; of the clumsiness of my own reactions and responses; above all, of the growing feelings of detachment.

We were at Covent Garden, for the performance of a special Christmas ballet. My father's mood had been only mildly truculent, and half-way through the performance he had embarked on a vaguely contentious diatribe about the myriad ills of English theatrical entertainment at Christmas time.

His very mildness of attitude contributed to my lack of ease. It was as though the evening, for him, simply did not matter. It was boring, it would all be over soon, and he would once again be liberated. For what, did not matter. And this itself almost induced a feeling of disgust. What possible warmth could life have in such circumstances?

'I just never could stand pantomime—in any form,' he said. The way he spoke the word made it sound as questionable as striptease. 'Never made sense to me. Hotch-potch of contradictions. I mean to say, what's it for? Who's it for? Tell me? Is it for children? If it is, then why the leg-show, and all the glamour? If it's not, then why the silly stories? I mean to say, it's obvious, they should think it out more. This principal boy nonsense. The whole thing is so futile.' He spoke the word 'futile' with a kind of spitting venom; and there was a gathering together of all human stupidity in the phrase he used, 'the whole thing'. And yet, did not a glimmer of desperation force its way through the mask of disdain, as even my father, a high priest of intolerance, recognised that a tradition as old as pantomime could not be wholly foolish? It must express something of humanity's infinite contradictions. 'I suppose there must be some that enjoy it,' he added, grudgingly, as an afterthought. 'Whereas this—' and he gestured around the great auditorium of the Opera House; 'quite different.'

He and Alice had bickered, almost comfortably, like any married couple, for several minutes already. It was not really for the purpose of extending knowledge in each other, of questioning opinions, expressing criticisms: no, their purpose was the simplest of all conversational objectives—the stirring of the pot of their own relationship.

There was a hectoring tone in my father's voice as he went on, piling up his scornful harvest of rhetoric, a mumble of complaint that I was determined to shut out and leave to Alice. He could be so shudderingly dismissive. And in that place, as far as possible, I wanted to be thought of as somewhat apart from them, even if I could not be seen as a completely detached party. I had so often experienced this gathering momentum of discontent, growing slowly during the course of an evening with Alice. It only happened, as far as I knew or could remember, with her. And yet strangely enough, I never recall the feeling that I blamed her for it. It was his belligerence always that seemed to be at the root of this; it was, to all intents and purposes, marital discord that I witnessed. He always blamed her. I never did.

Sometimes the evening storm died down again, the anger appeased. And it would all fade as we parted. And he and I, within minutes, striding away together, would laugh about it all; sometimes it cracked and raged, and ruined things completely. But increasingly Alice had learnt to capitulate. And though she often submitted with too great a measure of humility, her silence had become the wisest remedy.

I had learnt, more and more, to keep out of it; but I was also silent because I feared embarrassment in so public a place as a theatre. This was Alice's outing: ballet at Covent Garden. It was taking its predictable form. I almost felt an inclination to laugh at the slow, familiar ritual repeating itself. But I could not afford to risk even a grin lest I should anger my father or hurt her. Nor could I quite sustain my pretence that I did not belong with them. I was sitting, in fact, on Alice's side, and not between them, so that I was not directly involved in what was being said. I tried to fold myself away into a warm cocoon of other thoughts.

Alice tried to pour out the pacifying balm of compromise about the nature of entertainment. 'But George dear, *this* is a kind of pantomime. The story, after all . . .' Her gentle voice beside me tailed away. She, too, was conscious of the danger of a 'situation' developing. The second interval was drawing to a close, and people were already returning to their seats. With her usual prudence, Alice had chosen our places in the stalls carefully. We were in the front of one section, so that my father would have room for his feet; and we were more or less central. His approval of all this had been unqualified, but it did not stop the tide of his present condemnation.

'Pantomime?' he said, his voice rising, with that particular timbre in it which, had he been in the street or at home, would have stopped him in his tracks in order that he might strike an appropriately dramatic attitude, 'Pantomime? With Margot Fonteyn? And the finest company in the world?'

The questioning silence that followed his words attracted

attention around us. I sensed the interest of those behind us, who had returned to their seats from the bar, and who must have been feeling, from the tone of my father's voice, that they were missing an instructive debate upon the very nature of what they were there to experience. That peculiar, forced loudness with which limited remarks were uttered, and the plotted silences between, all symptoms of eavesdropping, accompanied the conversation.

'Well,' said Alice, 'it's a pantomime story, George. You have to admit—'

'They are light years apart.'

'But the comedy, George dear. The ugly sisters.' She spoke now without looking towards him, her voice, if anything, slightly more subdued; the expression on her face accepting a defeat which had not quite yet brought her to silence.

'Rubbish.'

'The make-up, too. That blond hair and red cheeks on Frederick Ashton.'

I was amazed at her daring. I had, on at least one occasion, heard my father tell Alice, in public, to shut up. And that had shocked me, but also prepared me for repetitions of the same kind of termination to other differences. And these had come. And I remembered, too, and was reminded particularly of it now, that there had been one bitter occasion when just such an argument had ended in my father calling Alice 'an old fart', and raising his hand as if to strike her. That had not been in public. Looking sideways, I noticed an expression of stubbornness in her plump jowl as well as a look of trepidation in her eyes. Yet again I asked myself the simple, unanswerable question: what made her stick by him? What conceivable happiness was there in a relationship that moved along in a manner that was so obviously discordant?

Fortunately, the house lights began to dim, and the 'performance' of these two beside me, which would last much longer in my memory than the details of Fonteyn in Prokofiev's *Cinderella*, was temporarily postponed in order to allow the fitting of the slipper and the conclusion of the fairy tale to be completed.

I thought of Alice, at that time, as a weak woman. And I thought that her capitulations, concessions, compromises, her eventual but inevitable bowing before his anger and his lordly acceptance of her money, together with his imperious gestures of disdain, were all part of a weak human character that stumbled along in service to a man who behaved badly towards her. I was wrong. But it would be many years—indeed, more than half a lifetime—before I would finally realise what might be called Alice's strength. It would only be after my father's death, news of which she herself would bring to me, that I would witness the dogged—indeed terrifying—steps of her journey to the end of her love for my father.

That lay in the future. Just then, sitting in darkness, and unhappy about the whole atmosphere surrounding us, my boyish resolve was the simple one: this had to end; it had to be replaced by something better, which was there for us both to grasp and make our own. Something must happen. Perhaps in the letter my father had received from the solicitors, and which I remembered seeing on the table, that first morning at home, lay the secret of our future.

I let my attention become absorbed in the final stages of the story. The prince arrived; ugliness was discomfited; the glass slipper was matched with its missing partner; beauty and goodness were rewarded; Cinderella celebrated her triumph; and the lovers were united for ever, under the wand of the fairy godmother, in an enchanted garden, far away from reality.

Mine was not a complete suspension of disbelief. I was conscious of the Prince's firm and muscular legs, his powerful buttocks, as he pranced the stage in attendance on the graceful, dancing figure of Cinderella, and I could not escape the faint feeling that this 'convention of the dance' was slightly ridiculous. This, in turn, bred a misgiving in my heart about the extent of my enjoyment. I had wanted to be entirely swallowed up. And to begin with I had been. The very luxury of our deep red plush seats, of the red and gold richness of the auditorium, towering around and above us, and of the people, had all impressed upon me the sense of great occasion. But I was gradually emerging from it, even as the last scene reached its climax, with a faint troubled sense of disappointment.

Originally, this particular ritual outing at Christmas had come about by accident. I remembered being asked, the first time by Alice, what I would like as a Christmas treat. We had known her for only a short while. She was untried then in the fire of my father's disapproval and disdain; and she had made a gentle and tentative move, with me, towards a decision about what our entertainment should be, conscious of the need to please all of us. I think, even then, I suspected that it had been decided beforehand, in the way that entertainment for children so often is. I did not complain. After that first time my interest in ballet became itself one of those strange schoolboy scrapbook hobbies which are self-perpetuating. And I suppose I was vaguely pleased by that. But it was really Alice, moved, as my father often suggested, by a secret yearning which derived from her dumpy, graceless figure, who had suggested *Swan Lake*. And *Swan Lake* it had been, that first year. *Coppelia* followed a year later. I still have, in some dusty drawer or cupboard, the scrapbook I kept then, with its brown photographs cut at school from the pages of the *Illustrated London News* of dancers and stage settings of that time. And they bring back as vividly as yesterday the strange determination with which, in childhood, we embark upon enthusiasms, not so much for their own sake—though that is what we think is happening—but in order to understand where we are going, and why.

The tide of music and movement finally came to rest, all white and gold and silver on the magnificent broad stage. In the stillness there remained the memory of movement, almost more powerful than the movement itself. The golden vibrating floods of light caught and highlighted the swelling of the dancers' breasts and shoulders, the infinitely desirable, supremely unattainable, downy softness of skin, the parted, triumphant lips. Yes, even with all my reservations, I was swept up in the climax, and imbued with feelings of the invincibility of my own imagination. The heavy red curtains came down for the last time; the lights in their brackets held by nubile slave girls glowed out across the crowded theatre; the clapping ceased. The performance was over.

A confident mood had been engendered in my father by Alice's money in his pocket, and once free of the constraints of the crowd he took charge of us with that measure of self-regard which is the prerequisite for gaining the respect and attention of others. We were soon ushered into a cab, and I saw a florin change hands. 'Trocadero, cabby,' my father said. We moved away.

It had snowed a little during the performance, and a few laggardly snow flakes were still spiralling down to settle and melt on the wet pavements. The wheels of the taxi hissed through the slush. I sat facing them on one of the pull-down seats.

'How did you enjoy it?' said Alice. She beamed at me, her cheeks dimpling slightly as they always did, and wobbling with the movement of the vehicle. She sat up straight, her hands folded around her shiny black handbag.

'I thought it was super,' I said. 'Terrific. I didn't expect it to be funny. But it's meant to be funny, isn't it? And Margot Fonteyn—she's our best, really, isn't she?'

My father nodded, sitting back into the seat, letting us talk on together. Alice agreed. 'Yes,' she said, 'you could say that. She danced very well.'

It was safe now to talk about it. I felt inclined to discuss the matter of the various performances with Alice, and to extend my knowledge a little more, as well as demonstrating my enthusiasm and my gratitude. But first I needed to measure out our relative positions.

'Have you seen her many times before, Alice? I mean, do you come to Covent Garden often for the ballet?'

'No. It's your special treat, and I save up my interest in ballet until Christmas so that we can go together.'

'And you never go between Christmases?'

She shook her head. 'Well, we did go last Easter, if you remember. Wasn't it then that we saw *Daphnis and Chloe*?'

I felt constricted by the fact that she was no better equipped by experience of the ballet than I was. I was of an age when conversation with even the most sympathetic of adults was difficult; and things were considerably more complicated when it was Alice and my father.

'I would love to go often,' she said, 'but I am really very busy. And it makes it special, just keeping it for Christmas.'

'For me it does,' I said, and the enthusiasm in my voice, even if ballet was not the ultimate aesthetic peak for me then, was still genuine enough. I wanted her to feel this. 'You should go more often, Alice, if you love it so much. Shouldn't she?' I looked towards my father for endorsement of this encouragement, but he was looking out of the cab window, and paying no attention.

She patted one gloved hand against the back of the other. 'Perhaps you're right. I shall think about your advice in the New Year. Perhaps George and I will go again during January.' And she looked a little hopefully at the back of my father's head.

The taxi turned down Shaftesbury Avenue, and I held on to the leather handle by the door to stop myself swaying over. It seemed to me that any prospective discourse upon the performance had by now been dismissed. I felt, however, that it was only right to try and make conversation. I turned reluctantly from the window, and the flow of people through the thin shreds of slush on the glistening pavements, and looked with compassion at the plump, inscrutable face of Alice as she waited, yet again, for time to pass between one place and another, between one experience and another. 'Did you have a nice Christmas?' I asked.

'Yes. But let's wait until we're in the restaurant. Then we can have an exchange of Christmas stories. I'm so looking forward to hearing how *you* got on. And I did like your present very much. It must have been a great undertaking, making that for me.'

'I enjoyed doing it.'

'It's so perfectly made. Did you hem the sail, and do the mast all by yourself?'

I nodded. 'I liked yours, too,' I said. 'And look at the watch Dad gave me.' I held out my hand, and she looked admiringly through the indistinct light as the cab pulled in beside the entrance to the Trocadero. The door was opened for us. The cab was paid off. I could tell, from the driver's 'thank-you', that the tip had been a generous one. We went in.

The entrance was crowded with people. The semblance of a queue had formed, and a busy headwaiter was advising of a delay of up to half an hour. My father crossed over and exchanged words with him, then came back.

'We will have to wait half an hour or so. He can't do anything.'

'Oh,' Alice said. 'That's a setback. I half felt we should have booked a table. What should we do, George?'

'We'll go to the Corner House. There must be room there.'

We followed him out into the night. I looked across at the lights of Soho, the dark corners, the groups of people, men and women, in idle, and to me sinister, conversations.

I had to admit to myself a secret preference for the Corner House even over the Trocadero. I had always liked the lights and coloured decorations of the huge, low-ceilinged room in the basement, with the band playing gipsy music. That was as I remembered it best from previous visits, usually with my father, though sometimes with women friends as well; and it was in that direction that I guided him now. It was as always, with the band playing vigorously and noisily. We were shown to a table beside a pillar. It was done with that strange instinct among waiters for detecting prospective benevolence. While we were settling ourselves, the band, sweating under the coloured lights, their faces and balding heads glistening with the heat they themselves were generating, reached the climax of their selection, suffered briefly the perfunctory applause spread unevenly across the large, low room, bowed once or twice, laid down their instruments, and departed.

'I hope they've only gone to wet their whistles,' my father said to the waiter, who smiled with knowing obsequiousness and nodded his head.

'They'll be back,' he said. 'Never you fear.'

Alice made more of a business of settling herself than we did, keeping clear of direct involvement in the exchange with the waiter, so that when he left us alone to peruse the large, stiff, folded menu cards, she 'came in', as it were, ready to play a leading role. 'Well,' she said, smiling at me across the table, 'this evening is for you. It is your outing. What would you like to eat?'

I knew already what I wanted, but searched the menu dutifully, as part of the expected ritual, confident that it would be there, my eyes going up and down the list of exaggerated descriptions. It was. I told her what I would have. Then I waited, watching them both.

Already, on my father's face, there was an expression of ill-concealed boredom, familiar to me from most, if not all, of the occasions in the past when the creaking machinery of celebration, initiated by Alice, paid for by Alice, and controlled by Alice, had been set in motion. Since we had known her, there had been at least one occasion in each of my holidays at home from boarding school when she had arranged some kind of similar outing.

They were occasions which strained my father's tolerance, occasions when he held in check, with determination, almost with a gritting of teeth, the urge to 'fly off the handle'; occasions also when Alice could claim at least one evening during which she exercised virtually total control. I played my part, peripheral, temporary, but important. Things had substantially improved in the stability of my life with my father since the advent of Alice, and basic need demanded that this should be sustained.

I suppose it was a natural enough part of my nature, cautious and careful as a result of so many things, that I should still want this security which resided in Alice while at the same time recognising that a fresh and energising zephyr had already begun to blow from another direction, offering a totally new and exciting and much wider kind of certainty. To outward appearances this had produced no change in me. But inside, as the evening progressed, I was becoming increasingly dissatisfied. This arrangement, 'liaison', call it by whatever name might fit, was not working. At the same time, what alternative was really in prospect? The question, which seemed to involve virtually every aspect of my life, gnawed at me.

Covertly, I watched Alice, her punctilious eyes carefully inspecting every word, her imagination savouring the different tastes, her secretarial mentality ticking off the items which she would not have, measuring out—for it was indubitably *her* money—the extent of our pleasure.

The waiter came. The order was given. Alice agreed on certain modest items of alcoholic refreshment, including a shandy for myself. The band returned, and began a halfhearted treatment of a medley of Strauss music, which seemed to please my father. We all relaxed a little more.

Alice looked at me, and smiled in a restrained and cautious manner. 'Well,' she said coyly, 'tell me about Babette.' With me she occasionally flirted with a mischievousness which she would never have dared to direct at my father. 'Is she still as much to your liking as when you went away?'

My father did not exactly raise his eyebrows at the question, unanswerable except in the affirmative, but the look he gave me across the table—that of a detached arbiter over this interrogation—was indulgent and patronising, and it sent a slight, pleasurable shiver of premonition about the future down my spine. And when I answered Alice, and said 'She's all right', it was with a secretive, almost conspiratorial half-smile across the table at her, specifically designed to register the feeling—a perfectly true one—that she was much, much more than 'all right'. I was vaguely conscious, then, of the direct imitation of my father's use of the same expression for a quite different purpose in describing Robert. I was also aware that in drawing Alice into the events and feelings, in attaching her to the fringes of these other relationships now enjoyed by my father and myself, I was performing something which she needed, if only out of curiosity and envy, and which my father could not perform, except in an awkward and unsatisfactory way. I could do it without emphasising any disparity in levels of enjoyment, except where pleasure in Babette's company was concerned; and this was something for which Alice could obviously offer no substitute. Alice responded, as we both knew she would, as my father had told me she would, with a catalogue of questions which carried us well into the meal.

Then, it was her turn. Her Christmas began, as she told us, with the office party. And being the senior partner's secretary, she was, of course, 'run off her feet'. It had been a Christmas Eve of errands and sorties into the dreadfully crowded and most inadequate shops around Fenchurch Street. And it was hardly surprising, she said, that by the time it came to the office party itself—a lunch-time affair, which petered out relatively early in the afternoon, allowing Bert, the doorman, finally to close over the double doors of the Merchant Bank at about three o'clock—Alice was in a state of 'total collapse'.

'I simply fell into a taxi—and that took some finding—and whimpered my way home, more like a drowned rat than anything else. It was not an auspicious start to my Christmas, my dears, since I had to get away down to my mother early on

Christmas morning. By dint of flashing here and there, hurling things into my overnight case, jumping out of bed at the crack of dawn, and simply racing as fast as my legs would carry me down to Victoria, I was just able to manage the trip out to Staines in time to help my mother with Christmas dinner.' She paused, and looked at us both. Satisfied, from the expressions of rapt attention which good manners imposed on me, and a look of absolute inscrutability on my father's face, she went on: 'Usually, we visit a friend's house, not far away, but mother hasn't been too well recently, so this year the friend came to us. It meant a bit more work, but at least there was no Christmas morning trouble over getting about. All in all, we had a quite jolly time.'

I tried to imagine what Alice meant by 'a quite jolly time', and could not. At times, her expressions brought me perilously close to laughter. I felt we would be on safer ground talking about food.

'And was it a nice dinner?' I asked.

'It was delicious. And I suppose, like everybody else, I over-ate. It's not often that one is fed by one's mother, and so well.' She tailed off, conscious of my attentive eyes anticipating everything she was saying, and perhaps feeling, over-sensitively, that her final remark constituted a *faux pas*; though this was far from being the case, as far as I was concerned. What I waited for, but did not get, was a more robust description of the relish with which Alice had 'over-indulged'.

I had long since disposed of my Corner House mixed grill; my father had done the same to his Hungarian Goulash; but not Alice. Her progress was regal, methodical and unhurried. She paused to think, to speak, to sip at her drink, to listen to me or to him, to cast around her the slightly wooden, politely surprised gaze with which she greeted the world, until finally, by tidy, small gestures with her knife and fork, she heralded the conclusion of the main course of our meal.

My father sat patiently enough through the meal, mostly in silence, leaving to me the job of sustaining our side in the conversation. Under her restraint he had not drunk much. He commented once or twice upon the music, but his expression, instead of softening or mellowing as the evening progressed, had become, if anything, more firmly set in lines of inscrutable hardness. His face, chiselled in reddish, weathered stone, embraced those hooded smudges of threatening fire, his eyes, which were made more penetrating by the shadow of the lid where it curved across the upper iris. And the very quality of stillness and repose surrounding him, extended even to the heavy, clumsy, powerful hands which were hanging, limp at the wrists and flaccid, over the wooden arms of his chair. This stillness had begun to oppress both Alice and myself. She looked more frequently at him as she spoke. I felt, myself, the possibility of some kind of disturbance bearing down upon our table.

It did not happen. My father did something which to me was almost more surprising. He turned to Alice, who was describing Aunt Jane's rockery—more for the benefit of father's temporarily dormant interest in alpine plants than for any feelings she herself had for gardens—and, raising his hand somewhat lazily, he brought it down in a gesture of familiar affection upon Alice's plump arm. She stopped speaking immediately, and turned to him.

Though his hand was on her arm, his eyes were fixed on me. Did I detect in them a sudden glint of benevolent mischief? Without looking at her, he said. 'Tell him about your childhood, Alice. Tell him about the redskins and the cowboys.'

She laughed, quite loudly, and with a sustained mirth. 'What a strange man you are,' she said. 'Whatever made you think of that?' She seemed inordinately pleased that he had thought of it, however, and she paused for some moments, looking into his face, seeking a meeting between their eyes to which only briefly did he respond before turning and fixing his gaze upon me once again. Even after looking away from her I noticed that she went on with what I could only think of as a visual caress of my father's face. Then suddenly she seemed to become aware of what she was doing, and turned towards me. 'Your father does exaggerate a good deal,' she said. 'Red Indians, indeed! The only Red Indians I ever saw were rather moth-eaten specimens.'

'Was it in America?'

'Yes, my dear, that is where I was born.'

'Come, Alice, you must tell him more,' my father said, disengaging his hand from hers and sitting back in benign contemplation of us both.

'It is such a trifling thing. My father was a dentist who went out to what I'm sure you think of as the "Wild West". It was wild, of course. But in a much less pleasant way than the films suggest. It was a place of illness and disease and high mortality, though generally not as a result of gunfights. There were those, too. We lived in Wyoming. My father and mother met there. I was born there.'

'When was that?' I asked. I faltered. 'I mean, *about* when?' I felt my cheeks redden. 'I don't mean to ask . . . it's just to know roughly, you know . . .' I tailed off into silence.

'No, of course not. It was in the days when there were still occasional gunfights. Though he was only a dentist, my father did have to cut out the occasional bullet, and bind up the occasional gunshot wound.'

'And did you ever see any of the fights?'

She shook her head and smiled at me. 'Wisdom dictated that one saw nothing,' she said. 'And I was very young. Just a child. It didn't happen very often, you know. Not the way it does in films. But it did happen once or twice. I remember it was very noisy, and frightening as well. You heard the guns from my father's house even if the fights themselves remained hearsay, and my father merely had to "patch up somebody".'

She said the words gingerly, as though she had been present on such an occasion, which could hardly have been the case. 'The town we were in was what is called, I believe, a "railhead". It was on a "spur" line, connecting up with the routes east, I suppose eventually to Chicago, and cattle were shipped through all the time. That meant quite a few cowboys coming into town.'

'Was it exciting?'

'My father didn't think so. We left when I was six and moved first to New York, and then home to Staines.'

'So there you are,' said my father, 'no magic. No glamour. No heroism. Life among the cowboys and Indians was like life in London or Manchester or Liverpool, nasty, brutish, and—if you are not careful with yourself, and take particular precautions when you are crossing the road—short.' He nodded his admonition to me, raising his hand to emphasise the point. Then it fell back on the arm of the chair, and a look of sadness came into his eyes. 'Those great plateaus of time,' he said. And he flattened out his hand, spreading the fingers, and drawing it horizontally across in front of him, above the table, as though he was conducting some last long muted chord of ineffable anguish. 'Of living, of working, of being. A Sargasso Sea of monotony. And unhappy, too, most of the time, bereft of any real satisfaction.' He paused, drawing in his hand, shrugging his shoulders, hunching forward and watching us both. 'Of course, I've had a good life myself. A full life. I've been lucky. Lucky to have met old Alice.' He stopped and looked, unseeingly, between us, his eyebrows raised so that his forehead was ridged with the horizontal lines and furrows of resignation, and so that his eyes opening wider than was normal, revealed more fully the world of unrequited hopes which they embraced.

'Dear, George. You are becoming melancholy. I'll have to cheer you up with a story, if only I can remember it.' She appeared to fuss around in her tidy mind for the details. 'Ah, yes. I think I have it. There was a Frenchman travelling in a train. He was on a journey from Paris to London, and he had crossed the Channel . . .'

I watched Alice, and tried to keep my mind on what she

was saying. But I could not. Instead, I drifted off into a reminiscence or daydream of my own. At first dramatic, it became sentimental, and in due course reverted to myself and Babette and the various adults on both sides who stood behind us.

I cannot say for certain, but I think this was the moment when I decided upon some kind of positive action. Coolly, without any great emotion or feeling of drama, I made up my mind to find out some part, at least, of what the future held. I knew that it would bring me, in due course, face to face with my father in a way not previously envisaged and with questions to be answered which had always seemed impossible up to that moment. But I think I resolved, then, to look at his private correspondence and see what his letters would reveal. It was a clear decision, taken deliberately and unhurriedly. Having taken it, I turned my attention, just in time, to catch the end of Alice's story about the Frenchman.

She told two more stories, and I managed to maintain my dutiful laughter. We left after that, and took a taxi, which first deposited Alice at her house, and then, after brief and hurried thanks and goodbyes, drove on. As was his style, my father overtipped the cabman outside the door, was warmly thanked, and responded graciously. It was late, and cold, and the sky had cleared so that it was possible to see the stars out across Kensington Gardens, above the glow of the city's lights. The surface of the street was wet, with the smudged reflections in it of the street lamps, and the untidy strips of slush still lying along the gutters and close in beside the plastered walls which ran along the areas of the tall, stately, converted buildings.

'She's a good woman,' my father said, as we climbed the steps of the house, 'very, very good. And so efficient. You can see how efficient she is, and what a godsend she must be to her boss. Correct, helpful, careful about everything. And not only her boss. Really helpful to us, too.' He stopped at the top of the steps, holding in his hand the keys to the house, an old and familiar expression of puzzled amusement in his eyes as he turned then towards me, his mind hunting for a conclusion to Alice's epitaph. Then he stared up into the pale and unresponsive face of the night sky. 'Yes, my son. I'm afraid it is true. She is so good, so very good. And so'—he paused—'so totally, infinitely, terrifyingly boring.'

Chapter Ten

I

The green morocco case lay in the centre of the table which my father used as a desk. To the right there stood the wide-necked, half-pint milk bottle, with its pencil, scissors and nail file. To the left there were two library books, one of them a collection of short stories by Somerset Maugham, the other a book about the British navy before the First World War.

Even among these things the leather case was isolated. It had come, I seem to remember, from my grandfather, and had been made for him before he went to India. And on more than one occasion my father's hand resting on its smooth warm surface had prompted recollections about that man I had never met. Last thing before leaving his room, wherever it happened to be, my father was in the habit of making certain small and precise gestures round and about the table he used as a desk, and the final one of these gestures was to 'square off', as he called it, the leather wallet in its central position. Equally, the first of his actions on returning in the evening—particularly at times like the present, when he was working hard and 're-organising' his temporarily shattered life—was to check his 'things', making sure that all was in order, everything 'just so', nothing interfered with or moved. It was a phobia. But it did have the outcome—desired or not, I could hardly say—of inducing in me respect for the sanctity of what the case contained.

He loved anyway the feel and texture of good leather. Did the case, as a result, glow with its own self-importance? I sometimes imagined so. It was old, and well-handled. The green had faded, and was stained in places. The corners were slightly bent, the leather buckled. And along one side where the stitching had frayed and opened up, he had carried out clumsy but thorough repairs which in turn had given a further possessive twist, a tightening of ownership, almost the vibrations of a living thing.

I sat that morning and looked at it.

I wondered, with the room empty but for me, with the dust hanging immobile in the still, lifeless air, with the door and the tall windows locked and the muffled sounds of life coming from outside, was there, in the case, some clue to the future? It was the substance of my father's identity. Just as, in Mrs Brooke's house, the essence of herself, as mistress of what surrounded her, emanated from the large, untidy desk in her study, so, for him, that function was performed by the green wallet.

Outside, I could hear the deadened rumble of morning traffic along the Bayswater Road, but it was distant and faint. Clanricarde Gardens itself was silent, and the closed windows, leading onto the balcony, shut out the already familiar sounds of morning, the sharp, clipped footfalls of people going to work, the very occasional noise of a starting car, the infrequent but unmistakable sounds of a taxi picking up or setting down a fare.

My father had already gone to work. I was to meet with Philpotts and spend the day with him. I had forgotten it, but on that first morning of the holiday, now so far away in time and in events, Philpotts had been given our telephone number by my father, and had asked him for our address and carefully noted it down. And before my return from the south coast a postcard had come, brief, almost peremptory, but precise, telling me that I would be collected that morning for a day to be spent in London, and deposited back, either early or later in the evening, depending on my father's wishes. It was to be early, since my father had arranged an outing in the evening, just for the two of us, celebrating his first pay packet. If Philpotts's suggestion could not be met then I had a telephone number on the postcard, and could ring and re-arrange the visit.

Initially, I had felt inclined to do this. In the wake of recent events, the recollection of Philpotts's very existence jarred upon me. Like the effect of the words of Moses on the shore of the Dead Sea, the days of Christmas divided the more distant past of Coppinger from the present. His card had been an unwelcome reminder that the seas of past and future would inevitably flow together again. And, since I did not want this reminder, I did not relish a day with Philpotts. Yet it had to be faced, and I accepted that it had its good side. Things generally seemed to be flowing my way. Instinct told me that events were in the air which would affect my life profoundly. And I suppose it was natural enough that I allowed my judgement and understanding to be confused by the firm and predictable way in which my own emotions had chosen to direct my thoughts.

All this made me accept Philpotts's visit, just as I was in the process of accepting my return to Coppinger, in that part of that return would be made warm and enjoyable by the prospect of letters passing between Babette and myself. Besides I wanted to talk with Philpotts about the possibility of my father marrying again. I needed to talk with someone more completely detached from my life at home. And I needed to talk from a position of knowledge, yet without any intention of disclosing too much.

I looked again at the green leather case. It seemed to loom out at me, divorced from any natural sense of scale. Its shape and shadow, reflected in the surface of the table, heightened the atmosphere of secrecy surrounding its contents, and of that distilled essence of my father coming from those few possessions which had travelled with him, from place to place, since my mother's death. For he was forever paring down, reducing to what he believed were bare essentials, the accoutrement of his life: people, possessions, places, tastes, habits, eventually even clothes, ties, photographs, the lot. But that lay in the future. At that stage I had not reached the point of laughing at it all. In relaxed moments, encouraged by him, I might join in amicable, amused acceptance of the fact that all these economies made life no less chaotic than it would have been had he indulged with prodigality in everything over which he so rigorously economised. My father's chaos, which at that time I was a long way from understanding, was simply chaos of a refined, economical, even methodical kind.

As I contemplated the leather case I prevaricated with myself, knowing well what I was going to do, yet having no idea of what I was going to find, and reassuring myself by pretending that there was no need to be frightened, its contents would be quite absurdly harmless. Then, quite suddenly, all nervousness, all hesitation, left me. I stood up and crossed to the table. Placing one hand on the edge of the leather wallet, I folded the flap back. It was a double envelope of leather; the first pocket opening to the left, the second to the right, and in the centre was a space for writing materials and a pen. The inside leather was a more vivid green and softer in texture. In the left hand side were the letters my father had received from the different firms to which he had applied for a job. I did not disturb them. In a smaller envelope above these were my own and my father's Post Office savings books, together with ration book and special emergency ration card, sent from school for the holiday. I did not disturb these either.

Cautiously, I lifted the right hand edge of leather. There were several typed sheets of paper, foolscap, and folded in half. On top of them were four envelopes held together by an elastic band. I recognised the top one immediately. It had the names WHARTON, REYNOLDS & SMEDLEY, across it in archaic capital letters, and underneath, in smaller type, the explanatory footnote: SOLICITORS. I let the flap fall, and rubbed my trembling hand down the front of my jersey. I could hear and feel my own heart beating. If I stop now, I thought, what will it be like tomorrow, and the next day, and the day after that? Perhaps, I thought, it is a matter of no real significance. But I must know.

In one swift movement I took everything out of the right hand side of the case and carried it over to my father's bed. I memorised the order of things, and laid them down neatly on the counterpane. I took the elastic band from around the four envelopes, marking in my mind exactly where it had been. They were all exactly identical, and I was aware of the need to keep them strictly in order. I laid them out, side by side, the top one on the left, the bottom one on the right, the others in between. I paused, and looked down at what I had done. I had gone too far to turn back, and I suppose I felt better because of that. I could take my time now. I looked at my watch and at the second hand clicking round with still unfamiliar newness. It was almost an hour before Philpotts was due to come....

The house was silent. It had long since given up its lonely tenants to their work in the city. I felt the soft, dusty, cushioning atmosphere of the dead house weighing down upon me. I had lived in so many houses like this already. I knew them, knew their neutral stillness, the cell-like isolation of each part, the suspicion, even fear, engendered between and among the residents, the echoing silence of hall and corridor, the unexpected, unwanted encounter on the corner of the stairs. Once all this had pulsated around one family: that was what a house was for. Now no longer. The stillness intensified my nervousness. Just suppose that my father came back, having had a row with the manager and lost his temper, and walked out, or having fallen suddenly ill? I shivered at the thought, then dismissed it. My father, strong as an elephant, and determined to make a fresh start, made the conception of such an idea absurd. I took what I thought was the first letter and looked it through. I saw from the date that it belonged to the summer. It could not have been the one that had arrived before Christmas.

19th April 1949

Dear Commander—,

Further to your letter of March 27th, we write to advise you that we have heard from your wife, through her solicitors, that, subject to the financial guarantees being satisfactorily resolved in co-operation with the Admiralty pensions department, she is prepared to allow proceedings for divorce. We have accordingly filed a petition which should come before the High Court (Probate, Divorce & Admiralty division) in the Trinity Term.

Yours etc.

I sat down on the edge of my own bed. I felt curiously elated. What I held in my hand was more, much more, than I had bargained for. It did not worry me, since it seemed to be on the right lines. But it left me bewildered. 'We have heard from your *wife* . . .' What wife? I looked at the date on the top of the letter. Yes, it said '1949'. It was *now*. Had my father married secretly at some time during the past five years? I thought of those dark, early days, after my mother had died, before the war ended, when Francis and I had been immured at Coppinger, and Melanie had vanished from all our lives. For close on three years we had not come home for holidays. There had been no 'home'. Those had been occasions—regularly shared with a number of other boys, no doubt seen in the eyes of the school as an even more neglected rump than the rest—when we had stayed back at Coppinger for long, empty, yet somehow not unhappy holidays. Could there have been, then, a marriage which had not worked? Up to the moment of looking at the letter, I would have regarded the question as ridiculous. And still I was puzzled by it. It was surely not in my father's nature to dissimulate about such things? I knew what he felt for Alice, and that eternity itself would never change that; I knew what my father felt for Ursula; and I knew what he had felt for other women in the past. But perhaps my knowledge did not go back quite far enough. Perhaps there, during that strange and distant time immediately following my mother's death, when in any case the world seemed upside down as the war drew to its close, he had made some fatal and futile effort at providing us with a home all over again, and it had not worked. And knowledge of it had been totally suppressed, only to come forth before us now.

Quite calmly, I opened another envelope. I was reading backwards in time. This second letter was dated March 4th.

Dear Commander—,

Thank you for your letter of February 20th with the copy of your application to the Admiralty pensions department for some form of guarantee preserving your wife's interest in your pension in the event of a divorce. Since that interest is of long standing, dating back to your retirement, we advise that this is an essential prerequisite for proceedings. If, and when, the matter comes to Court, and in the possible eventuality of the proceedings being contested, your willingness to give your wife agreed financial guarantees controlled by the Admiralty, will aid your case.

We have also taken the matter up with the Admiralty law department, and on receipt of satisfactory reaction from them we shall inform your wife's solicitors of the pension guarantee, or of such other firm arrangements as can be made within their restraints.

Yours etc.

Slowly, I put down that letter on the edge of the bed. It was typed on a thickish cream paper, and my careful unfolding of it to read had left it far from flat. I did not wish to smooth it out, for fear of tell-tale creases by which my father would detect my interference. I thought again of Berg, and the opening of the parcel, and the two polishing cloths, and the Double Clover Leaf Club. Reality was far more serious.

The letter rocked slightly on the edge of the bed in front of me. The room was very still. I felt awkward and yet suddenly endowed with the omniscience of a giant. Matters were even more perplexing than I had originally thought. What was meant by 'that interest is of long standing, dating back to your retirement'? I reached out for the third envelope. I was grotesquely conscious of my hand crossing the space towards the edge of the bed and beyond, as far as the letter. I trembled slightly as I took the third letter from the envelope.

It was dated March 12th.

Dear Commander—,

Your letter, together with other related documents, is to hand, and we have considered all the material, including the correspondence with Messrs. Heap, Mason and Shaw in the summer and autumn of 1946, when a previous attempt was made by yourself to obtain a divorce from your wife.

In the circumstances . . .

I stopped reading. 1946. I was confused again. When had my father 'retired' from the navy? I was under the impression that it had been much earlier, in the mid-twenties. Convinced of it, in fact. Yet here again was that strange, dark period in all our lives that had followed the death of my mother. What had happened? That had been the year of the school holiday in Wales, and the bell tents in the sand dunes, and the rain, the awful, unending rain. And we had spent Christmas at school that year, as well; and it had been very cold. And even then, infrequently—sudden, vibrant messages from an uncertain past, as it then seemed—we had received letters, Francis and I, and occasional parcels of food, from him. Had this mysterious marriage taken place then, or had it been much earlier?

I read on, and the darker suspicions hardened into fact.

In the circumstances we recommend that we take the matter up with your wife from the beginning again, making no reference to the correspondence of 1946 which you have sent us, nor to the earlier attempts made by yourself in 1931, details of which are now lost.

We do feel, from certain points made in that correspondence, that your wife's motives for refusing are primarily concerned with her financial security. Since this is affected only by your naval pension, it might be advantageous if some form of lifetime guarantee could be negotiated with the Admiralty. In the first instance we suggest that you make an approach to the officer dealing with pensions.

Yours, etc.
Wharton, Reynolds and Smedley.

I had read the first three letters in reverse order. I now picked up the last one. It was also the last one in time, the one I had seen that first morning. It was dated December 16th, 1949. It was the briefest of all:

Dear Commander—,

We write to advise that your divorce is now complete. The decree became absolute today.

We enclose our account, and would be grateful for early settlement of same.

Yours, etc.
Wharton, Reynolds and Smedley.

I sat perfectly still on the edge of the bed. I looked down at the array of papers. Though there were more documents which I still had not read, I had no wish to go on. I had seen enough for the present.

I was curiously light-headed. So this wife, obliquely mentioned in the letters as far as she, herself, was concerned, unnamed, with no address given, so casually introduced merely as a legal problem, a source of interference in my father's affairs, a potential source of interference in my happiness, was a figure from the distant past. She belonged to a period long before my birth. She had been my father's wife during that event, since then, and had only just relinquished that uncertain status.

The fact that her very existence as his wife, through all that time, meant that my mother had not been, could not have been, married to my father, struck me, as I sat there, unshaken, unmoved almost, as no more than a curious and interesting piece of additional information to add to an already large and complicated jigsaw puzzle of facts about myself. My mind simply accepted, with a calmness, a remoteness, that for long afterwards puzzled me, that my father and my mother had lived together as man and wife, and had given birth to three children before my mother's death two summers before the war's end. After that, we had been dispersed, my brother and I to Coppinger—a more fitting place to receive us, in the light of this information—and my sister to be adopted.

Briefly, an odd tableau pushed its way into my mind. It was of a summer's evening, a year or so before, and I had been standing at the door of a pub waiting on my father, who was drinking with Laurie. It had been my first meeting with her, and to a large extent my feelings about her, ever since, had been coloured by one tiny phrase. She and my father had been sitting at a table just inside the door, so that I was in their view, and half listening to their conversation. In a moment of idleness, Laurie's eyes had rested on me. She had smiled indulgently at me, then turned to him. 'How many children do you have, George?' she asked: and, quite obviously thinking that I could not hear, in the noise and bustle and laughter from the bar, she had added: 'legitimate ones, that is.'

I had turned away. Neither she nor my father had noticed. And he had made some broad and expansive and boastful answer, about not being able to count. Something vulgar of that sort. And the episode had passed away in laughter. But I had remembered. And it suddenly came to me, just then, clear, brief, chilling, before my mind moved on again to the firmer and more attractive territory of what this all meant.

The correspondence, which appeared to be at an end, was clearly pointing in one direction: that of my father's wish to marry again. Why otherwise would he have been getting divorced? I was filled with a deep sense of pleasure and happiness and exultation. I wanted to cry out. I wanted to shout. I did not really know what I wanted, or how to express my feelings. Instead, I clenched my fists so tightly that they hurt, and felt myself trembling at what it all meant. I knew that I had to be calm and careful and controlled. I knew that this discretion and restraint had to start right there and then, with small details, like putting all the documents away again. I folded up the letters and returned them to their envelopes. I looped them together with the elastic band. Then I returned the bundle to the green morocco case. I checked everything several times over: the order of the letters, the position in the side of the wallet, the position of my father's things on the table. I thought for a long time about what I had read; remembering the words and the details; absorbing the meaning. And then, after a while, when I could remember no more, and could check nothing any more than I had already checked it, I just stood there, looking down at the meagre, vital array of things on which turned so many important aspects of my father's personality. I felt a stab of pity at the way in which his life seemed to have been torn apart. And I blamed this unknown woman. I blamed her, I even hated her, at that moment. What I did not see, though the evidence was there in its bulk, and conclusive in what it said, was that my father was really distressingly ineffectual, thrashing about, as he was, in other people's lives, and unable to free himself. I suspect that subconsciously my understanding of him dated from those days during that Christmas holiday, and from the deep, and, in time, shattering, discoveries I was in the process of making.

Consciously, I grasped at the important and the immediate: itinerant days, it seemed to me, were drawing to a close. The moves from place to place, the new faces, the new interests, the new women, were slipping into the past. My mind was fixed firmly on Ursula, and of course on Babette. I hesitated for a moment or two. I could not be absolutely and completely sure; there had been sufficient disappointment in the past to have taught me an unusual degree of caution, and as I put on my macintosh and buttoned it, and carefully did up the belt, I told myself that I would have to be discreet with Philpotts that day. But sitting and waiting, even with my new leather gloves on, the poppers pressed home, the feel of them squeaky and stiff, I was suddenly overcome with a great wave of warm confidence about the future. It *would* be different this time.

II

Philpotts was a remote person about his private affairs, though in a positive way; he made a virtue—and a lively one—out of keeping himself to himself. In essence, I believed him to be my opposite in this, since deep down inside me there was a confessional instinct; in the right circumstances I was more than ready to tell to others things about myself which my older friend would have regarded as injudicious at the very least. Yet unconsciously I was learning from him; and I listened attentively when he discussed his own reasons for firm discretion, not just about personal and family matters, but also about ambitions and plans.

He was an advocate of secrecy and cunning. Yet his advocacy was open and forthright. There were good and complementary reasons for the attitudes he adopted, and I had an image at the time—possibly from some phrase or metaphor he had used—of his mind as a citadel, surrounded by fortifications built from impregnable and chinkless marble, glowing with its own justification. It pleased me to argue against the attitude he adopted, mainly because I could not fit into it my own desire to involve people like Babette and Ursula more fully in my life. At the same time I was attracted by the strength which it seemed to give to my friend.

It is strange to me now, looking back, that I should have thought of him so much more as a friend than I did boys like Danby and Kessner. Yet it was the reality. I was far closer to him than ever I could be to them in friendship.

I suppose it was fitting enough, given the sequence of events, that the argument, familiar to us both by now, should recur later that afternoon as we walked together through St James's Park on our way to Victoria Station. Philpotts was taking a train there which would bring him to his home near Lewes. He had wanted to come back to Notting Hill Gate with me, but had recognised, in my hesitation, not only a certain shyness about my home and my father, but also a gesture of independence which I would derive from seeing Philpotts off at Victoria, and then making my own way home, in my own time.

The day was almost over, and light had faded over the treetops and the high buildings along Birdcage Walk. The wintry mists which had persisted during the afternoon were now thickening into fog. It was cold and still.

We had been walking quite briskly. I suppose I must have talked for most of the day about my hopes for the future, no doubt telling Philpotts a great deal more than I realised I was telling him. On such occasions he was a good listener. When he himself had talked it had been on quite different matters, notably the theatre, which was an abiding passion with him. He loved everything about it, and on that afternoon we had been to a matinée of an unusual sort for me—I cannot remember its name, the revue, *Penny Plain* perhaps, or an Ivor Novello, or possibly a Noël Coward—and he had expatiated at length on the virtues and limitations of the English comic tradition. But now, walking along in the dusk, he was content to listen to my domestic recital. Most of the time I had successfully suppressed the urge to be comprehensive in the details I gave him, and partly because of this I must have seemed to him to be overstating my circumstances. Yet he listened patiently and without interrupting.

Suddenly, he was no longer beside me. I stopped, and turned. Some little way back he had also stopped, and was sitting down on a seat, staring through the dusk and lamplight after me. I went back to him. He shook his head. 'You are travelling too fast,' he said. 'And I don't mean the way you walk. Be careful. Keep your dreams to yourself.' He spoke softly, gently, shaking his head. I was nonplussed at first. In the sound of his voice I detected a wisdom, an understanding, which ameliorated the slight shock of his adopting the least expected of all attitudes—one that ran directly in the face of my present enthusiasm. Had I been less firmly set upon the impetuous course which the morning's discovery had outlined for me, I would have listened with more care to his gentle admonition. As it was, I took up the argument in my own defence, familiar with the broad outlines of both his approach and my own.

'I thought I was being cautious,' I said. 'I've only told you what I think would be nice if it happened. What's wrong with that?' I looked at his solemn face, pale in the shadowy, uncertain light from the lamps which lined the walk through the park.

'Don't set too much store by it. That's all.'

I felt crestfallen. As I saw things, this possible change could mean a great deal, and I felt that Philpotts was being unnecessarily gloomy. Perhaps he detected my feelings.

'Dreams are just better not talked about,' he said. 'They may not happen.'

'They may not happen; but they *can* happen,' I answered with a touch of defiance. I felt a strengthening in me of that surge of confidence which had been there throughout the day. And it was helped by the fact that I had, after all, told him much less than the full facts. I had merely hinted at a more stable and more firmly defined future.

'You're a fearful optimist!' he said, laughing. 'You'll need the angels on your side, even if you are right.' More seriously he went on: 'I make it a rule to keep dreams to myself. They are inexpressible, anyway, or so I believe. But you know all about that. We've argued it many times.'

We had. And at the root of his own position there was the belief that power over other people—something which even then had a devouring fascination for Philpotts—resided, in part, in knowing their inner ambitions. From these could often be deduced their plans and intentions, and presumably, when it came to it, mastery over another's destiny could be achieved.

It worried me that the argument was being related, for the first time, directly to me and my future. It seemed too sophisticated an approach. And perhaps I should have argued back. But I was silent. I waited, looking at Philpotts, feeling that I had been given a gentle admonition, a kind of affectionate verbal cuffing, aimed at teaching me a thing or two about life.

We tramped on.

'One should not make a habit of confession,' Philpotts said. 'It's far too important a human activity to be made a matter of routine.'

'But you can't keep everything to yourself,' I said. 'You can't always be bottled up and secretive.'

'Why not?'

I paused. 'I don't know really. My school report always seems to be making suggestions about "giving more" to others. And—'

'Oh, dear. Must I set you straight on that? Are you still taking your school report seriously?'

I did not know what to answer. 'I suppose—' I began.

'Don't,' was Philpotts's brief injunction. 'Don't suppose.

Don't take school reports as guidelines. They're merely the conscience-money of tired or negligent pedagogues.'

I listened as he talked disdainfully about the threadbare vocabulary of such reports. I wondered whether his view of things was not a bit extreme. I told him what the headmaster was accustomed to say. My last had contained something about 'not giving of his best'. It made Philpotts laugh.

'But surely he knows a little about us, doesn't he?'

Philpotts suddenly became quite serious. 'It may be the absolute truth,' he said. 'Giving of yourself may well be what you need to do. It's not that which I take exception to. It goes much deeper. It's the whole thing, the clichés, the repetitions, the narrow little range of comments which are made to summarise our desperate, packed lives at school. It's just so futile.'

'But there has to be something, Philpotts, some kind of comment or statement?'

He shrugged his shoulders. 'I suppose so. But when the headmaster writes on the lines you tell me, it could just mean that he has spotted in you a modicum of individuality and character which might, if it developed, become embarrassing for him and make his work more difficult. So unconsciously he must crush it out. But he doesn't know how. The days of flogging a school into conformity are gone, though he's not above trying. It must therefore be done by guile and cunning. Part of his armoury is the school report, and, through it, parental pressure.' Philpotts glanced each way along the broad winding walk, under the black network of a huge plane tree outlined against the glowing light coming up from the city. He turned with his arm up to restrain me. 'Forgive me for saying this, but I would wager that more than once in the coming year your father will use what Merchant has written in your report in order to admonish you for something you have done, or, more probably, for something you have failed to do. When he does you'll remember what I have said.'

In a way, Philpotts was right. Certainly, Merchant did work thus; certainly he deployed a form of fear within the school which, later, one came to despise. I also knew, and it made me want to blush, that my father would use the words of my report against me: indeed had already done so. But what I had not bargained for was the extent of Philpotts's cynicism. I simply could not accept that it was all quite as sinister and ruthless as he made out. His argument was about power, and the manipulation of people. It was dismissive of authority. I heard it out. I could not contradict it then, but I would in time bring myself to subscribe to it and use it for my own purposes.

We turned out of the park and down past the Palace. We were silent for a while. I wondered why he had wanted to spend the day in London with me. I was aware of the nature of our friendship, and accepted the affection he felt for me as a normal basis for being friends and spending the day together. Yet in addition I wondered briefly whether he was not a somewhat lonely boy among those at Coppinger, with his unusual and relatively sophisticated interest in theatre and the other activities of his imagination, rather than in the more muscular pursuits of the vast majority of boys of his age group. And I wondered, too, about his home. Was he equally isolated there?

'Do you live alone with your mother, Philpotts?'

He nodded.

'You've no brothers or sisters?'

He shook his head.

'When did your father die?'

'Who said he was dead?'

'Is he not? I always thought—'

'My mother wants me to think so. To her, he is dead. But don't let's go into that.' He looked across at me, a familiar, slightly mocking smile on his face. 'If you start asking questions I shall be forced into the unhappy position of having to tell you lies, which I would not wish to do.' Then he said: 'But with you, everything's been all right, hasn't it? Your father—?'

'Yes. Everything.' I said it with feeling.

'Good,' he said. 'You are lucky. Whatever happens, you'll be all right.' And he nodded to himself.

I felt completely at ease in his company, as the evening drew on, and we paced our way down towards the station. He seemed to be able to produce all the answers in a way that was curiously, even unnervingly, like my father. I felt relaxed and comfortable, and I doubt if I should even have worried if someone had suddenly told me that my father knew all about my morning's intrusion into the secrets of his life. Everything at home, at school, seemed to be moving in a graceful harmony that was more or less new to me, and which gave me a pleasure that was rich and seemingly more permanent than I had ever known.

We parted at the entrance to the Underground. He stood and watched me as I went down the steps. At the bottom I looked back. He was still standing there, and when he raised his hand I thought he was going to wave. But he did not. He put his forefinger up in front of his pursed lips, and, in spite of all the noise, I thought I could hear, coming down towards me, the hiss as he cautioned me to silence. I laughed back at him, and waved. His hand dropped, and slowly, not smiling, he turned away, and disappeared into the crowds of the main-line station.

III

I climbed the stairs slowly, my heart filled with a heavy sense of foreboding. My father would be home, and he would know by now if he were going to know at all, what I had done. Not for one moment did it occur to me that he might not be angry, or that he would simply ignore and suppress any acknowledgement of my interference with his things. There was just a simple and direct feeling of guilt as I mounted the stairs, the magnitude of it overwhelming me, the confidence I had felt when with Philpotts already evaporating. I relied simply on a skill preached directly to me by him that morning of being precise and exact with his things, and covering my tracks. I clutched the banister, and walked up slowly, rehearsing to myself the various answers I might give. I was flushed coming in from the cold. I had walked through Notting Hill from the Underground, and turning into Clanricarde Gardens I paced the pavement slabs more and more slowly, thinking about the day, reassured about my future, concerned simply to cope with the immediate present.

The door to our bed-sitting room was open, and the light shone through it into the hallway. I could see my father sitting at the table, writing. Even as I paused, for a few last moments, rubbing the gloved fist of one hand into the palm of the other, he suddenly turned his head, alert and frowning slightly.

'Is that you?' There was a note of tension in his voice.

I stood in the doorway, looking at him. He had not turned round. He remained sideways to me, perfectly still, waiting for me to approach. I did so, watching him carefully for anything indicative of anger.

'What time is it?' he asked, sternly.

I told him.

'Hmm,' he said. He paused. 'Well, you're in good time, I'll say that for you.' I had moved into his vision, and we now looked at each other directly. Then his body relaxed, the tension left it, he shifted in his seat, moved his hand which held the pen, and the expression on his face softened. 'Did you get on all right?' he asked. 'How was your friend? Where did he take you?' He paused again for a moment, suddenly concerned at the nervousness he must have detected in me. 'You're all right, aren't you?'

I relaxed, and nodded. 'Yes. I'm all right,' I said. 'It was a very good day. I'll tell you all about it at supper, Dad. Philpotts was great. He knows an awful lot about London. He sent you his regards. He would have come to see you, only he didn't feel he should since we hadn't arranged anything, and I told him we were going out. He said he wanted to meet you again.'

'A good fellow,' my father said. 'Philpotts. Yes. Odd name. Should have told you to bring him back. Didn't occur to me. He could have come with us.'

'It doesn't matter.'

'Take off your coat, just for a minute. I'll finish this letter, then we'll go.'

I felt a great sense of relief. I sat on the edge of the bed, still without taking off my raincoat, and watched as he went on with his writing, his lips murmuring the words and phrases, his large hand, massed in a great knotted lump, and pushing the slender pen, with its stubby 'relief' nib, across the page of paper with sharp, vigorous movements.

I knew that to go on watching him, to appear concerned at what he was doing, might betray the tension within me, and my sense of guilt, which was now subsiding. So I got up, took off my gloves and coat, moved round the room, and then took a book, and sat down in a chair.

The green case was open on his table, and papers were spread around. He had written two letters, which were in envelopes, sealed and stamped. He was now finishing a third. I watched him, the book—a Christmas present from my aunt —open on my knee; and I thought, in a very detached way, of my mother and of him together, living out the turbulent, stormy years of their shared life. It amounted to less than a decade. Three children, the rented house, the innumerable jobs, the disapproval of her family—the reason for which so much clearer to me now—and finally her death and the darkness that followed all passed swiftly through my mind. I had been concerned about being found out. Now, my original fears fading, the concern I felt spread further afield.

Then, quite suddenly, I felt a great wave of depression move over me. I felt bad. I had been dishonest and mean, prying into his life, and I felt guilty. There he sat, big and for the moment, reliable, dealing with the important affairs of his life, no doubt protecting me. And here was I, wizened by my treachery. He sat at the desk, writing, with that visibly rugged conviction about each word and phrase, so familiar a characteristic as far as I was concerned. And I thought of him being perpetually refreshed by a kind of innocence, which made him all the more vulnerable as a result; while I was sneaking among his privacies, probing his intentions. For an instant I felt I must confess. Then I quickly suppressed the feeling.

He finished at last, ending with his usual swift flourish of assurance, a sudden sequence of precise, prompt actions, putting away his papers, his pen, re-stopping the ink pot, sticking on a stamp, closing up the wallet, 'squaring off' his meagre possessions.

'Right,' he said, standing up and turning to me. He looked down at the letters in his hand. For a moment he frowned, tapping the three of them against his hand. 'I thought perhaps we might—' He stopped, and looked up at me again. Then his face cleared, and he smiled at me. 'No. I don't think so after all. We'll go and see *City Lights*. That's what we decided, isn't it?'

I stood up and put the book aside. I didn't say anything. I was curious about what was in his mind, curious as to what the three letters he was holding in his hand had prompted him to begin saying, and then to stop. But I felt that if I spoke I would lead him towards an alternative pursuit, that evening, which would be less pleasant for me. I wanted, believed, indeed knew that this recovery, this new job, this 'reorganisation' of his life, was more profoundly and lastingly different. And part of it had to be an increase of self-sufficiency, his and mine.

I picked up my coat.

'Wrap up warmly,' he said. 'It's a cold night.'

We walked to begin with, away from Kensington Gardens and the traffic westwards, cutting down a narrow street of Georgian houses towards Moscow Road. I reminded him, as we passed a letter box, of his letters. He took them out, and looked them through again, and then with sudden finality pushed them into the opening, feeling with his hand to make sure they had fallen. For a moment he stared at me; then he sighed, and we walked on together.

The hint of fog, which had lain thinly among the trees in St James's Park earlier in the evening when Philpotts and I had walked there together, had now thickened appreciably. The air had become thin and raw. It seemed possible to smell in one's cold nostrils, and to taste on one's lips, the bitter sharpness of impending cold as the temperature steadily fell.

I hugged momentarily his arm. My various feelings and attitudes of the day had settled themselves down into a general sense of well-being. The guilt had faded, and the fear. Whatever the past held, it was firmly imprisoned in the past. For me, now, and for him, the present seemed right; so did the future.

We came to the corner of the street, where it joined Moscow Road. There was a pub there, and from force of habit I felt both the tension and the tide of familiar signals—smells, sounds, the golden glow of warm light, the comfortable, cave-like safety—flowing over me. I looked in at the doors as we approached, with curiosity, I remembered the phrase—'legitimate, of course'—in Laurie's question, and I waited for the even more familiar faltering in my father's steps, the hand on the shoulder, the promise that I would only have to wait 'for a moment or two'.

And of course it did not come. Instead, he quickened his pace slightly, gripped onto my arm more firmly, and emitted a grunt of disgust. 'How can they?' he said. 'Hour after hour? Have they nothing better to do with their time and money? If there's one thing I can't stand, it's the smell of places like that.' He looked sternly ahead of him, but in the expression of his eyes I could see that even my father, a man who lived most immediately in the present, using the past with discrimination for pleasure whenever possible, rather than for guilt, and at the same time mastering new attitudes with well-practised skill, could hardly sustain my credibility without ameliorating in some measure the extremity of this revulsion for an establishment outside the very doors of which I had spent certain hours of my life. So he slackened his pace, looked at me, shook his great head, and began to laugh. Then he put his hand on my shoulder, until I laughed too, as we walked on together.

I was content to absorb his affection, enjoy his presence, and murmur to myself, under my breath, the words 'Moscow Road, Moscow Road'. They had a soft and lingering sound to them, like the gentle and distant beating of a drum. The tall, turn-of-the-century blocks of apartments, the proximity of the Greek Orthodox Church, and possibly something my father had said on some previous occasion, stumbling home from that very pub, though in a different direction, had caused me always to associate the district with fat and wealthy Jews climbing into large Wolseley cars, among the comfortable smells of leather, scent and cigar-smoke. It was a lost zone of the city, through which we forged together our determined way. I was confident, and happy. We were locked on a course together. We knew where we were going. We had no need to discuss it or plan it. It was there before us, as sure and firm and dependable as the street lamps which loomed out at us from the thickening fog as we strode along that winter evening.

The warm glow of an unknown yet inevitable future filled me with comfortable strength against the cold night. I had no need to take my father's arm, or to speak to him, or to exchange with him the smiles of pleasure which were secretly flooding through me. I had learnt something that morning from Philpotts; I was learning now from him. I paced the noisy pavement beside my father, measuring stride for stride with him, accepting with all my heart the rich destiny that lay ahead.

Chapter Eleven

I

It was the last day of the holiday. The train for Coppinger left Paddington at nine the next morning. I had gone to have lunch with Babette and Madge at their flat, but now Babette and I were alone for the afternoon. We were to go to Ursula for supper. My father would be there as well.

I could not escape a certain feeling of tension. Usually, this last day plunged me into a mood of deep dejection at what was ending, as well as filling me with presentiments about returning to the many different frictions and disciplines of school life. Yet this time, in spite of the natural sadness I felt at the ending of what had been a series of indisputably happy days, there was no question of my being dejected. I looked forward with tremendous confidence to the future. And I revelled in the thought that, side by side with my father's and Ursula's relationship to each other, there ran my own relationship with Babette. No, it was the more complicated tension produced by all this, together with the need to tell Babette enough of what I knew to instil in her the same faith as I had in what was to come, and what it would mean to us all.

I can only look back now and smile ruefully. How little I understood of how different I was from her. How little I realised, at the time, that the strange intensity which I brought to all these things was not shared by the others involved in that brief and clumsy drama. How little I perceived of what was really happening, and how completely I was the creature of my own need.

We were at the Tate Gallery. It was mid-afternoon. We had paused in front of a picture, and were discussing it. I told her I had seen it before, and had remembered it during our seafront walk at Christmas.

'Did you really think of it like that?' she asked.

She stood in front of the canvas, her head on one side, her teeth biting her lip. Her own intense interest in the painting—I could not tell what it was, the colours, the atmosphere, the light, the movement—made me question in my mind how much of what I was saying was really true. My voice hesitated.

'Yes,' I said. 'It is true. I did remember this. It did come into my mind.'

'And had you just seen it, before you came down to stay? Or was it much longer before that?'

'No. It was before.' I tried to remember. It must have been in the summer, on a visit up from Kent. Or even before that. 'It was in the summer,' I said.

'But it's so different,' she said.

'Not really.'

I was trying to work out how to tell her. I could not rely on our conversation turning, yet again, in the direction of ourselves or those nearest to us—though inevitably it would at some stage—and I did not know how to manipulate it.

She looked away from the canvas and at me. 'Where's Walberswick, anyway?'

I said: 'I don't know. I think it must be somewhere up north. It sounds like it. Perhaps the Yorkshire coast.' I ventured an imitation of what I thought might be the local accent: 'Let's go down't Walberswick, an' see lasses there, down't pier, with their skirts flyin' out all over.'

She ignored my feeble attempt at humour as an irrelevance. 'But this is summer,' she said.

'How do you know?'

'Well,' she said. 'The sails of the boats out in the sea, the sunlight flowing over everything. It must be summer.'

She was right. It was summer, that eternal, unending summer of the painter. And it was not really so like the pale, mistier light of that Christmas morning, hallowed for all time in my eyes.

'It makes me feel sad,' she said.

'Why?'

'It's something that no longer exists. It's gone and finished. And long ago. The girls are grown old and are dead now.'

It was my turn to look at the painting, hers to look at me.

I was looking at a glowing, golden moment in time. I was only beginning, during that holiday, and under the enthusiastic guidance of Ursula—she had already taken Babette and myself to see French paintings in the Wallace Collection—to comprehend just a little of what painting was about. And I suppose that much of what I felt and said in the Tate that afternoon was the product of half-digested ideas and reactions of that holiday.

'The girls are not dead in the picture. Look at them! They're alive. Happy. Enjoying themselves.'

'But the real ones, the ones Wilson Steer saw on the seafront that day, are dead and gone. Or, if not, they're little old ladies, living in Walberswick.'

'It would be fun to find out.'

She nodded, as we moved back from the picture.

'Do you think all four of them are sisters?' she asked. 'And that's their governess? And the two running away are off to buy some candy floss?'

'They didn't have candy floss.'

'Well, ice cream.'

'Not on the seafront when Steer painted that.'

I had a sudden consciousness of the need to open my heart to her. I wanted to talk. I wanted to explain things to her, quite what, I did not know. I wanted her to reassure me, with words and gestures, about ourselves. I wanted to store up enough memories and feelings to last me through the coming term until Easter.

Already, in my nostrils, I could smell the desks and lockers and cupboards: chalk, floor-polish, ink, soap, stale food, chocolate melting on radiator pipes, forgotten grasshoppers dead in cardboard boxes. I wanted to escape from the whole dismal anticipatory certainty of it, to run away, put it off right up until that moment at Paddington, when there would be nothing else to remember. I would have liked to have said to her, Babette, rescue me from thinking about it. I love you. Speak to me. Ask me questions. Tease me. Tell me about your school, your life, your friends, the secrets behind your glistening, laughing eyes. Break the silence. Make me forget. I will die remembering things.

As though she had read my thoughts, she asked: 'When you go back to Coppinger tomorrow, will you write to me?'

My heart leaped. 'Of course I will—that is, if you want me to.'

'I do. I wouldn't ask you otherwise. That's why I gave you the case.'

'And will you write?'

'Yes.'

'Your mother won't mind?'

'Why ever should she?'

'I don't know. There are some boys who write to girls from school, and it always seems to be so secretive. As if they weren't meant to. They say the girls aren't allowed to get letters.'

'That's for girls who are away at boarding school. Mummy says it's uncivilised.'

'What's a day-school like?' She told me briefly, and I envied her the coming home in the evenings, to the warm flat, and her parents, and listening to the wireless.

'Lucky beggar.'

She shrugged. 'I expect you often have quite a good time

yourself. You have warm fires, and read books, and listen to radio programmes, don't you?'

I admitted that this was so, grudgingly, not wanting the reminder; but realising that it was unfair to the school and to the Gaffer, whose fires and warmth and rough comfort on cold winter evenings I still hold in memory.

'Babette?'

'Yes?'

'Can you keep a secret?'

'Of course.'

'No, really. A proper secret. A life and death kind of secret. One that *really* matters.'

She looked at me, frowning slightly, her eyes grown suddenly serious. I noticed, as I had done before, the strangely ambivalent set of her mouth, a fulness which made it seem as though she was smiling when her expression was most serious.

'Yes,' she said again, 'I can.'

I thought of the four letters. How could I make the fact convincing without producing the evidence? I was certain that my father and Ursula would marry. But I could not tell her of the existence of the letters, or even hint at them.

'They're going to get married,' I said. 'They are. It's definite.'

Once the words had emerged into the open, they hung there, irretrievable. They seemed somehow clumsy and raw. Yet by being uttered, they made the truth of the statement more definite.

She looked at me, still frowning. I saw in her eyes vague evidence of doubt. I realised that behind her puzzled expression there must lie comments which had been made by Madge and Robert, perhaps unthinkingly before the child, and which had coloured Babette's guarded reception of my certainty. But I knew that my knowledge, backed up by perfect confidence in my father's passionate determination to have what he wanted, was a better basis for judgement than any doubts of hers.

'Are you sure?' she asked. 'How do you know?'

'You mustn't ask,' I said. 'I can't tell you that. And you mustn't ever mention it. But I am sure. I know. It's certain. I've seen certain things . . . documents. That's all I can say.' I paused, looking anxiously at her. 'You will keep it absolutely secret, won't you?'

She nodded.

'You promise?'

'I promise.'

'Are you pleased?' I asked.

Babette nodded, and smiled.

'No, really?'

'Yes, I'm pleased.' There was a look in her eyes which I could not understand. 'When they are, we'll be related. We'll be cousins by marriage, or step-cousins.'

I was faintly disappointed by her reaction to my news. She was not sufficiently impressed by it. I had expected greater enthusiasm. I tried again.

'It'll be very strange,' I said.

'What will?'

'Everything. After they're married. I mean, it was always him and me. Just the two of us. But now it'll be three; like you.'

Babette looked at me. Again I was conscious of a coolness in her reception of my news.

'You mustn't expect too much,' she said.

'Until now,' I said, 'there's only been him, just him.'

'No one else at all?'

'Well, Alice was there. And of course there were other friends he had.'

'Girl friends?' she asked. 'Women?'

I should have detected the slightly sharp note of inquiry in her voice. 'Sometimes I met them. Sometimes I only heard about them.'

'You knew? You mean he told you?'

'Yes. He'd mention names. It might be for some kind of outing. But it was always just him and me, really.'

I 257

She paused. We had begun to retrace our steps through the rooms full of pictures. She was wearing a coat, and swinging something in her hands, a bag or a scarf. And I still have this image of her in my mind, looking down as if to see where she should place her feet. And also as if lost in thought. When she spoke it was more quietly.

'What makes you so sure now?' she asked. 'Your father could still change his mind.'

I stood still, and thought. Ought I to tell her?

Babette said nothing. We walked on. We had looked at enough paintings. The mood for it was gone.

Quite suddenly she said: 'What is this document?'

I paused before answering. 'I can't tell you that. You promise you won't breathe a word of what I did say?'

'I've already promised that. Don't you believe me?'

'Of course I do.' I felt a growing sense of confidence that all the things I knew had triumphantly survived two challenging encounters, the one with Philpotts and now this one with Babette. If I had not told them, I assuredly would not succumb to the temptation to tell anyone else.

'Let's go back to Walberswick,' I said, 'and say goodbye to our friends. You're wrong, I'm sure, about them growing old. Shall we make a pact, now, to come here and meet them again at Easter? They won't have changed in the least.' And in the back of my mind was the thought: And we won't have either. Love doesn't allow people to change.

She nodded. We stood together in front of the painting. She put her hand into mine. I blushed, but held it tightly. It was warm, friendly, promising; she was pledging time, and the future, to me, and I was doing the same in return. The golden rays of that summer sun so long ago shone down on the bleached, weathered wood of the jetty; the yachts skimmed on for ever over the blue water, their white sails tugging and billowing in the warm, southerly wind; the girls laughed, and their bodies, soft, youthful, lithe, full of hope and wonder at all the goodness in their world, ran in angular, dancing enthusiasm down the pier towards us, their black-stockinged legs and pointed feet tripping across their eternal wooden stage, their sunburnt faces blurred by movement. Running for ever, they were still for ever, their youthful, laughing, dreaming lives preserved for ever from the tongues of fire and fringes of decay which time lays on us all.

II

'It's in Suffolk.'

'Not in Yorkshire? We thought it was in Yorkshire. It sounded like that. It's a funny name. Have you been there?'

Ursula nodded. 'Once. Yes. We spent a summer at Southwold. That's near to Walberswick. We were all there, Madge, Jennifer, me. Father was alive then. It was around 1932. I was your age, Babette.'

'And is it nice there?'

'Oh, yes. It's not a very seasidy place. I mean, it's not full of day-trippers or amusement arcades. I think that's why Wilson Steer went there. He liked the unfashionable.'

'And is it still the same now? I mean, would you recognise it if you'd seen the painting?'

Ursula laughed. 'I don't know. The painting doesn't show you much of Walberswick, does it? And it's a long time since I was there.'

Babette looked at me before she spoke. 'We wondered if the girls would still be alive.'

Ursula looked at us, a bit puzzled. 'You mean the girls in the painting?' We nodded. 'I suppose it's possible. It must have been painted around 1900. They'd be about sixty now, or sixty-five. You know, it's a long time since I was there. Why don't we all go again this weekend?' Ursula looked round at us, and then at my father, standing silent in front of the fireplace.

I looked down: 'I can't, Ursula, I'm afraid I—'

Babette cut in: 'He goes back to school tomorrow.'

'I forgot. I'm sorry.'

'It's all right,' I said, looking up at her. 'I'm quite looking forward to it.'

'That's the spirit! Back to work, with a will; nothing like determination.' My father brought his hands from behind his back and clapped them loudly together.

'Remember what Ellison said in your report.' He paused, searching the air for the exact words.

I tried hard to conceal my embarrassment, and the faint hint of misery that nibbled at me with each passing minute. Both Babette and Ursula noticed.

Babette called out. 'George . . .' It was half question, half warning. They looked at each other. She was as near as anyone could get to smiling and frowning at the same time, her finger raised in gesture calculated to silence any inappropriate delving into the oracular, hypnotic contents of school reports.

I thought of Philpotts, and his scorn for what he called the clichés of report-writing.

'He doesn't want to hear it again, George,' Ursula said. 'It's not important. I expect he said the same in lots of other reports. I expect, all over England this evening, Coppinger parents are quoting to their unfortunate offspring the identical sentiments you've just expressed.'

We all laughed.

'I doubt it,' I said, with feeling.

'What he wants to hear is what is going to happen next holiday. Isn't that right?'

I looked at my father. Before now, the mere idea of contemplating a next holiday, and considering the events which might fill it, would have been unthinkable. Today, for the first time in my life, it had become possible, even sensible, to think along such lines. The future had actually become tangible. This room, in which we sat, Babette close to me on the floor,

Ursula still at table, sipping a glass of wine, my father assuming a paternal stance in front of the warm glow of the gas fire, would be a part of it, a spreading tangle of lives, Madge, Robert, Mrs Brooke, Jennifer, and at the centre of it all, Ursula and my father. In my father's face I read clearly the realisation of this, the features softened momentarily by a slight uncertainty which of itself encouraged in me the conviction that he was approaching our new future with resolve and courage.

We looked at Ursula.

She said: 'I don't know whether it's possible, or even whether you'd like it, but usually at Easter Madge and Babette and I go down to the cottage on the coast. It's about fifteen miles along from mother. There'd be room for you both—if Robert was away.' She stopped and sipped at her wine. She put the glass down on the wooden table, and the sound of it was clear and precise in the stillness. Then she moved a fork slowly towards the glass until the two clinked together.

I wondered to myself what was happening inside her mind. I glanced only for a moment in her direction, and thought she was troubled. She was looking down at the polished surface of her table, one hand resting against her cheek, the other beginning to trace a vague pattern across the wood.

Remembering our Christmas visit, I said it would be lovely. My words, in their turn, seemed to hang timeless in the air. I looked at Babette, and she stared back at me, a questioning look in her eyes. In the stillness the tiny space that divided us could have been the distance between two stars. I faltered in my conviction about my father and Ursula. I questioned the secret I had told Babette. For a moment the gloom of going back to school was augmented terribly by this momentary, stabbing doubt; all my optimism to Babette could still turn out to be misplaced.

Then my father dispelled it completely.

'My dearest sweetheart!' he said. 'You are a most perfect

woman, and that is a wonderful idea. Of course we shall come. We would love to. We shall have Easter together, all of us!' He held out his arms. 'Come, Ursula, kiss me.'

She had turned to look at him, and was smiling, almost laughing. She was half-embarrassed as she got up and went across the room towards him. 'Really, George, it will embarrass the children,' and she laughed again, forgetting how she always tried to avoid using the word 'children'.

'Not at all,' he said, in mock astonishment. 'Why should it?' He took her in his arms and kissed her. It was a dramatic rather than a passionate gesture on his part. On hers, I was not so sure. She turned her lips up to him, and I imagined— for I could not see—the perpetual sadness which I had always detected deep in her eyes. Their bodies, standing together there in the soft reddish light of this now infinitely, eternally familiar room, in this decayed London street, reassured me. I was not surprised when Babette's hand closed over mine. I did not look at her. I turned my own hand upward and took hold of hers, and squeezed it, and let the waves of comfort and happiness and hope flow over me.

III

Philpotts was at the station already when we arrived, in good time for the departure of the schools special. He came up to my father, and shook his hand. They looked at each other, on Philpotts's face a slight frown of inquiry, on my father's an unexpectedly friendly expression.

'You had a good day together? You could have come out with us in the evening as well.'

'That's very kind of you, sir,' said Philpotts. 'Perhaps next holiday we could.'

'A good idea.'

I watched them as they talked. Philpotts was slightly taller than my father, but much less robust. Yet they stood together in the bustle of Platform One in an unself-conscious, man-to-man position which seemed almost to exclude me.

I was pleased. It was so much in contrast to the previous occasion. I wanted Philpotts to know him now that he had recovered. I wanted my father to rectify the damage possibly done before. The boys passing on their way to the Coppinger coaches in the train increased in number. One or two of them glanced in some curiosity at Philpotts talking with my father. The large, black hand of the clock moved up towards the hour.

There was not much time for conversation. Philpotts then took my case. 'I'll find him a seat in my compartment,' he said. 'You can follow me. We're only a few coaches down the train.'

My father placed his hand on my shoulder, and we walked slowly together along the platform.

'You have your money, and the chocolate, and fruit?'

I nodded.

'Don't stick your head out of the window. You'll get it knocked off.'

I looked at him.

'You'll work hard?'

Almost imperceptibly, I nodded again.

'Three minutes more,' he said. 'We'll shake hands now, and I'll go. We'll come down for half-term.' The slamming of carriage doors had already begun.

I made no answer. I felt warm inside. To see them together at half-term, would be the right beginning for our new and different kind of life, the details of which were still a long way from being worked out in my mind.

'I'll not stand about,' he said. 'Goodbye, old son.'

I climbed aboard and closed the door. He smiled up at me, and raised his hand. I had the window to myself, surprisingly, and leaned out, expecting him to turn and move away. But he stayed uncertainly below me, looking up. 'One minute more,' he said. 'Have a good journey. Play hard. Good fellow, Philpotts.

Have you got Alice's pound safe? Good.' There were shouts along the platform, and a whistle blew. 'Write to me. Mind how you cross—' He stopped, remembering that the roads around Coppinger were no threat, and that such warnings were for London. And as the train began to move out he smiled at his mistake, nodded to me, and waved his hand, then began to cross over the platform from the edge towards the various buffets and waiting rooms in order to have a more prolonged view of my departing head and waving hand.

Thus it ended, that time; and things were never quite the same again after that. Though the occasions on which we parted on station platforms, particularly that one, were innumerable, it is that parting I remember: him crossing to be able to see me, a strangely defeated lost look in his eyes and something peculiarly vulnerable in the way his figure, still to me that of a colossus, blended quickly into the crowds of people along the platform, was reduced to head and raised hand, and finally vanished altogether as the train gathered speed westwards.

Chapter Twelve

I

Those weeks, at the beginning of the new term, running well into February, seemed to race by. The weather remained bitterly cold, with heavy falls of snow. At one stage, in the high winds from the east, coming across the soft edge of the Cotswolds, from the direction of Banbury, it drifted; and for a few days the school was cut off completely from the outside world. There were no rugby fixtures during the first half of term: sport seemed to consist of long, gruelling cross-country runs, endless ploddings through snow-bound fields and along rutted, frozen lane-ways, gasping for breath in the frosty air.

Despite all the inconvenience and discomfort, there was a strange excitement engendered each morning as the persistence of the cold spell asserted itself in the unchanging white landscape into which, like grubby, grey, smudged insects, boys, staff, employees, were pushed on their school rounds each day. And even though the changes in the practical pattern of life, imposed by the weather, were small enough, they created an atmosphere in which everything had a temporary character. We knew it would all melt away soon enough, revealing once again the lifeless grass and undergrowth, the familiar open spaces and winding roadways that linked up the liberally spaced buildings of Coppinger. Yet that knowledge did not dissolve or dilute the strangely hypnotic effect of the grey light of snowclouds across a white landscape. People and things had more in common with the air than with the earth. This was the predominant reason for the unfamiliar atmosphere which prevailed.

Babette and I exchanged several letters. I became a kind of postal sleuth, searching expectantly and always too often for the blue, deckle-edged envelope addressed in her firm, almost flamboyant handwriting. She wrote about things that were on in London. We made various plans. Our expressions of affection were limited and tended to be conventional; but no less warm and sincere because of that. And I suppose that I basked in a glow of well-being: of loving and being loved.

Everything seemed to be moving swiftly. It was a shorter term than usual, anyway. At the end of it there was to be a production of *Trial By Jury*, coupled with something else, and I was involved in rehearsals for the part of the heroine, Angelina. My mornings were filled with expectation. I remembered the past, and particularly the Christmas holiday, and this helped to fill out my dreams of what Easter would be like. I worked well, and did not resent too much the compulsion of cross-country runs, cold sessions in the gymnasium, and the breaking of the thin skin of ice from our morning milk as we crowded round the school doors at break time.

Then it happened.

It was the night of choir practice. As term had progressed, more and more time had been given to practising Gilbert and Sullivan, less to chants and anthems and hymns. We were shortly to increase the number of practices, and start stage rehearsals and movements along with the music. But at that point we were still confined to singing out our parts in the school music room, where violin and piano lessons, and practices, were held.

I remember most vividly, of all the images of that evening, the expression of simulated anguish on Philpotts's face as he sang the few introductory lines to his opening song.

When Parker stopped him briefly for some small point, the expression vanished temporarily; then as he started again, his brow once more furrowed with histrionic appeals of heartfelt anxiety to be heard. He was singing the part of the Defendant, for which his voice was well suited. And he seemed supremely to be enjoying himself as somebody else; an unlikely, raffish character, at that. He had this capacity to lose himself within a part, impervious to the sniggers from other boys who could not throw themselves as fully into what they were doing.

I cannot explain why it is that I remember all this so vividly. It had so little to do with what happened subsequently. Yet now, on the infrequent occasions when we do meet, it is always to that time that Philpotts and I together direct our thoughts.

By that stage in the practice we had left our seats and were gathered around the piano, sharing copies and singing the parts as best we could. It was the Thursday before half-term. Five weeks would elapse before the performance would take place, yet already enthusiasm and tension were beginning to mount.

It came to my turn. I had practised on my own with Parker, and knew the music already. But I had suffered from a sore throat during the previous ten days; it had neither developed into a cold, nor gone away. It took the pleasure, which I had felt so keenly and for so long, out of singing. I knew really that my voice, and the weeks stretching away before the actual performance, were competing in a race, one against the other, and I was not optimistic as to the result. I was no longer comfortable when I sang high notes. I looked at Parker, and noticed a frown on his face as he bent forward towards the keyboard, playing softly, and listening to my 'Time may do his duty, Time may cast a shade.'

We sang on, all of us, stopping only occasionally to repeat brief passages. But practice time was nearly over, and, ragged though parts of the music still were, the rehearsal had to be brought to an end.

Parker was hot from his exertions, and his glasses, so many times pushed back from his nose, had once more slipped down as he gathered up his music and told Kessner and Davitt where to put the copies. The rest of the juniors left in some haste, anxious to get back to their houses, and not be too long delayed with prep.

Then Parker called me. 'I'd like a word with you. Just wait here by the piano.' He crossed to Philpotts and the other senior boys. 'Don't be too long getting back to your houses,' he said.

When they had gone, he sat down again at the piano and played softly. He had put his music away and was playing from memory. He did not look at me. He played only for a minute or two, then stopped abruptly. 'Listen,' he said, 'your voice is breaking. It won't last until the end of term. I'm making Kessner take the part of Angelina. He won't be as good as you would. And he certainly won't act as well. I don't mind telling you that. But he will be able to sing the part, and I can't risk you taking it, and having yourself voiceless when the time comes. I'm sorry. It can't be helped.'

We looked at each other. I had always liked Parker, and felt almost sorry for him, having to say this to me. I knew him to be, as schoolmasters go, timid. He was by no means good at discipline, and strident when situations overcame him. But I also knew that this had been coming for a long time, and I was half ready for it. I nodded. I still felt hurt at losing the part, and did not trust myself to speak. But in reality my disappointment was only superficial.

'I really am sorry,' Parker went on. 'It will be a disappointment.' He smiled, 'I don't suppose it will be much compensation, but I would like you to remain in the performance as one of the clerks of the Court. Would you do that for me?'

I nodded again. There was a further silence. Parker closed the piano.

'Can I go now?' I said.

Parker said: 'I'd just like to thank you for all your help in the choir during the past three years, and especially as the leading treble. I mean that.' He was embarrassed. So was I.

'You can go now,' he said.

I left quickly.

Outside, the snow gleamed white in the three-quarters moonlight. The frost glinted on its surface. The ice crackled underfoot around the main school entrance.

That main building stood higher than the houses and the other blocks. The ground curved away gently on either side; but immediately in front of the massive Victorian block of classrooms, hall and chapel, the ground had been artificially scooped and banked to make playing fields, and there was a dramatic fall away to the flat white surface below.

I crossed to the top of this bank and looked out. Beyond the playing fields there was a double line of trees, bare, leafless chestnuts in front—the source of conkers in autumn—and a mixed spinney of shrubs and conifers and occasional larger elms and oaks behind. Together they now made a dark, sombre boundary to the school domain. Far beyond, the gentle Cotswold hills rolled away into the distance; and at one point, where there was a slight declivity in the line of the horizon, could be seen the warm, enticing twinkle of lights. It was the nearest town; an unfamiliar place to us all, infrequently visited.

I felt that perhaps I should be experiencing, to a greater extent, the sense of change and transition. Yet all I could register was a persistent irritation in my throat. I felt no regret.

I remembered certain solos which had given me pleasure in church. And under my breath I repeated, in the still night air, the words I had sung in the wedding anthem: 'But as he which hath called you is Holy, so be ye Holy in all manner of conversation; pass the time of your sojourning here in fear; love one another with a pure heart fervently, see that ye love one another . . .'

I would write to Babette, and with a clear conscience, perhaps even with a hint of pride, explain why I could not take the part of Angelina. I had lost my part in the play, and suddenly the terrifying thought occurred to me that everything in life is subject to loss and that I could lose her. I turned cold at the notion. Standing on the edge of the school forecourt, the ground banking quite steeply away before me to the playing fields below, and beyond them to the sharp dark line of shadows from the trees, I shivered and stamped my feet in the crunching snow. The building behind me stood up dark and silent. Parker had already left by a staff entrance on the other side. Elsewhere, I could see the warm glow of light from other houses, reflected across the white ground.

I set off at a run down the gentle incline that skirted along the edge of the steeper banking. My boots squeaked and I kept to the softer margins where the tufts of rank, dead grass, attempting to push their way through the layers of soft, frozen snow, gave me foothold.

It was over. No more solos. No more practices. No more tense occasions. A new departure, I would tell my father, and he would say something like 'Not a bad show, old skin; you've done your bit.' And that would be that. I could depend on him to take it well.

He had not been as much in my thoughts lately as I would have wished. I was still not sure whether he was definitely coming down with Ursula for half-term, to take me out, as he had promised. It was only three days away, but it was two weeks since I had heard from him. I had become anxious. Silence at this time, I felt, meant danger. I clattered down the house steps, and in at the back door. It was quiet inside. Prep was still on, and I had my own work to do.

I gave my boots a quick rub, then took them off, and pushed my feet into my house shoes. There was the smell of polish and leather all around. The walls were painted black. I stuffed the boots hurriedly into the correct locker. Then I went into prep.

II

'Would you come with me for a minute?' It was the Gaffer, his head thrust in at the common-room door. There was a rustle and commotion as people turned, first to the housemaster, then to look at me.

I got up and went out.

Forrest, his hair a bit tousled, preceded me down the hall to his own study. 'Your father's telephoned. A bit irregular. I try to discourage it, as a rule. But he wants to speak with you. It's probably about half-term. In there. Call me when you've finished. I want to check the boiler.' He ambled off down the passage.

I pushed the door to, but I did not close it. I crossed over to the desk, and picked up the telephone. I felt relieved, and reassured.

The voice was slurred. My heart missed a beat. I had not expected a return to drinking again now that everything was all right; and so soon.

'That you, old son?'

I said that it was. I was tense with fear.

'We got married today.'

I recovered immediately. I felt a great surge of comfort and relief. 'Oh, Dad,' I said, 'I'm so pleased. That's super, really super. Can I speak with Ursula?'

There was a pause, quite short. His voice, when it came again, was different. It was suddenly as though he realised that he was speaking to another person, not just to an extension of himself. 'Ursula?' he said. 'What do you mean, Ursula? It's Laurie. I'm married to Laurie.' The slow, slurred, only slightly drunken words filtered through my brain. I could visualise the bland, expansive expression on his face. For a brief moment I hated him more than anyone else in the world. I felt that my brain was capsizing. I clutched the telephone, remaining silent. Then he said: 'Are you there? Hello? Hello?'

I said: 'Yes, I'm here.'

He said: 'Good. Wonderful. You must speak with her, old son. Say how pleased you are.'

I was once more tense, and filled with bitterness against him. 'Dad—?' I said. Then stopped.

'Yes?' he said. 'What is it?' His voice had that slow, patient, deliberate quality that I had learnt, over many years, to fear. He was himself detecting my reaction.

'Nothing,' I said. Then, quickly, and again fearfully, 'Are you coming down? Half-term?' I asked.

'Of course,' he said. 'Both be there. Saturday. We'll take you out.'

'That's good,' I said. My voice was blank and dead. I had nothing more to say myself, and I could hardly bring myself to bear another word from him. In the distance, I could hear them exchanging words. Then Laurie's voice came over the line, and I was surprised at how familiar it sounded, since we had met so little. It was crisp and flat in tone. She wasted no time. 'Hello, dear,' she said. 'This is Laurie. I hope we're going to get on together, you and me. I hope we'll make a go of things.'

'Hello,' I said. 'I want to wish you all the best. I hope you'll be happy.'

She laughed. 'We'll muddle along, I expect. Two of a kind, if you ask me.'

'You're coming on Saturday,' I said. It was a statement of fact. I could think of nothing else to say.

'Yes.' Then her voice, initially so matter-of-fact, softened briefly. 'You're a bit taken by surprise, aren't you? I'll hand you back to your father. George?'

I heard their voices again. I wondered where they were. I felt completely indifferent to them both, and yet curious, in a detached sort of way, to see or hear what would come next.

My father came back on the line. 'Laurie says I've had one over the eight,' he said, and laughed. 'But can you blame me? Celebrating. Important day. Are you all set for half-term?'

I said that I was.

'We're coming. Saturday. Train from Paddington: taxi from the station: with you about 11.30. That O.K., old son?'

I told him I would be waiting for them.

'You'll love Laurie,' he said. 'She's sound as a bell. She understands me. Heart of gold. Doesn't mind the odd drink. Broad-minded.' There was a pause, and I could hear my father answering a question from her which I did not hear. His answer ended with 'Don't worry. It'll be all right on Saturday.' Then he came back on the line again. 'Keep your chin up. Until Saturday.' And he rang off.

For a long time I just stood there. Illogically, I thought first of Forrest, and where he was, and what trouble it could be that he was having with the boiler. Then the awfulness of everything hit me, and the impossibility of any remedy. No single moment in my life has been worse than that one. Never again would I feel the same complete sense of loss that I felt then, standing beside my housemaster's desk, holding the lifeless telephone in my hand.

What had happened had stopped, totally and completely, and without any warning that I had been able to discern, the whole direction and purpose of my life. For me, at that moment, there seemed to be nothing at all; Babette, Ursula, Madge, their mother, the refined and gracious set of circumstances of their lives which had seemed to me so right and proper, and at the same time so miraculously attainable, had been, quite simply and completely, taken away. They were all struck from my grasp and without warning. I could pretend to myself that it would be possible to hold on to Babette. I could try. But how could I sustain a role that must be seen by everyone of her family as that of an intruder, bringing unfortunate messages out of a brief and unsatisfactory past? I was still too young, too dependant. No. It had gone, all of it. And she whom I loved, the focus point of it all, must inevitably be blotted out with all the rest. Even that did not conclude the pointless summary of loss. For with his marriage my father took from me part of himself. I sensed this was happening from the tone of his voice, and the fact that he had sprung the news on me as a dreadful *fait accompli*. Just how great the deprivation would be, I had yet to learn.

But certainly all those moments of warm intimacy right at the beginning of the Christmas holiday, waking to see him shaving and to listen to his singing, were now part of an irrevocable past.

I was still holding in my hand the telephone, trying to think of someone, or something to which I could turn. Philpotts? Danby? Religion? Alice? They all seemed dreadfully remote, compromised, useless. I raised my eyes from the desk. Forrest was standing at the door, watching me.

'Well, you've finished,' he said. 'Bad news?'

I stared back at him. In a sudden moment of insight, touched with irony, I realised just how well he would understand me if I decided to tell him my 'bad news'—that I had acquired a step-mother, stability, a permanent home in London, a half-term visit in three days' time, and was feeling as unhappy about it as I had ever felt in my life. Would not he, who knew me and my kind so well, grasp things fairly quickly? In fifteen years at Coppinger, before the war, through it, and up to that time, he had watched so many pupils passing through minor emotional casualties, and had judged and measured the degree of hurt, the extent of damage. He would so judge me if I let him, and to give him credit, would not be lacking in compassion.

'Sorry, sir, if I held you up. It was just my father saying he'd be down on Saturday. At around eleven.' I was going to add that my father was married, then decided to say nothing.

'Good,' he said. 'Good. That's another of you fixed up. With a bit of luck I shall have everyone out of the house.'

'May I go now, sir?'

'Yes. Get back to your work. I hear you won't be taking the lead in *Trial*. Voice breaking. A bit of bad luck, that.'

'Oh, I don't mind too much, sir. It had to happen.'

'Mm. I suppose you're right. Boiler's playing up. Clinkers. Not your bath night, I hope?'

III

It was the lipstick on the end of her cigarette: too much of it, and sharp in colour, scarlet.

She said: 'It's a nice house. Of course I don't have it all to myself. Not by a long chalk. That'd be asking too much. But it's comfy, the basement.' I was being given details of my future home.

'Is there a garden?' I asked.

'Yes, there's a garden. Well, we call it a garden, don't we, love? It's really a yard. But your father's got ideas for it. He's determined to quite transform it, aren't you, George? He's going to put trellises against the walls and grow climbing plants. What I like are the climbing geraniums. I like 'em even when they start tumbling down. And even the few flowers now are pretty, aren't they, love?'

'Wait till we have roses. You'll see. Queen of all flowers, the rose. Absolute perfection. Nothing in creation to beat it.'

My father took a drink from his glass. We were sitting together in the lounge of the Randolph Hotel. It was evening. We had come from the theatre, and eaten, and were now passing the time before departure. The weather had turned warmer. A thaw had set in.

'I have a separate entrance, of course. The tenants use the main door.'

'What are they like?' I asked.

She looked at me, frowning slightly. 'What are they like? Well, there's a salesman, and a ballet dancer, and two sisters. One of 'em works in a bank. And there's an Indian student.'

'And you collect the rent from them?'

She nodded. 'Well, your father does it now.' She looked at the man in question: that seemed to me to be the way in which her eyes designated him. 'I'd like another gin and tonic, George,' she said.

'Righto.' He looked round the lounge for a waiter. Eventually he saw one, and waved him over. After he had ordered the drinks he said to me, 'You don't mind about us going back, old son, do you? We've a lot to do, you see.'

I chose my expression carefully. In my heart I was relieved, but did not wish to reveal the fact. 'No,' I said, 'it's all right. I understand.'

'You're a very understanding young fellow,' Laurie said. 'I'm glad to meet someone with so much understanding.'

'Well, you did say how you had the house and everything, and that it hadn't been easy to get away.' I was flustered. I had not come quite to terms with my step-mother's manner.

She became pacified. 'It's true,' she said. 'I have my problems like everybody else. And you are good to see them.' She paused, staring at me. Then she added, as though suddenly aware of my inevitable physical presence in her future, 'You'll have a room of your own, of course, when you come home at Easter.'

We talked about the school. Laurie was obviously a manager, in the same way, but more than Alice. She enjoyed broad generalisations about life, a pragmatic woman, whose concern was very much with the present. Unlike Ursula, she did not reminisce; unlike Alice, she did not hope. Trellises, geraniums, collecting the rent: I wondered how it would be possible, not just for me to fit into her way of living, but for my father to go on sustaining it in the future.

He was watching me as we talked, a strange look of compassion coming into his eyes from time to time, and then he would seem to pull himself together. He sat up and took a mouthful of beer, then spoke: 'We'll have a grand holiday at Easter,' he said. 'I'll find some new friends for you. A better life. Stability. Certainty. Moderation. Laurie doesn't frown on the odd drink or two, do you? But moderation and balance in all things. That's the answer.'

I did not like the way she smoked. She held her cigarette in the middle of her mouth, and kept it there, the smoke rising from it into her eyes, which blinked often. The ash grew longer and longer. Sometimes it fell off onto her coat. Then she would stub the cigarette out in an ashtray already overfull.

'Perhaps we should be making a move, love,' she said.

I got to my feet obediently. We gathered up our things and left.

I was to go back by train. There would probably be other boys with me, though some would have their parents as well, committed to a longer stay than my father, and spending the night in the village near the school rather than in Oxford.

It was still cold outside, coming from the hotel. But the pavements were wet, and there was a dampish gleam from them as we set out together from the station. Occasional gusts of rain blew in our faces.

I walked beside Laurie.

My father said, 'I'm sorry about the voice. But you're growing up, old skin. It has to be faced.'

I said nothing. I felt very distant from him. Even if there had been only the two of us I did not think that there would have been much to reply. But there would have been some gesture, a squeezing of my arm, a glance, a smile, a passing, laughing phrase. Now that there was this third walking between us, casting a shadow, things were different.

I felt suddenly a flood of reaction and bitterness against the whole wasted and hideous day. I had been restrained, careful and polite. I had tracked my cautious path between their feelings. I had dissembled. I had lied. And in God's mercy we had all survived.

And now that it was drawing to a close I felt resentment. She had drawn him away. Why? Alice never did that. Nor Ursula.

I yearned for his hand on my shoulder, or for some other sign of physical affection. I wanted the laughter, the reminiscences, the jokes, the stories. Moreover I wanted it all to myself. I did not want to share it.

We tramped on under the lamplight.

'When does your train leave?' I asked.

'When does it leave, George? About an hour after his, isn't it?'

'What will you do? Will you wait?'

'I expect we'll sit there and have a drink, won't we, love?'

'You could have stayed in the hotel,' I said.

She did not answer.

My father said: 'You'd like Laurie to come and see you off, wouldn't you?'

'Of course; if it isn't keeping you out in the cold.'

'I'm all right,' she said. 'You mustn't worry about me.'

We came to the station. My father bought my ticket.

The old familiar feelings which I associated with partings, and with trains and stations, were not there. I did not feel tensed-up and nervous. My reaction leading up to this half-term encounter had resolved itself into a cold, sharp detachment. I had no vain regrets. I had no wish to talk or joke. I just felt for the first time in my life relief at the impending departure. I wished desperately that she had said goodbye earlier. But she insisted on coming right onto the platform, and accompanying me to where the short, unimportant looking little train with its ancient, corridor-less carriages and snub, wheezing engine, was gathering up its energies for departure. For an instant amid all my cold resignation, I felt a stab of desperation in my heart, the sudden panic of a trapped animal. If I let this occasion pass in my new mood of coldness, then it would tend to repeat itself the next time, and the next. And I did not want that. I wanted to hurl myself at my father, just one last time, clutch at him, reassure myself that all was as it had been before. I wanted to demonstrate my own love at least, and its superior claim upon my father's heart. For I doubted their affection for each other.

What was it that appealed in Laurie to him? I knew, by instinct, by his words, by his gestures, that it did not encompass the same feelings that my father felt for Ursula. I could see no romance: only a certain earthy tethering together; a companionship that was uncomfortably real after the uncertain passion I had witnessed between Ursula and him during the Christmas holiday. But after that an incompleteness intruded, and it nagged at my heart. Would it last? Could it last? What lay ahead for me? Where should I turn?

I saw Davitt ahead of us with his parents, and I slowed up. Danby was also there. Davitt had asked Danby out for the day, since Danby's mother had been unable to come down from Yorkshire.

Davitt was clutching packages, presumably of sweets, against his fat body. He was speaking a little too loudly, and his gestures and words were oddly at variance with his friend's shy attitude. His parents—both were apparently alive since they were there—watched him with pride and complacency. They were, like him, short and fat.

I slowed up, and my father looked at me, alert to the possibility of some kind of subtle conflict that might arise.

I said, quietly, 'I'd prefer to travel alone.'

'Are they friends?' my father asked.

'They're in the choir.'

He paused. He looked at me, then glanced at Laurie. 'No. Go with them. It will be better.'

I nodded slowly. Everything was happening with such ponderous delay. I was fretting with impatience. Every movement of Davitt's fat mouth, Danby's eyes, Laurie's hands, even my father's head as he turned and watched the gathering signals of departure, seemed impossibly slow and studied. It brought to me a feeling of nausea. What did it all signify? Was it necessary? How many days in one's life would be wasted thus? Was happiness something that could be taken away as arbitrarily as it had been given in the first place? Was it the same for Davitt? For Danby? Was it the same for this woman who would now presumably be permanently part of my life? And would the days and months and years ahead develop in this way, folding up my joy like a scarf, washed and ironed and stored away for another winter which might never come?

I kissed Laurie on the cheek. She told me to be a good boy, and to work hard. I looked her straight in the face and said nothing. Gently I disengaged my hand from hers, and held it out towards my father.

'Goodbye, Father.' It was the first time I had called him that. It was our first farewell without an embrace. It shocked me briefly that I had been able to do it. There had been no decision as such. The near presence of Davitt and Danby helped. But it was Laurie who accounted for it, her shadow cast between us and before us; not an object of hate—in my eyes she did not yet merit that—just a new disposer of my ever-uncertain future.

My father took my hand, held it tightly, and looked into my eyes. For the first time I saw there a new appeal. It was as if he was apologising. Life would change: it had changed. But whereas his control over it had lessened, mine, though I did not fully realise it, had grown.

'Look after yourself, my son. Square your shoulders, keep your chin up. I'll write.'

Doors were being closed. It was time to go. I climbed in with the others, to share the window with Davitt. Smiles were exchanged. Laurie stood back a little, watching us, her face in repose, careworn, tough, faintly suspicious of feelings and changes she did not fully understand.

The train began to move. My father did not speak again, but raised his hand in salute, his weight shifted onto one foot, his appearance, seen from the carriage window, faintly diminished. He stood there with Davitt's parents and Laurie, a little group under the pale white light of the station platform which grew smaller and smudged and indistinct as the train gathered noisy speed and headed out into the night.

IV

We sprawled across the seats and stared at each other. The three of us were alone.

Davitt puffed, and patted his belly, and went on chewing. He had a bag of sweets beside him and was replete with the satisfactions of the day.

I also had a small package of things my father had given me. I said to Davitt, 'Are your parents staying at the Randolph? Will you go out with them tomorrow and Monday?'

Davitt nodded. 'Yea. We're going to Worcester tomorrow. I have to be down to get on the train in the morning on my own.'

Danby asked: 'Where are you going tomorrow?'

They both stared at me, waiting for an answer. I felt self-conscious. I did not altogether like Davitt, and would not tell him the things I might tell Danby. I was sorry I had not been able to ask Danby out. I felt I needed to explain, but could not. I felt grateful for the dim light in the compartment. 'I'm not going out tomorrow,' I said.

'Why not?'

'My father has to go back to London. He has business there in the evening.' The invention seemed reasonable enough. What in reality puzzled me most about the day I had just spent, was the fact that my father had the sense to realise that one day was enough. It was in itself an immense relief to me, even then, sitting there, to know that I would not have to face Laurie again for several weeks.

'Couldn't your mother stay on?' Davitt asked.

I looked directly into his eyes, set deep above the fat, red, slightly shiny cheeks. A host of answers filled my brain, embracing a whole catalogue and recital of my life before they finished. For some unknown reason I began to feel a tenderness for this lumpish, fat, ignorant boy, and I let it grow. How could he possibly be expected to understand!

I just shook my head.

Danby looked across at Davitt and said, 'It isn't his real mother, Dav. Didn't you know that?'

'No.' Davitt paused. 'Do you want one of my sweets, then?' He held out the crumpled bag of toffees. I took one wrapped in green cellophane; I knew the peppermint flavour, and despite all my depression my mouth watered.

The train trundled on along the valley floor. We could see little from the windows in the darkness. We passed through occasional stations, stopping at Charlbury and the two Wychwoods. Under the pale and inadequate light the surfaces of the platform and of the sloping roofs gleamed moist in the beginnings of the thaw. There were slight, intermittent spatterings of rain, and strong gusts of wind.

I become more conscious, with the passing of time, of the invisible mist of regret which will forever overhang that valley. Ancient memories are locked up there in churches and houses and hills and ruins, and the great forest of Wychwood, long since hacked away. To anyone, moving there, it seems that one is moving along the fringes of the warm and comfortable west, looking out, maybe a little fearfully, at a harder and a colder England.

Sitting there, with the other two, after conversation had died between us, and listening to the regular, unhurried clicking of the wheels across the rail joints, I was filled with a deep, hard sense of loss and despair that could not be dissolved in tears, because of the presence of the others, could not be dissolved in tears, anyway. I was overwhelmed by a sense of my own frailty and irrelevance. Vibrant feelings of force and passion and direction in life had lapsed into indfference and uncertainty; and even the relief that might have been offered by the opportunity to give way, wholeheartedly, to grief: even that was suspended by the fact of the three of us sitting there, in the train's inadequate light, jogging flatly along beside the slow, winding river.

Had I been completely mad, I wondered, to think of my father, on an equal footing with Robert, perhaps even superior to him in some respects? Had I clutched at something ridiculous since that first encounter with Babette, in the upstairs room at the wedding, looking out upon the moonlit snow?

It seemed now infinitely distant, and quite irrecoverable. I was seized by a sense of having been trapped into a quite different, earthy life from now on; having been made somehow grubby and tarnished by what I had learnt through reading the letters. I had become, more so than Davitt, Danby, Philpotts, more so even than Eagle, an appropriate subject for the Coppinger foundation's benevolent pity.

And yet I felt increasingly detached about it. Everything had become so factual. I remembered Philpotts' warning in the park that night; I remembered Jennifer's sparse outline of predestination. I saw how right they both were, although the one conflicted with the other.

I realised that the whole period of time, from the first glorious wedding to the second hideous one, had covered no more than a single winter, a few months of frost, cold, and snow, and occasional relenting sunshine. It had started with snow; and now, when I think of that time, I have the sense of being encompassed and blanketed over by snow, grown to obsessive proportions.

It has become the symbol of inevitable loss, spreading over every episode, touching the lives of each and every one of those people, most of whom are now gone for ever; and melting away, just as they melted away, with my father's marriage to Laurie.

Along the road from the station there were other boys from the school, and Davitt drifted away from Danby and myself.

We were not sorry, though we said nothing. Danby had evinced some discretion during the journey, but he allowed himself to say now: 'I didn't expect your new mother to look like that. Not from what you said.'

'No?'

'After what you told me—'

'Forget what I told you,' I said. 'It doesn't matter. Just forget it.'

'Is something wrong?'

'I'm sorry, Danners. I don't want to talk about it.'

It was cloudy, and there were gusty rain-filled scuddings of wind in our faces. From behind the low levels of cloud the moon gave us sufficient light to see our way along the road back to school, and to perceive groups of other boys, ahead of us and behind.

We trudged on in silence. Occasionally I bent to pull up my socks. I had lost a pair of garters. My feet were cold. One of my boots leaked. I clutched in my hand a brown paper bag with a box of Sharp's toffees in it. I felt a sudden longing to be grown up, to be free, to be on my own. But there was tomorrow to live through, and Monday, and then school again. I wished the time would pass more quickly. But towards what? Towards what I had always had: the certainty of uncertainty. Only more of it. Much more.

'Danners,' I said. 'I'll tell you about it one day. I promise. But not now.'

'It doesn't matter. I don't want to know.'

'You're my best friend. If I can't tell you, who can I tell?'

'I didn't mean it like that. I just thought you might want to talk.' He walked on beside me, looking ahead of him in the uncertain light.

'Have we rehearsals next week?' I asked.

'Yes. Thursday.'

'What are we doing tomorrow?'

'There's a game of Cornish football arranged. It's for the whole school. Seems a mad idea, doesn't it?'

'It'll be fun, though.'
'Yes, I suppose so. What's happening on Monday?'
'I don't know,' I said.
'I suppose something'll be arranged.'
'Yes,' I said. 'They'll arrange something for us. They always do.'